Catherine Chidgey's novels have been published to international acclaim. Her first, *In a Fishbone Church*, won the Betty Trask Award and was longlisted for the Orange Prize. Her second, *Golden Deeds*, was a Notable Book of the Year in the *New York Times Book Review* and a Best Book in the *LA Times Book Review*. She has a degree in German literature and lived in Berlin during the 1990s. She now lives in Ngāruawāhia, New Zealand, and lectures in Creative Writing at the University of Waikato.

REMOTE SYMPATHY

Catherine Chidgey

REMOTE SYMPATHY

Europa
editions

Europa Editions
8 Blackstock Mews
London N4 2BT
www.europaeditions.co.uk

This novel was written with the generous support of a grant from

creative nz
ARTS COUNCIL OF NEW ZEALAND TOI AOTEAROA

A catalogue record for this title is available from the British Library
ISBN 978-1-78770-371-1

Chidgey, Catherine
Remote Sympathy

Art direction by Emanuele Ragnisco
instagram.com/emanueleragnisco

Cover design by Ginevra Rapisardi

Prepress by Grafica Punto Print – Rome

Cover image: © EyeEm/@Imagelldem

Printed and bound in Great Britain by Clays Ltd, Elcograf S.p.A.

CONTENTS

for Alan,
again

In Weimar there are no distances.
—THOMAS MANN, *Lotte in Weimar*

. . . the past is not preserved, but is reconstructed
on the basis of the present.
—MAURICE HALBWACHS (Buchenwald prisoner 77161), *The
Social Frameworks of Memory*

There is no such thing as an innocent memory.
—JORGE SEMPRÚN (Buchenwald prisoner 44904), *What a
Beautiful Sunday!*

REMOTE SYMPATHY

PART ONE
ALL THE BIRDS ARE HERE

FROM LETTERS WRITTEN BY DOKTOR LENARD WEBER
TO HIS DAUGHTER

Frankfurt am Main, September 1946

L ook at the picture, Lotte: the Palmengarten in midwinter. How pretty the trees are, their branches sugary with snow. I have a pile of pictures just as pretty; my neighbour gave me a stack of old calendars, and so, in the absence of any other paper, I'll write to you on the backs of all the vanished years.

Did your mother ever tell you that we met at a museum in Dresden? It was 1930, and I was studying medicine and working on my machine that would save the world. Recently I've thought about returning there, to the place where I first caught sight of her, but the museum is in ruins now, the exhibit we visited destroyed. A mass of melted wire and plastic and bone, buried in the rubble like some strange fossil.

I remember the ripple of her black hair. Her butter-yellow dress.

During my studies I'd read about the early therapeutic uses of electricity: Mediterranean torpedo fish applied to the temple for a headache; the limbs of hopeless paralytics shocked back to movement. I'd read, too, of more recent experiments in America and France and Italy, where electrotherapy promised relief from epilepsy and anaemia, neuralgia and chorea, and, some suggested, even cancer. But it was the eighteenth-century writings of John Hunter, the great Scottish surgeon, that sparked the idea for my machine: his theory that the cure as well as the disease could pass through a person by means of remote sympathy; that the energetic power produced in one part of the body could influence another part some distance away. Each evening in the parlour, I sketched out my plans for the Sympathetic Vitaliser, and I listened to recordings of Lotte Lehmann as I worked, partly to keep myself awake, and partly because her crystalline notes allowed me to worry away at my central premise. In fact, one of her arias – 'Come, Hope', from Beethoven's *Fidelio* – was playing as it first became clear to me: if a singer could shatter glass when her voice reproduced its resonant frequency, couldn't we shatter a tumour in the same way? By causing its cells to vibrate in sympathy, couldn't we turn it to dust? No need for the knife, just the correct dose of destructive energy delivered to growths crouched in the pelvis or breast or brain, or lodged in the lymph nodes like pearls. *Come, hope – let not the final star of the weary fade away . . .* While my mother slept, I remember, I placed a pile of books on the pedal of my father's grand piano, then lifted the lid and ran a finger across the taut strings; the instrument let out a soft falling sigh. I peered inside the open cavity and smelled the mahogany and lacquer and wax, and the secret chill of the wires. For a moment I feared the lid might fall on me, shut me away in that dark box, and I steadied it with my hand. Then I sang middle C and the middle C wire vibrated, and I moved down the scale, note by note, and watched each string begin to move in turn, to quiver and blur as it recognised its own frequency in my voice. For all the earth was alive with energy; every atom of every single thing sang with its own resonance, and this was as true of flesh as it was of piano strings.

Electrotherapy was starting to catch on in Germany by that time too, and I suppose I fancied myself a radical young researcher. An innovator. As nearby as Giessen, Erwin Schliephake was trialling his short-wave apparatus, and I remember I wrote to him to question the safety of its thermal effects: perhaps it did kill the bacteria in the milk, I remarked, but it killed the mice as well. I pored over the dozens of photographs in Carl Franz Nagelschmidt's publications: carcinomas of the ear and tongue healed by his high-frequency treatment, which also offered a miraculous resolution of pain – though Nagelschmidt insisted that inoperable tumours remained inoperable, and that a patient with metastatic cancer had as little chance of survival as ever. Except I knew he was wrong. I *knew* it, Lotte. I saw for myself the veins of light that leapt from Tesla coils – coronas and streamers that seemed to depict the very pathways of the body, the blood vessels and nerves that led far inside a person to where the scalpel could not reach. Sing into the open piano: watch the wire shiver.

In May 1930 I travelled to Dresden specially to see the exhibit at the new German Hygiene Museum. He was in all the newspapers, the Transparent Man: a real skeleton sheathed in a hard, clear skin, with the circulatory and nervous systems wrought from twelve kilometres of wire, and every plastic organ packed into place. I told my mother that I thought seeing the model might help me design the prototype of my machine, and she burst into tears.

'If only you could have found a cure in time for your father,' she said.

'I'm sorry,' I said.

On the train ride from Frankfurt, I watched my reflection slip across fields sprouting with barley and wheat and corn so bright the green might have been painted on. My aunt and uncle met me at the station – my mother's sister and her husband. They lived not far from Dresden's Großer Garten, and day after day the crowds streamed towards the exhibition hall there – it seemed the whole country wanted to witness the body's secret workings. The Transparent Man hung on every advertising column, face upturned, arms lifted as if to catch hold of the sun.

It was a clear May morning the first time I went to see him;

I know that. Soft white fluff from the poplar trees flecked the air and gathered in drifts on the pavements, stirred by the movement of feet before settling once more into downy mounds. I made my way past office workers and factory workers and young mothers with all the time in the world. My final examinations weren't far away, and I whispered the anatomy of the ear to myself as I hurried along: *tympanic membrane, malleus, incus, stapes* . . . There was too much to remember about the human body: how it functioned and how it failed. There is still too much to remember.

I'd brought only heavy clothes with me from Frankfurt, unsuitable for the warm day, so my aunt had given me some of Onkel Alexander's to wear; the jacket, which smelled of tobacco, hung loose across my narrow back, flapped across my chest. I had just turned twenty-five but I felt eight years old again, standing in my dead father's clothes while my mother pinned them up and drew dusty lines at my wrists and waist with her tailor's chalk. It was a rectal carcinoma in his case – painful and humiliating – though all I knew at the time was that Papa had been very sick, and sometimes very sick people don't get better, and we would have to make do.

Despite my rush, once I reached the exhibition hall I lingered in the tuberculosis room and the cancer room and the primitive races room; I took my time over the mechanical model of the heart. I delayed visiting the very thing I'd come to see, worried that it might disappoint. I suspect you'd understand that feeling, Lotte. I suspect you inherited my twisting anxieties, though I always hoped you'd be your mother's tranquil daughter. When finally I made my way to the room that held the Transparent Man, I was surprised to feel the tug of tears; I had not expected him to be so beautiful. He stood on his circular plinth, his clear arms raised, his chest laid bare, plastic organs lit each in turn by tiny bulbs, every nerve pathway and every blood vessel on show. I followed the branching networks of wire and imagined the waves from my machine passing along them until they hit the tumour they were calculated to destroy, and I felt a great surge running through my own body: what if it worked? What if the Sympathetic Vitaliser worked? It really might save the world. It was all I could do to keep still, to keep quiet: in the other rooms, in front of the other exhibits, the crowds chattered away in their usual voices, but here before the naked figure they whispered as if in a church – even the sniggering schoolboys, even the blushing fiancées. And indeed, he stood in a kind of apse, a kind of chapel, shining beneath a pointed archway, lit only from overhead in the otherwise darkened space.

'Like an angel,' a young woman next to me murmured.

Her companion said he couldn't see any robes and he couldn't see any wings, but I knew what she meant: the figure shimmered above us, seeming to float in the shadows, a creature of water, a creature of light, like us but not us, like us but perfect.

'Yes,' I murmured, even though the young woman hadn't been addressing me.

I felt rather than heard the couple behind me – they were irritated because they couldn't see past my lanky frame, I knew. Since I was about fifteen years old I'd stood a head taller than my peers, and I was always conscious of the space I took up, the way my arms and legs encroached on the aisles in buses and trains, the way I blocked the view. I'd developed a stoop to my shoulders, and my mother told me I would be a hunched old man one day. I turned and nodded to the couple, then moved to the side. They rushed at once into my spot, scowling at me.

I stayed at the museum for hours. After some lunch and a glass of beer, I jotted down notes on modifications to the Vitaliser – the size of the contact plates, their best placement. Then I bought two postcards of the Transparent Man: one to send to my mother, and the other for me to keep, so I could remember him exactly. I kept circling back to his room – I couldn't stay away – and found myself watching the crowds as much as I watched the figure itself. They stood and wondered at him, and lightly touched their own clavicles and jaws, and studied their own hands as if they might see right inside themselves. And I started to *understand* what I had already known: that the body wasn't a collection of separate parts, each performing its own solitary task, but a circuit, a machine, an exquisite and collaborative machine. The fold-out illustrations in my anatomy textbooks had never shown me this, and nor had any of the surgeries I'd observed, and nor had the work I'd done in the dissection room. Here I could see every organ at once, every artery and vein, every nerve, as large as life.

I didn't want to leave, didn't want to return to my aunt's apartment with its squat sofa and its fringed lamps and its framed prints of horses. I could hide myself somewhere in the exhibition hall, I thought; emerge again once everyone had left and the building had been locked for the night. I wouldn't have to jostle past the crowds and worry that I was too tall. I could climb onto the plinth and stand right next to him, measure my height against his. I could touch his glassy skin, trace the route from the stomach to the brain, from the hand to the heart.

I did no such thing, of course. When the time came to leave, I exited the building with everyone else, blinking at the sunny late afternoon.

'There you are,' said my aunt. 'We thought we'd lost you. I made Streuselkuchen, you know. Where have you been all this time?'

I showed her the postcard I'd bought to send to my mother.

'You'll give her a heart attack,' she said. 'Won't he, Alexander. A heart attack. Now, how much room do you have in your suitcase? I've sorted out a few bits and pieces for her. Does she still like plums? Of course she still likes plums, who doesn't. A few jars of my plums, and some of my pears, and what about some peas? Peas? And carrots? And look, take some chocolates – she always had a sweet tooth, and we've only eaten the nut ones. And orange marmalade? Some people find the peel too bitter. Well, she can try it, and then I can send more. She just needs to say. She just needs to sing out.'

Every time I visited it was the same – Tante Miriam loaded me down with food for my mother. This had started some two decades earlier, when my father was diagnosed and my mother began to wither away alongside him. She was a statuesque woman before he fell ill, but the flesh vanished from her bones, and she had to take in all her own clothes as well as cutting his down for me. Tante Miriam had let out a shriek when she saw her for the first time. 'I'd not have recognised you,' she said. 'I'd have walked past you in the street. Would you have recognised her, Alexander?' And her husband shook his head and said no, he wouldn't have recognised her. After that, Tante Miriam started sending jars of preserves and slabs of cake, tins of fish and wedges of cheese. My mother packed it all away in the pantry and always wrote a thank-you note on her best paper, but I was the one who ended up eating most of the food, or throwing it out when it turned bad.

'*Electricity?*' said my aunt when I tried to explain my machine to them over supper. 'Sounds very dangerous.'

'*Very* dangerous,' echoed my uncle.

They frowned at me, chewing on their black bread and waxy slices of Gouda.

'And how would you know what you were doing?' said my aunt. 'You can't even see it.'

'Quite right, quite right,' said my uncle, spearing a gherkin. 'Invisible.'

'But that's just it,' I said. 'No surgery. No trauma to the surrounding tissue. If you came to see the Transparent Man I could show you how the human body—'

'No,' said my aunt, shaking her head. 'No no no.' Didn't I remember cousin Norbert – not a real cousin, of course, but that was neither here nor there – who'd lost the use of his arm when he thought he could rewire a table lamp himself? He should have taken it to a professional, to someone with the proper training and qualifications. This was what happened when you tried to cut corners. Now everyone assumed he'd been wounded in the war, which wasn't a bad thing in itself, she supposed, but he still couldn't tie his own shoelaces. She had no wish to accompany me to the exhibition, and certainly no wish to see a Transparent Man – I don't need to know what goes on inside me, she said. She'd heard that it was very graphic, and that people were lining up outside the door and down the street to see it, and that a woman had fainted and had to be fanned in the face with a lottery ticket. She sniffed. Some things were better kept covered up.

The following morning, I went straight back to the museum. It was a Saturday, and the crowds were even worse, and I couldn't get close to the Transparent Man; people bumped into me as they wrestled their way to the front, and I hunched my head into my neck and my neck into my shoulders. I stood at the back of the throng and waited for a gap to open up while the bulbs inside his body kept on illuminating each organ in turn. The Transparent Man reached his arms up and away from all the people as if praying for rescue. And then I noticed her – the young woman from the previous day, who'd thought he looked like an angel. She was by herself this time, as far as I could tell, and she wove through the crowd, saying excuse me, pardon me, excuse me, until she was standing directly behind the plinth. She was partially hidden by the figure, though I could make out the butter-yellow of her dress through his legs, and her black hair and pale face rippling through his pelvis. I moved so I could see her better. She lifted her head to look up at the Transparent Man, and the light hit her face and her long, fine neck, and she stretched out a hand and touched his calf, first with a fingertip and then with a cupped palm as if to warm him. Another woman saw her and began to shout: 'You can't do that! It's not allowed! Stop it! Stop it!' An attendant came rushing over, and the scolding woman pointed and said, 'She was touching it. *Touching* it.'

'There are signs,' said the attendant. 'Anyone touching the exhibits will be asked to leave, and prohibited from returning. It's quite clear.'

The other members of the crowd began to back away, as if they might be implicated somehow, blamed for a crime they hadn't committed. Before I knew what I was doing, I was striding over to the rule-breaking woman and placing my hand on her shoulder.

'I do apologise, sir,' I said to the attendant. 'She's a student of mine, an anatomy student. You can understand the interest.'

The other woman snorted. 'What difference does that make? I'm interested in it too. We're all interested in it – that's why we've paid to come and look at the thing. But you don't see us grabbing it. Leaving our grubby fingerprints all over it.'

The attendant peered at the Transparent Man.

'As mentioned, it was motivated by a professional interest,' I said. 'A *scientific* interest. It won't happen again.'

I pressed my fingers into the young woman's shoulder, and she said, 'No! Absolutely not. I do apologise, sir.'

'Well,' said the attendant, 'in future, please remember where you are.'

'Of course,' I said.

'Of course,' said the young woman.

'Now,' he said, turning to the woman who had complained, 'where did she touch it?'

'Just here, on the calf,' she said.

'Now *she's* touching it,' said the young woman.

'That's different,' said the attendant.

'Quite different,' said the woman.

The attendant took a clean handkerchief from his pocket and scrubbed at the spot.

'We should keep going. There's still so much to see,' I said, and guided the young woman away.

'Why did you do that?' she said when we were out of earshot.

'I . . . I don't know. People like that . . . they can make things very difficult, once they get an idea in their heads.'

'I expect it made their day,' she said. 'Anyway, it was very nice of you to help, but I would have been all right on my own.'

'I can see that.'

'And you need to come up with some better lies. You look far too young to be my anatomy professor.'

We were at the café by now, and she insisted I let her buy me a coffee to thank me.

'I thought you said you would have been all right on your own.'

'So I would have. But it was still a nice thing to do.'

'I saw you here yesterday,' I said as we waited for a table.

'It's my third time.'

'It's my second. He's . . . he's . . .'

'Perfect.'

'Yes. Perfect. And also . . . I don't know. Defenceless.'

'Yes,' she said.

'Yes,' I said.

'So, am I a diligent student?'

'The best in your year. With the steadiest hands.' I still have no idea, Lotte, why I mentioned her hands, but I remember that I blushed. I began telling her about the machine then, outlining for her the principle of remote sympathy, and as I spoke I could feel – I could almost *see* – the heat of her hand lying close to mine on the café table.

'So if something is wrong with my knee,' she said, brushing her fingers over the knee-length hem of her yellow dress, 'you might apply the contact plates to my lower back? Here? And here?'

'Exactly,' I said, trying not to imagine her lower back. And then, before I could stop myself: 'But there is *nothing* wrong with your knee.'

I noticed the way she looked at me: as if I had already cured the disease. As if I had already invented the miracle.

'I've seen it work on geraniums,' I said, and she laughed.

'You can cure a plant of cancer?'

'I'm sure of it.'

'Extraordinary.'

'I still don't know your name,' I said.

'I'm Anna. Anna Ganz.'

Twelve months later she left Dresden for Frankfurt, and we were engaged.

From then on, more than ever, I willed my machine to work. It felt like praying.

All through 1931, when I began working at the Holy Spirit Hospital, I spent my evenings at home labouring over the prototype of the machine. I experimented with triodes and condensers and meters, fine-tuned the copper coils and wires that would lie at the Vitaliser's heart. When I burnt myself with the soldering iron, and the smell of my own seared skin merged with the resinous scent of the flux, I hardly paused for long enough to allow my mother to dress the wound. I spent months on the contact plates that I would apply to my subjects' palms, chest, forehead, temples, back and feet; if I made them too large they'd be unwieldy to attach, but if I made them too small I increased the chance a patient might feel some discomfort from the current. I tried silver and copper – even a thin layer of gold, for its non-corrosive properties – and I tested them on myself, Lotte, as well as on your mother. Buckling the straps around her bird-thin wrists and ankles, her pale stomach, asking, 'Does it hurt? Does it hurt?'

My mother watched on, shaking her head. 'Poor Anna!' she said. 'What kind of honeymoon is this?' But I could tell she had high hopes for the Vitaliser too. 'A villa on Zeppelinallee,' she said. 'A motor car! A maid!'

After my father had died we'd moved to the suburb of Nordend, where we rented a four-room apartment on the top floor; the piano took up most of the parlour. In summertime, when all the windows were open, the pealing of the bells from St. Bernhard's coursed through the place, set the very bones humming. I loved the sound, but my mother said it put her teeth on edge, and I knew she would have liked to move somewhere smart.

When I finished the mechanism itself, I built the box to house it, cutting dovetails from pearwood I had chosen for its hardness; I imagined the machine would need to withstand decades of use. I scored the shapes of the controls into the fine grain – the needles and the dials, and the switch that would bring the whole thing to life – and then millimetre by millimetre I formed the holes until they were just big enough. Then I sanded the wooden walls so they were ribbon-smooth, and fitted the corners together, and they locked one into the other exactly as I'd calculated they would. In the recess of the lid I fitted slots to hold the copper contact plates and their straps and cords as well as the little chamois cloth for cleaning them. Like a proud father, I photographed the Vitaliser at every stage of its development. The brass handles were an afterthought once I realised the size and weight of the finished machine – in fact, it was Anna who suggested them.

'It's not going to sit in a laboratory,' she said. 'You'll be shifting it around. Taking it to the bedsides of your patients.'

And I kissed her for her easy belief in it.

I experimented on geraniums first, just as Georges Lakhovsky had at the Salpêtrière in Paris, inoculating them with *Agrobacterium tumefaciens* so they produced tumours on their stems. These were small and white to begin with, the size of cherry stones, but grew rapidly into large multilobar masses. At that point I treated three of the plants with the Vitaliser, applying the contact plates to the area around the roots. The results astounded me: two weeks after the first treatment, the tumours began to necrotise. Three months later, all the plants in the control group had perished – all the untreated geraniums – while the three that received treatment were not only free of their tumours but flourishing.

I was aware that at some stage I would have to persuade real patients to let me try the Vitaliser on them, but I didn't foresee any difficulties in that regard: a dying man will drink the sea; a dying man will swallow glass. I was going to save the world.

I started to fill page after page with graphs that calculated the resonant frequencies of the human body – the chest wall sixty cycles per second, the eye eighty-nine cycles per second. On graphs, too, I estimated the frequencies needed to kill the cells of different carcinomas – hundreds of thousands of cycles per second – the waves rising and falling, rising and falling, rippling from the tip of my pencil and across the paper and, it seemed, into the very air around me. I could sense the whole world vibrating: oysters and oak trees and paper and hummingbirds and fruit knives and moths all tuned to their own particular notes, and yes, brains and tongues and lungs and hearts too. I stopped working each night only when I fell asleep at my table – and even then, I saw waves curling and breaking on my eyelids' black meniscus, shivering through my dreams.

At the start of 1932 I requested permission from the Holy

Spirit to conduct a small trial of the Sympathetic Vitaliser; the director, Herr Baumhauer, was an ambitious man, eager to expand the hospital's reputation as well as his own.

'Do you know, at the Charité, they suspect vitamins?' he said. 'They're looking into low-vitamin diets for cancer patients.'

I nodded. Everyone was trying something new: viral therapy, heliotherapy, Chinese rhubarb, fruit-juice injections – even hemlock. But electrotherapy, I told him . . . we could corner the market there.

'Valentin Zeileis,' he said. 'Isn't he the chap? With the castle in Austria, and the lightning machine?'

Zeileis was a former metal worker who had set up an electrotherapy institute in Gallspach; his approach to every ailment involved blasting patients with arcs that streamed from a kind of showerhead.

'He claims a very high rate of success . . . ' I began.

'A total charlatan, from what I hear,' said Baumhauer. 'The German League to Combat Quackery wants him shut down.'

'He has no medical training, it's true. But the University Hospital in Vienna—'

'And I read that he lights the place – the treatment room – with lamps held in the jaws of giant stuffed snakes.'

'I don't know anything about that,' I said, though I too had heard stories. Zeileis had been bitten by a cobra, and the saliva of an Indian holy man had saved his life. Zeileis was descended from an ancient dynasty of Indian princes. Zeileis had used electromagnetic waves to set fire to a pile of wood six thousand kilometres away. I said, 'The University Hospital in Vienna has one of his machines – the patients flock there.'

'It's always the same,' said Baumhauer. 'What the miracle doctor actually does is far less important than what the people believe.'

I thought that was the end of it, but then he said, 'They flock there, eh?'

'In their thousands, I'm told.'

'Do they. Do they now. Well, you can't argue with the numbers.'

That spring he invited me on a staff excursion to the Taunus, where he made sure I danced with the prettiest nurses who wore flower crowns in their hair. We had egg-and-spoon races and sack races and a tug of war – I remember thinking that I wasn't sure if I wanted to be on the winning side, which meant falling backwards, or the losing side, which meant falling forwards.

I convinced fourteen patients to take part in the trial, treating them with the Vitaliser while they also received conventional therapy. There was a melanoma on a forearm, I remember, and a transitional cell carcinoma of the bladder. A colonic carcinoma, a cervical squamous carcinoma. A lymphoma, I think. And even though the outcome was inconclusive, the survival rate after three years statistically insignificant, the *Monthly Journal of the Struggle Against Cancer* published my findings; it was new and trying to prove itself too. But young men are full of vast ideas that wither to nothing, Lotte; passions that shrink and perish. While there was some interest on the fringes of the medical community, most of my colleagues dismissed the experiment as quackery. *There is no miracle hidden in young Doktor Weber's varnished box*, wrote a Berlin specialist. *The fact that two of his patients appear to have entered remission must be seen for what it is: pure chance.* Another cautioned against *offering false hope to those fighting the number one enemy*, and suggested that my machine was *as reliable as a ouija board.* The editor of the *German Medical Weekly* even questioned its safety: *It is all very well for Doktor Weber to declare that he has tested the device on himself and his young wife with no ill effects, but how can we be certain that a patient whose health is already compromised will not worsen or even die when exposed to his 'healing frequencies'? Surely conventional treatment alone offers better results than a gadget cobbled together by a junior physician in his spare time?* Far better to focus on prevention, they said. *The most important measures of the government – in genetics, education, sport, home hygiene, the Hitler Youth, the SA and SS – can all be regarded as prophylactic against cancer.*

My mother told me I shouldn't take their comments to heart; they were just jealous. I kept on sitting up late every evening, listening to my recordings of Lotte Lehmann and adjusting and refining my machine, attaching the contact plates to myself to test them – though no longer to Anna, who by that time had fallen pregnant with you and was quite unwell. Mama tended to her when I was at the Holy Spirit, fussing about with chamomile tea and hot-water bottles and cold compresses as if she were still a nurse. She adored Anna, adored having her under our roof after we married. I started a list of patients I could select for a second, bigger trial – but Herr Baumhauer kept delaying his approval. It was our duty to wait and see what became of the two from the first trial, he told me, and that's what I told Anna and my mother as well. In reality, though, I suspected he didn't want me drawing attention to myself and his hospital given I was married to a Jewess. Every week, another of my colleagues appeared in a brown or black uniform.

In January 1936 I requested another meeting with Baumhauer, and we sat in his office with its hulking furniture carved in the Black Forest style, all boars and stags. Framed hunting scenes covered the walls, and above the desk a painting of the Führer glistened as if the paint were still wet.

'I was wondering if you've reached a decision on the second trial,' I said. 'I have a list of almost thirty suitable candidates, and just this week another promising case has arrived.' In my mind I was already buckling the contact plates to their bodies; I was already flicking the switch.

'The thing is,' he said, 'we'd need proof it would be of value to the Reich. To the German people. You'd need to show me some convincing numbers. The two survivors have both died, I understand?'

'Later than they should have,' I said. 'Between them they achieved six years of remission. Six full years of extra time.'

'It's certainly something,' he said. 'It is. It is. But I don't know that it's enough.' And then, finally, he came out with what he actually meant. 'If you could resolve your domestic situation, perhaps we could consider it.'

'My domestic situation?'

'A divorce, Doktor Weber. That would clear the way for you to stay on here.'

'What do you mean, stay on here?'

He spread his hands. 'You know how difficult things have become. It's out of my control. We may not be able to keep someone with your sort of connections.'

'What would you do, in my position?' I asked. I wasn't looking for advice; I really wanted to know.

'Well, I wouldn't have married a Jewess in the first place.'

I knew if I lost my job it would be impossible to find another. I stopped pursuing a second trial; I packed the machine away in the attic and just kept going to work, hoping things might improve. Every morning I passed the painting from the original hospital's old collection box, though the box itself was long gone: the Holy Spirit descending in the form of a dove, wings spread wide, a host in its beak. *Give to the poor in hospital, as God commands.* I didn't tell Anna that Herr Baumhauer had suggested a divorce; for months her pregnancy had confined her to bed with a nausea that left her as limp and pale as a paper doll. Your body was drawing on her own flesh, it seemed, Lotte, paring away her muscles and binding them into its new little self – and I sat at her bedside and felt you move beneath my hand, an unknown pulsing orb, and I loved you already. You were born in the springtime of 1936, and we named you after Lotte Lehmann on account of your extraordinary lungs.

We should have paid closer attention. By that time, Jews could no longer marry Aryans. They couldn't raise the national flag; they couldn't vote. They couldn't hire German maids under the age of forty-five. Our mayor had been especially eager to enact the new legislation even before it was passed: all Jews employed by the city lost their jobs at the law courts, the schools, the university and the hospitals. Our neighbours stopped greeting us, and Anna's oldest schoolfriend crossed the street to avoid her. Businesses advertised their *Pure German Skin Cream*, their *Aryan Shoes*. Each time I met with Herr Baumhauer, he asked me if I had come up with a solution to my *domestic problem*. We had to think of the greater good, he said. In November 1938, when I was at the Holy Spirit, I heard the news: they were burning down the synagogues, ransacking the Jewish shops, throwing people's belongings from the windows of their apartments: gramophones, bedding, sewing machines – even a piano. I ran to the synagogue on Börneplatz to see if it was true, and yes, there on the square, a crowd of people watched the smoke and flames bursting from the great dome. Next to me a group of Hitler Youth boys were jostling one another and laughing. *We caught one of them, and cut off his beard and ear locks. He looked like a turnip by the time we finished with him.* Two fire engines came, but they didn't turn their hoses on the fire – only on the burning debris that fell too close to the neighbouring buildings. After that, the authorities arrested thousands of Jews, picking them up on the streets or at the railway station, even in their homes. Anna's parents and her brother left Dresden for Shanghai, where they would admit Jews without visas. We should have known. We should have felt it coming. All the parades and the torchlit marches, the blaring trumpets and the thudding drums, the voices roaring *Heil! Heil! Heil!* The shudders in the ground beneath our feet.

And then, early in 1939, Herr Baumhauer called me to his office.

'I've been doing a bit of digging,' he said. 'And the thing is, it seems you're part Jew.'

'I beg your pardon?' I said.

'It's a terrible shame, of course. I was hoping there'd been some kind of mistake, but the records prove it. This polluted blood – you never know where it'll turn up.'

'But I was baptised,' I said. 'And confirmed. My parents, too. We have the certificates.'

'Your mother's father is the sticking point,' he said. 'I'm afraid it does make things tricky.'

'But there must be something you can do . . . '

'The thing is,' he said, 'you're still married to a Jewess.'

'She's baptised as well,' I said.

'Makes no difference.'

'There must be something . . . ' I said again.

'I can keep it quiet for now, but as I've already mentioned, it would be much simpler all round if you had your marriage dissolved. Much safer – and then you could keep working here. Have a think. I'll need an answer before too long.'

'Well, yes,' said my mother at supper that night. 'There was something like that with Papa. But look at you – blond hair, blue eyes, just like me. You couldn't be more German.' She accepted another tiny serving of herring from the platter Anna passed her. 'I really shouldn't, but it's too delicious.'

'Your father went to church every week, though,' I said.

She nodded. 'He was no Jew – he'd be horrified.'

Anna burst into tears.

'Oh,' said my mother, 'oh – no no, my dear – that came out wrong. You're not a real one.'

'What does that mean?' I said.

'Just – well, they *are* different. And they must have done *something*, otherwise they wouldn't be in so much trouble. Maybe it would be better for everyone if they went back to Palestine.'

'Back?' I said. 'Back?'

A tight little shrug.

Anna wiped her eyes with her serviette. 'I hope you've left some room,' she said. 'There's Pfefferkuchen for dessert.' She began to clear the plates.

'So if your father was Jewish, Mama,' I said, 'that means you're Jewish too. Legally speaking.'

'What?' she said, staring at me, eyes wide with fright.

I avoided Herr Baumhauer as much as possible for the next month, though twice when I passed him in the corridor he reminded me that time was running out, and that he would need an answer very soon. Finally, in March 1939, it was Anna herself who suggested we divorce.

'A lot of couples are separating,' she said, her voice too bright. 'It wouldn't mean anything. Not really.'

'It would mean we couldn't live together,' I said. 'Couldn't see each other. Wouldn't it?'

'Only for a little while.'

'How long? Months? Years?'

'Nobody knows.'

'What about Lotte?'

'We'd be doing it *for* Lotte.'

And the truth was, we had no other way of earning enough to live on.

We had to act as if it were a real divorce. We couldn't tell anyone, not even our closest friends, not even my mother – though she died of cardiac arrest soon afterwards, and I still believe it was the separation that killed her. I packed my photographs of Anna away in the attic; I dared not keep them on display, since the merest hint of contact with her could see me tried for race defilement and Anna sent to Ravensbrück. If people asked, we hinted at an infidelity that was too painful to discuss. On our last night together, as we lay for the last time in our bed, we made up the woman who had led me astray.

'A French duchess,' said Anna. 'I don't want my replacement to be just anybody.'

I smiled into the dark. 'How did I meet her?'

'She came to the hospital for some kind of embarrassing operation. She didn't want her social circle in Paris to know about it.'

'No, I think I want a healthy one,' I said. 'A cleaning woman? I saw her on her hands and knees and couldn't help myself.'

'A *cleaning* woman?'

'All right, not a cleaning woman.'

'A cleaning woman! You might as well say the toilet attendant at the Hauptbahnhof.'

'I'm sure she's not unattractive . . . '

'I don't think you're taking this seriously.'

I felt Anna turn onto her side and pull the covers up over her shoulder. 'You're letting in the cold,' I said.

'And you're having an affair.'

'All right. A chorus girl? A tap-dancer? I saw her perform at the Schumanntheater and it was all over.'

'You never go to the Schumanntheater.'

'Maybe I do, but in secret. You thought I was up late, working on my machine.'

'Not a chorus girl, though. A famous actress, celebrated for her beauty.'

'Or a magician's assistant?'

'I'll make her disappear, if I ever get my hands on her.'

'She's terrified of you,' I said. 'She's always looking over her shoulder.'

'So that'll never last. What about the heiress to a family fortune?'

'Perhaps. How have they made their money?'

'Chocolate,' said Anna. 'We'd have an endless supply of pralines.'

'Well, I would,' I said.

'Oh. Oh yes. I forgot.'

'Not chocolate. I'd get too fat, and then she wouldn't love me any more.'

'And then you'd come back to me.'

'Would you love me if I were fat?'

'How fat?'

'Enormous.'

'Hmm.'

'Not chocolate, then. How else could they have made their money? Tanks? Or paperclips. Something in demand.'

Anna rearranged her pillow, punching it into shape, and again the cold air rushed into the bed. 'This replacement,' she said. 'What does she look like?'

I turned onto my side so I was facing her, though I couldn't make her out. 'You. She looks like you.'

Anna's hand brushed my cheek just for a second, then withdrew. 'Maybe she's a youth leader from the League of German Girls. A Hildegard or a Waltraud.'

'Mmm. Those uniforms . . . '

'Tall and blond and blue-eyed. Nothing like me. Mind you, she salutes so frequently that her right arm's twice the size of her left. You don't mind that, do you?'

'All the better for hitting the children.'

'Or she's an older woman. The wife of a high-ranking Party member. She's going to leave him and run away with you to Romania, where you'll farm goats.'

'We'd be stopped at the border. Taken outside and shot.'

We both fell silent. The only sound was our breathing. Then, in the next room, Lotte, you let out a single high cry, the way children do in their sleep. Some small nightmare, over before it began.

'Good night,' I said at last.

'Good night,' said Anna.

We did not embrace.

Since Anna couldn't take over our apartment – the owner of the building decided he wouldn't rent to Jews – she looked for a new place for the two of you, finally moving into a small flat in Ostend. You were too young to understand what was happening, and on the day that you left we behaved as normally as possible, calmly packing your clothes and toys, your favourite blanket. You thought it was a game and brought us other things to pack in the suitcase: my winter scarf, the egg timer. And then, at the last minute, you started to wail. You ran to me and flung your arms around my legs. You wouldn't let me go.

'No, Papa, no no no no no,' you cried.

It took both of us to prise you free.

All these years later, I can still feel your arms tight around me.

We agreed that it was too dangerous for me to visit you at the new flat, but I sent money every month, folded into letters from an 'Onkel Theo' who was living a life nothing like mine. I didn't even dare write that my mother had died. I left the envelopes in the old part of the cemetery in Nordend, under a rock hidden in the bushes, and occasionally Anna wrote back to Onkel Theo, also using a false name and no return address. You were both in good health, she said, and enjoyed going to the Jewish symphony orchestra and the Jewish swimming pool. Even when the war began, I still thought we would be all right. With so many doctors called away to the front, Baumhauer couldn't do without me, and so I was able to keep sending money from Onkel Theo, securing the envelopes under the rock.

Then, in October 1941, the mass deportations began. I saw the people herded together at the Großmarkthalle in their best coats, their suitcases strapped shut to hold everything inside.

'Where are they going?' I asked an elderly man standing next to me.

'Palestine, I expect,' he said. 'Or maybe Madagascar. Who knows? Anyway, good riddance, eh?'

I scanned the crowd for you and Anna. I didn't see anyone I recognised, but there were so many people, so many hundreds of them, the mothers holding on tight to their children's hands.

Anna's letters still found their way to the rock in the bushes at the cemetery, though. The two of you were still in Frankfurt.

One December day, a woman bumped into me in a quiet corridor of the Holy Spirit and dropped all her papers.

'I'm so sorry,' she said. As I bent to help her pick them up, she glanced over her shoulder, then said, 'Anna has had to leave the flat, and she has remarried. A man called David Hirsch offered – he works at the Reich Association of Jews.'

'What?' I said. 'What are you telling me?'

'Because of his job, he won't be deported. So his wife and any stepchildren won't be deported either. Understand?'

I nodded, and she told me their address – a shared Jewish house, where they crammed families in together, one on top of another. Before I could ask anything else, she had gone.

For a few months after that, things settled down, and there were no more deportations – until May 1942, when they began again. The same thing was happening all over Germany, and I received word from Dresden that Tante Miriam and Onkel Alexander had been sent east. I couldn't stand it; I knew it was dangerous but I had to see you both. To hold you both. In the hospital courtyard I walked around and around the pond with its little fountain. What would they do to us if we were discovered? Send us to a camp – all of us. And we'd be together.

I waited until dusk, when the day was neither one thing nor the other, and then I caught the tram over to Ostend. The city was closing its eyes; one by one the blackout blinds came down, and by the time I reached your address it was difficult to see two steps in front of me. I made my way to the back building, where clouds of steam from a barred basement laundry escaped like smoke.

A dark-haired man around my own age answered the door, and when I explained who I was he said, 'You shouldn't be here,' and hurried me inside a stuffy flat. In the passageway he held his finger to his lips and gestured for me to follow him. 'The children are all asleep,' he whispered.

Other people passed us in the passage: an elderly couple in their dressing gowns; a young woman who stopped to ask where the coal bucket was. 'And you are?' she said to me, and I said, 'An old friend of Anna's.' At the end of the passage we came to a small bedroom, and there she was, your beautiful mother, beneath a bare bulb that made her hair shine like liquorice. She sat unravelling a worn-out jumper, stopping at the end of every few rows to wind the crinkled wool into a ball. I watched her for a moment. I thought that she might vanish if I spoke – that I might wake to find myself back in my own house, alone. Then the man said, 'Anna? Lenard is here,' and from the way he spoke I knew who he was: David Hirsch. Her new husband. She looked up, and her hands sank to her lap, and the ball of wool dropped to the floor and rolled away, undoing itself. 'I'll give you some time,' David murmured.

'What's happened?' she said to me, and I realised that she was terrified. 'Has someone died?'

'I wanted to see you. In case you have to leave.'

She was in my arms then, and I felt the thinness of her, the edges of her shoulder blades, her spine hard beneath my hands. We were both of us smaller.

'And Lotte?' I said.

'I'll wake her.'

You stumbled blinking into the room, wearing a nightdress with a pattern of ladybirds on it; I remember that. I suppose I should have known that after three years you wouldn't recognise me: when I knelt and embraced you I felt you struggling to escape – and then you started to scream.

'This is Papa,' said Anna. 'It's all right. It's all right. It's just Papa.'

I let go, and you ran and crouched behind the bed, and I could hear you sobbing.

'There's nothing to be frightened of,' said Anna. 'Don't you remember him? Your papa? See, you have the same ears.'

That was untrue; Anna and I had never been able to find anything of me in you – not in your looks, at any rate. Still, it was enough to get you to come out from behind the bed. I couldn't believe how much you had grown. You were six years old by then, and Anna said you had excellent handwriting, and could sing every verse of 'All the Birds Are Here' from memory. How beautiful you looked, with your wavy black hair hanging down your back, and your right cheek flushed where you'd been sleeping on it. You glanced up at me from beneath your dark lashes, and when I gave you the book I had brought – *The Story of the Rabbit Children* – you turned to Anna before you took it and said, 'Is it my birthday?'

'It's just a present,' she said.

'Why?'

'Just because.'

You said, 'Thank you, Papa,' and held on to it with both hands, as if someone might take it away again.

'It must be nice, living with so many friends,' I said.

'Sometimes,' you said.

'Only sometimes?'

You fiddled with the spine of the book. 'Rachel Metz calls me a dirty Jew.'

'Oh!' gasped Anna, and her hand flew to her mouth.

'You didn't know?' I said.

Anna shook her head. I could see that she was trying not to cry; in truth, I could have wept myself – for you, and for Anna, and for Rachel Metz too, who didn't seem to understand that she also was Jewish. But I said, 'Rachel sounds like a very rude little girl.' I sat on the couch then, and we opened your new book to read about the hunter's children, who had fallen out of their basket and were taken home by a mother rabbit. In fact, it wasn't a new book at all; my aunt in Dresden had given it to me when I was a boy, and I knew every page. I used to read it to you at home, before you moved away, but you didn't remember. You settled in next to me and leaned your head against my shoulder, and I could feel the little ridges of your ear, the ear that was nothing like mine, and we laughed at the pictures of the hunter's children in their fuzzy rabbit suits, eating the berries with the other little rabbits, and wasn't it lucky the hunter's dog recognised them before it was too late?

Afterwards we crept into the bedroom where you slept with the rest of the children, and you showed me the single bed you shared with Rachel Metz.

'What's all this?' I whispered, gesturing to the wall above your bed. Drawings covered it, pinned to every blank space, right to the edge of the window.

'They're the places we can't go,' you said, and pointed out the pools where you couldn't swim, the cafés where you couldn't drink hot chocolates, the parks where you couldn't collect leaves – all rebuilt from Anna's memories, since you'd never seen them yourself. Even the Italian ice-cream parlour on Frankenallee, where Anna and I used to go on summer afternoons, only you'd drawn the ice cream as snow. And the Palmengarten, with its rowboats drifting under weeping willows and its manmade grottoes, only you'd turned it into a jungle, with great choking vines, and black sockets in the rock.

David was in the bedroom when Anna and I returned, taking a pair of pyjamas from a drawer.

'I'll leave you alone,' he said. 'Good night.'

We lay on the bed in each other's arms then, the two of us, husband and wife, as if no time had passed, and Anna looked at me with her dark eyes, and I knew she saw right inside me to my every nerve.

'No one will disturb us,' she whispered.

And too soon it was almost dawn, and we must have fallen asleep; a little clock woke us as it struck five A.M.

'I wish I could have a photograph of you,' Anna said into my chest.

She went to wake you so you could say goodbye. 'Remember, Lotte,' she said, 'we can't tell anyone about Papa's visit. It has to be our special secret. Understand?'

You nodded, and took my hand and swung it in yours as I walked to the door, and when I bent to brush the hair from your forehead and give you a kiss goodbye you whispered in my ear – my ear that was nothing like your ear – 'I don't want to be a dirty Jew.'

PART TWO
EICKEWEG

FROM THE IMAGINARY DIARY OF FRAU GRETA HAHN

February 1943

We wouldn't have to pack very much apart from our clothes, Dietrich told me; the villa was fully furnished. Some small personal items – favourite cushions, a few framed pictures – were all we needed. Some books, if I wanted any. The villa came with its own domestic, too, which meant we couldn't take our maid with us when we left Munich.

'Oh,' I said. 'I just assumed Erna would be coming.'

'I'll see she finds another position,' he said.

'No, but I mean – it would be easier for Karl-Heinz to settle in if he had a familiar face.'

'He'll have us.'

I suppose it was silly, but I felt jealous about Erna going to work in another household, adapting to the routine of another family. Since Dietrich's career had begun to take off, we'd come to rely on her – and because neither of us came from money, I think we valued her all the more. She knew how I liked the beds made and how Dietrich liked his vests folded. She made sure the coffee came with cream as well as milk and that I never ran out of the bright-blue ink I used for my letters, and she knew to unscrew the lightshade from the bathroom ceiling every month and shake out the dead moths that had found their way inside. She knew never to overwind the alarm clock that sat next to our bed, and to rotate the china from our wedding service so that some plates didn't wear more than others. Well, I supposed we wouldn't be taking our wedding china either.

'But what about when we come back?' I said. 'We'll have to find a new girl. Start from scratch.'

Dietrich said we'd deal with that when it happened and I needed to stop worrying about it, because there were excellent servants available at Buchenwald, and many good reasons not to take an outsider there.

'*We're* outsiders,' I said. 'Karl-Heinz and I, at least.'

'You're family.'

'How close is it?' I said.

'Not very.'

'Can you see it?'

'Not from the house. But I'm more worried about the troops stationed there – we can't have you fraternising with all those young men.' He pulled me onto his lap and softly bit my neck. Our age difference bothered him far more than it did me.

'When you're a hundred, I'll be eighty-four,' I said, just as I always did.

In the photos I'd seen of the villa it looked like a ski lodge in a magazine or a film. It had a solid stone wall at the front of the property and broad steps leading to a pretty front door, and a large terrace so that we could sit outside and enjoy the fresh air – and even a conservatory, which we could fill with potted plants. It was one of ten houses built specially for the officers and their families, Dietrich said, so there'd be plenty of other people – our sort of people – to get to know. They named the street Eickeweg after Theodor Eicke, who'd taken Dietrich under his wing at Dachau. He was the one responsible, really, for Dietrich's rise through the ranks, from a lowly bookkeeper through to an administrative officer; he'd seen something in him, and Dietrich looked up to him the way a son looks up to his father. All Eicke's men loved him for his insistence on absolute loyalty, absolute devotion to duty, and the way he prepared them for the work they had to do. When they talked about him, they called him Papa Eicke.

'The villas are on one side of the street, and the forest is on the other,' said Dietrich. 'It'll be like living in a little village.'

It did sound nice, being so far away from the noise and smoke of Munich, though our apartment there was very smart. We'd moved into it when we married – Dietrich was doing well by that time – and he secured the apartment downstairs, too, for his mother. She hadn't taken to me at first, even though I brought her chocolates from Dallmayr's, and bunches of lilacs in spring, which I knew were her favourite flower. I even embroidered her initials onto a set of handkerchiefs, but I never saw her use them. Oh, they're too special to wipe my nose on, she said, but it was because she didn't approve of my marrying her son.

'She could be your daughter,' I heard her saying soon after we moved in.

'Their line is pure back to 1700, Mama,' said Dietrich's voice.

'She'll go to fat,' she said. 'Her sort always do. And a Catholic!'

A little later, though, after Karl-Heinz was born, I could do no wrong.

Karl-Heinz was allowed to choose one box of books and one box of toys to take with him to Buchenwald, but he couldn't decide what to pack and what to leave behind; all morning he kept changing his mind. In the end I told him it didn't really matter, because we wouldn't be living at the camp forever, and when we came home again all his things would be here waiting for him.

'I'll be too big then,' he said, and I didn't know whether to laugh or cry. I looked around the apartment: already it seemed unoccupied, the armchairs and mirrors and the crystal chandelier covered with dust sheets. Karl-Heinz was traipsing from room to room, saying goodbye to the empty spaces.

'He'll love it up there,' Dietrich said. 'You can take a picnic lunch and go walking through the trees and hear nothing but birds. Never even see another human being.'

'Goodbye kitchen. Goodbye bathroom,' Karl-Heinz was saying. At last he returned to us.

'We can go hunting,' Dietrich told him. 'Up in the hills, just like the dukes of Weimar.'

'What can we hunt?'

'Oh, bears, lions, elephants, I imagine.'

Karl-Heinz studied his father's face. 'You're teasing,' he said.

'Not at all,' said Dietrich. 'You'll see.'

'How big are the bears?'

'Enormous.'

'Bigger than me?'

'Certainly. Bigger than Oma Hahn, even.'

'Oh,' said Karl-Heinz, and was quiet for a moment. 'Do they eat little boys?'

'Only the curly-haired ones.'

'*Dietrich*,' I said. Sometimes he didn't realise he was going too far. 'Papa's just making it up, Karli.'

'They eat honey,' said Dietrich. 'And jam, straight from the jar. They have no manners whatsoever.'

Karl-Heinz was laughing now.

'They chew with their mouths open,' I said. 'They never wash behind their ears.'

'They forget their pleases and thank-yous,' said Karl-Heinz.

'Yes, all the time,' I said. 'Even when their mamas have knitted them lovely warm jumpers.' I tried to close his box of books, but there were too many crammed inside. 'You'll have to leave some of these, darling.'

'In fact,' said Dietrich, 'there really are bears. But they're kept in a pit, inside an enclosure, inside a zoo.'

'A zoo?' I said.

'A zoo?' said Karl-Heinz, and the word started to sound strange, nonsensical. He picked through his books again, opening each one and running his finger down the pages as if checking their worth.

'Oh yes,' said Dietrich. 'Specially for the families to enjoy.'

'And . . . where are the inmates?' I said in a low voice. 'Is it safe?'

'Of course,' said Dietrich. He seemed surprised I would even ask. 'As I said, from the villa, you can't see a thing.'

Above us the shrouded chandelier hung like a rain cloud, all the little droplets quivering inside.

'Taking a child to a place like that,' said my mother.

'It's quite safe,' I told her. 'We'll be living well outside the enclosure. We won't even be able to see it. Apparently the villa's beautiful – you can come and stay whenever you like.'

'Will you bring me dry bread for my dinner? Slide it under my cell door?'

'Mama, it's not like that,' I said.

And it wasn't.

Often I find myself regretting I haven't kept a diary of our time at Buchenwald – for my mother to read, for Karl-Heinz to read, or even so that I can remember what it was really like – but it's much too late for that now. All I can do is imagine what I might have written.

I think I would have described the house first.

With its steep gables and its log-cabin walls and its windowboxes heaped with snow, the villa reminded me of the dollhouse I'd owned as a girl, and as I looked up at it I had the feeling that the whole front might swing open, the icicles working themselves loose from the eaves, and inside I would find little figures posed stiffly on couches and beds, warming themselves beside cellophane fires and gazing into mirrors of tin. Tall, snowy spruces and pines surrounded the house, as well as bare beeches and a few oaks, and across the street, guards with guns patrolled the edge of the forest. I had never lived in a wooden building before; I wondered how safe it was, especially in an air raid, but – as Dietrich said – why would they attack a camp that held thousands of prisoners?

'Thousands?' I said.

'You don't need to worry,' he said. 'No one escapes.'

'But the weapons factories . . . ?' I hadn't seen them, but I knew they were nearby.

'Too close to the prisoners,' said Dietrich. 'They wouldn't risk it. Isn't that clever?'

There was a mirror just inside the entranceway; we had one in the same place at home, so we could make sure everything was in order before we went out, but this one was larger and much nicer. In the spacious hallway – a room in its own right – an expensive carpet shimmered on the parquet floor, and twisting wrought-iron light fittings jutted from the walls. I peered through to the formal dining room, and the conservatory with its seagrass chairs, and the living room with its built-in window seat. A model sailing ship from centuries ago gleamed on the mantelpiece, and a chandelier made from stags' antlers hung from the ceiling.

I darted back into the entranceway and helped Karl-Heinz off with his duffel coat and mittens. 'Is this real?' I whispered.

Dietrich drew me to him and scooped up Karl-Heinz, and we looked at our reflection. 'Well, Frau Sturmbannführer,' he said, 'what do you think?'

I stood up straight and sucked in my cheeks – I'd always hated how plump they were, though Dietrich loved to pinch them. On the table under the mirror a pretty oak clock began to chime the hour, and there was a little card, decorated with beech trees and lavish calligraphy: *Welcome to the Hahn*

Family. It sat next to something covered up with swathes of white netting, like a bridal veil, and when I lifted it away I found an elaborate cake with three sugar figures on top.

'Is that me?' said Karl-Heinz, pointing to the smallest one.

'I think so,' I said. I was still whispering, as if this weren't our house, as if we might wake the real family. It was only then that I noticed a pair of men standing in the shadow of the door to the kitchen, and I jumped.

'Who are you?' said Karl-Heinz, wriggling free of his father to gaze up at them in their zebra-striped uniforms.

'Come back here, Karli,' I said, grabbing at his jumper. The men simply inclined their heads.

'Just some of the workers,' said Dietrich.

'Who?' I said, but he didn't reply.

They brought in our luggage and between them began to haul it up the stairs to where I assumed the bedrooms were, speaking to each other in very broken German.

Karl-Heinz ran on ahead to the living room.

'Be careful! Don't break anything!' I called.

I wanted to go upstairs and change out of my travelling clothes, but I could hear the workers up there, dragging things around. I wandered through the other rooms – so much more space than in Munich. Although I knew another family had lived here before us, everything seemed brand new. The kitchen looked untouched.

'A horse!' Karl-Heinz shouted. 'Mama, a horse!'

I thought he must have seen something out the window, but he'd found a rocking horse. 'Do be careful,' I said again. As he rocked, he was moving closer and closer to a porcelain vase on a shelf; already it was trembling.

'If it breaks, we just ask for another,' said Dietrich. 'That's the way it works. You'll get used to it.'

While Karl-Heinz was still occupied I took Dietrich aside and said, 'What *does* happen if we're attacked?'

'There's an air-raid shelter,' he said. 'A proper one, just across the road. Very solid. Very safe. And we have our own cellar, too.'

I looked for it but couldn't find the door. I had the idea that there might be all sorts of hidden rooms.

When the workers finally headed downstairs, they were carrying my suitcases.

'No,' I said. 'They go upstairs. In the master bedroom.' I didn't know where that was, of course, so I just pointed at the ceiling.

They gave the smallest of nods and continued bringing my suitcases down.

'Dietrich,' I called. 'Dietrich!'

When they reached the bottom of the stairs, they opened the lids: empty.

'Where are all my things?' I said.

'Yes,' said one of the men. They both kept their eyes on the floor.

'What is it?' said Dietrich.

'They've . . . I think they've unpacked my clothes.'

'They're Polish,' he said. 'Go on!' He waved them away. 'I'll deal with them later.'

Upstairs I found an elegant bathroom: oyster-coloured tiles on the walls and thick towels hanging ready on the rails. There were three large bedrooms – one with aeroplane wallpaper, and a model train set looping its way across the floor, and a bed sweetly carved with oak leaves and runes. The master bedroom opened off to the east and had its own balcony, and furniture in the latest style – all bright chrome handles and polished veneers. I was expecting to see my things stacked on the bed, but the blue satin eiderdown was clear and smooth, as empty as a summer sky. The bedroom curtains were grey velvet, like the ones in my grandmother's house; when I was a child I used to hide behind them while she looked everywhere else for me.

Where is Greta? Where could she be? She was here a moment ago. Oh dear, I must have lost her. I would wrap the fabric around and around me until I could hardly breathe, listening for my grandmother's footsteps, trying not to give myself away. *What shall I tell her mama and papa? How can a little girl just disappear?* Once she pretended to cry because she couldn't find me, and even when I called out to her that I was wrapped up in the curtain, that I was right there in the room with her, just a few steps away, she wouldn't stop sobbing. *Oh no, oh no, I have lost her. She is gone for good. I'll never see her again.* I tried to unwrap myself, but the fabric tightened around my body, binding my arms to my sides, filling my mouth with the taste of dust. My grandmother must have released me when she realised I wasn't laughing any more, but I don't remember that part. I don't remember getting out.

I threw open the door to the balcony and stood on my tiptoes: winter trees, all spangled with snow and ice, and the hillside falling away to the glittering Thuringian countryside. If not for the guards with their guns, we could have been anywhere. One of them looked up at me, and I didn't know whether I should wave, or call out a greeting. I hurried back inside, feeling my cheeks burning – really, Dietrich should have told me what to do, how to behave. I ran my hand over the eiderdown, smoothing out wrinkles that weren't there, feeling all the little feathers bending inside. The bedroom really did look like a picture from a magazine – one of those drawings of a woman sitting at a mirror with a jar of miracle lotion, touching her face, marvelling at her skin. On the dressing table I saw a hairbrush and comb – *my* hairbrush and comb, I realised, and my bottles of scent, and the manicure set Dietrich had given me for my birthday. Even the little photo of Karl-Heinz when he was a newborn, held in Dietrich's arms. I opened a drawer and found my handkerchiefs in precise stacks, and in another my gloves, fingers all pointing towards the dark space at the back. Everything had been put away. My skirts and blouses hung in the wardrobe, arranged according to colour, evening gowns grouped at one end and my shoes lined up in their ranks. Even my underwear had been dealt with, the little pieces of silk folded and sorted, the garter belts coiled next to the paired stockings. I sat down on the bed and stared at the open cupboards and drawers. In the distance I could hear Karl-Heinz giggling in the frantic way he did when Dietrich tickled him without mercy. And, closer, I could hear the alarm clock I'd brought from our bedroom in Munich, ticking away on the bedside cabinet. Next to it, my father's volumes of Goethe and Hölderlin.

When I came back downstairs a young man stood in the hallway with Dietrich – a boy, really. His fine, fair hair flopped over his forehead, and he had bright-blue eyes set into a pale face. He must have been fifteen or sixteen.

'This is the domestic,' said Dietrich. 'I ordered him specially – a surprise for you.'

The boy made a small bow. He was wearing a purple triangle stitched to his shirt, I noticed, and a number – but surely he was far too young to be a prisoner.

'Do you speak German?' I asked.

'Yes, madam. I'm from Magdeburg.'

'And what is your name?'

'Josef Niemand, madam.'

'And where is the cellar door, please, Josef?'

'Right there, madam.' He pointed to a door set into the wall under the staircase behind me. Once I'd seen it, I didn't know how I could have missed it, and I felt foolish for asking.

'Thank you, Josef,' I said. 'That will be all for now.'

'Do we hide in the cellar when the bombs come?' said Karl-Heinz.

I laughed, too loudly. 'There won't be any bombs,' I said.

'The cellars are mainly for storage,' said Dietrich. 'Do you like your surprise?'

'He seems very nice,' I said. 'Karl-Heinz, I think I saw a train set upstairs. Why don't you have a look?'

Off he ran.

'And I should sort out my office,' said Dietrich, and started to put on his coat.

'Wait a minute,' I said, then lowered my voice. 'Is the servant – is Josef – a *prisoner*?' I whispered the last word.

'Of course,' he said.

'When were you going to tell me?'

'Greta, it's quite usual. And very economical. I thought you'd be pleased.'

He put on his cap, kissed me on the cheek and was gone.

I pushed open the cellar door and stepped onto the little landing. Almost no daylight reached it from the dim hallway, and I felt around for a light switch. As the cool air rushed up at me, something tapped my face: a moth? A spider? I scrabbled it away, forcing myself not to cry out, and when my hand met with it again I realised it was just a cord for the light. I shut the door behind me and peered down into the space that opened up under the house. I could smell something rich and smoky – something I recognised though couldn't quite name.

At the bottom of the stairs I found a low-ceilinged room lined on every wall with shelves. Those nearest to me held bottles: row upon row of wines and liqueurs you could no longer buy in the shops. There were baskets of pears and apples that gleamed under the electric light, and four large wheels of wax-dipped cheese, and, on a bottom shelf, a first-aid kit in a bulky square tin with a cross on it. I opened it and ran a finger over the brand-new bandages and slings, the bottle of iodine as black as poison, the tiny tube of salve. And still I could smell it: that rich, smoky something, a little sharp, a little greasy. Was it the cheese? Two wooden benches stood in a corner, underneath a narrow window that showed a strip of garden at eye level, snow pressing against the pane. I sat down and closed my eyes for a moment. I would have to remember to telephone my mother when I went back upstairs; I'd promised to let her know we'd arrived safely.

'It's just a train trip,' I'd told her. 'It's hardly the African jungle. It's hardly the moon. We're only a few hours away.'

'All the same,' she'd said.

My stomach rumbled, and I took an apple and bit into it: cold and sweet, with the faintest taste of earth in the skin. I could make out something long and pale hanging in the far corner of the cellar, where the light didn't quite reach, and as I got closer and it took shape I knew what the smell was: meat. A whole side of cured pork, the trotters and the halved head still attached, and strings of blood sausage and liver sausage, too, and three limp-necked birds – large ducks? Small geese? – hanging ready to be plucked. Surely it was far too much for one family; surely it would spoil. I touched the soft back of one of the birds, which set them all swinging, and for a moment I had the feeling that they were just waking up, that they would tilt their heads and open their wings and begin to fly around the cavernous space, looking for a way out. I thought of our cellar in Munich; how makeshift it seemed in comparison, and how small. Well, that was because we shared it with everyone else in the apartment building – we were hemmed in by our neighbours' suitcases and trunks and bicycles and baby car- riages, and, during an air raid, by our neighbours themselves, chattering away until the all-clear. I stopped chewing my apple and listened: nothing. Even my footsteps sounded muffled, deadened by the weight of the earth pressing in, and the beau- tiful house pressing down from above. We would be happy here.

I decided to take Karl-Heinz for a walk so we could stretch

our legs. We headed along Eickeweg and into the forest across the road from our house – I nodded at the men with their guns – and we hadn't gone very far at all before we found the falconry, set among the trees. The falconer's half-timbered house was so lovely, like a fairytale house, and from the roof of the long aviary a giant falcon watched us. I thought it was real at first, until I realised it was as tall as a person, and carved from wood.

'If you come back on Sunday afternoon, we can show you the birds,' the falconer told us. 'That's when we put on a bit of a show, with the ferrets and the rabbits.'

'Can I have a pet ferret?' said Karl-Heinz.

'I don't think so, darling.'

'You can see some of the animals today, though,' said the falconer. 'There's even a mouflon, all the way from Sardinia. Just follow the path.'

And yes, a little further on through the trees we found them: foxes and wild boars, chickens and pheasants, and a red-coated ram with big curling horns.

'Is that the mouflon?' said Karl-Heinz.

'I think so.'

A pair of deer came right up to us and nuzzled our hands, completely unafraid, and I wished I had brought some of the apples from the cellar with me; they could probably smell them.

'Where are the bears?' asked Karl-Heinz. 'Papa said there were bears.'

'So he did,' I said.

'At the zoo.'

'Yes. I'm not sure there *is* a zoo.'

'But this is the zoo.'

'Maybe it is.'

A terrible shriek sounded, and we both jumped. Karl-Heinz grabbed my hand.

'It's all right,' I said, but my skin was prickling, and I could feel my heart stumble. The shriek sounded again, louder this time.

'Mama!' Karl-Heinz held his arms up to me. At five years old he was getting too heavy for me to lift, but I bent and picked him up, and he pressed his face into the crook of my neck the way he did when he was sleepy or frightened. Another shriek. His little body jolted. Then I saw it: a peacock perched in the branches, loosening rushes of snow when it flapped its wings.

'It's just a bird,' I said. 'The noise. Look, it's just a peacock.'

'Where?'

'Look. Up there. Let's go back to the house and start unpacking our things, shall we? Then we'll ask the servant to make us some hot chocolate, and we can read a book together. Would you like that?'

He said something I couldn't catch, and tightened his grip around my neck. I felt my arms begin to fail. 'I'll have to put you down, darling,' I said, but he held on even tighter. 'Come on now. I don't want to drop you.'

'We didn't *bring* the book I want!' he sobbed.

'Which one?'

'The one about the funny *dog*!'

'No,' I said, 'we didn't have room for that one.'

I had just settled Karl-Heinz into bed for a nap when the doorbell rang. I froze, listened, but he didn't stir. Quickly I checked my reflection in the mirror in the entranceway; I was still wearing my travelling clothes, and wisps of my hair had come loose, and there were dark rings under my eyes. I could have done with a nap myself; the last thing I felt like was guests. To buy some time, I found the servant and asked him to answer the door. Then I darted into the living room and sat on the L-shaped window seat, smoothing my creased skirt over my knees, and a moment later Josef showed in a tall, attractive woman. She must have been around thirty; her smooth auburn hair was caught in a twist at the nape of her neck, and she wore a well-cut navy dress with long rows of pearl buttons at the cuffs and the back. She set down a large bunch of dark-pink tulips.

'Emmi Wolff,' she said, extending her hand. 'I'm the wife of Sturmbannführer Wolff – the prison compound commander. We're just next door.'

'Greta Hahn,' I said. 'How nice of you to stop by. Josef, would you bring us a pot of tea? And some of the cake. And put the flowers in water.'

Frau Wolff sat on the window seat too, and we looked out at the front garden and the trees beyond, the snow bright white in the late afternoon sun.

'Where did you find tulips so early?' I said.

'They grow them here,' said Frau Wolff. 'Masses of them, in the greenhouses.'

'Greenhouses? How lovely. And what happens to them all?'

'They're sold, of course. Much nicer than what you find down in Weimar.'

Maybe we could have our own greenhouse, I thought, and I could try growing exotic flowers like my mother did, to pass the time – though she had no greenhouse, just the deep windowsills in the dining room, and wet towels over the radiator. One of her orchids looked like clusters of little naked men, mottled purple arms and legs extending from pale bodies, and little hooded faces too. I remembered the warm, moist air in the room, the dizzying fragrance. My mother told me I must never lay a finger on them; even the lightest touch could bruise the petals. One day I crept to the dining room on my own, thinking I would pinch at the waxy flesh, pick a flower and hold it to the light so I could peer in the mouth and see its insides. What was its name? I can't remember now. And I couldn't bring myself to pick one; all the little eyes watching me, all the little mouths readying themselves to tell tales.

'Beautiful, isn't it?' said Frau Wolff, gesturing at the snowy trees in the garden. 'But you must notice the cooler climate this high up. You've come from Munich today?'

I nodded, tucking a strand of hair behind my ear. 'It is a little bitter.'

'It's much milder on this side of the Ettersberg, though, believe me. Over there, on the northern slope—' she gestured with her head and shivered her elegant shoulders.

Josef brought in some of the cake with our tea, and I studied his face and his eyes and his hands. He wore a decent shirt, and his nails were clean and trimmed. He didn't look like a prisoner. 'Oh!' I said when I saw the sugar figures from the top of the cake all cut up into pieces.

'You'll get very used to it, I'm afraid,' said Frau Wolff, accepting a plate. 'They have a first-class pastry chef. It's terrible!' She laughed and stabbed a silver fork into a slice. As we drank our tea her fingers kept straying to a gold bangle on her wrist, turning and turning it.

'What a pretty thing,' I said, and she seemed pleased I had noticed.

'Don't you think? Otto had it made specially for my birthday.' She unfastened it and handed it to me.

It was engraved with three names – Ada, Margot and Felix, chiselled as fine as hair, each name followed by a tiny oak leaf that grew out of the final letter.

'My children,' she said. 'Try it on, if you like.'

I slipped it over my hand and snapped it together, admiring the shine of the gold against my skin. 'Exquisite workmanship,' I said.

'You can get anything here. We have the finest craftsmen in Europe.'

'In Weimar?' I said. It was not a very big town.

She gave a little laugh. 'No, *here*,' she said. 'Right on your doorstep.'

Already I was imagining a bangle of my own: Karl-Heinz's name picked out in the same hair-fine lettering, and the rest of the space left blank for names still to come.

'Stonemasons, bookbinders, carvers, sculptors – and the goldsmiths and silversmiths, of course . . . ' Frau Wolff was saying. 'I've ordered a painting of our family tree for our hallway. It'll be over six feet high.' She pointed at the model ship on the mantelpiece, its sails filled with the gust of an unseen ocean. 'That's their work too.'

Just then Karl-Heinz wandered in. 'I don't like my bed,' he said. 'I want my real one.'

'Come and meet Frau Wolff,' I said. 'She's our new neighbour.'

'Hello there, young man.'

He climbed up beside me and hid his face behind a cushion.

'Don't be rude, Karl-Heinz. Shake hands with Frau Wolff.'

'What's wrong with your bed?' she said.

'It's too soft,' he mumbled from behind the cushion.

'Oh dear,' she said. 'Yes, that's a serious problem. Could we find you an ironing board to sleep on? Or the dining table perhaps?'

A giggle.

'Or something to distract you from the softness? Hmm . . . what about a book to read?'

Karl-Heinz lowered the cushion, and she opened her bag and gave him a small, flat parcel.

'Oh, you really didn't need to,' I said.

'It's nothing.'

Karl-Heinz pulled away the paper. 'My dog book! Mama, look!'

'Well I never. Did you say thank you to Frau Wolff?'

'Thank you, Frau Wolff.'

'It's nothing,' she said again. 'But you have it already?'

'We left it at home. We've been a bit upset about it.'

'Ah.'

'Karl-Heinz, fold up the paper. We'll start a new pile, for the soldiers.'

'What do they do with all the paper?' he said. 'The soldiers?'

'Well,' I said. 'Well, I imagine they use it to make more paper.'

'You know,' said Frau Wolff, 'I have a little boy about the same age as you. It'll be nice for Felix to have a new friend. His sisters are just that bit too much older.'

We watched as he turned the pages of his book; he was mouthing the words to himself, though he couldn't yet read. Frau Wolff turned to me, lowered her voice. 'He'll be fine, don't worry. He'll adjust in no time. Children are very resilient.' She looked around the spacious room, taking in the fine carpet, the porcelain vases and the oil painting of the sea breaking on rocks. 'How do you find the accommodation?' she said.

'It's lovely. Dietrich told me it would be, but – I had no idea what to expect. Given the circumstances.'

'I was the same when we moved here. I was so relieved when I walked into the villa. A pleasant surprise, isn't it?'

'She has cake on her chin,' said Karl-Heinz.

'Darling, where are your manners? I'm so sorry – it's been a long trip, and—'

Frau Wolff waved a hand and dabbed the crumbs away with her serviette. 'You know,' she said, 'you can do whatever you want to the place. New floors, custom-made furniture, a sculpture of Karl-Heinz . . . Do you still have those grey velvet curtains in the bedroom? Very dreary.'

I nodded, though I liked the curtains. 'What do you say, Karli? Shall we get a statue of you? Oh, I think one Karl-Heinz is quite enough.'

'But honestly – just put in an order. A mural on the wall, a fresco on the ceiling – God and all his angels, if you like, and all for the price of some cigarettes. There's a famous Dutch painter here who's done several pieces for us – he's in demand. Well, our husbands work hard enough. They need to come home to somewhere nice.' She popped another morsel of cake into her mouth.

'My mother's friend had a games table when I was a little girl,' I said. 'You could fold out an inlaid chess board, and a backgammon board, and there was a baize top for playing cards. I thought it was the cleverest thing.'

'There you are, then,' said Frau Wolff, clapping her hands. 'They could make that for you, no problem. And then I'll come and play mah-jong.'

Yes, over by the bookshelves; that would be just the spot for a games table. I could throw mah-jong parties, with glasses of champagne, and little cakes made in the shape of mah-jong tiles. All the elegant ladies in their shimmering gowns, finger-nails tapping on the pieces of bone as they planned their next moves.

'Of course, there is one bigger house,' said Frau Wolff.

I nodded; I'd seen it when we walked to the falconry. 'The Kommandant's?' I said.

'The *former* Kommandant's,' said Frau Wolff. And she told me about Karl Koch, who'd been investigated for corruption and moved east in a series of demotions. His wife Ilse had stayed on in their Buchenwald villa, though: Frau Wolff said that she bathed in Madeira; that she had a personal masseur rub her naked back with fresh lemons; that she'd ordered a private riding hall built behind the SS casernes, at vast cost, and had it lined with mirrors so she could see herself from all angles. And Frau Wolff had heard other things, worse things.

'Why is she still living here?' I said.

'They're still looking for a house for all of them, apparently. And the children, I suppose – she doesn't want to uproot them. This is the only home they've ever known.'

'Not so resilient, then.'

She smiled. 'Perhaps not.'

We sipped our tea.

'She lost one, you know,' she said quietly. 'A child. A baby. It was only two months old, and she went skiing, and it fell ill and died.'

'Skiing?' I said. 'What sort of mother . . . '

'Exactly. And she's kept a bank account in the dead child's name, for the funnelling of various funds. *And* . . . ' – she lowered her voice still further – 'I heard that they put the Kommandant's son from his first marriage in the Bunker. You know – the punishment block.'

'Oh yes,' I said, as if I did know.

'Completely alone. A tiny space, bare concrete, for a whole day. And he could hear them torturing prisoners in the next cell. All because he talked back to her.'

'What do you mean, torturing?'

'Well, they were criminals.'

'Oh yes,' I said again.

'A dreadful thing.'

'Yes,' I said. 'Do you . . . were you . . . friendly with her?'

'I wouldn't say friendly. Kommandant Koch was not a popular man.'

Somewhere a telephone began to ring, and I jumped to my feet, but Frau Wolff said, 'The servant will answer it.'

Sure enough, a moment later Josef appeared at the door. 'A call for you, madam,' he said. 'Your mother.'

'Oh dear. I was supposed to let her know we were all right.'

'Why wouldn't you be all right?' said Frau Wolff.

'You know how they worry. She thinks I'm still a little girl.'

Once I was out in the hallway I realised I had no idea where the telephone was, and Josef had vanished. I returned to the living room. 'I don't suppose you know where—'

Frau Wolff laughed. 'In the entranceway, opposite the door to the kitchen. The same as ours.'

'Hello? Mama?' I said into the receiver. The line was very bad; now and then I thought I caught my mother's voice, but it was all broken up, and I could make no sense of it. 'We're here,' I said. 'We've arrived, we're here. Everyone is fine.' I paused. Nothing but the crackle of the bad connection. 'We haven't found the zoo yet, but there's a falconry just across the road, with eagles and hawks. And some deer. They nuzzled our hands.' Nothing. 'They're quite tame. Completely tame.' Still nothing. 'What was the name of the orchid you used to have? The one with all the little men.' But she couldn't hear me, or I couldn't hear her. I hung up.

I found Frau Wolff sitting next to Karl-Heinz on the couch, looking at his book with him. His head rested against her shoulder, and they were laughing at the pictures of the funny little dog with the legs of a dachshund, the mouth of a pug, the coat of a poodle and a single pinscher ear.

'You have a very bright boy, Frau Hahn,' she said. 'He can already read some of the words.'

'Which words?' I said. He'd never read any for me.

'Lots of them,' said Frau Wolff. 'Can't you, Karl-Heinz? Shall we show Mama?' She pointed to the page and he said, 'Dog.' She pointed again and he said, 'Stone.'

'I had no idea,' I said.

'Oh,' she said, seeing my face. 'Oh, I didn't mean to spoil anything.'

I blinked away the tears I could feel forming. 'I'm being silly. I'm just tired after the trip.'

'Of course you are. Of course.'

'Was I naughty, Mama?' said Karl-Heinz. He was screwing up his face, about to cry too.

'No, darling. Mama's tired, that's all.'

'Did you talk to your mother?' said Frau Wolff. 'Is she happy now?'

'I couldn't hear her. I assume it was my mother.'

'Well, the servant said it was.'

'Yes. Yes, it must have been her.'

'I want to talk to Oma!' said Karl-Heinz, starting to wail.

'Now then, darling. Oma says hello, and she says you're to be a good boy. She'll come and visit us soon.'

'I want to talk to *Oma*!'

'That's enough, Karl-Heinz. What will Frau Wolff think?'

'I should go,' she said. 'Leave you to settle in. Let me know if you want to come shopping in Weimar one day, though – I'll order a car.'

'Is that allowed?' I said. 'The petrol?'

'It's allowed,' she laughed.

It wasn't until I was seeing her to the door that I remembered the bangle; I was still wearing it. 'I do apologise,' I said, and knew I was blushing.

'I can see I'll have to keep my eye on you.'

Just then a shriek sounded down the street, and even though I knew what it was, I started. Karl-Heinz leapt behind me, snatching at the back of my skirt; I thought I might lose my balance.

'Peacocks,' said Frau Wolff. 'Over in the falconry. They make a terrible noise, but they're lovely for the children.'

'We saw them earlier. Didn't we, Karl-Heinz? I don't know why I jumped. How silly of me.'

'Don't worry, you'll get used to it. After a while you won't even notice. And you know about the zoo, over by the camp? Felix adores it.'

'I thought Dietrich was making it up,' I said.

'No no. Just at the edge of the camp. There are monkeys and bears, and deer too. We even used to have a wolf . . . perhaps we'll get a new one. You can feed them if you want to. Would you like that?'

Another shriek. Karl-Heinz shook his head.

I lowered my voice. 'When you say at the edge of the camp . . . how close is it?'

'Just a few metres away,' said Frau Wolff.

'So . . . so you can see through the fence? Children can see through?'

'Oh yes, easily.'

I was still searching for the catch on the bangle, but it was too tiny; it seemed to have melted into the names that encircled my wrist. 'I can't quite undo it. Oh dear. There must be a trick . . . '

'Here,' said Frau Wolff, and took my arm, her fingers soft and cool. 'Hidden in the veins of the oak leaf. Isn't that clever?' The bangle sprang apart, and she put it back on her own wrist, and I felt its absence then; all afternoon I kept checking to see if by some sleight of hand I still wore it.

'Why did she have my book?' said Karl-Heinz. He had taken it to bed with him and was tracing the picture of the dog on the cover.

'It's not your book, darling.'

'Yes it is. She gave it to me.'

'Well, yes, *now* it's your book, but it wasn't before. It's not the same book as the one at home.'

He looked at the picture, frowning.

'I met Emmi Wolff today,' I told Dietrich. 'I liked her very much. I think we'll be friends.'

'Good,' he said. 'That's good.' He'd loosened his shirt and put his feet up, and the newspaper drooped in his lap, only half read. More dreadful stories about Stalingrad, I supposed: I didn't want to know.

'She has a son the same age as Karl-Heinz. Felix.'

'Mmm.'

'She brought me those flowers.' I nodded at the vase that Josef had placed on the end table next to his armchair. 'Dietrich, what did he do? The servant?'

'He's an enemy of the Reich.'

'What does *that* mean?'

He sighed. 'He's a Jehovah's Witness. Calmly waiting for the end of the world. They're very reliable, and they never try to escape.'

'He's working in our house, though.'

'Would you prefer one of the professional criminals? I went to quite some trouble to order him for you.'

I didn't reply.

'The stupid thing is, he'd be set free if he'd only sign a piece of paper renouncing his insane beliefs. They all would be. Just a piece of paper.' He rested his head against the back of his armchair. He looked tired. 'Sometimes they make them kneel on the mustering ground for hours.'

'What?'

'Hmm? Nothing. I don't know.'

'Did you hear the peacocks before?' I said. 'A terrible noise. Karl-Heinz was quite scared. But Frau Wolff says you get used to it.'

'I didn't notice,' said Dietrich, his voice sleepy.

'Maybe he'll stop asking us for a little brother. Now that he has Felix to play with.'

'Maybe.'

The logs in the fireplace shifted and hissed.

'I thought I might have our bedroom curtains replaced. Something a bit brighter.'

He glanced up, as if he could see through the ceiling. 'Didn't you say you loved the grey velvet? That was the first thing you said when you walked in. Like a soft forest at dusk, wasn't it?' He settled himself further into the armchair. 'Anyway. Whatever you want.'

'Oh, but the kitchen,' I said. 'There's almost nothing in the cupboards. Almost no equipment at all – not for proper cooking, at any rate. Doesn't anybody eat here?'

'They use the officers' club,' he said, eyes closed. 'It's very economical.'

'I don't want to go to a restaurant for every meal! And how will I make your Pflaumenkuchen? And Karl-Heinz's noodles?'

He didn't answer. I lifted the newspaper from his lap and skimmed the page he was reading: the 'Funny Stories' section. *An elderly farmer stood before the judge. The judge asked, 'How, at your age, did you come to stab a fork in the innkeeper's chest?' The farmer replied, 'It's precisely my age that's to blame! I can't see so well and thought it was a knife!'*

The tulips looked almost black in the low light, and they cast their huge shadow on the wall beside Dietrich, their huddled heads the size of his own.

The Hanging Man orchid. That was the name of it.

When visitors came here to the heart of Germany – the Athens on the Ilm – we showed them the places where eminent citizens once lived: Goethe's garden house in the park, with its bee-filled beds of flowers, and Cranach's house on the Marktplatz, with its winged serpent just above the arch, if you knew where to look. Nietzsche and Herder, Wieland and Bach, Richard Strauss, the Duchess Anna Amalia – oh yes, the finest Germans have called Weimar home. And although the Führer never lived here, he visited many times, and our Platz Adolf Hitlers was the first Platz Adolf Hitlers in the whole of the Reich. We didn't bother showing our visitors the Bauhaus cube, which looked more like a coffee grinder than a house – it was not only ugly, it was also un-German – but see, we said: that is the actual bed in which Schiller died; this is the very chair in which Goethe breathed his last. Here is the clock that displays on its golden face the age of the duke, down to the last elapsed minute – some find it morbid; others declare it a masterpiece of German mechanics. Stand in the Marktplatz and listen: the town hall's chiming carillon, its bells made not from bronze but from Meissen china, as fine as our best dinner sets. And pause for a moment in the old ducal library, in the centre of that soaring rococo hall: see how the spines of the books seem to hang in the pale air above? But shall we wander past the royal stables? Who is kept shut in there now, in place of the royal horses? Let's keep walking. Let's follow Ludendorffstraße north, past the railway station to the foot of the Ettersberg. See, up ahead of us, the green hill rises, here in the green heart of Germany, thick with beeches and spruces and oaks and thrumming with birds. And what is that other sound, louder as we climb? Can we make out the chipping of pickaxes and hammers? We've heard there is a quarry not far from here. If we were to ignore the rules, the signs that say *BEWARE!*, we might draw closer and closer to the place where the trees have been felled to make way for fences and watchtowers. The Goethe oak still stands, though, not far from here – the tree beneath which the poet wrote some of his most celebrated verse, and rested with Charlotte von Stein. They say that if it falls, Germany also will perish . . . but what is that sound? The splitting of stone from stone? Now night is fast falling – we have not kept track of time – and the shadows are dropping from the branches, and we don't dare draw any closer to where we think the Goethe oak must be. And did he write 'Wanderer's Nightsong' in its shade, or the Walpurgisnacht scene in *Faust*, with its witches riding to the peak of the Brocken? No one is certain, no one can say, and perhaps it was both. And what *is* that sound? Men bent double, hewing their own headstones? Or the tinkling of Meissen bells?

5 October 1954

[tape corrupted in places]

Have you started? Am I close enough?

I was talking about the numbers: you had to get the numbers right. Then the place not only paid for itself, it functioned as a successful business. By March 1943 the prisoners totalled twelve thousand five hundred – I have rounded to the nearest hundred – and the weekly meat allowance was two hundred and eighty grams per head. Each prisoner could work twelve hours per day, in theory, and German companies paid four to six Reichsmarks per worker per day. Siemens, Krupp, BMW – even Ford! – all recognised the bargains to be had. The trick, then, was to keep the running costs well below our revenue, taking into account such variables as deliberately slow work, death, and the skimming of funds by the occasional dishonest SS man. It was a delicate balance: we needed the workers, but they cost money to keep. And yes, there were always more workers – they arrived in their hundreds, their thousands, though not all arrived alive – but Berlin was very clear about wastage by that stage of the war: it was our duty to keep the death rate at an acceptable level so we'd have enough prisoners to rent out. Buchenwald's first Kommandant, Karl Koch, had failed to grasp this; he was too busy lining his own pockets, setting a terrible example for the men – and his wife Ilse was no better, parading about in skimpy clothing and taking down the number of any inmate who glanced at her. Koch had left by the time we came to the Ettersberg, of course, so I had nothing to do with him, and nothing to do with the death rate of one in three – I should make that very clear. Yes, he'd been shunted on by that point, first to oversee the camp at Lublin and then, when he bungled that, to guard the military mail at some obscure outpost in the east. Ilse, though, remained in their villa on Eickeweg, playing chess with her gold chess set and carrying on with her married lovers.

'Probably not your sort of person,' I said to Greta when she asked if we should invite her over for coffee and cake. I didn't elaborate; I knew that the Higher SS and Police Leader – Prinz zu Waldeck und Pyrmont, no less – had investigated the couple. He'd scrutinised the accounts for anything that didn't add up, and all sorts of unpleasantness had come to light, including the pair's adulterous affairs – Ilse with camp doctor Hoven as well as with Florstedt, the prison compound commander, and Koch himself with a dancer in Weimar. More important, though, were the brazen black-market dealings with civilians, which . . .

[corrupted]

. . . have heard of human soap, of tattooed lampshades with bases made from human leg-bones. Of light switches made from mummified thumbs. I ask you! People need to ensure they don't let their imaginations run wild; nothing of that nature was ever found, though when the Americans tried us in 1947 they devoted hours of court time to a few bits and pieces recovered from the camp, manufactured purely for scientific reasons, as I understood it. Admittedly, it is the case that Koch allowed some terrible crimes – the thousands of Russian prisoners of war who thought they were lining up for a medical examination, for instance, and the indiscriminate shootings in the quarry. A Jew catapulted from a tree. Two Austrian priests crucified in the Bunker. Before my time, and not my area – I was merely in supplies – but I heard about them. And yes, he turned a blind eye to some high-spirited behaviour on the part of the men, but if you give a keen young German a pistol, won't he want to fire it? If you give him a whip, won't he want to crack it? At any rate, after Koch's departure, Kommandant Pister made it clear that while he understood the need to let off steam now and then, the more extreme frivolities would no longer be tolerated – and as I'm sure you know, all guards had to sign a declaration that they would not maltreat the inmates. Buchenwald was a labour camp, essentially, not one of the bone mills in the east, and just as our housewives were saving the fat from their stews, just as our children were collecting paper and rags, so we went to great lengths to conserve the prisoners. Who else would assemble the rifles? Mine the clay? Break the stones? I for one welcomed this sensible approach, and I'm proud to say that due to my careful budgeting, all prisoners were fed a decent diet – in the satellite camps as well as the parent camp. No rotten potatoes, no soup made from turnip greens. No meat from sick or condemned animals. The written records bear me out, despite what the American prosecution argued. Regularly I entered the spotless kitchen to check the charts, taking note of the little red tabs that indicated every ten deaths, so the cooks could prepare precisely the amount of food required. Not a gram less.

I oversaw the large vegetable gardens that supplied the SS kitchens, too, as well as the piggery and the poultry farm, and the sheep pen where we kept a hundred and fifty head of sheep, and I ensured that these also were economical operations: a special team of prisoners, for example, transported excrement to the plots, so that nothing was wasted. And I did not neglect our zoo creatures, either; they continued to receive the fodder necessary to keep them in good condition for the enjoyment of our men and their families. Mashed potatoes with milk for the monkeys, honey and jam for the bears. It gave me pleasure to pass by the enclosure and see them looking so healthy, so sleek. But yes, naturally, when a prisoner could no longer work, we had to redirect the food to one who could. That's just common sense.

*

When I told Greta we were moving, she asked what on earth she would do there.

'It's a large house,' I said. 'A villa. Plenty of room for children.'

She gave me a sad little half-smile, and I thought I should not have mentioned it – though we were both beginning to wonder if something was wrong. With Karl-Heinz it had been so easy; he was a true honeymoon baby. After his birth, Henning Rost, one of my coarser friends, had clapped me on the back and said, 'You've hardly had a chance to enjoy her,' which should have made me furious – but I couldn't stop smiling. I'd always wanted a big family, and so had Greta; she pored over the pictures of the Goebbels children in her magazines, all six of them dressed in white and beaming as they presented flowers to the Führer or played with Göring's lion cubs. We'd planned just such an army for ourselves, but five years had passed since Karl-Heinz was born, and we had nothing more to show for it. We knew he wanted a little brother; he kept asking us when we would get him a baby, and we overheard him ordering his toys about often enough. Sometimes, also, he talked of – and to – a boy named Ingo, who was not real. When we found muddy footprints on the carpets, or spots of jam on the tablecloth, he told us Ingo was to blame. I mentioned this to our doctor, who said it was quite common in a boy his age, and there was nothing to worry about. There was nothing to worry about with Greta either, he informed me – physically she was in perfect health, as far as he could tell, and he felt certain that another child was just a matter of time. A change of scene would do her good: a move away from the city. Plenty of fresh air.

'We'll pack them in like herrings in a jar,' I told her. 'You'll see.'

We had just finished our midday meal and we could hear Karl-Heinz out in the hallway, chattering to Ingo, asking questions and then waiting for a reply.

Greta was toying with the greeting cards lined up on the windowsill, I remember: messages of congratulation on my appointment to Buchenwald. She held up the one from the Rosts, and asked me if I'd read the nice note from Susannah. Henning had scribbled his name at the bottom too.

'As if it were one of his arrest warrants,' I said.

She laughed and told me I was very wicked.

I went to school with Henning Rost, and we fought together at Passchendaele in the Great War. He'd always scored better marks than I had, always run faster, jumped higher. He even had a scar on his cheek, which he told everyone was a duelling wound, but I'd seen him slice into his face myself. I was supposed to do the same – it would help us in our careers, he said – except I lost my nerve. After Passchendaele he received the Bavarian Bravery Medal in Gold, whereas I had to make do with the Military Merit Cross Third Class.

'Third Class with *Swords*,' my mother said.

'That just means awarded in wartime,' I told her.

'Oh,' she said. 'Well, not everyone is the hero. It's still something to be proud of.' But her voice was uncertain, as if she needed to convince herself. She displayed the medal on her mantelpiece, next to a china dog with a chipped ear.

Henning had the sense to join the Party very early on. By the mid-1930s he'd been hand-selected by Reinhard Heydrich himself to work in Berlin, first for the Security Service and later for the Gestapo, and he'd bagged himself a villa in Grunewald and produced a family of five. My start was slower; after my commercial apprenticeship and some clerical work for an engineering factory I was unemployed for a time – which is no reflection on a man's character or worth, given the period – and I didn't feel I could provide for a wife and children. I watched my two brothers marry and start families, and whenever I saw Henning he asked me if I'd found a decent woman yet, and said that if I left things much longer it would shrivel up and fall off. I joined the Party eventually too, in the big scramble in 1933, and I told him that I had no time for a family and instead was concentrating on my career for the good of the Fatherland. Even as I spoke the words, I knew he would let out one of his big yelping laughs. He shoved at my shoulder and said, 'That only works if you're the Führer – and you're definitely not the Führer.' Then he showed me the latest photograph of his children: the eldest boy looked just like him, and Henning assured me he was beating everyone else in his class.

'Maybe if you changed your name,' he said. 'Maybe that's what's putting the girls off.'

'Why on earth would I do that?' I said.

'Well,' he said, 'Hahn's a Jew name.'

'No it's not,' I said, 'I have all the paperwork. It's an ordinary German name.'

But although my bloodline couldn't be faulted, it turned out he was right. And I probably should have taken his advice and changed it, because I began to feel I had to explain things to people when meeting them for the first time. *I know, it does sound Jewish. One of those strange corruptions: we're honest Germans through and through. Farmers on my mother's side, and bakers and blacksmiths on my father's.*

The only time I ever outdid Henning was when I married Greta.

'She could be your daughter,' he murmured in my ear. 'Good man. Good *man*!' I saw the way his eyes travelled over the curves of her body as she chatted with Susannah, who at thirty-eight was already turning grey. 'That'll take your mind off the Fatherland all right,' he said.

I knew she would miss Munich when we moved. She said she wouldn't know anyone at Buchenwald, and she'd be leaving behind all her friends, and her sister, and her mother. I reminded her it wouldn't be just us – there'd be other families there too, the best sort of families, and children for Karl-Heinz to play with. 'Just wait till you see the house,' I said. 'You'll fall in love with it, I know you will.'

She asked if we could afford it, and I assured her it was very reasonable. Ten per cent less than the going rate, because of where it was. And could we see anything from the house? Just the forest, I said. Mostly the forest. They chose the site specially. But we couldn't see anything else? No, nothing else, I told her. And it was a labour camp? Yes, I said, essentially just a labour camp. A protective custody facility. The inmates – beggars, vagrants, wastrels, drunkards – got to work outside in nature, in the fresh air, chopping wood and digging holes and so on. And after they'd received the proper political instruction, they were released back into the community as better men.

You look surprised – oh yes, there were releases; plenty of them. People don't seem to realise that, but the records will confirm it. It bolstered morale.

Karl-Heinz wandered into the dining room then, wearing my cap – I had a habit of leaving it next to the mirror in the hall when I came home for lunch, so I could check my reflection before I returned to work. He was always asking to wear it, but Greta told him no, it was Papa's special hat, not a hat for little boys, and Papa needed to keep it spick and span. Anyway, on this particular day he'd found it when nobody was watching, and he was very pleased with himself.

'Oh – no, darling,' Greta started to say, but I waved my hand. How could we punish him for wanting to be like his papa? He was only five, and the cap kept slipping down over his eyes so he couldn't see where he was going. We laughed as he staggered around the room.

'I'm going to get you!' I cried, following along behind him and grabbing at his back. 'Just wait till I catch you! Then you'll know all about it!'

He laughed so hard I thought he might be sick. Finally I snatched him up and sat him on my lap, and when he had quietened down he examined the cap, holding it close to his face the way that children do when they're studying the things that fill the world, learning how they work: earthworms or acorns or money, or the hand of someone they love. He crept his fingers across the braid and the visor and the eagle that looked to the left, returning again and again to the little silver death's head, which was his favourite part. He brought it so close I could see his eyelashes brushing it as he blinked, and then he peered inside, running his fingers over the satin lining.

'I hope your hands are clean,' said Greta, and he nodded – but when I took the cap back from him I noticed a smudge on the visor.

'It was Ingo,' said Karl-Heinz.

Greta and I glanced at each other.

'I didn't see him,' I said.

'What does he look like?' said Greta.

Karl-Heinz said, 'He's hiding.'

'Where does he live?' I said.

He shrugged. 'In the wardrobe, under the bed, behind the curtains . . .'

I rubbed the smudge away with my handkerchief; it was time to return to work. Greta and Karl-Heinz came to see me off, but when I opened the front door he squealed.

'Be careful, Papa! Ingo is hiding there. You'll squash him.'

'Oh dear, we wouldn't want that,' said Greta.

'Say sorry,' said Karl-Heinz.

'I'm sorry,' I said, making a little bow to him.

'No, say sorry to Ingo.'

Greta was trying not to laugh, I could see. I leaned behind the door. 'I'm sorry, Ingo,' I said to the empty corner. 'I didn't notice you there.'

Later, I remember, when I was alone, I held the hat close to my own face, squinting at the braid, the visor, the silver death's head – but despite their closeness, they blurred out of focus and did not look like the things they were.

The following month, when we were leaving Munich, Greta told Karl-Heinz that Ingo would stay behind, to look after our apartment. The strategy appeared to work: Karl-Heinz waved up at an empty window as we climbed into the car to go to the train station, and he kept waving until we turned out of our street. It seemed we really had rid ourselves of his imaginary friend; he didn't even mention him the first night, when we'd expected him to feel unsettled, and I remember I had the strange idea that his absence had made room for a new child to take his place: a real child.

'A fresh start,' I said to Greta.

'A fresh start,' she said.

I could tell she was impressed with the villa.

'The size of the garden!' she said. 'It's practically a farm!'

'Not quite a *farm*,' I said – but certainly, it was big enough for a dog. A lot of the senior officers owned one, and I decided we should have one too. I chose a Weimaraner, to commemorate the move to our new home, and I put Karl-Heinz in charge of her water bowl. We named her Freya.

I don't know what happened to her.

Greta did her best to make the house ours, arranging our own cushions on the couches and armchairs, hanging our favourite pictures on the walls: the print of Hohenschwangau in our bedroom, the swans on the Bodensee at the top of the staircase. Next to the bed she placed our own alarm clock and our wedding edition of *Mein Kampf* in its carved oak box. She had the beds made up with our own linen, too – before we were married she'd spent months decorating it with lace as fine as sea foam, and she couldn't bear to leave it in storage. It was helpful, she said, for Karl-Heinz to have a few things to remind

him of home – and if I'm honest, I too appreciated these familiar little sights. But the kitchen, apparently, was a disaster.

'Look,' she said. 'How on earth will we manage?' She listed
for me all the things that were missing, peering several times
into every cupboard and drawer as if she might find what was
not there. No measuring cups, no scales, no sharp little wheel
for crimping pastry. No baking tray for my Pflaumenkuchen
and no strainer for Karl-Heinz's noodles. No crank-handled
mincer. No mixing bowls, no roasting pan. No skillet. Not
even a sieve. Her mother would be shocked when she saw it,
she said, but I doubted that Elisabeth would visit. She hadn't
even come to our wedding, which wasn't a wedding at all, she
told us, because it was in an oak grove and not the church, and
we were not married in the eyes of God. But I had seen Greta's
face lit by the flaming torches; I had felt her hand tight in mine
as we passed beneath the saluting arcade.

That first week she and Emmi Wolff went into Weimar and
bought all the items on her list that they could find, given the
shortages. They were chattering and laughing when they
returned to the villa, their cheeks bright from the icy February
air, and they unwrapped their purchases and washed them and
dried them and spent quite some time deciding on the best
place for each one: whisks in the middle drawer, along with the
little notched scoop for separating eggs, and the apple corer in
with the sharp knives, and the set of china measuring cups
shaped like geese displayed on the dresser, because they were
charming as well as practical.

'He'll expect miracles from you now,' I heard Frau Wolff say.

At supper Greta told me they'd visited the Hotel Elephant,
which was just as nice as the Bayerischer Hof in Munich, in its
own way. 'It's where the Führer stays when he visits,' she said.
'He had a special balcony added so he could address the crowds.'

'I'm glad you're settling in,' I said.

Then she remembered she'd brought me a piece of

Schwarzwälder Kirschtorte from their konditorei – they told her it was the Führer's favourite. 'Josef!' she called, and the boy appeared. She asked him to bring me my cake, and thanked him.

I waited until Niemand had scurried off, and then I said, 'Don't speak to him as if he were an ordinary person.'

From the look on Greta's face, you'd have thought I'd struck her. 'I was just being polite,' she said. 'If we lose our good manners—'

'He's an enemy of the Reich,' I said. 'I've told you that already.'

'Yes, you have,' said Greta in a tone I did not care for – but the SS families *needed* to be careful about how they engaged with their servants; Kommandant Pister had made that quite clear.

When Niemand returned with the cake he placed it in front of me and backed away, almost bowing.

'For goodness' sake,' I said. 'I'm not the Führer!' Greta shot me a look. I noticed a thumb-sized dent in the side of the cake, where someone had tried to press a cherry back in. It loosened itself again and plopped onto the plate as I watched, and bright juice sprayed the side of my hand. Still the boy was retreating towards the door; he would not turn his back on me. 'It looks delicious,' I said to Greta, lifting my fork. And it was; I finished it in just a few bites.

I suppose I should have apologised to her properly, but that afternoon had been particularly trying; no wonder I was start-ing to lose my hair. The camp's senior inmate had been nagging me for this, that and the other, as if I had an entire department store filled with towels and bowls and blankets at my disposal. Then I found out there was a problem with the camp's water, which was my responsibility. Water issues had dogged Buchenwald ever since it had opened – issues with the pumps and tanks, the rainwater purification plant, the removal of sewage – and were probably the reason the famous Goethe oak was looking so sickly. This time it was the water supply to the camp laundry, which meant the prisoners' clothing couldn't be washed, which meant I had to find a solution quick smart. Kommandant Pister called me into his headquarters and told me as much – it was my duty to ensure that the camp maintained basic hygiene, he said, to avoid the spread of disease, which could very well jump the fence. We sat in his conversation area, on the cushioned banks surrounding a small pool. It was sunk into the ground and bordered with tropical plants that wouldn't survive outdoors but seemed to flourish here at the edge of the water. I could see them reflected in its surface: spidery shadows, strange and shifting tentacles, bits of tusk. Sometimes tunnels, sometimes faces. How pleasant to have such a space at your disposal during the difficult working day. I told Pister I would fix the problem so that the laundry workers could clear the backlog of dirty washing as soon as possible. As a matter of principle I was always mindful of the inmates' basic needs – make sure you include that – but like all the other officers, I preferred not to have to visit the compound unnecessarily; you risked seeing something, or catching something. And the laundry was far too close to the disinfection facility, where a new transport of prisoners was being deloused; as soon as I entered the grounds that afternoon I could feel myself itching – so the last thing I felt like when I came home was having to remind my wife of the correct protocol with servants.

The thing was, I couldn't close the office door at the end of each day and leave, as other men could – bankers or dentists or bakers, or indeed men like Henning, who didn't live at their place of work. Even if I drew the curtains, turned on the gramophone and grabbed Greta by the waist for a waltz around the living room or took her upstairs to bed, it was all still there, just outside, just minutes beyond the officers' villas that lined the gentle curve of Eickeweg and just minutes from our little garden where Karl-Heinz had built a snowman with stones for eyes – my office, the hunched rows of barracks, the mustering ground, the electrified fence. And it was a rare evening that I wasn't interrupted to sign some document or other, to make some difficult decision or other; difficult decisions were just part of the job. Goethe himself sent a Weimar woman to the scaffold – not many people know that. She'd been convicted of killing her unborn child and sentenced to death, and Goethe was asked if, as Staatsminister, he supported the sentence, and he said yes. I'm not complaining – don't get me wrong. I know that many men would have given their eye teeth to be in my position, difficult decisions and all. Did I miss our life in Munich? Of course, yes, and I knew Greta did too, especially at the start; she tried not to mention it, but I saw the look that came over her face when her sister wrote of skating on the Nymphenburg canal, and how pretty the Chinese Tower looked in the snow. In demanding times, however, one must make sacrifices. We can find somewhere to skate here, I told her, and the Chinese Tower isn't going anywhere. Even Karl-Heinz knew that Buchenwald was our home for the time being. 'We have to stay until Papa has won the war,' I heard him tell his ark animals one day. I had never felt so proud.

And after all, I was doing exactly the kind of work Obergruppenführer Eicke had prepared me for at Dachau. I still count myself fortunate to have learned from him, even now. He'd had his writing paper printed with the motto *Only one thing matters – the command given*, and that was the attitude he passed on to his men. Papa Eicke, those in the guard unit called him, and so did I. He was a true statesman but never minded getting his hands dirty, never hesitated in doing whatever his duty required – you'll recall that he stepped in without question to solve the problem of Ernst Röhm. He would have gone on to even greater things, I'm sure. I couldn't believe it when the news came through that his plane had been shot down in Russia, but it made me all the more determined to do the best job I could at Buchenwald. I think he would have been proud of me; certainly, I was proud to live on the street that bore his name. Yes, you can include that. I'm not ashamed, have no reason to be ashamed – the American trial was a farce, as you know, and had nothing to do with justice. For instance, they were charging us with victimising their citizens, but they failed to furnish the defence with the name of a single American victim! They refused to stop the public from leaving wreaths outside the courthouse, making the whole thing look like a funeral, and they called us *the accused* rather than *the defendants*; so much for the presumption of innocence. Even before the trial began, they published our photographs in the newspapers as if we were master criminals, already convicted, and we had to sit in the dock in front of crowds of gawking spectators with numbers hanging from our necks. All the real criminals, though – the ones who issued the orders – had taken the coward's way out. Shot themselves or poisoned themselves or hanged themselves and left people like me to wait for the punishment. Locked up at Dachau, a stone's throw from my home, right where Papa Eicke had taken me under his wing. And after that, Landsberg, no less. *Dietrich Hahn has been convicted of the offence of aiding and participating in the operations of the Buchenwald Concentration Camp and has been sentenced by the General Military Court to serve a sentence of death by hanging.*

And yet, here I am.

PART THREE
THE ANIMAL KINGDOM

Frankfurt am Main, September 1946

But I wanted to tell you about the miracles, Lotte. There are three in this story – I'll start with the first.

In the autumn of 1942, when a Herr Erling came into my care at the Holy Spirit, they had given him less than a year to live. As I approached his hospital bed I could tell he was a very ill man; his eyes seemed to look in rather than out, and his skin had grown so thin I had the feeling, just for a moment, that I could see right through it to where the tumours lay like bulbs buried in black soil. His face was all shadows cast by its own bones – all sockets and teeth – the face of my father at a similar stage of the same disease. The nurse unbuttoned his pyjama shirt and exposed his chest. He didn't clutch at me as I examined him, the way many terminal patients did; instead, he placed his hand on my forearm like a close friend about to share a secret.

At first I thought he wanted me to end his suffering – it was not an uncommon request in the cancer ward, though of course I could never agree to that line of treatment.

'I would swallow glass,' he said. 'If you advised it, I would swallow glass.'

'We can ensure you are free from pain, Herr Erling,' I told him – or rather, I told the hand that was resting on my arm; I had never succeeded in cultivating much of a bedside manner.

'Is there any hope at all?' he said.

I became uncomfortable when patients began to discuss things other than their immediate physical symptoms; my training didn't cover such affairs. They are not people, my old professor used to say – they are diseases. You are of most value to them if you approach them as such.

'I'm sorry, Herr Erling,' I said, and began to note something down in order to free myself of his hand.

'You could open me up again and cut it all out.'

'I'm sorry,' I repeated.

The other patients looked away, pretending they hadn't heard. The nurse tidied his bed, brushing at the spotless pillows, lifting his blanched hands and placing them under the blanket before tucking it in as tightly as the flap of an envelope.

'Can nothing else be done?' said a voice. I hadn't noticed his wife sitting white-faced in the corner of the room, obscured by a spray of chrysanthemums. She was small and plump-shouldered and wore her grey-blond hair set into finger waves, like my mother used to. 'What about your electrical machine?' she said. 'Your Sympathetic Vitaliser?'

By then I'd all but forgotten about it – or so I said, at least, if the subject ever came up. Truth be told, Lotte, I was embarrassed about that chapter of my professional life, about my belief that I might really have discovered an effective treatment for cancer, and the machine remained packed away in the attic like a memory.

'That was just an experiment,' I said. 'An idea I had when I was a student and thought I could save the world. It came to nothing.'

'Two of the patients survived,' said Frau Erling, crossing to her husband's bedside. 'That's not nothing.'

'Not nothing,' said Herr Erling.

'They entered remission for a time,' I said. 'It wasn't statistically significant.'

The nurse withdrew, stealing away on her cork-soled shoes that made no sound. The Erlings' eyes would not let me go.

'We'll sign anything you want,' said Frau Erling. 'At the very least, it can't hurt.'

'Can't hurt,' echoed Herr Erling. He was trying to sit up in his bed, but the nurse had secured him too snugly, and he sank back into the pillows once more. They puffed up around his hairless skull like rising dough.

'Don't exert yourself, Karsten,' said his wife, stroking his cheek. It was scattered with grey stubble, as if he'd spent the day at the beach, lying on grey sand, though his pallor recalled the inside of a shell.

'The machine has been in storage for years,' I said. 'Some of the rubber may well have perished. It would need recalibrating . . . and I would need permission from the hospital director, who is unlikely to grant it . . . ' I trailed off.

'Please, Herr Doktor,' said Frau Erling. 'Perhaps we might even make a donation to the hospital . . . ? For further research. We have substantial means at our disposal.'

She was standing so close to me that I could smell the face cream she'd rubbed into her pale cheeks – lily of the valley, the same one Anna used.

'I can't make any promises,' I said. 'I'll have to ask for permission. And I'll need to inspect the device. Make sure I wouldn't be exposing Herr Erling to any danger.'

'And how soon . . . ?' said Frau Erling.

Time was always the most difficult subject for my patients and their families to broach. I was used to unfinished questions; questions too terrible to articulate. *How soon . . . ? How much longer . . . ?*

'If we are going to try the Vitaliser – *if*, Frau Erling – then we have no time to lose.'

I thought she was going to kiss me, and once again I turned to make a note on Herr Erling's chart.

'Thank you, Herr Doktor,' she said. 'You don't know what this means. Thank you. Thank you.'

'Thank you,' said her husband, his voice little more than a whisper.

I didn't tell them that the two patients who had entered remission had died; don't ask me why. And don't ask me why I let them think Herr Baumhauer might approve the treatment. Perhaps I felt a quiver of that old energy begin to hum in me – and besides, remission was something, wasn't it? If not a cure, then at least a little more time.

In the evening I climbed the narrow stairs to the attic. It was just above our kitchen, where the ceiling was lower than in the rest of the apartment; once it would have been the maid's quarters, but we used it for storage. The air was thick and warm in that stooped space, and I opened the tiny window in order to breathe more freely. I thought I could hear Anna practising her scales in the parlour on the floor below – but of course, Anna was gone by then, married to David Hirsch, and you were gone too, Lotte, and I was living alone. It must have been a neighbour I could hear; the ghost notes drifted up to meet me, as soft as the voice of a distant bird, but whenever the pianist made a mistake a crash of keys sounded, discordant and angry, hammered out with the fists. I picked my way around collapsed armchairs, trunks of clothes, a butterfly net, your old high-chair, a cheval mirror that used to stand in our bedroom until a gust of wind toppled it and it cracked, cutting our reflections in two. Anna refused to part with anything; she said you never could tell when you might need it again. I worried about the weight of the contents of the attic, the hillocks of old and broken things piled above our heads. 'One day it'll all come down,' I told her. 'It'll bury us alive.' She smiled and said that just because I always expected the worst, the worst didn't always happen.

I was sure the Vitaliser was packed in a trunk, but the first one I opened contained only my books and papers from university. The silverfish had made a meal of them; I held a page of my notes to the window, and the daylight spattered through my careful sketches of the parts of the human cardiovascular system. I remembered reciting them to myself over and over as a student, inventing all manner of desperate mnemonic tricks. I'd feared I would only ever be a mediocre doctor; perhaps that was why I was so drawn to electrotherapy, which seemed to promise an invisible shortcut, a magic trick. Deeper in the recesses of the attic I opened another trunk, and my fingers met with something soft – something feathered. A wing, I thought at first, and for a split second I imagined that one of the pigeons that cooed on the guttering had found its way in and become trapped, and here beneath my fingers lay its slight remains. A closer looked revealed my grandfather's full dress uniform; his fine serge trousers and tunic folded into perfect squares, his boots glinting like ebony, the Pickelhaube helmet trimmed with feathers. He had never discussed his time in France, as far as I could remember, but once a year, on Sedan Day, he put on the uniform and pinned his medals to his breast. I'd thought that war must be an elegant affair, conducted by gentlemen with scented pomade combed through their hair, and wax on the tips of their moustaches, and extravagant plumed helmets on their heads. Somewhere in the family album was a portrait of me, aged four, wearing the Pickelhaube: a rare moment of indulgence on the part of my grandfather and my parents, who'd agreed to the photographer's suggestion, they said, because it seemed the only way to stop me crying. They sat me on a velvet chair that had lions' heads for arms, and I brandished a wooden sword, which showed in the photograph as a grey blur: a strange slice of rain.

I lifted the helmet from the trunk and held it out in front of me, and the feathers stirred: a sudden current of air from the window, or perhaps just the imperceptible movements of my hands. I thought I could smell my grandfather's tobacco, which he used to tamp into a curling meerschaum pipe carved with a mermaid; he told me the smoke was her breath, when I was young enough to believe such stories. Anna's scales reached me again – little waves rising and falling, rising and falling – and then the bells of the nearby St. Bernhard's. I moved further into the corner of the attic, to where the roof met the floor and I could no longer stand upright. The worst place to be if there was an air raid. Behind a tapestry fire-screen made by Anna's mother – the wooden frame was sound but the silk had frayed and rotted; Anna said you might stitch a replacement one day, Lotte – I could make out a third trunk. Hunchbacked, I crept towards it and opened the latches – and yes, there lay the Vitaliser in its pearwood case. The contact plates huddled inside the lid; I remembered winding their cords around my hand so they wouldn't kink when I packed it away, and rolling up the soft chamois cloth, too, then bedding the whole thing down in a nest of frayed woollen blankets Anna had kept for just such a purpose. I turned the dials, although it wasn't plugged in, and I felt it again: that old quiver.

With some difficulty I transported the machine to the Holy Spirit on the tram, and then I went and knocked on Herr Baumhauer's door.

'Yes, Doktor Weber?' he said. 'I don't have much time.'

'I've had a request for alternative treatment,' I told him. 'With the Sympathetic Vitaliser.'

The director sighed. 'Everyone died last time.'

'It's Herr Erling and his wife.'

'Then there's definitely no point.'

'They've offered to make a large donation.'

He opened his mouth, closed it again. 'A donation?'

'They have substantial means at their disposal, they say.'

'So they do. So they do. He should be in a private room, of course, but what with all the wounded . . . '

I knew that Baumhauer wanted to expand the hospital – his legacy to the sick of Frankfurt, he said – and I knew that he'd been negotiating with the authorities to lease the closed Jewish Hospital in Gagernstraße.

'The Vitaliser might put us on a more equal footing with the Berlin researchers,' I said. 'Allow us to compete. Minister Goebbels gave one of them a hundred thousand Reichsmarks.'

He bristled. 'Well, perhaps in this case an alternative treatment could be approved. Yes, I think we might allow it. The Führer has a special interest in cancer research, after all – you'll be aware that his own mother died from the disease.'

'Is it a radio?' said Frau Erling as I wheeled the Vitaliser into the ward. 'Is Mozart to cure my husband?'

Before I could answer, Herr Erling spoke.

'I had a beautiful singing voice,' he said. 'Clear as a bird – that's what the choirmaster told my mother.'

Like many patients in his condition, he was plucking at the past as it slipped by in an opiate drift.

'Is there a lark loose in the church?' he said. 'Flitting about the rafters like a prayer?' He paused for breath. 'Until my voice broke and another boy took my place. *Laudate Dominum, omnes gentes . . . Laudate eum, omnes populi . . .* '

I recalled such meanderings from my father when he was nearing the end and imagined himself back on the battlefields of Africa – like my grandfather, he too was a military man – but it was impossible to tell what was memory and what the conjuring of the drug.

'A word, Herr Doktor?' said Frau Erling, and drew me aside and whispered too softly in my ear.

'I beg your pardon?' I said.

She leaned in closer. 'Will it *hurt* him?' she breathed, looking not at me but at her husband.

'Not at all,' I said in a brisk voice that was meant to reassure.

'Some patients report a little pinch, at most. A little sting – a rubber band flicked against the skin. The majority feel nothing.'

I saw the nurse casting a sceptical eye over the machine as I steered it to the edge of the bed and plugged it in. The other patients craned their necks: restaurant patrons regretting their choice when they see the dishes served to another table.

'To answer your first question, Frau Erling,' I said, 'it's not a radio. The wooden box houses the control unit that generates the frequencies, and I adjust these via the dials to achieve the correct dose, which the contact plates deliver to the patient. We can't see it working, just as we can't see the oxygen we breathe that keeps us alive.'

As I looked at the Vitaliser in that bright white room, I saw that it was as beautiful an object as ever – and at the same time I knew that it could do nothing for Herr Erling, no matter how glossy its varnish, how bright its brass handles. I wondered what had possessed me to resurrect it. The patients in the other beds were still watching, all eyes in the ward on my useless invention. It was too late to change my mind now.

'Sister?' I said.

'Yes, Doktor.' The nurse folded back the bedding and positioned Herr Erling's feet for me, and his face creased – in laughter or distress, I couldn't tell.

He was murmuring to himself again, of choirs and rafters, and his wife took his hand and said, 'Shhhh, shhhh. It's all right. Everything is all right.'

'Please stand back,' I said. 'You must not make contact with him during the treatment.'

I strapped the plates to the soles of his feet, and his skin was cool, as bloodless as the tripe Anna used to cook for herself in our low-ceilinged kitchen when I wasn't at home. She was forever urging me to try it, but I couldn't bear the smell.

'*Quoniam confirmata est . . . Super nos misericordia eius,*' said Herr Erling, half singing, then lapsing into silence.

I switched on the Vitaliser. It started to hum its familiar hum, and I turned the dials, watching the needles waver and sway behind their little panes.

After a few moments Frau Erling whispered, 'When will you begin, Herr Doktor?'

I used the Vitaliser on Herr Erling once every two weeks, for ten minutes at a time, rotating between his feet, his hands, his thoracic and lumbar spine and his abdomen.

'I don't mean to question you, Herr Doktor,' Frau Erling said one day, which always meant a question was to follow, 'but why don't you treat his chest? Since the cancer started in his lungs.'

I tried to explain to her the theory of remote sympathy – that treating one part of the body could affect a seemingly unconnected part. 'The body is a circuit,' I began, but I could see she couldn't understand me – or didn't believe me. 'This is the procedure I developed,' I said. 'The correct procedure. And besides,' I added, unable to help myself, 'we do not wish to stop his heart.'

I don't know why I said that. The Erlings were perfectly decent people who had never done anything to me, and it was clear they loved one another. Well, perhaps that was why I said it.

The patients in the other beds gasped.

'What did he say?' asked one.

'He doesn't want to stop his heart,' replied another.

'I thought I must have misheard,' said the first. 'Stop his heart!'

'Of course not, of course not,' said Frau Erling. 'No, Herr Doktor – you know best. Of course not.'

After three months, however, by December 1942, her husband showed no improvement. Indeed, he seemed to be deteriorating; his colour was worse, his voice fainter, he wouldn't eat – not even the appetising broths and jellies Frau Erling brought from home – and he flinched at my touch. I had the feeling I was applying the contact plates to bare bone.

'We don't have to continue,' I told her. 'If it's too uncomfortable.'

'What will happen if we stop?'

'Nature will take its course, regrettably.'

'And if we continue?'

'At this stage, I would expect the same outcome.'

'Is the machine making it worse? Spreading it around more? Since the body is a circuit.'

The thought hadn't occurred to me. 'No,' I said. Was it possible? 'No.'

'Then we'll continue. Won't we, Karsten?'

Herr Erling was gazing up into a corner of the room and gave no reply. I recognised that look, had witnessed it many times over the course of my career: eyes resting on a blank ceiling, an unadorned wall, as if it were the wide sky. As if it were home.

And then, a few days later, he sat up unassisted and said he would like some vanilla pudding. His wife fed him the tiniest of dobs, tinier even than those you might offer an infant who knows nothing other than its mother's milk, but he grasped the spoon and began to feed himself great gulps of the stuff. In a moment he was scraping the bottom of the dish, sucking at the spoon and asking for more.

One month after that, around the time he should have died, my first miracle rose from his bed and packed his suitcase. His chest X-rays showed no evidence of the tumours that earlier had spotted every film.

Herr Baumhauer called me to his office and shook me by the hand, then took a tray of little red glasses from the top of a massive sideboard. 'These have been in my family for a hundred and fifty years,' he said, pouring me a schnapps. 'I'm told that Frederick the Great drank from one of them before the Battle of Liegnitz. We don't know which one, of course – but I rather like that, don't you? It could be any of them.'

I suspected he'd recounted this story many times before. 'Remarkable,' I said, though I didn't think the glasses looked that old.

'Ruby glass,' he said. 'Made by the Great Elector's alchemist. He couldn't make gold, but he discovered the secret to ruby glass. Prost, Doktor Weber.'

He took a sip of schnapps and motioned for me to do the same. The late afternoon light had turned the contents of the little glasses a deep and sticky red.

'Prost,' I said, and swallowed a few drops.

'It was a sensation, this ruby glass. Nobody had seen the like of it since ancient times. The Great Elector gave the alchemist his own laboratory on his own island.' He took another sip, and so did I. 'What I am saying, Weber, is that innovation is the thing. Experimentation. This machine of yours, this, this Sympathetic Volumiser – it could really make our name.'

Hadn't I dreamt of such a moment, Lotte? Hadn't I imagined it a thousand times? 'Herr Direktor,' I began. I didn't know what to do with my glass, so I continued to hold it, the fluid inside warming to the temperature of my blood. 'I'm delighted with my patient's progress, of course – but we must be cautious. Spontaneous remissions do occur. It's too early to tell if the Sympathetic Vitaliser played any part.'

'Did you read the Führer's last speech?' he said. '*The miracles we have achieved in the last three years are unique in history.* This could be our miracle.'

'I don't think we can talk of miracles quite yet, Herr Direktor.'

'Of course we can!' He sat back in his chair beneath the painting of Hitler that still didn't look quite dry. 'Did you know they're making a second donation, the Erlings? The *Völkischer Beobachter* want to do a story.' He drained his glass. 'It's a shame he looks so Jewish. Even though he's not – that's all been checked, of course. Perhaps we can find a stand-in for the photograph, or—' He stopped short. 'Ah. I always forget,' he said, gesturing at my blond hair, my blue eyes. 'Well, nobody need know.'

FROM THE IMAGINARY DIARY OF FRAU GRETA HAHN

February 1943

I spent the day after we moved in cleaning the house from top to bottom. It wasn't at all dirty, but I felt more comfortable knowing for certain that everything had been washed and wiped down, from the empty shelves in the kitchen cupboards to the tiles in the bathroom to every last light switch. When Josef saw what I was doing he came rushing over, and for just a moment, before I remembered who I was, I thought he was going to scold me.

'I'm sorry, madam,' he said. 'I should have told you. That's been done – I cleaned everything, before you arrived. Everything. There's no need.'

'It's all right, Josef,' I said. 'I want to. It makes me feel more . . . at home here.'

'At home,' he said, nodding. 'Yes, madam. Of course.'

'But how am I supposed to cook, do you know?'

'I'm not sure, madam. I'm new here.'

I gave Karl-Heinz a little cloth of his own, and he followed me around, making a show of dusting the skirting boards and the radiators and then grizzling because he couldn't reach any higher.

'But they look so clean!' I said. 'Well done, darling. What a help you are. We'll have to think of a reward.'

He brightened at that and asked if I would take him to the zoo.

'Not just yet,' I said. 'But maybe we can go and meet the little boy who lives next door.'

'And then we can go to the zoo with him.'

'Mmm,' I said.

When we'd finished our work we made ourselves presentable and went to see if the Wolffs were home.

'What a lovely surprise!' said Frau Wolff. 'Come in, come in. Felix! Look who's here! You can take Karl-Heinz to see the fish pond and the alligator. Oh, it's not a real one.'

Their house had exactly the same layout as ours; even the view looked the same, though I knew it must have differed by a few degrees. On a table in the entranceway, a model sailing ship just like ours. As we passed the kitchen I said, 'Is it true that nobody cooks here?'

'Nothing more than boiled eggs,' she said, showing me to the living room. 'Marvellous, isn't it?'

'So everyone eats at the officers' club?'

'You can eat there if you like, but most families have them deliver their meals. It's unbelievably cheap.'

'Is there somewhere in Weimar where I could buy a few pots and pans, though?'

'If you must,' said Frau Wolff. 'I can take you. I'll order a driver.'

A servant entered and set down a tray of coffee and pralines. After he'd left I said, 'I can't get used to that.'

'Ugh, don't tell me you're the guilty type,' said Frau Wolff, unwrapping a chocolate. She looked me up and down. 'And you can afford a chocolate or two. And we deserve it.'

'I mean the arrangement with the servants. The prisoners. I thought they'd be locked up.'

Frau Wolff laughed and told me I'd have to learn how things worked here. Thousands of them were let out every day, she said, to work in the quarry, or on building the rail link to Weimar, or at the new Gustloff armaments works, only a short stroll away. We watched the children through the glass, the girls throwing snowballs while Karl-Heinz and Felix leapt over a stone alligator.

'But having one in your own house,' I said.

'It's quite safe – Kommandant Pister doesn't really approve, but Otto explained that I need the help because of the children. And your husband obviously made a case too.'

'Don't you worry he'll steal something?'

'He knows what will happen if he does. Anyway, you just have to make sure you have the right kind. You wouldn't want any of the greens, and obviously not the blacks.'

'What?'

'Asocials are the black triangles, and professional criminals are the green ones. The reds and the purples are the best choice – the politicals and the bible worms.'

'What are bible worms?'

'Jehovah's Witnesses, of course! Oh, but Frau Koch's servant . . . I shouldn't really say.'

'What? Shouldn't say what?'

'Well . . . one day she came home to find him blind drunk and dressed up in her underwear.'

The Kochs' villa sat on the corner of the path that led to the camp. The largest house on Eickeweg, it had a trio of whimsically carved musicians fixed to the front gable and a stone turret at the entrance gate – it looked like a watchtower, but Frau Wolff said it was just ornamental. I waited for the former Kommandant's wife to come and introduce herself; we'd been at Buchenwald for almost two weeks before I so much as laid eyes on her, and I was beginning to think she was just a rumour. Then one morning, when Karl-Heinz and I were heading out on a walk – he wanted to see if he could find some acorns in the forest, though I told him it was the wrong season and they would all be hidden by the snow – I saw her front door open and she stepped outside. She was small and red-haired, and despite her features, which were a little too pinched to be beautiful, she carried herself like royalty. I raised my hand to her, but maybe she didn't notice. A little boy and girl followed her out onto the front steps, and she paused to pull hats down on their heads. The boy took his off and threw it on the ground, and she picked it up and put it on his head again. This routine played out twice more. I recognised it well; Karl-Heinz still did the same thing sometimes, because he thought it was funny. I remembered smacking him for it once, the sting pricking my palm long afterwards. Ilse Koch did not smack her son. She bent down to him, showed him the knitted hat, pointing to the ducks stitched along the border – I wasn't close enough to see the pattern, but it would have been something like ducks. The little boy stood there quite obediently while she pulled the hat on him one more time, and as she tied it under his chin, he looked over at us and smiled.

'Mama,' said Karl-Heinz, tugging at my sleeve. 'Mama!'

'Yes, darling?' I said, taking his hand and setting off in the direction of the forest. Hoarfrost like chips of glass under our feet.

'Are they going to look for acorns too?'

'Maybe they are,' I said. I nodded at the guard on the sentry line. 'Wouldn't that be nice?'

'No!'

They were a little ahead of us now, and I could see Frau Koch's red hair shining against her red fox-fur coat, as sinuous and sleek as the pelts themselves. In the cold air, her breaths drifted towards us in clouds. 'No?'

'They'll take all the acorns.'

'We can share.'

'They'll find all the good ones.'

'Acorns are acorns,' I said.

It was quiet in the forest. Colourless. Snow-covered trees, white sky. Karl-Heinz found a stick and started poking around, but all he unearthed was brown muck, decaying leaves – and, once, a long pale worm that twisted blindly on the end of his stick. He held it up for me to see.

'Put it back where you found it,' I said, trying not to shudder in front of him; I didn't want him to learn to be afraid of the world. 'Make sure you cover it over. Keep it nice and warm.'

'Where did the other lady go?'

'I'm not sure,' I said, though I'd been wondering the same thing. Every now and then I thought I heard the snap of a twig, the crunch of a shoe on new snow; I thought I glimpsed coppery fur stealing between the trunks. But it was nothing.

They'd made a beautiful job of the new bedroom curtains; I could see that even before they were hung. I'd spent days looking at different fabric samples, rubbing them between my fingers to assess their weight and sheen, holding them up to the windows and trying to imagine how they would look full-size. In the end I'd decided on a French floral print: red and yellow roses, to brighten the room.

'This way,' I told the two prisoners. 'Don't let them drag on the floor.' They followed me up the stairs, and I had to resist turning to check on them: were they drawing knives from their sleeves? Preparing their home-made garrotte? I told myself not to be so silly, but I was much happier when we reached the bedroom. As we entered I could see them behind me in the cheval mirror, holding the curtains high so they didn't drag, just as I'd asked. One of them noticed his reflection and stopped dead for a moment, his mouth an open hole – I thought he was going to say something, but then he met my eyes, blinked, and kept walking. He and the other prisoner had been tailors, Dietrich said, and when they spread the curtains over the bed for me to inspect, I saw how they'd matched the pattern along every seam. Leaf to leaf, rose to rose, so you could hardly see the joins – and the hems were hand-finished, the stitches almost invisible.

Josef fetched a step-ladder, and they began taking down the

old curtains, one prisoner unhooking them while the other gathered the velvet in his arms.

'What will happen to them?' said Karl-Heinz from the doorway.

'I'm not sure,' I said. 'Go back to your toys.' But he came in and watched the men too, placing himself at the foot of the ladder, as stern as the guards who patrolled the forest just across the road; it was all I could do not to laugh.

Gently the men lifted the first curtain from the bed and hung it hook by hook. I stood back and admired the fall of the fabric – all the way from Paris, I said to Karl-Heinz. It was as pretty as a summer dress, and already the room felt lighter, brighter. Yes, I'd made the right choice.

'What's that?' said Karl-Heinz, peering at a spot on the curtain the prisoners were still hanging.

'What?' I said.

'That.' He pointed to one of the roses a handspan from the inner edge, and I saw that part of it was shrivelled, deformed, as if attacked by insects.

'Josef, do you see this?' I said. 'It's a mistake, isn't it? A manufacturing flaw.' I sensed the prisoners pause in their work for just a beat.

'Perhaps you won't notice it once it's hung, madam,' said Josef. 'The pattern is so dense . . . '

'But I was told this fabric was the finest quality. It came all the way from Paris.' I could feel my voice rising, my face starting to flush. All I'd wanted was pretty curtains, to brighten the room. To make it feel like ours. And here was this mistake, spoiling everything. 'It's the exact spot my hand will go to every day, to pull them across,' I said. 'No. No. I can't look at that every single day.'

The prisoner on the step-ladder stumbled and let out a small cry; for a few seconds he scrabbled at the air before pressing his hand to the windowpane to steady himself.

'Do be careful!' I said.

'Yes, Frau Sturmbannführer.' He was standing there looking down at the floor, and the other one was looking at the floor too, the unhung section of the ruined curtain still folded over his arm so as not to wrinkle it. 'Shall we take them down, Frau Sturmbannführer?' said the first one.

'Of course, yes, take them down! Please.'

They moved slowly, cautiously, arranging the curtains over the bed once more; they seemed not to understand that it no longer mattered if they creased. The little brass rings sewn to the lining twinkled like a row of wedding bands.

'Shall we hang the old ones back up, Frau Sturmbannführer?'

'Of course!' I said. 'Of course, hang them up! I don't want bare windows!'

I couldn't be in the room with them any more. I went downstairs and lay on the couch, and I must have fallen asleep, because when I woke the light had changed and I knew it was much later. I could hear Dietrich moving around upstairs.

In the bedroom the grey curtains were back in place and the floral ones had been taken away.

'I thought these were going today,' said Dietrich.

'There was a problem,' I said. 'A manufacturing flaw.'

'A flaw? What do you mean? There shouldn't have been any flaws.'

'Something must have happened when the fabric was printed. The machine must have slipped, or there must have been a bubble in the dye. One of the roses was wrong.'

'Wrong?'

'Sort of . . . mangled. Josef said the pattern would hide it—'

'Why were you discussing it with him?'

I shrugged. I could feel tears forming.

'Well,' said Dietrich, 'whether the pattern hides it or not is beside the point. You'd always know.'

I nodded, then started to cry. 'I think they can just replace that panel.'

'Of course they can,' he said. 'And we'll make sure it's perfect. We'll check every rose, don't you worry.' He waited until I was quiet, then said, 'But you really mustn't talk like that with Niemand. Never forget what he is.'

The next morning Emmi Wolff called in, wanting to see how the new curtains looked. We were on first-name terms by then, and she was halfway up the stairs, already on her way to the bedroom, before I could tell her about the fault.

'Surely not,' she said, and kept climbing, refusing to believe me until she saw the room with her own eyes. 'Oh!' she said. 'What a shame! What a disaster!' She fussed with the grey velvet curtains, peering behind them as if the new ones might be there after all. 'Still, I'm sure it won't take long to fix.'

'They have to order more fabric,' I said. 'It came all the way from Paris.'

'It won't take long,' she said again. 'Not if they know it's for you.' She glanced up at the top windowpane. 'What's that?'

I followed her gaze – and yes, there was something, way up high. A smear on the glass, as if a bird had flown into it at full speed. I couldn't bear it when that happened; I didn't want to look outside for fear of what I might see. I'd have to ask Josef to bring a dustpan, send him to remove the little thing while I looked away.

'It's a hand print,' said Emmi.

I squinted, craned my neck. The smear vanished and reappeared depending on where I stood, sometimes hidden against the sky, sometimes white against the treetops. To begin with I couldn't make out the shape, but as I slowly changed my position – slowly, slowly – I could see Emmi was right. It was just a hand print, and there was nothing outside the window; no clump of cold feathers, no eyes like dots of glass. I remembered then: the prisoner stumbling on the step-ladder, grabbing at the air. 'I'll ask the servant to wipe it away,' I said.

After lunch I left Karl-Heinz with Josef and had a car take me into Weimar so I could go for a walk along the river. I didn't feel like company. I followed the Ilm through the park and came to an arching stone bridge, and I saw how its reflection in the icy water made a perfect dark O. Then I doubled back into the old town centre and explored the narrow streets with their houses that seemed to lean into one another as if to share secrets. I stopped to buy a postcard for my mother: the famous statue of Goethe and Schiller on the Theaterplatz, though I hadn't found it in person yet. *You see?* I wrote on the back. *We're quite civilised here.*

The afternoon had turned very cold, but I wasn't ready to go back to the villa – to return up the hill. As I made my way along I couldn't shake the thought that people were staring at me. Was it just my imagination? I checked my reflection in a shop window: my collar was sitting flat, my hat straight. It was new, the hat, and the smartest little thing: dark-blue felt with a bit of netting hung along the front – a make-believe veil, though it didn't hide anything. And no, it wasn't my imagination – weren't those two women at the café looking over and whispering behind their hands? And that man walking his little white dog – didn't he speed up when he saw me, anxious to get past? And that group of soldiers exchanged glances too, didn't they? I realised I'd reached the Theaterplatz, and I searched for the statue of Goethe and Schiller.

'Excuse me,' I said to a passer-by. 'Pardon me, but where is the statue?'

By way of reply she cocked her head towards a big brick structure in the centre of the square, and as I approached it I realised that it held the statue; that Weimar's two most famous citizens were walled in for the duration of the war. On I walked, not really knowing where I was going, and soon I found myself at the door of Herz-Jesu, the Catholic church. I went inside.

Straight away I could smell incense, fresh flowers, brass polish, candles: if I closed my eyes, I could have been back in Munich with my mother and my sister, all lined up in our pew, our hair combed flat with water, our patent-leather shoes gleaming like tar. Helena and I holding our christening missals edged in gold with imitation ivory covers; mine showed an angel in a garden. I can remember my mother reaching for my hand once when it was time to pray for the brave men fighting the war and the brave men already fallen – I must have been only four. She squeezed my fingers until I thought she would stop my blood. I knew I couldn't pull my hand away, though, because she was praying for Papa, and so I closed my eyes as tightly as she did and prayed for him too. But it didn't work.

I hadn't attended Mass in years; not since I'd met Dietrich. The churches were the enemy of the Reich, he told me – that's what Papa Eicke had taught him at Dachau – but there in the fragrant half-light, before I knew what I was doing, I dropped to my knee and genuflected. Then looked over my shoulder. High above me, a vaulted dome as smooth as the inside of an egg. A rose window, its stained-glass panels shining with angels, and in the centre the shining face of Jesus caught on Veronica's cloth. A statue of Saint Elisabeth, her bread for the poor turned to roses. Around the altar the patterned floor-tiles teemed with fabulous creatures: wings and fins and snouts, and long curling tongues. On another window, Jesus raised a boy from the dead, and on another, a pelican pierced its own breast to feed its young. I sat in a pew and watched the parishioners come and go: mostly women, and mostly there to clean or confess. One of them took away vases of camellias, pausing and bowing each time she passed the tabernacle. The flowers didn't look dead or even wilted to me, but maybe I was too far away. And maybe they weren't camellias; I'm not sure. When the woman returned with the fresh arrangements she set them down and tugged at a stem here, a bloom there, stepping back and considering the effect, nudging a final length of ivy into place. She bowed again, then made her way down the aisle – towards me, I realised. She stopped at my pew. 'Pardon me,' she said. I moved my knees to one side and she brushed past, the hem of her coat trailing across my lap like a cat. I thought she would keep going, but she knelt down next to me and began to murmur. I strained to make out the words. The stresses and pauses sounded familiar; a verse I used to know, though I couldn't quite remember it now: *and my sin is ever before me . . . wash me, and I shall be whiter than snow . . .* Over at the confessionals, a line of women waited their turn. I couldn't see the priest, but I knew that he was shut in the middle of the three little booths, listening to the sins of the woman on his left and then to the sins of the woman on his right, and as each woman left a new one took her place, with a new list of sins. I looked at them: ordinary housewives in ordinary clothes, their hair neat, their faces scrubbed. What on earth could they have done wrong?

Helena and I used to play Confession, climbing into our father's massive wardrobe and dividing it in three with his hanging clothes, which our mother couldn't bring herself to give away. We both wanted to be the priest, who had to retain his composure in the face of even the most shocking sins – robbing countesses of their jewels, strangling our French teacher until she turned blue – and who had the power to forgive. 'You have made a good confession,' we'd say in our deepest voices. 'I absolve you of your sins. For your penance, braid your sister's hair and eat her string beans.'

I must have shifted in my seat, or cleared my throat, because the woman next to me paused, turned her head. She stared at me for a moment, then returned to her prayers. Who was she, this murmuring woman kneeling so close? The church was almost empty; there were dozens of other pews. I decided to leave, but before I could gather myself the woman rose to her feet and said, 'Pardon me,' again, and as she moved past me she placed a hand on my shoulder. Then she was gone. It lasted for just a second or two, that strange touch, but I felt a lightness, a kind of relief, as if I'd confessed to something and been forgiven.

Before I left I stopped at a statue of Mary to light a candle for my father. There were already so many flames burning at the shrine that I could feel the heat push against my cheeks; row upon row of little dots of light, far more than I expected, far too many to count. I lit my father's candle from one of them, careful to hold my sleeve well clear. It's hard for me to remember his face, and I think I most often remember him from the photos taken when he was home on leave. Other times, when I try to bring it to mind, I see my mother's face instead, twisting and collapsing as she told us the news: that he had died of his wounds in France. As I left the church I glanced back, but I couldn't tell which candle was my father's. And on the way home, as the car made its way up the hill to Buchenwald, the shape of the shrine stayed in my eyes, a single block of flame.

I knew I wouldn't tell Dietrich where I'd been.

In the bedroom, I could still see the smear on the window-pane. 'Josef!' I called. 'Would you mind cleaning that, please?'

'I did clean it, madam.'

'But I can still see it.'

He frowned, peered up at the spot. 'I'm sorry, madam – I can't see anything.'

'It's right there.'

He followed my finger, shook his head. 'I'm sorry . . . Would you like me to have another try?'

I sighed. 'How can you clean something you can't even see?'

He appeared to be thinking of an answer, but I said, 'Never mind, Josef. If you fetch me the step-ladder and a cloth, I can do it myself.'

I had to stand on the uppermost step to reach; there was nothing to hold on to. For a moment I pictured myself falling through the glass as if into water, palms working against the weight of it, eyes wide open, waiting for the shoals of bubbles to clear so I could get my bearings. I looked out to the trees and the ever-present guard. Behind the house, only a moment's walk up the slope, so Emmi had said, were the Isolation Barracks, where they kept prominent people they didn't want mingling with the prisoners in the main camp. A former Reichstag deputy and his wife lived there, shut away behind the tall wall. I breathed on the glass, and there it was: the ghost of a hand. I rubbed at it till my chest ached.

'Have they ordered the new fabric?' I asked Dietrich later that day. 'So they can fix the curtains?'

'They'll be finished by the end of the week at the latest,' he said. 'Probably before.'

'They were tailors, you said . . . ? I thought I might have them make me some new blouses. The work was very fine.'

'They're no longer here,' said Dietrich.

'What do you mean, no longer here?'

'They've been moved to another camp. It happens all the time.'

'Well, it's very inconvenient. Who'll fix the curtains?'

'Someone else.'

And he was right: before the end of the week, the new ones were in place.

8 October 1954

[tape corrupted in places]

I was going to talk about the ark animals, though – are you interested in that side of things? I carved them for Karl-Heinz myself. I'm still pleased with the animals.

I made the tiger first. There was so much fallen wood on the Ettersberg that it seemed wasteful not to use it: whole thick branches lying beneath the trees. Karl-Heinz came with me so he could pick up some of the smaller pieces – we didn't need to go far beyond the house – and I told him it was for firewood so as not to spoil the surprise. With the tip of my knife I cut his initials into one of the beech trunks. 'That'll last forever,' I said, and showed him how thin the bark was, and how it would never heal. Then I carried all our raw material home and dried it in our garage until it was ready to carve; it would take my mind off other things, I decided. I'd have liked to work in beech – I thought it would make a nice memento of the place when we were no longer living there – but it was so dense and hard and fine, such an unforgiving wood. I couldn't get it to behave, and I was forced to dispose of my first disappointing attempts. Once I decided on oak instead, the basic shape of the tiger took me only an evening; it seemed to grow from the grain, as if it had been waiting for my blade all along. I spent the rest of the week getting the finer features right – the muscled flanks scored with stripes, the pricked ears, the teeth, the claws – and I kept holding it at arm's length, considering it from every angle. How do you know when an animal is finished?

'He'll love it,' said Greta, stroking its back. Now I just had to make its mate, she told me. And then the rest of the animal kingdom.

The following Saturday night we left the pair of tigers on Karl-Heinz's pillow so he'd find them when he woke – and sure enough, he came running into our bedroom in the morning, one in each fist.

'Mama! Papa!' he cried. 'Cats!'

'Let me see,' I said. He gave me one of the figures, and it was as warm as his own little body. 'Hmm,' I said. 'Is this a pussycat, do you think, Mama? Or is it a fierce *tiger*?'

'Look at the teeth,' said Greta. 'The claws. Definitely a tiger.'

Karl-Heinz made a growl in his throat and hopped the second figure along Greta's arm and up to her neck. I waited for him to ask where they had come from, but the question never occurred to him; it was quite normal, apparently, for a five-year-old boy to wake to tigers in his bed. Instead he said, 'When can we go to the zoo? To see the wild animals?'

'Soon,' said Greta.

'You'll have to come and see my office, too,' I said. 'It's very smart. You can tear off the day on my calendar, Karli.' I was a little disappointed that they hadn't been already. I wanted to show . . .

[corrupted]

. . . and Karl-Heinz was looking at the tigers side by side now. 'Which one is the papa and which one is the mama?' he said.

'Well now,' we said – but they were both the same size.

'So she should be a bit smaller?' I asked. I could fix that – whittle one of them down. Sand away the face until it was blank; find a new one underneath.

He was no longer listening. 'This one is Thomas, and this one is Rudi,' he said. The names of his friends back in Munich – but at least Ingo was keeping his distance. He wouldn't let me correct the problem, though; when I took out my knife he threw himself on the floor and screamed and thrashed. I had never seen such behaviour; it was very unlike him.

'Darling, darling,' said Greta. 'You'll hurt yourself.'

I crouched down, peered into his tear-streaked face and said, 'Come now, Karli. What will the neighbours think we're doing to you?'

He took the tigers back to his room and tucked them into bed. 'Good night, Thomas. Good night, Rudi,' he said.

'Good night, Thomas. Good night, Rudi,' Greta and I repeated.

I tackled the bears after that, making sure one turned out bigger than the other, and when I made the lions I gave the male a mane, and when I made the chickens I gave the rooster a comb. Karl-Heinz squealed in delight at each new pair, rushing to show them to me as if I didn't already know their every whorl and hollow.

'Aren't you a lucky boy,' I said. 'Which animals will be next, do you think? What are we still missing?'

'Elephants!' he said. 'Horses!'

And so I carved him a pair of elephants, and then a pair of horses, and if I say so myself, it was as fine a collection as any you might see for sale at Hertie in Munich.

But the tigers always bothered me.

If you don't eat your soup, we'll send you up the hill: that was something we told our children when they misbehaved. Most often they laughed, and then we laughed too, but there was no denying the proximity of the camp; we knew very well that it lay in the clearing just beyond the Bismarck Tower. Back when the authorities were planning it, they wanted to call it Konzentrationslager Ettersberg, after our lovely hill on which it would stand. We objected, however, given the name's association with Goethe – we weren't making trouble; we weren't objecting to the camp itself, only to the name – and so Reichsführer Himmler approved the change, and they called it after the beech forest that grew there.

After they built the camp we still went walking on the Ettersberg, even though we'd lost part of it. The forest was in our blood, but we took care not to get dirty, aware of our rationed soap and bathwater. How pretty it was up there amongst the trees. Frau Topf said the fresh air kept her complexion bright, and Herr Ziegler swore that it cured sore throats. If we kept our distance, we could pretend that nothing had changed. In winter our children rode their sleds down the slopes of the Devil's Pits, and in summer we brought our picnic lunches, our watercolours, our notebooks in which we rhymed *Blut* with *Mut* and *Liebe* with *Fieber*. We spread out our blankets and sat in the dappled quiet, and we ate our bread and cheese, our Mohnkuchen and our sour little apples, which somehow tasted better away from home. We threw crumbs to the robins and the wrens, drawing them closer and closer to us until we could almost reach out and grab them. Then we lay down and slept for a while, and we dreamt that we were running late; we dreamt that we were falling. We dreamt that we had buried something precious and couldn't remember where. We dreamt that we were home again, in the houses we grew up in, only there were other rooms to these houses, rooms we knew nothing about. Or we dreamt that we were flying, the forest a green ocean far below, and we were not afraid. When we woke, we blinked at the pale trunks surrounding us, and for a moment we thought that they were people, quiet grey people. We wondered why they did not speak. Later we laughed at our mistake – talking trees, indeed. *Don't tear off my leaves! Don't carve your name in my side! Don't chop me into pieces!* We packed away our things, shaking the twigs from our blankets, and then we peered around and tried to remember the way back down. All the trees looked alike; why had we not taken more careful note? We knew that if we made a wrong turn, or began to wander absent-minded, we'd find ourselves at the camp before too long, our path coming to a halt at the sentry line or the edge of the quarry. We grabbed our children's hands then and told them there was nothing to worry about. The air shivered and sparked.

It was possible, of course, to visit the falconry up on the Ettersberg. Most of us went at least once, if only to satisfy ourselves that there really were trained raptors so close to home. We hoped we might catch a glimpse of Reichsmarschall Göring, Master of the Hunt, and we paid our fifty Pfennigs and strolled the length of the aviary with its cages lined with cloth so the birds did not hurt their claws. We viewed the round gazebo, where they could shelter in bad weather, and we let our children feed the deer, only they kept snatching their hands away at the last minute, scared they might lose their fingers. The falconer showed us an albino ferret, and told us how it drove the rabbits from their burrows for the goshawks to catch: the birds swooped lightning-fast on their prey, and the falconer rewarded them with a piece of the liver or the lungs. And we all wanted to see Thea the golden eagle, presented to Reichsführer Himmler for his birthday, and so dangerous and wild that it tore the meat from its trainers' hands and attacked it as if it were still alive. Before we caught the bus back to Weimar, we walked through the hunting hall built in traditional Germanic style. It might have stood there for centuries, though the great trunks of oak had been felled only a few years earlier, when the land nearby was cleared. We admired its heavy oak furniture and its iron sconces and its fireplace big enough to hold a man, and we imagined that this was our home, that we could trace our lineage all the way back to Hermanfrid, King of Thuringia, and that the trophies mounted on the wall were things we had killed ourselves.

Frankfurt am Main, September 1946

Here's another month with a picture on the back, Lotte: *View Across the Riffelsee to the Matterhorn*. The mountain mirrored in the lake, a submerged twin.

At the start of 1943 Frankfurt hadn't yet been hit by heavy bombing, though everyone said it couldn't be much longer. One April morning, after a scattered attack that failed to cause much damage, a flurry of leaflets descended: *Last night you experienced only the first drops that announce the coming storm. But it will pelt down on you, more and more powerful, more devastating, until you can no longer withstand the hurricane's elemental force.*

I decided to write you a letter – or rather, Onkel Theo decided to write you a letter – in which I mentioned that most Sundays my family commitments took me to Hanauer Landstraße, near Allerheiligentor. *Perhaps I'll see you there one week*, I said.

The following Sunday I waited at a tram stop on Hanauer Landstraße, pretending to consult the timetable. I wore my collar turned up and my hat pulled down so you wouldn't recognise me and give us all away – but a year had passed since I'd visited you and Anna, and you probably didn't remember me by then. I caught sight of the two of you for only a moment as you walked past on the other side of the street, the yellow stars stitched to your chests. Certainly, there was no opportunity to speak to you, to hold you. Anna glanced across the traffic and gave me a tiny nod, then paused to rearrange the knitted scarf

you wore, winding it around your neck a second time so it covered your ears. You struggled away from her and unlooped it,
and almost collided with a woman carrying a cake box, a little
terrier on a leash scurrying along at her heels. She snatched the
box to her chest, then inspected it for damage or dirt, though
you hadn't touched it. I could see her saying something to Anna
while she jabbed a finger at you, the tatty feathers on her hat
shaking. I wasn't close enough to hear her. I looked down the
street for the tram I didn't need. The little dog leapt and pawed
at the air, waiting for someone to throw a stick for him to fetch.
He licked your hand at one point, and you bent down and
stroked his ears, but the woman yanked on the leash. She
scolded him with the same finger she had jabbed at you, and he
sat. Other pedestrians glared and frowned as they made their
way around you, and you started to fiddle with the tassels on
the end of your scarf. Anna stood silent while the woman had
her say, now and then glancing over at me. I stayed on the other
side of the street. I looked at the tram timetable. I checked my
watch. A tram pulled in, and everyone boarded it but me.

'Well?' said the conductor, a hand on her hip. 'We don't
have all day.'

I shook my head. 'I made a mistake,' I said.

When the tram pulled away you had disappeared, and it
took me a moment to find you in the crowd. Then Anna
turned and looked back over her shoulder, and the two of you
kept walking further and further down the street, becoming
smaller all the time.

And I should have gone after you.

And I stood there and did not move.

And everyone who passed by stared at me, and I knew they
could see I was up to no good, and I knew they were already
thinking about reporting me.

And I stood there and did not move.

The next letter I retrieved from under the rock at the cemetery contained only one line: *Will you send a photograph of yourself?*

That night I emptied out all the drawers in my desk at home, looking for the postcard I'd bought in Dresden back in 1930: the Transparent Man. And when I found him, I slipped him into an envelope and hid him under the rock.

FROM THE IMAGINARY DIARY OF FRAU GRETA HAHN

May 1943

I wanted to find the perfect present for Dietrich's forty-fifth birthday – something special, something he didn't already own – so one morning a few weeks beforehand, Emmi and I took a car into Weimar and went from shop to shop.

'What about cufflinks?' said Emmi. 'Or a fountain pen? Or a wristwatch? Engraved on the back: *With my undying love forever and ever, amen.*'

'He has all those things,' I said. 'He has everything.'

There wasn't much on display – or not much that was actually for sale – but the shopkeepers did their best to find the right thing for me, opening locked drawers, scurrying to back rooms and returning with items far nicer than the ones in their windows and cabinets. Their movements were hurried – anxious, even – and they spoke too quickly, I thought, glancing at me every so often but mostly keeping their eyes lowered. 'Let me see,' they said. 'Let me just put my mind to it. I'm sure we have something. Yes yes. Let me just look.'

We were in a little shop on Kaufstraße; it must have been the tenth place we'd visited, and I was starting to feel off-colour – I'd probably eaten too much cake at the café we stopped at, but the girl who served us had brought extra-large slices piled with cream, and she kept coming to our table to check if everything was all right; I hadn't wanted to seem rude. 'I'm trying to watch my weight,' I said to Emmi when the girl had gone, and she said, 'Don't be silly. You have nothing to worry about.'

'What about a letter opener?' she asked when the shop-keeper produced a tray of them. She grasped one in her fist, jabbing it at me. 'En garde! Your money or your life!'

'A fine choice, madam,' said the woman behind the counter. 'Solid silver, and genuine amber from the Baltic in the handle. German workmanship, though,' she added. 'Exquisite German workmanship from before the war.'

Emmi said, 'En garde!' again and sliced through the air next to me. 'You have to defend yourself, you know, otherwise it's not fair. Isn't that right?'

The woman gave a nervous smile. 'Well . . . ' she said. 'Well . . . '

'I think he has a secretary to open his letters for him,' I said.

'Of course. Yes,' said the woman, and whisked the tray away. 'Perhaps a schnapps flask? Very fine. You can tell by the weight of it. You can have his initials engraved, or a small sentiment of your own choosing – we have a list, if you can't think what to say. A lot of people can't think what to say. Or a fine pair of binoculars? In a presentation case?'

Emmi snorted. 'He can go bird watching, Greta! In his free time.'

'He likes carving,' I said. 'Maybe a chisel? In a presentation case?'

'A chisel. A presentation chisel,' said the woman. 'I'm afraid we don't really stock . . . Well, let me just see. Let me just check.' She scanned the shelves as if a chisel might appear; perhaps she had forgotten about a whole cache of tools in presentation cases. 'No,' she said at last. 'No. I'm terribly sorry. We don't appear to sell chisels, madam. But may I ask how much time you have?'

'Time?'

'Until the special occasion. We could try to order something in . . . '

'Oh,' I said, and couldn't think. 'What's today?'

'The nineteenth, madam,' said the woman. 'The day before the Führer's birthday.'

'Of course,' I said.

'I'm sure we could arrange something quite quickly. Under the circumstances. Shall I make some enquiries? It would be no trouble. It would be my pleasure.'

I felt a sudden pain in my side, and I stifled a gasp. 'Do you have a chair?'

'A chair, madam?' The woman frowned. 'If it's a piece of furniture you're wanting, you might try Marktstraße. Do you know the place? It's not far, not at all. If you turn left—'

'I need to sit down,' I said, steadying myself against the wall.

'A chair!' cried the woman, her voice too loud now. 'A chair!' She flung aside a curtain behind the counter, revealing a small dark room. I could make out an old man sitting at a table slicing a loaf of bread – was it a loaf of bread? I think so – and a girl of about fifteen peeling carrots. They both froze in their work and stared through the little doorway at me as I stared back at them. I blinked.

'I need a chair!' said the woman, grabbing for the one the girl was sitting on. She scrambled to her feet, but the old man still stared through the doorway at us. The pain shot at my side, and I heard myself cry out.

'Here,' said the woman, rushing around to the front of the counter. 'Sit down. Sit down.'

'What is it?' said Emmi. 'What's wrong?'

'Nothing,' I said. 'Too much cream. Too much walking.' I closed my eyes for a moment and waited for the pain to pass. Yes, we must have done too much walking, trying to find the perfect present for Dietrich. I wished I were back in Munich – back home, where they had proper department stores, not strange little places with strange little hidden rooms. When I opened my eyes the old man was still watching me. Then the girl shut the curtain. I looked around: all the other customers had left.

'I'm sorry,' I said. 'Nothing is quite right.'

'No,' said the woman. 'Of course. No.'

The pain disappeared as quickly as it had arrived, and I waved away Emmi's offer of an arm for support.

'Why did you apologise?' she said when we were back out on the street. Nearby a clock was striking twelve.

I shrugged. 'We didn't buy anything. I don't imagine business is very good – and they were so eager to help.'

'They know who we are,' said Emmi.

'What? What do you mean? Who are we?'

'Are you joking?'

'Emmi. Who are we?'

She laughed, shook her head. 'Anyway, you can order anything through the camp, remember. Think of what you want, and abracadabra, someone will make it for you. You know Doktor Hoven? Ilse Koch's special friend?'

'What does he have to do with it?'

She looked over her shoulder, lowered her voice. 'He's only a doctor because he got two of the prisoners to write his dissertation.'

'But that's terrible!'

'Like I said, you can order anything.'

'I thought I might be able to find the perfect thing on my own, that's all.'

'He's a carver, you said?'

I nodded. 'He's making Karl-Heinz the most adorable Noah's ark. Well, just the animals at the moment, but I imagine he'll get around to the actual ark too. He says it relaxes him.' I stopped; all of a sudden I wasn't sure Dietrich would want me sharing such details.

'A Noah's ark?' said Emmi. 'Isn't that Jewish?'

'Oh,' I said. 'I hadn't really thought . . . Well, he's only done some animals. He hasn't done Noah.'

Emmi laughed again. 'I'm *joking*. He's a good father – anyone can see that. I wish Otto would stay at home carving animals, but he spends all his time at the officers' club.'

I didn't know how to respond. We were walking to the corner of the street, where our driver was waiting for us, so I said, 'There's the car.'

'Yes,' said Emmi, 'there's the car.'

'Home, is it, ladies?' said the driver as we climbed in. Arno Rehbein was a young farmer from Hesse, around our own age: tall and tanned, with green eyes and thick black hair, and the broadest hands I had ever seen. It was clear he was on comfortable terms with Emmi, and I noticed that she made sure to ask for him whenever we needed a car.

'Can't you just picture him hard at work on the farm?' she liked to say to me.

'Don't get too attached,' I said. 'He'll be off to the front soon enough.'

She smiled. 'Not if he has friends in high places.'

It turned into a game between us, coming up with imaginary jobs for Arno; whenever he was driving us into Weimar she'd lean over to me and whisper *swinging an axe* or *shoeing a horse*. 'Have you had a successful morning, ladies?' he asked.

'Yes, thank you,' I said at the same time as Emmi said, 'Not really.'

'Well now,' he replied, looking at us in the mirror, 'which one of you is lying?'

'I am,' said Emmi. 'Can't you tell?'

'Milking a cow,' she breathed into my ear as we drove back up the hill.

'Hammering in nails,' I whispered back, and she giggled.

'You ladies and your secrets,' said Arno, shaking his head. 'I can see I'll have to report you.'

'Twenty-five lashes!' said Emmi. 'Shall we bend over?'

I elbowed her in the ribs. She was always taking things too far; poor Arno was blushing all the way down to his collar.

'Oh for goodness' sake,' she said. 'Arno knows I'm only joking. We need a bit of fun, don't we?' The car slowed as it turned into Eickeweg. 'Anyway,' she said. 'Carving. There's an inmate who used to do the most beautiful work. A real artist. He made the signposts around the camp – the zoo one, with the animals on it, and the one on Carachoweg with the prisoners all dashing along. And the one at the bus stop, too – SS men on one side, prisoners on the other. In case anyone was confused.'

I nodded, though I hadn't seen the signposts myself; I hadn't explored very far beyond our villa. 'What does that mean, Caracho?' I said.

'I think it's Spanish. It means double time – they make them scurry along there at breakneck speed, right down to the gatehouse.' She clapped her hands. '*Carrrracho! Olé!*'

'Why Spanish, though?'

'Hmm. I don't know. Arno, why Spanish?'

'I don't know, Frau Wolff,' he said. 'I always thought it was Russian.'

'It doesn't sound Russian,' said Emmi. 'Maybe it's Italian. One of the many mysteries. You'll find you can exhaust yourself by wondering about these things, Greta. Anyway, I'm sure you could have him carve something special, if he's still around.'

I thought of an article I'd read on home interiors, back when Dietrich and I were furnishing our Munich apartment. I'd flicked through pages of footstools and mirrors, candlesticks and clocks – all the elegant things you could buy to put in rooms – and I remembered an oak desk set carved with shells and birds and the figure of a young woman in a bathing costume. She clasped one leg to her chest and stretched the other out in front, her head tilted back, a serene smile on her lips as she gazed at the sky – or at the ceiling, I supposed. An owl perched on her knee, and smaller owls rested either side of her, guarding the ink bottles. There were little indentations designed to hold stamps and nibs and paper clips, and a border of carved scallop shells encircled the base. Something like that would be just the thing for a man of Dietrich's standing. I wondered how long it would take to make one; I didn't have much time. But then, hadn't the curtains been fixed in a matter of days?

I asked Emmi if her husband Otto could find out about the prisoner – and the next morning she telephoned and told me to come over to their house, and to bring a sketch of the desk set with me.

Otto Wolff was in the hallway when I arrived, supervising the hanging of an enormous picture: the family tree Emmi had ordered. A thick, straight trunk of oak divided the canvas in half, and leafy branches extended to the left and right, dotted with names painted on ribboned shields. On a hillside in the background stood a castle.

'Up a bit on the left,' he was saying. 'No. No, it's still crooked.'

'Greta's here, darling,' said Emmi, and he said, 'You're just in time! What do you think? It's crooked, isn't it?'

'I'm not sure I have the best eye,' I said.

'You and Dietrich should have yours done,' said Emmi. 'There's an office right here that will trace your ancestors.'

'Well, we already submitted mine, before we got married,' I said. And the character reference, too: *Is she reliable or unreliable? Is she fond of children or not fond of children? Companionable or domineering? Frugal or wasteful?*

'Yes yes, but the office here will go back hundreds and hundreds of years! The Czechs do it – they're very thorough. Or are you worried what they might find?'

'It's no laughing matter, Emmi,' said Otto.

'They can just saw a branch or two off, if need be,' she said. 'Just clip a twig here and there.'

'*Emmi.*'

'Or you might be aristocracy. Greta von Hahn. Do you know, they released some of the Polish child prisoners because they found out they had Aryan blood?'

'Child prisoners?' I said.

'They gave them to good German families. So that's a happy ending.'

'Is that true?'

Otto said, 'Come with me, ladies,' and directed us into the living room. 'Wait right there,' he told the men holding up the painting. I thought he was going to explain to me about the released prisoners, the children with Aryan blood who would be Germans now. But he said, 'The prisoner who carved the signs is still in the camp. He's assigned to pathology these days.'

Strange images flashed into my thoughts: knives carving long ribbons of flesh. I blinked them away. 'Pathology,' I said. 'He doesn't do the carving any more, then?'

'Well, not officially,' said Otto. 'But I'm sure you could make a request. And it's fair to say his patients can wait a while, don't you think?'

'Otto can place the order for you,' said Emmi. 'So Dietrich doesn't find out.'

He nodded. 'You only have to say the word.'

'That's very kind,' I said. I blinked again, then showed him my sketch of the desk set.

He looked at it and frowned. 'Should he make it exactly the same?'

'Yes,' I said. 'I'm not much good at drawing, but yes, just like the picture.'

He tilted his head, peering at it.

'Is something wrong? Is it not clear?'

'No no. Quite clear, and he's very skilled,' he said, but he was still frowning.

'It was in a magazine,' I said.

'Only . . . ' he said. 'Only the owls. Why are there owls, if she's in her bathing costume? I've never seen owls at the beach. Or is she in her bathing costume in the forest?'

He was starting to annoy me. 'It's allegorical,' I said. 'That's how the magazine described it.'

'I see,' he said. 'Yes, allegorical.'

'And if he could model the girl on this,' I said. I felt myself starting to blush as I handed him a photo Dietrich had taken of me years earlier, just after we met; I was sitting on the beach on Rügen, smiling into the sun, my arms and legs bare and my hair still damp from the sea. 'Do you think he can manage it?'

'Of course, Greta,' he said, looking from the photo to me and back again. 'He's the best you can find. A real artist.'

'But can he manage it in time?'

'I'll see to it that he does.'

'And not a word to Dietrich.'

'Not a word.'

Out in the hallway, the men were still holding up the painting.

In the two months we'd been at Buchenwald, I hadn't visited Dietrich's office once. He'd offered to show me around, but I told him I had too much to take care of with the house: making sure Josef did things the proper way, making sure Karl-Heinz was happy.

'I thought you might like to come and have a look now,' he said one night. 'Now that you've settled in. Karl-Heinz can have a stamp on his hand. Or water my potted plant.'

'I'm sorry,' I said. 'I do want to – it's just I've organised quite a few things with Emmi and the children.'

I knew he was disappointed, but I didn't want to tell him how dreadful I'd been feeling; he had enough to worry about with his work.

Maybe it was the higher altitude that was affecting me; that week I felt so feeble I had to ask Josef to brush my hair, and help me climb the stairs to take a bath, and even zip up my dress – not that I told Dietrich.

'Hmm,' said Emmi. 'I was like that when I was pregnant. When did you last bleed?'

'I'm not sure,' I whispered, glancing at Karl-Heinz and Felix, who were playing marbles on our living-room floor.

'Oh, don't worry about them,' said Emmi.

'I suppose it was . . . a few weeks ago?'

'Are your breasts tender? Any morning sickness?'

'No. I don't think so.'

'What about with Karl-Heinz? Was it the same then?'

'I was fine. Hardly knew I was pregnant.'

Now that she mentioned it, though, I *had* felt a bit sick recently. 'It's possible,' I said.

Emmi squeezed my arm. 'Think of all the things we can dress it in! Do you want a boy or a girl? Wouldn't a little girl be lovely? She can marry Felix!'

'Slow down,' I said. 'We don't know anything for sure.' But already I was imagining silver rattles and carved cradles, tiny lace-trimmed gowns and dolls that closed their eyes. Another child! Dietrich would be so pleased with me – and my mother would *have* to visit.

'That pain you had when we were in Weimar,' said Emmi. 'That can happen when it's taking root. Burrowing in. My sister had the same thing.'

'If that's what it was, it's still very early, then,' I said. 'I don't think I'd be feeling sick yet.'

'You never know,' she said.

I made an appointment for May with a Doktor Lang in town. I needed to let some time pass before I mentioned anything to Dietrich, in order to be sure.

'We'll arrange for Arno to drive you there,' said Emmi, 'and I'll come too.'

'Because you're concerned about me,' I said.

'Exactly,' she said.

Karl-Heinz helped Ingo onto his rocking horse – he had returned – while Felix chattered about rabbits. There were cages and cages of them inside the camp, he said, with fur that grew right down to the ground.

'Rabbits?' I said. 'In the camp? I don't know about that, Felix. I think you might be making things up.'

'It's true!' he said. 'They want to make them into socks for the soldiers.'

'It is true,' said Emmi. 'It's Himmler's big plan – angoras, bred for their fur.'

'Papa's sending some to the zoo tomorrow for me to play with,' said Felix. 'Because it's Easter. You can poke them and feed them lettuce leaves and even pick them up, but you have to be careful in case they kick.'

'We haven't been to the zoo yet,' said Karl-Heinz.

'What?' said Emmi. 'Why not?'

'Karli, let Felix have a turn on the horse now, please. And don't slip on the marbles. Maybe you should tidy them away, yes?' I waited for him to obey, then whispered to Emmi, 'It's so close to the camp. I'm worried about what he might . . . what he might see. He has a very vivid imagination.'

'Greta, it's good for them to see. It teaches them what they should be afraid of. They might as well know what our enemies look like.'

'I suppose so . . . '

'And it's there for the families to enjoy. That's what it's for.'

'I know.'

'And you can't visit the falconry any more.'

'I know. I know.' She was right; they'd closed it so they could use the falconer's house for high-ranking prisoners.

'Can we go and see the rabbits?' said Karl-Heinz. 'And the monkeys and the bears and the elephant?'

'I'm not sure there's an elephant, darling.'

'I can take him,' said Emmi. 'If you need to rest.'

'No, I'm fine,' I said. 'I'll be fine. I should come with him. Let's make an outing of it tomorrow – take a picnic.'

'A picnic, a picnic!' sang the boys.

'I'll ask Josef to pack us some sandwiches,' I said. 'And some of his apple strudel – it's delicious.'

'And we need lettuce, for the rabbits,' said Felix.

'All right,' I said. 'Some lettuce, too. Shall we take the cake forks? For the strudel? It can be a bit messy otherwise. And then, I suppose we'll need little plates, and some serviettes. Do you have a picnic blanket? Or we can use my travelling rug.'

'That sounds like quite a lot to carry,' said Emmi. 'We might need some help. Don't you think?'

'It's not far, is it? Only about five minutes?'

'Longer with the boys. We'll definitely need some help.' She caught my eye, grinned.

'Shall we see if Scharführer Rehbein is free?' I said.

'What a good idea!'

The following day was blue-skied and warm, perfect spring weather, and as we set out along Eickeweg we could hear the birds singing in the forest. Emmi was wearing a belted georgette dress that showed off her waist and legs; the sheer pink fabric lifted and drifted as she walked, split sleeves parting now and then to expose her pale upper arms. Arno hoisted the picnic basket onto one shoulder, and Felix and Karl-Heinz took turns carrying the blanket, but they kept squabbling over it, and in the end we had to threaten them with no picnic at all.

'Scharführer Rehbein will decide whose turn it is, all right?' said Emmi. 'When he orders you to swap, you must swap. No questions, no arguments.'

'My brother and I were the same at their age,' said Arno.

'Always fighting over who would collect the eggs and who would put the money in the bag at church.'

'You have a brother?' said Emmi. 'Younger or older? Or perhaps a twin!'

'Two years older, Frau Wolff. He's in North Africa.'

'So you're the baby.'

'He's not a baby!' said Felix.

'He'll always be his mama's baby, though,' said Emmi. 'Just like you'll always be mine.' She stroked Felix's hair, and he grimaced and said, 'Ugh!' and darted away from her. 'Now then,' she said, 'don't make me dress you in a bonnet and give you a bottle for your supper!'

Karl-Heinz laughed and chanted, 'Baby, baby, Felix is a baby.'

The boys ran on ahead.

'Not too far on your own,' I called, though Eickeweg was as quiet as quiet could be. Just the sound of the birds, and the brush-brush-brush of the men from the camp as they swept the street. I had to keep reminding myself that this was not Munich, where the cars and buses hurtled past, and the trams came out of nowhere.

'I'll keep an eye on them,' said Arno, and soon we heard him talking to the boys. 'Question: What must the prisoner feel? Answer: That the guard represents a better worldview, a faultless political stance and a higher moral position, and that he – the prisoner – can use him – the guard – as a role model in his efforts to become a useful member of society again.'

Emmi took my arm, and we breathed in the scent of the lilacs growing in the front gardens. 'He has a *brother*,' she whispered in my ear as we watched him striding along after the boys. 'One each.'

'Shh,' I said.

'Rubbing down a horse,' she giggled.

'Shh!'

'Guiding a plough.'

'He'll hear you!'

'Never mind picnic baskets – I bet he could throw both of us over his shoulder.'

'You're very wicked,' I said. But I was laughing, and it was spring, and somewhere a bird was singing its heart out, and the air was full of lilacs and nothing else.

We made our way towards the Kochs' villa and through the cool patch of forest to the north of our street, and the shadows of the trees fell across us. Arno stopped to change the picnic basket to his other shoulder and told Karl-Heinz to give the blanket to Felix to carry, and Karl-Heinz handed it over and didn't scowl or complain. As we paused, something caught my eye on the edge of the path: a tiny severed paw, the colour of a sparrow's breast, the claw-tips as clean as my own nails. It was a strangely perfect little thing. Before anyone else saw it, I kicked it into the undergrowth. Then, when we set off again, Karl-Heinz took Arno's free hand and swung it back and forth in his own. The way he usually did with me. I stopped for a moment as a coldness spread across my chest, and I wanted to be out of the forest with its shifting shadows and its severed paws and all the trees so close.

'Greta?' said Emmi. 'What's the matter? Did you forget something?'

'No, nothing. Nothing.'

'Thank goodness for that. I thought you were going to say you'd forgotten the strudel. Disaster.'

'Hey!' shouted Felix, pushing in between Karl-Heinz and Arno. 'I want a turn!' He tried to grab Arno's hand.

'You're carrying the blanket!' yelled Karl-Heinz. 'You can't have both!'

He shoved Felix away, and Felix threw the blanket aside and shoved him back.

'Boys, boys!' I said. 'That's enough!'

'It's all right,' said Arno.

'He started it,' said Karl-Heinz, wrapping himself around Arno's arm.

'Did not,' said Felix.

'You did start it! You did!' said Karl-Heinz.

'It doesn't matter who started it,' I said.

'He did,' said Karl-Heinz.

'Mama, he won't let me have a turn!' said Felix.

'Poor Scharführer Rehbein,' said Emmi. 'Everybody wants him.'

Felix scowled and kicked at the blanket.

'Pick that up, please,' said Emmi. 'Look, it's covered in leaves now. Pick them all off. All of them.'

Karl-Heinz laughed and swung on Arno's arm. '*All* of them,' he echoed.

'Karl-Heinz!' I said. 'What's got into you? Honestly, I've a good mind to turn around right now. Feed the picnic to the birds.'

'We're terribly sorry, Scharführer Rehbein,' said Emmi. 'Aren't we?'

'Aren't we?' I said. 'Boys?'

'Sorry,' said Felix.

'Sorry,' said Karl-Heinz.

'Nobody will hold Scharführer Rehbein's hand,' I said. 'Karl-Heinz, you'll walk with me, and Felix, you'll walk with your mama. And I'll carry the blanket.'

We set off again, the boys dragging their feet, leaning behind us to pull faces at each other. Felix picked up a stick and aimed it at Karl-Heinz, closing one eye and squeezing an imaginary trigger. Karl-Heinz let out a yelp and began to slump and stagger, pretending to die.

'Come along,' I said. 'We don't have time for that.'

When we emerged from the trees we crossed a street, and Emmi said, 'Let's go past the parade ground, so Greta can see it.'

We skirted another patch of forest, passing the walled area she'd told me about, which housed the high-ranking prisoners, and then another enclosure where, Arno said, members of the Romanian Iron Guard were kept. Emmi stopped to pick a crocus flower and slide it behind her ear. Finally we came to the parade ground and the semi-circle of huge casernes. Officers looked on as groups of soldiers balanced rifles on end, stacking them into perfect teepee shapes. Outside the central building, others sat at tables under sun umbrellas, just as if they were relaxing at a café. Karl-Heinz and Felix began to march along, left, right, left, right. A man in civilian clothes raised a glass of beer at us, and Arno called out a greeting. 'Herr Nadler, from the brewery in Weimar,' he told us. 'Nice fellow. He always stops for a drink when he makes his deliveries.'

'They have a table soccer game in there!' said Felix. 'I've played it with Scharführer Rehbein.'

'The officers' club is just inside too,' said Emmi. 'You'll have to come with me some time.'

'When can I have a turn with the table soccer game?' said Karl-Heinz.

'Well, I'm not sure I know what it is,' I said.

'All the little men in a row,' said Emmi. 'When one kicks, they all kick. Oh, and there's even a cinema, and a proper stage – the Nationaltheater comes up from Weimar to put on shows.'

'How lovely,' I said.

'And other budding actors have performed there. Isn't that right, Arno?'

He laughed.

'He's too modest to mention it, but he's already made his debut – only a chorus girl so far, but destined for stardom. You should see how high he can kick.'

'Just a little act some of the boys and I put on, Frau Hahn,' said Arno as we continued on our way. 'Just a bit of fun.'

'Shall we go and say hello to Papa?' said Felix.

'No, he's very busy,' said Emmi. 'But he promised he'd arrange for the rabbits to be sent to the zoo. Don't you want to see the rabbits?'

The rabbits! The boys had almost forgotten about them. Yes, yes, they wanted to see the rabbits – to poke them and feed them lettuce leaves, and maybe even hold one. How much longer until they could see the rabbits?

'Not much longer,' said Emmi. 'Look, there's the bus stop. We're nearly there.'

A bus from Weimar was just pulling in, and Emmi waved at the driver. Just beyond it, the signpost that directed SS men in one direction and prisoners in the other. The boys raced to the stone eagle at the start of Carachoweg, where another signpost marked the street that led through the camp command area to the gatehouse. *Yet always a cheerful song rings out*, carved in pretty script, and across the top a group of hurrying prisoners. Karl-Heinz stopped to climb on the carriage of an old field gun from the Great War that sat on the verge like a garden ornament. 'Look at me!' he called. 'Mama, look at me!'

'There's the zoo sign!' cried Felix – and yes, up ahead of us a third signpost pointed the way. It was decorated with a pair of bears, a monkey running off with a banana, and a – well, what was it? A rhinoceros? A warthog? A wolf? I can't remember now, but the carving showed the same fine workmanship as the girl with the owls on Dietrich's desk set. Little wooden bird boxes sat in the branches of some of the trees, though I couldn't see any birds.

And then, the camp, right there. The gate was painted white, like the gate to a park or a private garden. A motto ran across it in red, and it took me a moment to decipher it, because from where I stood it was backwards: *To Each His Due*, picked out in smart modern lettering. On the lintel above, another motto: *My Country, Right or Wrong*. Through the gate I glimpsed a great empty space which had to be the mustering ground, where they counted the prisoners each day to make sure none had escaped. Beyond that, rows and rows of wooden barracks began.

'You've gone too far!' called Emmi. 'It's in here.'

When we entered the zoo a cage of monkeys started screeching, jumping up and down and waving their arms as if they had something important to tell us. Just across the pathway, the electrified fence: *Danger! High Tension!* Further along, a watchtower – and a chimney, too, pointing into the sky like a vast brick finger. It gave off thin wisps of smoke, hardly visible in the bright spring air. As we drew closer Felix said, 'That's where they bring you if you're naughty.' I noticed a little twinge again: the baby, burrowing in. Three men in prisoners' uniforms rushed by us with buckets of fodder, their feet slipping in wooden clogs. They were filthy and lean, and there was something rattish about them.

'Which way are the rabbits?' I said. 'Arno? The rabbits? I don't know about you, but I'm hungry. It must be nearly time for our lunch.' I took Karl-Heinz's hand and dragged him along. 'We have some of Josef's strudel, don't we, darling? Your favourite. What a treat! I might even let you have two pieces, if you're good.'

There really were bears, as large as life, ambling around a bear pit: a walled complex of concrete caves and tunnels. I could see shreds of raw meat, bits of bone – the remains of their dinner, I supposed, but I decided not to look too closely.

'That one's called Martin,' said Felix, pointing. 'He likes dancing.'

'He really does!' said Emmi. 'When the brass band plays, he gets up on his hind legs.'

I began to feel light-headed as I peered into the enclosure; I hadn't had much of an appetite at breakfast and had eaten only a few bites.

'What if they get out?' said Karl-Heinz.

'They can't get out,' I said.

'But what if they do?'

'They can't.'

'There they are!' Felix called, and he rushed over to another prisoner who was setting down a cage of rabbits.

'Is he the zookeeper?' said Karl-Heinz. 'Is that his zookeeper's uniform?'

'I think so,' I said, and held his hand until the man disappeared.

I hadn't expected quite so many rabbits; there were stacks and stacks of them crammed into the hutch, nervy and twitching. And they smelled, too. Maybe I was just more sensitive to these things, because of the baby, but I didn't want to get anywhere near them.

'Where's a good place?' I said. I looked around for a bit of shade; the sun was blaring from the hot blue sky, and I needed to sit down. I spread the blanket out in the shadow of the bear pit, and Emmi took the head of lettuce from the picnic basket and tore off a leaf each for the boys, and we watched them pushing it through the wire of the cage. The rabbits swarmed towards it, shoving and scrabbling, climbing across one another's heads, sharp little mouths all snatching at the same scraps of leaf. I shivered.

'You can't be cold,' said Emmi.

'No,' I said.

We unwrapped the sandwiches and the strudel, and I set out the cake plates and the silver cake forks.

'What's that *smell*?' I said. 'Not just the animals, surely.' It was fatty and smoky and too too sweet, worse when the breeze picked up. I felt a little ill, and I waved away the fat black blowflies that had appeared out of nowhere. 'We need to eat this, boys,' I said, shooing away a fly just before it landed on the strudel.

Arno was opening the cage and reaching inside. 'You,' he

was saying. 'Yes, you. Come on.' He dragged out a rabbit by the scruff of its neck and held it up for the boys. It struggled for a moment, twisting and bucking in his fist, hind paws kicking at the air, and then it fell still.

'Do you think he'd like a piece of strudel?' said Karl-Heinz.

'No, darling,' I said.

'But why not? It's delicious.'

'Well, because it might make him sick.'

'Why?'

'Because it's human food, not animal food. Humans eat human food, and animals eat animal food.'

'And humans eat animals,' added Felix.

'Yes. Well, yes,' I said.

'Can we keep him?' said Karl-Heinz.

'No, darling.'

He reached out a tentative finger and touched the rabbit's belly, then jumped back, letting out a shriek.

Arno laughed. 'You can't be scared of such a little thing,' he said. 'You're not scared, are you?'

'No,' said Karl-Heinz, keeping his distance.

'What about you, Felix?'

'I'm not scared,' he said, but he too hung back.

'What if I told you he's the Easter Bunny?' said Arno.

'Is he? *Is* he the Easter Bunny?' said Felix, inching closer, peering at the creature. He stroked its tufty ears.

'He might be,' said Arno. 'We don't know that he's not.'

'That's right,' I said. 'We don't know that he's not. And if you're good, he might hide some eggs in your garden on Sunday.'

'At any rate, he won't hurt you,' said Arno. 'Look, he's terrified – you can tell because he's stopped struggling. He's playing dead. Do you want a turn?'

Karl-Heinz shook his head, but Felix said, 'I do! I do!'

'Wait a minute!' called Emmi, and she took out her camera.

'Hold him like this, behind his neck,' said Arno. 'So he

doesn't escape. And put your other hand under his hind legs. That's it.'

The rabbit was trembling, and pushed its head into the crook of Felix's arm.

'Make it look over here,' said Emmi. 'Hold still. Wait, I'll come around the other side. All right. Smile. Felix. Felix. Smile.'

'He licked my finger!' said Felix.

'That means it likes you,' said Emmi.

'Your turn now, Karl-Heinz,' I said, but he shook his head again. 'Just for the photo,' I said. 'We can give it to Papa, for his birthday. He can put it on his desk. Wouldn't that be nice? Look, I'll be in it too. Just pretend for a moment.'

He stood motionless while Arno passed him the rabbit.

'Behind his neck, remember,' said Arno.

'Look at Frau Wolff, darling,' I said, putting my arm around his shoulder. 'Quick, Emmi.'

She took the picture, and Karl-Heinz let go. The rabbit dropped from his arms and shot away.

'Shit!' hissed Arno.

'Scharführer Rehbein said a bad word!' said Felix.

'I'm sure he didn't,' I said.

'I heard him. Karl-Heinz, did you hear him?'

Karl-Heinz looked from Arno to Felix to me. 'I don't know,' he said.

'Shit,' said Felix. 'That's what he said. Shit shit shit.'

'Felix!' said Emmi. 'Stop telling tales. Come and have some lunch, before the flies get to it.'

'I'll have to find it,' said Arno. 'We can't have rabbits running around the place.'

Emmi waved a hand. 'It's just one little rabbit.'

'What if it's one little female rabbit?' said Arno. 'There could be dozens of them in a few weeks. Hundreds in a few months. The rats are bad enough.'

'Rats?' I said.

'Rats?' said Karl-Heinz, looking all around us.

'You enjoy your lunch,' said Arno. 'I'll be back soon.'

'Hands!' I said as the boys reached for the sandwiches. I made them wait while I found the damp cloth Josef had packed.

'You think of everything,' said Emmi.

'Here,' I said. 'Give them a good scrub. Fingers and thumbs too. And in between.'

Finally we sat down to eat, and I bit into a sandwich. The bread had gone dry in the heat, and the butter tasted curdled; nobody else seemed to mind, but it coated my tongue with a slick of grease, and I wanted to spit it all out. I swallowed, and felt it shifting down inside me in a hard lump. I swallowed again. Beyond the electrified fence, the smoke from the chimney was thickening, darkening. A blur of grey feathers.

Emmi slipped off her shoes and moved into a patch of sun on the grass. She pulled up the hem of her dress to mid-thigh and lay down, flinging an arm across her face.

'Careful you don't burn,' I told her.

'You're so lucky with your skin.'

'He wasn't the Easter Bunny, anyway,' Felix was saying. 'The Easter Bunny is much bigger, because he has to carry all the eggs.'

'I found one in a tree,' said Karl-Heinz. 'Didn't I, Mama?'

'What did you find, darling?'

'An Easter egg.'

'That's right,' I said. 'In the chestnut tree at home. Do you remember that?'

'Papa told me. He had to lift me up.'

'So he did.'

'Rabbits can't climb trees,' said Felix.

'I climbed it,' said Karl-Heinz. 'Papa lifted me up.'

'But how did the egg get there?'

'Hmm,' said Karl-Heinz.

'Emmi, aren't you having anything to eat?' I said.

'I'm watching my figure,' she said from behind her arm.

'She measures herself every day,' said Felix. 'With no clothes on. Can I have her strudel, please, Frau Hahn?'

'It's delicious,' said Karl-Heinz.

'Emmi?' I said.

'Finish yours first, and then we'll see.'

'We have to save a piece for Scharführer Rehbein,' said Karl-Heinz.

'I brought a piece for him,' I said. 'There's enough for everybody.'

'He doesn't deserve it,' said Felix.

'*Felix*,' said Emmi.

When they had finished their sandwiches the boys stabbed at the strudel with their cake forks, chasing it around their plates, blobs of apple oozing from the pastry.

'Like this,' I said. 'See, you use the edge of the fork like a little knife.'

'Why can't we use our fingers?' said Karl-Heinz.

'That would be rude.'

'We ate our sandwiches with our fingers.'

A blowfly landed on my wrist, and I shook it away. Emmi turned over to try to get some colour on the back of her legs. The air was still and hot, and the smell of the place was in my hair and clothes and mouth. I took out the book I'd brought with me – my father's Hölderlin – and tried to read. *The fruits are ripe, dipped in fire . . .*

'Where's the elephant?' said Karl-Heinz.

'There's no elephant, darling,' said Emmi.

'It's not a real zoo, then,' he said. 'I saw an elephant in Berlin, when we visited the Rosts.'

'We should think about packing up soon,' I said.

'What about Scharführer Rehbein?' said Karl-Heinz.

'He might not know the way back to our house,' said Felix.

'Of course he does,' I said, but Emmi said, 'I can wait for him. I'll show him the way.'

'I'll see if I can find where he's gone,' I said. I must have stood up too quickly; for a moment the world went black. I blinked, blinked again – and yes, there were the boys with their silver cake forks, and Emmi stretched out on the grass, and the rabbits packed into their cage, fur poking through the wire, and the chimney huge and high on the other side of the fence. I shooed away another fly, and it collided with my hand, and even after it zoomed off again I could feel the thud of its black body in my palm. I walked a little way, but there was no sign of Arno. The only person I could find was the man who'd brought the rabbits; he was mucking out the monkeys' enclosure. I knew I wasn't supposed to talk to prisoners – Dietrich didn't even like me chatting to Josef – but there was nobody else to ask, and I wanted very much to go home.

'Excuse me,' I said, and the man started, looking up at me for a second before training his eyes on the ground. 'I'm trying to find Scharführer Rehbein. Have you seen him?'

He shook his head.

'It's a lovely day, isn't it?' I said, and he nodded. 'A lovely day to be working out in the fresh air.'

Still he did not raise his eyes.

'Well, if you do see Scharführer Rehbein, would you tell him I'm looking for him?'

He nodded again.

'Oh, how silly of me. It's Frau Hahn. I'm Frau Hahn.' I could hear shouting in the distance, and dogs barking, and then what sounded like a gunshot. 'What was that?' I said, but the prisoner seemed not to notice; he returned to his work, shovelling the excrement into a pile. The monkeys screeched and cackled and grabbed at his clothing. 'Well, thank you,' I said. It *was* a gunshot, wasn't it? I was starting to feel faint; everything was too hot, too bright.

I headed in the direction of the watchtower to the left of the gatehouse, but they hadn't seen Arno either. 'What was that noise just now?' I asked.

The guard shrugged. 'Probably someone trying to escape,' he said.

A voice blared from a loudspeaker then: *Corpse carriers to the vegetable gardens.* I should have gone back to the bear pit; I should have gone back to Emmi and the boys and bundled everything up and returned home. But I found myself walking along the fenceline, back towards the main entrance to the camp. Soon enough I was at the gate.

'Good afternoon,' said a guard. 'Can I help you, Frau . . . ?'

'Frau Hahn,' I said.

'Frau Hahn, of course. Are you looking for the Sturmbannführer? I can take you to his office if you like.'

'Thank you, no. I'm looking for Scharführer Rehbein. He was with us at the zoo, but we appear to have lost him.'

'I haven't seen him down this way,' said the guard.

Beyond the gate I saw a pair of prisoners hurrying past, carrying someone on a stretcher. His arm trailed along the ground, and there was a dark stain across his chest. I didn't want to look, but there was no avoiding it at that distance.

'Was there an accident?' I said.

The guard glanced over his shoulder. 'You don't need to think about things like that, Frau Hahn.'

'But is he . . . is he dead?'

'You don't need to think about it.'

The two prisoners stopped to get a better hold on the stretcher, and their patient thumped against the ground. The sound of it shook me; it seemed to shake the whole place.

'What happened to him?'

The guard glanced over his shoulder again. 'I'm not sure. Might have tried to escape. Or steal from the Reich. A carrot. Some dog food.'

'A carrot?' I said. 'A carrot?'

'I know. They never learn. *Our* job is to eat the vegetables, and *their* job is to spread the shit on the gardens.'

'What?'

'I apologise, Frau Hahn – the manure.'

I'd seen only one dead body before – my grandfather, tiny in his coffin. But the dead prisoner wasn't small in death. He filled the scene; he was everywhere I looked. I could make out the curled dark hair on his wrists and the dirt under his nails, the white of his teeth and the wide stripes on his jacket and trousers, and the wooden shoe that fell from his foot and thudded to a stop, a little abandoned boat.

I needed to get away. I hurried back to the zoo entrance and ran towards the bear pit, keeping pace with the prisoners as if we were competing in some strange race. I pushed myself to run faster, though the pain had returned to my pelvis; I wanted to get to Karl-Heinz and distract him as the men passed. Out of the corner of my eye I could see the dead prisoner's arm jerking and jolting, his fingers brushing the ground, touching it one last time. I couldn't keep up. Karl-Heinz was probably turning to look even now. And then, just as I reached the bear pit, the monkeys cackling and pointing at me, the prisoners disappeared behind a fence and were gone. I stopped, caught my breath. The pain was sharper now, and I found myself praying for it to leave me. I closed my eyes.

I thought of my grandfather laid out in his shroud, white hair combed into wings at his temples. I'd been allowed to attend his vigil Mass with my sister the night before his funeral, and because it was a special occasion my mother had given me her rosary beads to carry in their little rose-shaped celluloid case. It hung from a chain that had a ring at the top, and you slipped your finger through the ring, and the rose swung as you walked, and everyone knew that you must be a trustworthy girl, a good girl, to be permitted to carry such a thing.

There were two figures on the lid of the case, pressed into the brass: a bearded man, and a child sitting on his lap. Both wore haloes around their heads, and I never could decide who they were meant to be. Joseph holding the baby Jesus? Or Jesus holding a child? If you unhooked the tiny clasp that said MADE IN BELGIUM in letters almost too small to read, you could see the backwards image of the figures on the inside of the lid, as if they could be two different people at once. My mother told me it would be mine to keep when I made my confirmation, but I was still only seven, and that was seven years away, which was forever. The beads themselves were as tiny as seeds – little dots made from blue and white glass that warmed in your hand as you prayed – and at the bottom the silver cross with the silver man on it, who was Jesus, who was God. It was thin and sharp, the cross, and weighed almost nothing.

My grandfather had died in midsummer, and the church was hot with candles when we arrived, and my legs cooked in their thick black stockings. I had to shift the rosary-bead case to my left hand when I dipped my fingers in the holy water so it wouldn't hit me in the face when I blessed myself. Helena was already crying, and my mother took a handkerchief from her purse and gave it to her, but it was mostly lace, and very small, and not very useful. I wondered if she was crying for our father; we'd never had a funeral for him because he never came back from France, so my mother had said we could imagine him in Opa's coffin too, and sing for him, and pray for him. I followed her down the aisle, and I didn't see the coffin until we were almost upon it, and it loomed up at me like a dark ship, Helena's sobs coming in gales now. I fiddled with the ring of the rosary-bead case, putting it back on my right hand, looking at it on my ring finger and pretending I was married. As we reached the front pew I saw my grandfather wrapped in his linen shroud like bread in a bag, and I had to wait there for a few moments while my mother and my sister genuflected and filed into their seats. And then, as I took my place and arranged my stiff skirts, keeping my ankles and knees together, making sure not to bang the rosary-bead case against the worn wood, I caught the smell of something strange and sweet in the hot church, like a jug of milk on the turn, like an apple liquefying at the core; something the incense and the flowers couldn't quite cover. I glanced over at my grandfather in his linen. Everyone says that people look smaller when they are dead, don't they? And he did; my grandfather did. And I knew that soon he would become smaller still, because Helena had told me that was how it worked: he'd shrink and shrivel in his bag, in his box, until he was only bones. I found myself thinking of the bread bag I'd made my mother for her birthday: I'd embroidered a sheaf of wheat on it, and the words *Give us this day our daily bread*, only I'd made the wheat and the first word so big that I had to squash the rest of them, and there was hardly any space in between. 'Didn't you measure it out?' said Helena. 'Didn't you count the threads? Mark it with chalk?' No, I hadn't planned it in the proper way, the way we'd been taught. 'Well then, what did you expect?' I wanted to rip the thing to rags, throw it into the fire, but then I'd have had nothing to give my mother. When she unfolded it and held it up I watched her face for signs of disappointment, but she didn't notice my mistakes – or if she did, she kept them to herself. 'Clever girl!' she said. 'Thank you, darling. It's just the thing.' And she showed the awful bag to every visitor.

I opened my eyes. The monkeys were chattering nearby, and the pain had eased off again. At the bear pit, Arno was waiting with Emmi and the boys, eating his piece of strudel. Emmi was holding his tunic for him, dusting it off, and I could see patches of sweat on the back of his shirt and under the arms.

'There you are,' I said. 'I thought you'd disappeared. Is everything all right?' He was panting, and there was a scratch on the back of his hand and a small tear in his sleeve.

'Everything is fine,' he said.

'You found the escapee?'

'I dealt with it,' he said, nodding towards the boys in a way that stopped me from asking anything further.

I began packing away the picnic things, but I couldn't get them to fit back in the basket; I couldn't remember where everything belonged. I was so tired by then that I wouldn't have cared if we just left it all behind for the flies. I wanted to get away from the heat and the smell, and the red chimney, and the gate with its mirror-writing.

Emmi took the plates from me and started wiping them with the damp cloth one by one.

'Why is it backwards?' I said. 'The motto on the gate.'

'It's not,' said Emmi. 'Not if you're inside. If you're a prisoner.'

'But it's not even clear what it means,' I said. '*To Each His Due.*'

'Everyone gets what he deserves,' said Arno. 'That's what they told us.'

I watched Emmi wiping the plates. I wanted to tell her that she was doing it wrong, that the cloth was for cleaning our hands, not our dirty dishes, but she'd already finished the last one and was stacking them in their proper place and fastening the little straps to hold them in position.

'Do you know what I deserve?' she murmured to me. 'What I deserve is a muscular young farmer from Hesse.' She did the cake forks next, smearing them with the cloth that must have been quite filthy by that point, then bundling them up in a used serviette. 'No point carrying this back with us,' she said, handing the remains of the head of lettuce to Felix. 'Feed it to the rabbits, there's a good boy.'

But Felix was bored with the rabbits. He kicked the lettuce head to Karl-Heinz, who kicked it back; in a moment the thing split apart and disintegrated, and the boys jumped up and down on it until you could hardly tell what it was.

Back at home I pulled the curtains and climbed into bed, though I didn't sleep. I stared at the print of Hohenschwangau hanging on the wall, a castle-shaped hole in the dark forest. Every now and then the pain came, dragging and twisting at me, and I couldn't get comfortable; the sheet was too starched and the mattress too soft. I wanted my own bed, back in Munich. I rolled onto my side and studied the pattern on the curtains – the rows of roses – except with the light behind them they were just silhouettes, and might have been the tops of trees, or heads of lettuce, or clenched fists.

'I heard you went for a walk today,' said Dietrich. I jumped; I suppose I must have fallen asleep after all. The room was almost dark, and I couldn't make out his face. 'I thought you might have stopped in to see me.'

'The boys dragged us to see the zoo,' I said. 'And the rabbits. Karl-Heinz wanted to keep one.'

'And what did you think?'

'I told him no.'

'No, I mean – what did you think of the camp? You must have had a look through the fence.'

Something in his voice made me smile; he sounded like Karl-Heinz when he was showing me a drawing he'd done of huge-handed faceless figures that were meant to be us, or a papier-mâché animal he'd made, the lumpy body still soggy with paste, caving in on itself. Then I remembered the man on the stretcher, the stain spreading through the striped cloth. I sat up, turned on the bedside light. 'They shot a man, I think,' I said.

'Where?' said Dietrich.

'In the chest, I think. Possibly because he ate a carrot.'

'But where? Did you see it happen? Did Karl-Heinz see it?'

'Oh,' I said. 'No, we didn't see it.'

He stretched and yawned. 'That's all right, then.'

'He must have done something, though, mustn't he?'

'Oh yes, he will have done something.' He was unbuttoning

his tunic, hanging it on the wardrobe door and brushing it with the little clothes-brush he kept just for that purpose. He did this every day; I told him he'd wear holes in it.

The pain jabbed at me again, and I sucked in air through my teeth.

'Greta?' he said. 'Are you all right?' He'd stopped brushing the tunic; it was long since spotless, anyway.

I exhaled, smooth and slow. 'I think I overdid it today.'

'Are you in pain?'

'A little.'

'You mustn't go off on these walks all over the place.'

'It wasn't far.'

'All the same. You must take care.'

We dined at the White Swan in Weimar for Dietrich's birthday. The Wolffs came too, and Otto pointed out the Napoleonic cannonball still lodged in the front façade. While we were waiting for our meal I gave Dietrich the carved desk set. He took so long to unwrap the parcel that I could hardly bear it; I felt my whole body fluttering.

'Such fine work,' he said at last. 'Finer than anything I could ever make. Wherever did you find it?'

I just smiled, and Emmi said, 'Your wife can be very devious, you know.'

'Look at the girl,' I said, and Dietrich ran his fingers over the figure in the centre: me on the beach just after a swim, smiling into the sun.

'The photo of you, that day on Rügen,' he said.

'Do you remember? We climbed to the top of the Königsstuhl.'

'Have you been?' he asked the Wolffs. 'You can see right across the Ostsee.'

We stayed at the restaurant until well after midnight, long after everyone else had left.

'Shouldn't we let the owner close up?' I said, but Otto said they were always happy to stay open for people like us.

'I think Greta means she's tired, darling,' said Emmi – and yes, I had to admit that I couldn't keep my eyes open, and I fell asleep in the car on the way home.

Dietrich took the desk set to work the following morning, and he told me he'd look at it and think of that day on Rügen whenever he wanted to imagine himself somewhere else. His job did require a lot of him, I know. The disgraced former Kommandant, Koch, had almost run the place into the ground with his stealing, and it was up to Dietrich to show that the areas of the camp under his control weren't costing more than they should. Sometimes he brought his paperwork home: pages and pages covered with columns of figures. Such huge numbers to balance. He had to account for everything, he said, and it didn't help that Prinz zu Waldeck, who'd investigated the Kochs once already, was still asking difficult questions about corruption at the camp.

'You're being careful, aren't you?' I asked, and he said of course he was; of course.

'You have nothing to worry about,' he told me. 'We've done nothing wrong.'

He rubbed at a spot between his eyes and let out a long sigh – so that was when I told him about the baby, even though my appointment with the doctor was still a few days away.

I said, 'I think I'm pregnant.'

He stared at me for a moment – and then, in two strides, he was at the side of my chair and grabbing my hand. 'Greta! My little Gretalein! Really?'

'I think so.'

'Clever, clever girl!' He kissed me on the mouth, his lips cool and soft and tasting faintly of smoke. 'I knew coming here was the right decision,' he said, as if the place had planted the child in me.

'I don't know for certain yet,' I said.

'Karl-Heinz will be so excited!'

That was true; he was still asking for a little brother to play with, and we were still avoiding the question. Maybe now he'd stop talking about Ingo. And Dietrich must have read my thoughts, because he said the same thing: 'Perhaps Ingo will die a death.'

'But we won't tell him yet,' I said. 'To be on the safe side.'

'Yes yes,' said Dietrich. He laughed. 'Your mother will have to visit us now.'

The pain knifed at my pelvis again, and I winced.

'What is it? Greta?'

'Nothing. Nothing. Just the baby, burrowing in.'

The next day Emmi and I took the children to the swimming pool down in Weimar. I stayed in the shallow end for a while and watched her and the girls climb the diving tower and leap off the board. She convinced Felix and Karl-Heinz to try it too, and soon they were all hurling themselves into the water, fearless.

'Come on, Mama,' called Karl-Heinz. 'I dare you!'

When he was still a baby, we left him with Dietrich's mother one afternoon so we could go out to a film together, just the two of us, for the first time in over a year. We went to see *Olympia* – the one with the diving sequence at the end – and those slow-motion scenes returned to me as I pulled myself out of the water and climbed the ladder to the board. I remembered sitting in the dark cinema with Dietrich, the athletes high above us in our seats, bright gods twisting against the sky. They didn't leap; they flew. It seemed they might never descend.

And then I was crashing into the water, and it was forcing itself into my throat, and for a few seconds I couldn't breathe.

'I jumped off the diving board!' Karl-Heinz told Dietrich that night. 'I might be a fish when I grow up. Can you make me some fish for my ark?'

'They didn't have fish on the ark, darling,' I said.

'Then how do we still have fish?'

'Well, the fish could swim.'

'I hope Mama didn't go jumping off the board,' said Dietrich, and Karl-Heinz said, 'She did! She did!'

'Greta!' he said. 'The baby! Why would you take such a risk?'

It had never occurred to me that something might go wrong.

'What baby?' said Karl-Heinz.

On the day of the appointment I had Arno drive me to the doctor's clinic with Emmi. We asked him to let us out on the next street over, so he'd think we were just going shopping, but even such a short walk exhausted me, and I had to keep stopping to rest.

'It's hot today,' said Emmi, fanning me. 'You're wearing too many clothes.'

She came into the waiting room with me, and I took off my blazer and held it in my lap.

'Raising the second one is so much easier,' she said, flicking through a magazine. 'You stop worrying that you're going to kill it.'

'I used to check Karl-Heinz every hour at night-time,' I said. 'To see if he was still breathing.'

'Such nonsense! Did you read Johanna Haarer too?'

'Of course,' I said. All new mothers read Haarer's child-rearing manual and followed her advice to the letter. If the baby started to wail, we were not to respond. *With lightning speed the child will recognise that he need only cry in order to summon a sympathetic soul and become the focus of all attention. After a short time he will demand this attention as his right, and will allow you no peace until you carry him again, or rock him, or push him in his carriage – and thus the tiny but merciless house tyrant is born!*

I felt the bleeding start as we sat there in the waiting room; a warm gush that I feared would soak through my light-grey skirt. That was my first thought: not that I was losing a baby – or losing maybe just the thought of a baby – but that the stain would show. 'I'm bleeding,' I whispered to Emmi, and as she helped me to my feet we both glanced at the chair I'd been sitting on. There was nothing to see.

In the lavatories she spoke to me through the cubicle door. 'How bad is it?'

'Not bad. A few spots.'

'That's good! That's fine, probably. A few spots.'

I could see her shoes at the bottom of the door: soft cream leather pierced with little decorative holes, and the tips of them open to show her toes. She'd had them sent from Florence.

I blotted the spots with paper – really, it had felt much worse than it was – then took my handkerchief from my purse and folded it into my underwear. It looked very small; I didn't trust myself to make it back to the villa.

'Could I – do you have a spare handkerchief?' I said through the door.

'Of course. Of course,' said Emmi, bending down and passing it to me.

'I'm sorry,' I said.

'Think nothing of it. I've forgotten already.'

Doktor Lang pulled a curtain around the bed and waited on the other side of it while I removed my underwear. I squashed it into a tight bundle so he wouldn't notice the handkerchiefs, then climbed onto the bed and lay very still, afraid the bleeding would start again. He felt all around my stomach and pelvis, then pushed two fingers inside me and kept pressing into my pelvis with the other hand. I stared at the ceiling, trying to make out the exact borders of an old water stain. After he finished, he told me that I definitely wasn't pregnant. 'But you're still young, Frau Hahn,' he said. 'You should have no problem conceiving a second child. We might need to have a little look inside, that's all.'

'You just did,' I said.

'A little operation, I mean. I'll refer you to an excellent surgeon. All right? Good.'

'Was it my fault?' I said. 'The bleed?'

'The bleed was probably nothing,' he said. 'We don't know anything for sure.' He scribbled a few words on a piece of paper and gave it to me: *Chamomile tea. Bioferrin iron tonic.* 'In the meantime, these should help you feel better.'

'No new hats?' said Arno when we returned empty-handed to the car.

'We couldn't find anything we liked,' said Emmi. 'We looked and looked.'

'I'm sorry,' said Arno.

'Oh, it's not your fault! We're too fussy – that's the problem. Or Weimar is too dowdy. Well, have you seen the women? You'll have to drive us to the Champs-Elysées, Arno!'

On she chattered, inventing a trip to Paris, filling his arms with imaginary boxes of hats and shoes and dresses. 'Could you carry all that, do you think, Arno? Of course you could, without even working up a sweat. And then off to the Ritz for champagne!'

I was still holding the note Doktor Lang had given me, and when I folded it to put it away in my purse I noticed something printed on the back: the name of another doctor, a Doktor Abraham, who had rooms at the same address. Yet there'd been no other doctor in the building. Someone had drawn a single stroke of ink diagonally across the page, crossing this other doctor out.

Back at the house I went to lie down, and Emmi arranged for Josef to bring me some lunch on a tray, but when the food arrived I had no appetite.

I must have slept right through the evening, and I didn't even register Dietrich coming to bed. Much later I woke with a blade in my side again, and although the day had been so hot the air in the bedroom felt icy. It rushed into me as I sat up and gasped and held my breath, afraid to exhale. Dietrich lay on his back, undisturbed. I had no idea how to tell him there was no baby. Shadows fell into his open mouth, the sockets of his eyes, but the rest of his face was as white as bone. It frightened me.

In the morning the pain was gone, and Dietrich beamed at me over breakfast and said perhaps we would take Karl-Heinz to the park on the Ilm and let him sail his boat.

'You're not feeling sick?' he said. He smiled, flesh and blood, the man I had married.

'I'm sorry,' I began. 'I made a mistake. I got it wrong.'

'What?' he said, spearing a thick slice of ham with his fork. 'What did you get wrong?'

I glanced at Karl-Heinz, who was daubing great dollops of jam on his bread, dripping it all over the tablecloth.

'I had a *bleed* yesterday.' Soundlessly I mouthed the word at him.

He put down his knife and fork, wiped his mouth with his serviette. 'Are you sure?'

'Certain. I've seen a doctor.'

'Here?'

'Down in Weimar.'

He nodded. 'We don't want word getting around.' Then he said, 'It'll be that diving you did.'

I'd been wondering the same thing, but I said, 'No. The doctor told me that wasn't the reason.' A lie. 'He said there might not have been anything there at all. He said it was probably nothing.'

'What do you mean?'

'I'm not *pregnant*.' Again I mouthed the word. 'I'm not, after all. Well, not any more. Maybe I never was.'

'No baby?' said Dietrich.

'That's right.'

'What baby?' said Karl-Heinz.

'Nothing. It's nothing,' said Dietrich.

'No, nothing,' I echoed.

That afternoon I found my underwear and the two hand-kerchiefs folded on the bed, spotless.

PART FOUR
REMOTE SYMPATHY

FROM AN INTERVIEW WITH FORMER SS
STURMBANNFÜHRER DIETRICH HAHN

13 October 1954

[tape corrupted in places]

You'd be surprised, perhaps, that the families of deceased prisoners routinely asked for the gold from the mouths of their dead. I don't know how many letters my secretary brought me to sign: *[Prisoner's name] died in this camp; the corpse was cremated on [date]. Any return of dental gold is therefore impossible.* Well, perhaps it's not so surprising that the families of criminals would make such indecent demands. At any rate, I was bound by the decree handed down from the Reichsführer, which meant that all such material deriving from prisoners of the Reich remained the property of the Reich.

Once a month the camp dentist delivered the gold to me for safekeeping, and I issued him a receipt for the correct recorded weight, and then, every six months, sent it on to Office D IV in Berlin. It was to our benefit that so many of the inmates had failed to take care of their mouths: we amassed three hundred and thirty-eight grams in May alone. Most of it was in the form of roughly cast ingots, but now and then I found a whole crown or a bridge. I kept the best examples for myself, in a chocolate box in the spare bedroom, locked away in a writing desk. I found it relaxing to sift through the pieces at the end of a long day – as a boy, I used to sift through my mother's button tin – and before you say anything, let me tell you that one way or another, every single officer at Buchenwald skimmed off his share. Prinz zu Waldeck himself placed an urgent order for a large refrigerator to be installed in

Block 50 so he'd have somewhere to store the deer he shot, though the paperwork said it was for serum to protect our troops. And I know for a fact that Adjutant Schmidt organised for butter, eggs and milk to be brought to him from the hospital kitchen on a daily basis, and nothing much happened when the Kommandant found out he was stealing supplies – just a reprimand. You see the corruption I was up against. How impossible it was to run a decent sort of place. My goodness, I wasn't taking food out of anyone's mouth; I was simply keeping a few trinkets. It was easy enough for me to have one of the inmates correct the paperwork that went to D IV, and I made sure he received his due in the form of cigarettes or blood sausage – and so you see, in this respect I helped him, and possibly even saved his life due to the extra nutrition.

Perhaps don't put that in.

You may think I'm stating the obvious when I say that Buchenwald was a prison camp; the individuals held there were prisoners – but many of them seemed to forget their role. They started to believe that because we permitted them to oversee their individual blocks, or run the records department, or distribute the food, they had some kind of real power. The instant one of them got his hands on a kapo armband, let alone a camp senior one, he strutted about as if wearing full dress uniform. The newcomers supposed they would stay for a few months, after which time, depending on their conduct, they'd be released. And their conduct *was* noted, in regular reports for the Gestapo; to simplify this process it was easier not to meet with the actual prisoners, but merely to fill in the most likely words: *disobedient, irredeemable, not suited for release*, et cetera. When we did let one of them go – to bolster morale, as I said – he had to agree to have no contact with other former inmates, and never to speak of the conditions in the camp. For security reasons, you understand.

In 1943 more and more of them began attempting to

escape, and so in accordance with regulations the appropriate punishment had to be meted out. In every case, we made sure we followed the rules: three forms of different colours went to Berlin, and two copies came back. If Berlin expressed approval, then and only then could we take action. It was a valid means of keeping thousands of men in line: if fifty tried to escape, one might succeed, and if one succeeded then a hundred might try and three might succeed, and if three succeeded then five hundred might try, and on and on until the entire camp was in chaos and the Ettersberg so full of men on the run that it was no longer safe for family excursions. At times, though – I'm not afraid to say it – I feared what might happen if they decided to stage a rebellion. They were brutes, most of them, hard-bitten criminals and drunkards with little respect for authority and even less for human life. Who knew what they might attempt?

We had done our best to introduce reasonable measures, to ensure that Buchenwald was a model camp. Proper dental care was made available to the prisoners, for instance, and if a tooth containing gold was ever extracted from the mouth of a living inmate, he was compensated for it as a matter of principle. All very fair, all above board. Goodness me, they had their own library, their own infirmary and their own cinema, and once a year, on the Führer's birthday, they received a hot chocolate. Every prisoner had a bed to himself, with clean sheets and two woollen blankets – there are photographs of this – and the infirmary rivalled any decent hospital; again, there are photographs. We let them stage concerts and listen to the radio over the loudspeaker – sometimes music, certainly the Wehrmacht communiqués and all the important speeches – and we broadcast songs on the gramophone. The brass band played cheerful tunes for them when they marched to and from their work, too, and from the middle of 1943 they would even have a brothel. And we'd had a permanent crematorium built, capable of continuous operation, after one of our vehicles lost a couple of corpses on the way to the Weimar crematorium – they fell out in the middle of town, in full view of a coffee house. The manufacturer supplied us with urns so ashes could be returned to relatives at their own cost – oh yes, we saw it as our duty to handle the dead with dignity, despite what you might have heard. Despite what you might have seen in the footage the Americans shot. They screened it on the first day of their show trial at Dachau: piles and piles of bodies in the crematorium courtyard, but no admission that most of them had died *after* the SS had left! And no admission, either, that people of eastern countries – yes, let's say it, though it's no longer fashionable: the Jews – were largely responsible for the dirty conditions. They refused to use the flushing toilets, preferring to defecate in their food bowls – that's just one example. I could go on.

The trouble was, there were simply too many prisoners. The water supply and the sewerage system, for instance, which were my responsibilities, caused me considerable suffering; no one had foreseen the sheer numbers. As long as the gate still shuts, the camp is not overfilled – that's what Wolff said, but ultimately it was my problem when there wasn't enough water to sluice out the pathology rooms, or when typhus threatened to spread from block to block because the prisoners couldn't wash. Or when a group of Poles tried to saw through the grating on one of the sewerage pipes and escape like giant turds. Pister had tried instituting morning calisthenics, for the good of the inmates' health, but was forced to cancel them altogether because too many participants were collapsing. When we were in sore need of new clothing for the prisoners we applied through the correct channels and filled out the correct documents, and we did receive several hundred thousand surplus garments from Auschwitz – but on inspection almost half had to be thrown away because of bullet holes and bloodstains. These were the sorts of obstacles we faced. We tried . . .

[corrupted]

. . . told me she was pregnant, then, I felt an immediate easing of my mood. Let them forge ahead with their corruption investigations! Let the prisoner population swell by the thousand every week; let sewage drown the place! Nothing had changed about my work, and goodness knows the balance sheet was as difficult as ever, yet I no longer dwelt on such petty problems. I no longer brought them home with me. A baby! A baby would make us a proper family. I didn't let on, but I longed for a daughter – a pretty little thing to win my heart with her cooing and her curls, like Kommandant Pister's little Edda. We could name her Gudrun, or Hermine – a good strong German name.

'I'll be happy with a girl or a boy,' I told Greta. That's what you're supposed to say, isn't it?

As I walked home through the forest that week I felt that things were finally starting to go my way. The trees had unfurled their new leaves, and the wind was blowing in the right direction, the air fresh and new and untainted by smoke from the camp. I would have to write to Henning Rost and tell him how successful my move to Buchenwald was proving. Perhaps I'd even invite him for a visit, so he could see our model camp. We could go walking in the hills, along the old hunting trails cut into the beech groves for the dukes of Weimar, and I could show him the spot at the summit where the royal hunting parties used to wait with their rifles while their quarry was driven straight to them. Napoleon himself was a guest, I would tell him. Tsar Alexander I, too. I imagined a shooting expedition with Henning, signalling to him to stand clear while I took down a great stag. We'd hack off the head between us, and I'd have the antlers made into a chandelier even bigger than the one in our living room. I felt the ground drumming beneath my feet; my own future galloping straight for me.

Only a few days later, though – and over breakfast, when Karl-Heinz was sitting right there, and the servant was within earshot – Greta announced that she'd been mistaken, and there was no pregnancy. I know it was cruel of me, but I asked her if she thought her trip to the swimming pool might have had something to do with it. I couldn't help it. She *should* have taken more care. At that moment I was very aware of the difference in our ages.

At first I didn't register who the doctor was when he telephoned me.

'Doktor Lang, from the clinic in Weimar,' he said again, and then apologised. He'd seen Greta the previous day, and he assumed she would have told me.

'Of course she told me,' I said. 'Yes, yes she told me.'

In that case, he said, I would know he'd referred Greta to a colleague – an excellent, excellent surgeon – because he was a little concerned. He suspected he'd felt a mass in her pelvis when he'd examined her.

'The baby?' I said. For an instant I thought perhaps Greta had misunderstood, and there really was a baby, and the doctor had done some tests to confirm it.

'Ah,' said Lang. 'No, not a baby. A mass. A growth.' He thought it was probably harmless – she was very young, so statistically speaking they were unlikely to find anything – but they needed to check.

'A growth,' I said.

'Yes, Herr Sturmbannführer,' he said.

I asked if they could cut it out, and he said they'd know more once she'd seen the surgeon. I knew he didn't want to mention what he thought was wrong, but I insisted. And so he told me.

Ovarian cancer. That's what he suspected might be growing in her. Not a child: a tumour.

'But where do these things come from?' I said. Greta was of excellent stock – a very hardy German line.

'It can be difficult to pinpoint the cause,' he said. 'Arsenic pesticides, artificial fertilisers. Smoke inhalation. Lead from toothpaste tubes and water pipes, perhaps, or dyes in pudding powder. X-rays.'

'X-rays?' I said.

Radiation could cause genetic damage, he explained. Sterility, yes, but also mutations in future offspring.

'She doesn't eat pudding,' I said.

When I hung up the telephone I stood there for a moment, my hand still on the receiver, and I did not move. The entranceway around me seemed to retreat, opening out into some vast and empty room, the walls and floor too distant to see. I felt my breath leaving me in quick little pulses, out of step with the ticking clock. Still I did not lift my hand from the receiver. The death's-head band on my ring finger glimmered. It was a present from Greta for my fortieth birthday, and I never took it off. At first, I remember, it felt strange, uncomfortable, and I kept worrying at it with my thumb, turning it, tilting it, trying to stop the press of it against the bone. Eventually, though, I grew used to it, and hours could pass without my giving it a second thought, and then, after a time, I didn't notice it at all. It wasn't a real one, of course – only small numbers of those were ever issued, awarded by the Reichsführer himself and engraved inside with his signature, so rare that they had to be surrendered on the owner's death. No, Greta had mine made for me; I'd mentioned that I wanted one, that a number of officers were commissioning such rings, singling themselves out as men who were committed to their careers, their advancement. And the jeweller did an excellent job: it certainly looked the part.

'The only thing he couldn't include was the signature,' she said. 'That would have made it a forgery, not a replica.'

I wasn't sure I understood the difference – but yes, it was blank inside. I must have let my disappointment show, because she said, 'You deserve a proper one. They'll recognise all your hard work one day. They will.' Then she took the ring and put it on my finger and said, 'There. In the meantime, nobody will know.'

But you don't want to hear about that.

I decided not to tell her about the doctor's suspicions, and later that day, when I spoke to Amsel, the surgeon, he agreed it would be better if we kept them to ourselves. Kinder.

'And besides,' I said, 'it might be harmless, mightn't it?'

'Yes,' he said. 'Yes, it might be.' He paused. They wouldn't know exactly what they were dealing with until they could look inside her. In the meantime, they'd call it a cyst.

'A cyst that needs to be removed,' I said.

'Exactly,' he said. 'And the sooner the better, just to be safe.'

I asked if we'd be able to have another child if it were a tumour.

Possibly, he said. It depended on how radical an approach they took. Usually it was safer to remove everything and follow up with a course of radiation.

'Everything?' I said.

'Both ovaries as well as the womb,' he said.

I told him no: I would not support the radical approach. Still, he tried to persuade me, and so I had to repeat myself: I would *not support* the radical approach. And no radiation, either. I didn't want her giving birth to a monster.

I still stand by this decision.

I wrote to her mother to tell her about the surgery, but I downplayed the seriousness; I didn't want Elisabeth turning up for a visit. I knew she disapproved of where we were living and what I was doing; if she arrived out of the blue on our doorstep, wanting to see the patient, Greta would surely suspect something was wrong.

I don't think I slept at all the night before the operation. There was a mosquito trapped in the room; it kept finding me in the dark, homing in on my hands, my cheeks, my neck. I pulled the covers over my head, but I couldn't breathe. Every few minutes I heard the insect approach, sensed it alight on me, and I swiped and slapped, then settled back down to sleep – and there it was again. Whenever I turned on the light, though, it disappeared. I must have looked like a madman, swatting at myself, trying to kill something I couldn't see. Greta groaned and put her hands over her eyes. 'I can't even hear it,' she said. 'Just go to sleep.' But all night I listened to it singing for my blood.

Emmi Wolff looked after Karl-Heinz for a few days; she wouldn't have been my first choice, but my mother was by then too elderly to come, and we needed the help. He cried when I dropped him off at their house, and I had to prise his hand from mine.

'Just until Mama's better,' I told him – and then, when I went to collect him, he didn't want to come home.

They'd been to the zoo twice, he said, and a monkey grabbed his finger, and he held a Lügner – that's what he called it, a Lügner – and he pulled the trigger, bang bang bang!

'It's *Luger*, stupid,' said Felix.

'Yes, a Luger!' said Karl-Heinz. 'I held a Luger!'

'What's all this?' I asked.

'They wanted to try out my pistol,' said Wolff. 'It wasn't loaded, of course,' he added.

Karl-Heinz could hardly wait to tell me the rest. They saw all the robbers lining up behind the fence, he said, and Martin the bear was dancing to the music! And then the robbers weren't going fast enough so they had to crawl on the ground, and they got all dirty!

He and Felix lay on their stomachs on the carpet to demonstrate, pulling themselves along by their elbows, laughing and laughing.

I asked him how long they stayed there.

An hour or two, said Wolff. Then they came home for hot chocolate.

It must have been a late night, I said, and he shrugged. The boys had begged, and once in a while didn't hurt.

The next day, when Greta was due back from the hospital, I said to Karl-Heinz, 'We won't tell Mama about seeing the robbers, all right?'

'Doktor Amsel is very pleased with you, darling,' I said, and this was not a lie; he was confident he'd cut out all of the growth. I made no mention of the exact nature of that growth, though: a tumour, stuck fast to the right ovary, which he'd removed in its entirety. According to my instructions he'd stopped short of a full hysterectomy, and he assured me we should still be able to conceive a second child.

She didn't need to know it was cancer, I told him. It was kinder that way. And no radiation, either.

'If that is your wish, Herr Sturmbannführer,' he said.

That was my wish, I said. And at any rate, hadn't there been studies? I'd heard – I'd *read* – there could be a better outcome for cancer patients if they didn't know what was wrong with them. If they didn't give in to the disease.

He'd heard of such studies, he told me uncertainly. But yes, it was astounding, the things we could talk ourselves into.

'You'll feel back to normal soon,' I said to Greta.

'I feel eighty years old,' she said, clinging to my arm as we climbed the front steps. 'How long have I been gone?'

In the entranceway she stopped in front of the mirror and stared at her reflection, leaning in so close that the glass started to fog. I helped her up the staircase, slowly, slowly; we had to pause three times so she could catch her breath.

'I'm fine. I'll be fine,' she said. She looked up ahead of her to the top of the stairs, where the print of the swans on the Bodensee hung: three little smears of white suspended in the dark, their necks hooked like question marks.

Karl-Heinz wanted to climb into bed with her and have stories, the way he did on Sunday mornings, but I told him she would need a bit of time, and we had to be careful not to hurt her.

'Ingo could get in, though,' he said.

I started to remark that it was high time Ingo returned to his own family, wherever that was, especially since Karl-Heinz would be a big grown-up schoolboy soon, but Greta said, 'Yes, there's room for Ingo,' and she pushed back the covers.

'Don't squash her,' Karl-Heinz said to nobody.

The completion of the railway should have been cause for celebration. It ran from Weimar up the Ettersberg to the new Gustloff Works – the armaments factory – on the edge of the camp, making the transport of all kinds of material much simpler and more cost-effective. Reichsführer Himmler ordered it finished in just three months, by June 1943, and there was a great scramble to make sure we achieved this, with twelve-hour day and night shifts conducted at a hectic pace. We lost a lot of prisoners because they weren't used to such work; many of them had never put in a day's honest physical labour in their lives. Still, despite the wastage, we met the deadline, and the railway opened with great fanfare on the longest day of the year – the most important SS involved received decorations and promotions, and the prisoners had their reward as well, in the form of a wash. All the officers turned out in their dress uniforms, and the dignitaries came too, even Reichsführer Himmler, and I shook hands with him and exchanged a few words, and somebody took our photograph. The sun shone, and the SS band, which had been rehearsing for weeks just for the occasion, played 'Old Comrades' and 'My Regiment, My Homeland'. I felt such a lightness as I watched the first train arrive from Weimar; we needed some good news, after the disaster at Stalingrad earlier in the year, and the end of the North African campaign, which nobody liked to mention outside their own homes. As the locomotive approached, hung with fat garlands of greenery, I read the placard fixed to the front: *First Trip to Buchenwald*. I tapped my foot in time to the band and applauded the train's arrival, and I knew that Greta was waiting for me at home, getting better all the time, and I decided that any day now she would be well enough to put on the sky-blue dress that I liked and join me at the officers' club for dinner. And then, perhaps even in time for my next birthday, a little daughter.

'A sign of good things to come,' I said to Hans Schmidt, Pister's adjutant, who was standing next to me.

'If it holds, it'll be a miracle,' he muttered. I could smell the schnapps on his breath, and I suppose I shouldn't have tried to engage him in polite conversation; he was a crude individual who liked reading low-brow novels and throwing his weight around, yet never seemed to put a foot wrong in his career – though of course, things would not go well for him in the American trial.

I was unsure what he meant by his remark, and I was about to tell him that he should take care, since such comments had the ring of defeatism, but the train had hissed to a stop and the mayor was alighting and coming to shake our hands. He showed us a commemorative folder Pister had presented to him and the other dignitaries: photographs of the railway under construction, with strong, healthy prisoners shovelling soil and securing the sleepers. SS men watched over them, hands behind their backs. No whips. No cudgels. No dogs. All this can be verified.

Later there was a get-together at the Pisters' villa, and out of duty's sake I stayed for a few drinks, to keep up appearances. Adjutant Schmidt made a lengthy toast to the Kommandant for completing the railway on time, and then Wolff made an even longer one. All I wanted was to return home to Greta. Though it was past nine when I walked through the front door, it was still light, and I could see her sitting in the conservatory.

'Have you eaten?' I asked.

A little, she said. She offered to make me something, but winced when she started to get up from her chair. She sat down again, her breathing heavy. The sinking sun flooded through the western window and turned her skin transparent.

'You just need some time,' I said, and I brought her a little of the medicine Doktor Amsel had prescribed if we needed to keep on top of any discomfort.

She breathed in and out, in and out, her eyes fixed on the garden just beyond the open French doors. It was in full bloom: little patches of cornflowers and clusters of purple pansies, and the apple-scented climbing roses trained over a wire archway that led nowhere in particular. And the geraniums: abundant spatters of pink and red, brighter and more profuse than any we'd grown in our Munich windowboxes, glowing in the last of the light. 'Was it really a cyst?' she said, picking at one of the knots that had started to unravel on her seagrass chair.

I felt something seize inside me. We had agreed, Amsel and I, that she didn't need to know. It would be better. Kinder. But it wasn't so much out of kindness on my part: rather, I understood that it is human nature to do what is expected of us. We tend towards obedience; if we're told we have six months to live, then in six months we die.

She'd been overdoing things, I said. She just needed to rest.

From the Pisters' villa, a cheer went up.

'It was a cyst though, wasn't it?' she said.

'Yes,' I said, 'a cyst.'

The next day I heard that the new railway was unusable. The prisoners had built it too quickly, and after the first loco-motive had passed, the foundations began to slide. It would take months to repair the damage.

By late July, the weather had turned stifling. I found a sun umbrella for the garden, and I had Niemand set up a daybed for Greta in the shade. Karl-Heinz and Felix were trying to make Freya shake hands, but she wouldn't learn the trick, so they started throwing sticks instead.

'*To* her,' I called. 'Not *at* her.'

I noticed something crawling over Greta's foot and up her shin – a red beetle, with a black pattern on its back like a Zulu mask. I brushed it away.

'What was that?' she said.

'Nothing,' I said.

She was pretending to read a book about Constantinople that I'd borrowed for her from the prisoners' library. She changed position, drew up her legs, shifted the cushion at her back. I could tell she wasn't comfortable.

'Darling?' she called to Karl-Heinz. 'What are you eating?'

He ran over to show her: some of the wild raspberries that had crept in over the wall.

'Spit them out,' she said.

He tried to explain that they were just raspberries, but she wouldn't listen.

'Spit them out!' she said again. 'They might be poisonous!'

I told her I'd have someone come and weed, and carefully she settled herself on the daybed once more.

'Something's not right,' she said.

I asked if it was the scar, but she wasn't sure. 'We just need to let it heal,' I said.

'Yes, heal,' she nodded.

I gave her a kiss on the forehead. 'I'm sorry,' I said. 'I have to go to the office. Catch up on some things.'

I didn't go into detail; I didn't want her to know that on top of everything else, the authorities had ordered a second investigation into corruption at Buchenwald. They'd asked a Judge Konrad Morgen to sniff around for evidence, and in particular for evidence of Karl Koch's embezzlement of Reich funds, which carried a death sentence. Morgen questioned me at length about the sourcing of camp supplies, and then he announced that he needed to visit our villa so he could inspect the perfectly legal wines and liqueurs in our cellar, the slabs of ham and the smoked sausages and the jars of peas and carrots, for goodness' sake. I had no choice but to tell Greta he was coming – I said it was just a formality. When Morgen arrived I explained to him that we needed such provisions for the entertaining of important guests, and I made sure I could produce receipts for it all, as well as for every leaf of cabbage the prisoners ate, every chunk of horse meat; I was proud of my impeccable books, though the level of detail Morgen demanded made me feel that I, like Koch, was under suspicion. I had to show him through the warehouse, too, where we stored the clothing and shoes and eating utensils and so on, and he kept stopping to make notes in a little notebook. Obviously, I told him, if there were any irregularities with the supplies, other parties would need to be questioned: the kapos of the prisoners' canteen and the storage warehouse, and Otto Wolff as well, since he was the one who oversaw what actually went on inside the fence. I stressed to him that I was merely in administration – which is quite true, as you know. As far as I was aware, for instance, every prisoner had his own bed and his own bedding; if Wolff shoved two or three inmates in together, that was out of my control. The Americans spent many tedious hours going over such details, trying to trip me up – but the fact is, when I was awaiting trial at Dachau they forced us to share beds too! I tried to point this out in my testimony.

I can't say I was sorry to hear that Morgen suffered minor burns when he interfered with the hinges on the steam-bath box and it snapped shut. He accused the inmate operating it of intentionally harming an SS officer, which should have meant a death sentence, but Morgen was so unpopular that nobody felt the need to avenge him. I thought of all the pieces . . .

[corrupted]

. . . about what Amsel had told me after the surgery. He said he was confident – no, certain, he said – I am *certain* – that he'd removed the cancer, and that it had not spread any further. Now I wonder whether he believed that at all, or whether he was afraid of what might happen to him if he gave me the wrong answer. People will say anything to save themselves. I heard that when Karl Koch was arrested the first time around, Ilse Koch turned on her husband, calling him a crook, a murderer who belonged behind barbed wire, and revealing information about his crooked dealings – the vastly inflated prices at the prisoners' canteen, the profits skimmed from the camp piggery. The selling of camp supplies to Weimar citizens. And then, when Himmler ordered him released, and Ilse realised he might be useful to her, she staged a nervous breakdown, becoming hysterical and insisting that she couldn't remember what she'd said, and therefore couldn't be held responsible. It was no way for a German wife and mother to behave.

Over summer I suggested taking a holiday to Baden-Baden or Paris – somewhere far away from the Ettersberg, far away from Morgen's snooping – but Greta said she thought it might be better to stay where we were.

'Who does Morgen think he is?' I asked her one evening; I couldn't help myself. We were sitting in the conservatory, the French doors open to let in the cool of the garden. He'd taken a suite at the Hotel Elephant, I said. How much did that cost? And now he'd moved up to Buchenwald, and they'd given him an office right in the middle of everything, so he could pry to his heart's content.

Greta was picking at the seagrass chair again, winding a bit of twine around her fingertip till it turned bright red.

'Don't do that, darling,' I said. 'You'll pull it apart.'

'Hmm?' she said.

Morgen had planted himself where he could see the whole operation, I told her. The prisoners' compound as well as our side of things. Sitting there like a spider in a web. Reading any files he chose. And he had a massage every morning before he even thought about work! I wasn't exaggerating – despite the way Morgen presented himself after the war, as righteous as you please on the witness stand at Dachau, he was just as willing as the next man to take advantage of the perks.

'You could have a massage,' said Greta; she knew for a fact that Otto Wolff got the masseur to come to his villa.

'It's how it *looks*,' I said. And anyway, did she want even more of them visiting?

She asked me what I meant.

The masseur was a prisoner, of course, I told her. A Dutchman. She realised that, didn't she? And so was the barber who came to the Wolffs' every morning with his scissors and his razor. Who was to say he wouldn't just slit their throats one day?

She studied me for a second or two. 'I thought you said there was no risk,' she murmured.

'Well,' I said, 'I wouldn't let them near me with a blade.'

But remind me – what was your question?

One night a few weeks later, in August, I was sitting in the living room in the dark, staring out the window at the lightning that flashed along Eickeweg every few minutes. The trees in the garden and the forest beyond seemed closer and larger than they should. Karl Koch was due to return to Buchenwald that night, summoned by Morgen, and just before midnight his car lights shone in our window as he headed for his former home, where Ilse still lived with the children. I slipped outside and peered down the street; yes, it was definitely Koch, letting himself in the front door. I watched from the shadows for a while, and then, as the lightning flashed, I saw Morgen and another man arrive. Pistols ready, they rang the bell, but when nobody answered, Morgen rapped on the door with his boot. It opened – and there stood Koch, casually dressed and quite relaxed, as if he'd been home all evening, as if he were an ordinary, decent man. Morgen arrested him, and as he led him away, Koch glanced down the street in my direction. Apart from the lightning, it was a very dark night, but I had the feeling he was looking right at me. I went upstairs then, stealing into our room as quietly as I could. Greta groaned when I slid into bed.

Up until that time I'd managed to keep my distance from the corruption investigation, more or less, but Morgen requested that I accompany him when he searched the villa, along with Kommandant Pister and a representative of the Criminal Police. We sent the children over to the neighbours' house, and then we combed the place from cellar to attic, opening every drawer, looking in every cabinet and cupboard. Piles of money lay around, and articles made from gold and silver, and the cellar was crammed with luxury foods and fine wines and liqueurs – far more than we had stored in ours for absolutely legitimate purposes. In the wardrobes, Persian lambskin coats and leather coats and furs. Pister did find a shrunken head in Koch's office; I won't dispute that. The pathology department made them on special request, for research purposes, according to the traditional headhunters' method whereby the skull was crushed and emptied then filled with hot sand. Or that's what I heard, at least; pathology wasn't my area. What a curious object it was:

no bigger than my fist, so the hair seemed all the thicker, and the eyelashes too appeared longer and more abundant than on a real person. I'll remind you of this, though: we never found any lampshades made from human skin, nor any photograph albums bound with it, nor any tattooed gloves or manicure sets or knife holders, as some have suggested. How the Americans lingered over these phantom items when they tried us, when all they really had were a couple of shrunken heads, a few pickled medical specimens and plenty of hearsay! And how quickly the prosecution backed off when the witness – a former prisoner who worked in the pathology department – said they cured rabbit skins there. People want to make us into monsters, but it's easy to accuse someone else of atrocities to deflect attention from your own involvement – to salve your own conscience. I can see you know what I mean.

I was there when Morgen took Frau Koch into custody, too. She answered the door in a dressing gown, her hair uncombed. 'You'll pay dearly for this,' she said, and she began to shout and swear and again became quite hysterical. Her husband had been cleared back in 1941, she yelled; the Reichsführer himself had exonerated him. She threatened us with terrible revenge.

Afterwards I went home for lunch with Greta, and then we started out on one of our short walks – Amsel said she needed plenty of fresh air. We'd only gone a little way down the street when we saw the Koch children playing in the neighbours' garden.

'How much did they steal?' she whispered.

'Hundreds of thousands of Reichsmarks,' I said. Perhaps millions. So I'd heard.

We walked a little further along Eickeweg, but I could feel her tiring on my arm.

'The air's not very good today,' she said, and so we returned home.

One morning that same August, without warning, Emmi Wolff came to see me in my office. My secretary – a decent girl from Weimar – was filing a massive lot of paperwork, and I knew she needed to keep on top of it, but I dismissed her and made sure she shut the door behind her. Then, before I had time to invite Emmi to sit down, she asked me point blank if Greta had cancer. The word hissed around the room like something poisonous, and she stood before me in her coquettish little hat and said, 'I have eyes, Dietrich. I'm no fool.'

'Your behaviour towards Arno Rehbein would suggest otherwise,' I said. I had eyes too.

That threw her, but just for a second. Taking her time, she sat down in one of the chairs opposite me and said, 'Greta is my friend. We've become very close, and I'm worried about her.'

'Does she suspect anything?' I said.

'Anything?' said Emmi.

'About a disease,' I said.

'Oh,' she said, 'the disease. I don't know.'

I told her there was no disease. The surgeon was certain he had removed it all.

'It's cancer, then.' A statement, not a question.

She couldn't tell Greta; I made myself very clear about that. As far as my wife knew, it was a cyst. We had to bear in mind the power of belief.

She nodded. 'And Scharführer Rehbein is just a friend.'

'Very well,' I said, tearing the previous day off the calendar on my desk. 'And I'd advise you to keep it that way,' I added. 'By rights he should be doing his duty at the front.'

At home as well as at work I tried to carry on as normal. I travelled to the new satellite camp near the Harz Mountains to check that the accommodation and furniture and kitchen facilities and so on were up to standard – nobody discussed with me the quartering of prisoners in tunnels, by the way, and I saw no evidence of it. Before Karl-Heinz started school in September, I asked Emmi to buy a satchel for him and wrap it up, and to organise the big paper cone of sweets he would receive on his first day.

'These are from Mama,' I told him at breakfast, and he threw his arms around her neck and said, 'Thank you! Thank you!'

'Gently,' I said.

'My baby,' said Greta. 'I can't believe it. My tiny baby.'

Karl-Heinz asked her why she was crying, and she scrubbed at her face and said she wasn't.

He didn't believe her, he said. She wasn't telling the truth.

When he posed for a photograph on our front doorstep, I had Niemand take a family shot of us as well. Greta dabbed on some lipstick and a little bit of rouge, and I clicked my fingers at Freya so she lay at our feet. I clicked my fingers at Karl-Heinz too, which he knew meant stand up straight. He wore the satchel on his back, and said it was exactly the one he wanted, and how had Greta known? And she said a little bird had told her. We must have looked like a perfectly ordinary family with not a care in the world.

After that, for a time, Greta even talked about taking Karl-Heinz to visit her mother in Munich for Christmas. I heard her telling him about it one day, when they were planting tulip bulbs I'd brought home from our camp greenhouses. They were pushing them into the soil while Freya ran about the place and barked at nothing. Though I had contacted Elisabeth following the surgery to tell her it was cancer, I still hadn't elaborated on the seriousness of her daughter's condition in case she blurted the truth to her – and I made her agree not to breathe a word, for Greta's peace of mind. By early December, however, it was clear a trip to Munich would be impossible. I wrote to Elisabeth and asked her to come to us;

I said I thought it might bolster Greta after her difficult year. But sure enough, the barbed reply came straight back: *How lovely – on Christmas Eve we can all break rocks together.* Typical Elisabeth. Well, it was probably for the best – Greta had lost so much weight, and the dark rings were so deep under her eyes, that I feared what her mother would say if she saw her in person.

'I think there's another cyst,' she said one night as we lay in bed.

'I'm sure it's nothing to worry about,' I said. We'd go back to Doktor Amsel, and he'd fix it. He was a very clever man.

And I turned out the light.

I didn't mention the disease to Karl-Heinz, naturally, but even he noticed she had changed.

'I bet I could beat you in a race,' he said to her one Sunday as we were finishing lunch. 'First one to the front door and back.'

'Finish up your carrots, Karl-Heinz,' she said – though she herself hadn't eaten much at all.

'I don't like them,' he said.

I reminded him we grew them right there, just for him – the pork, too – but he pushed his chair away from the table and said, 'On your marks—'

'There won't be any racing, Karl-Heinz,' I told him. Sit down. Mama's tired.'

'I'd win, though,' he said.

'I'm sure you would,' I said, because Greta let him win whatever game they played together – I never approved of that, as a matter of principle. I told him to go and wash his hands and tidy his hair, and I'd take him over to Felix's. He galloped off to the bathroom, racing himself in the absence of anyone else to beat. 'Don't you like your carrots either?' I said to Greta.

'They're very nice,' she said. She rolled up her serviette –

unused, unmarked – and threaded it back through its silver ring.

Out of nowhere, Niemand appeared and began to clear the plates.

'Can't you see we're not finished?' I yelled, but Greta said, 'It's all right, Josef. I don't want any more.'

Karl-Heinz ran back into the dining room, panting, already pulling on his coat and hat.

'Slow down, slow down,' I said. The Wolffs weren't expecting him till two. We had plenty of time.

'I was chasing Ingo,' he said. 'He never lets me win.'

I glanced at Greta – we hadn't heard of Ingo in quite some months – but she was pinching her serviette into pleats.

'That's enough about Ingo,' I said. 'He's not real. He's imaginary.'

Karl-Heinz wasn't listening. Outside he started to run on ahead of me and down the front steps, calling, 'First one to the front door, Papa!'

So I bolted past him.

When we walked into Amsel's rooms I could tell we were the last people he wanted to see. He examined Greta, then ordered some X-rays and said that occasionally a patient took a bit longer to recover from an operation. He prescribed more medicine.

I returned to see him on my own a few days later and he showed me the X-rays. He could make out a little fluid on the left lung, he said, but no evidence of bowel perforation.

I squinted at the films; how strange it was to be peering at all the dark places that seemed as empty as caves. 'Where is the heart?' I said.

He pointed.

'That doesn't look like a heart,' I said, and he told me I had to use my imagination. The more I stared at her ribs, though, the brighter they glared, until they looked as bright to me as the searchlights that crisscrossed the camp when anyone tried to escape.

'However,' he said, 'based on my examination of your wife, I believe we'll need another surgery.'

'Another one?' I said. 'Will you be able to leave her intact?'

His recommendation – his *firm* recommendation, he said – would be an entire hysterectomy.

'But there'll be something else you can try,' I said. 'German doctors are the finest in the world. They're looking into these things all the time. Conducting experiments . . . there's some highly innovative research happening at my place of work.'

So he'd heard, he said. This was such a complex disease, though; there was so much we didn't understand.

'Still,' I said, 'there must be new treatments. Things not available to the average German, perhaps.'

He looked at me sharply. 'I'm sorry,' he said again.

'No more children, in other words,' I said.

'Unfortunately not,' he said.

Unfortunately! 'And if we take a less radical approach?' I asked.

Then I should make the most of my time with her, he said. Ensure she was comfortable. Even if he did remove everything, that may be the only remaining course of action.

I asked him what he meant.

'We'd probably only be gaining a little more time, Herr Sturmbannführer,' he said. 'I'm sorry.'

I could not believe what I was hearing. Did the man not know whom he was addressing? I could make things very difficult for him. A few phone calls, and he'd be arrested in a matter of hours. Shut down within a week. I began to tell him so, but something stopped me. I closed my eyes for a second, and I could see the after-image of the X-ray, the lengths of rib spreading to fill every space.

'How much longer?' I said.

But he wouldn't even give me that.

'I can't put a precise figure on it,' he said. 'Perhaps as long as twelve months, if luck is on your side.'

I told no one about Greta's condition. Following the appointment with Amsel, I threw myself into my work – well, I had little choice, given the rapid expansion of the camp. And it felt like a kind of escape, for a while, to think of ways to deal with the over-burdened sewerage system and the constant lack of water, the proper provision of food for the transports to the satellite camps, the maximisation of profits from the prisoners' canteen – so we could continue to source decent goods for them to buy, you understand – and the administration of the brothel. That's another good example of our humane treatment of the inmates: as long as they weren't Jewish, Gypsy or Russian, they could make a request via their block officer; they had to pass a physical examination, and then they paid two Reichsmarks for a written permit. The approved inmates were informed of their successful applications over the loudspeaker at evening roll call, and after that they could enjoy twenty minutes with a medically sound female from Ravensbrück. And it should have provided a decent stream of income, but despite the trouble we'd gone to for them, the prisoners seemed loath to make use of it – even after we sent the women marching around the camp by way of advertisement, singing National Socialist songs. More than a few inmates began depraved connections with the very young Poles and Russians; these doll-boys were devoid of any morals, engaging in the most perverted acts in return for a little food. I could not understand why they – the inmates – didn't just visit the brothel, with its pleasant situation amongst the trees and its vases of flowers on the tables – but then, what do I understand of the criminal mind? And it's true, there were times when it had to shut its doors: whenever there was a water shortage, for instance, or a broadcast by the Führer.

In fact, it was a water problem that brought Arno Rehbein to my office just before Christmas. The showers in his barracks were blocked, he said, and when he removed a drain cover and fished around he found a rat, not quite dead. He stamped on it and then burned it.

'So that fixed the problem,' I said. I was keen to return home for lunch – coax Greta to eat something.

'If there's one, there'll be others,' said Rehbein.

'Certainly,' I said. 'They come from the camp. There's not a lot we can do, given the short distance.'

'But the risk of disease,' he said. 'I'm lucky I wasn't bitten. They can turn vicious when they're trapped.'

'I'll look into it,' I said.

He fell silent then, and didn't seem to have anything to add, but I knew he was circling around something else by the way he clasped and unclasped his hands, glanced at the photograph of Greta and Karl-Heinz with the angora rabbit as well as the one of myself with the Reichsführer. When he cleared his throat as if to dislodge something and began to say, 'I understand that your wife—' I cut him off. I imagine it was Emmi Wolff who informed him, but Greta's health was none of his business; I kept my home life separate from my work life, as far as possible, and I didn't want anyone knowing that a disease had struck our household. A reproductive disease.

'I have work to do,' I said. 'Dismissed.'

Rehbein glanced at the door, then at the photographs, then back at the door. Again he cleared his throat. 'I know of a doctor who may be able to help,' he said all in a rush. He was looking straight at me by this point. 'It was a long time ago,' he said, 'around 1933. This doctor invented a machine—' and here he began to stumble. 'A machine to treat it, to shrink them, the, the growths . . . ' He could not say the word.

'What machine?' I said.

A man in their village near Frankfurt, he said. He'd been given three months to live – it was stomach cancer – and he looked like he'd swallowed a boulder. His brother Horst dragged him along to visit this man – he was a real do-gooder, Horst – and they sang him his favourite songs, and he vomited blood right in front of them. Horst told him it was his singing.

'And the machine?' I said.

There was a doctor at the hospital in Frankfurt, he said. He couldn't remember his name, but he had a machine to attack the growths. He was looking for patients to try it, and this man from their village volunteered. And it worked.

'Worked?' I said.

That's what he heard, Rehbein said. He was cured. The growths disappeared. And he wasn't the only one.

'Where is he now?' I said.

Still in the village, he supposed. He remembered he took up watercolours – he was really quite good. Old barns, fields of wheat . . . he couldn't do the front of horses, though, only the back.

'The *doctor*,' I said. 'Where is the *doctor* now?'

'Oh. I don't know,' he said. He lowered his voice. 'Maybe he was a Jew. Lots of them were.'

The new camp physician, Schiedlausky, had never heard of such a machine. He asked me if I had the doctor's name, and I shook my head.

'Well,' he said, 'if it's as wondrous as you suggest, don't you think everyone would know about it? And about him?'

We were in his office in the infirmary; a shelf of specimens ran along one wall, packed into jars like preserves for the winter. Schiedlausky sat at his desk and signed a pile of death reports, his name nothing more than a wavy line.

'He may have been a Jew,' I said.

Still, he pointed out, someone else would have taken over if it was any good. And he imagined the doctor would have published about it. He stopped signing for a moment then, I remember, and looked up at me. 'What's your interest in it?' he said.

I shrugged and peered at a specimen of white tissue sliced as fine as muslin. I wasn't about to discuss such private matters with him – such *intimate* matters – and have the whole place gossiping.

'Stomach,' he said, by way of explanation.

'Wonderful,' I said, but I felt a little sick, and moved a few steps away from the shelf.

'They're not mine,' said Schiedlausky. 'I inherited them from Doktor Hoven.'

I was surprised to hear his name; Waldemar Hoven had become an embarrassment at Buchenwald. Quite apart from his lengthy affair with Ilse Koch, he'd also been investigated by Judge Morgen and jailed on suspicion of murder by lethal injection, about which I of course had known nothing. I wasn't sorry; he loved giving me his opinion on the prisoners' nutritional requirements, and how we could best allocate the food supplies in order to improve the camp's working capacity – all without any thought of the cost. He'd lived in America for a time and worked as an extra in Hollywood, and with his thick, slicked-back hair and his deep-set eyes he carried himself like some kind of film star. He used to get about the place wearing a ring that came from Egypt, or perhaps it was Mexico, and told everyone it contained a secret compartment for poison – only when they arrested him it was quite empty. 'A terrible mess,' I said. 'The kind that gives the rest of us a bad name.'

Schiedlausky nodded – but Hoven, he said, had been able to track down all kinds of obscure medical information. He'd got the state library to interloan certain texts for him, on certain things he wanted to try out. I could always ask if they might be able to find my doctor's publications.

'Where is it?' I said.

Just down in Weimar, he told me. The old ducal library. A pretty place.

I could still see the pieces of grey and white matter out of the corner of my eye. 'Imagine, though,' I said, 'if we could treat cancer. Cure it. Imagine if a German invented the miracle machine that could do that. Do you know, the Führer's own mother—'

He laughed. 'Every doctor I've ever met has wanted to save the world,' he said. 'At the start, anyway. But the world can't be saved. Sooner or later we realise we're just bandaging wounds. Lancing boils. There are no miracles.'

He returned to his pile of death reports, and I understood that I was to leave.

At the library the woman behind the desk started when she saw me. She jumped to her feet, knocking over a pile of books.

'Heil Hitler!' she shouted, and the patrons all looked up from their reading.

'Medical journals,' I said. 'I need everything from the mid-1930s.'

'I'm terribly sorry, Herr Sturmbannführer,' she said, and her hand flew to her throat and worried at the bow on her blouse. They weren't that sort of library: they had poetry, novels, all the classics. The newspapers, of course, and non-fiction, but medical journals . . .

At that, a man reading the *Völkischer Beobachter* rushed to the desk to return it. 'Thank you, Frau Topf,' he murmured, and then, without looking at me, hurried out. *Churchill, War Criminal* read the headline. *Unmasked by His Own Admissions.*

'You can order them for me, though,' I said. 'The medical journals.'

Oh yes, Herr Sturmbannführer, she said. As long as it was for essential war activity. And I'd need to register with the library, and tell her the names and dates. She had a form. She began to stack the toppled books, nudging them into a neat pile.

'I don't know the names and dates,' I said.

'Yes,' she said, 'yes, but you see, I have a form.' She licked her lips.

I told her simply to write that Sturmbannführer Hahn of Konzentrationslager Buchenwald was requesting all German medical journals from the mid-1930s. For essential war activity.

'Yes,' she said, again licking her lips, 'but is there anything specific you're looking for?' She glanced at the death's-head ring on my hand.

'I don't know what I'm looking for, Frau Topf,' I said. 'I'll know what I'm looking for when I find it.'

She nodded, took a form from a drawer. 'Mid-1930s,' she said. 'Mid-1930s . . . Would that include 1932? Is that in the middle? Herr Sturmbannführer?'

I was aware of the eyes of the patrons on me, but when I turned to leave they were all studying their books and newspapers, and nobody looked up as I walked out.

Lenard Weber: that was the man's name. It didn't sound Jewish, so perhaps there was hope. 'On the Curative Potential of Electrotherapy via the Principle of Remote Sympathy in Subjects with Metastatic Carcinoma' spanned over a dozen pages, and while I didn't understand the finer scientific details of the paper, I understood the results well enough: of the fourteen patients, two were still alive a year after treatment with his Sympathetic Vitaliser. As far as I could tell, it worked on certain waves – certain frequencies that resonated within a tumour so that it began to break down, much in the same way a glass can break if a soprano hits the right note. It made a kind of sense: aren't some sounds so uncomfortable, so painful to an individual that he feels they might cause him damage? Don't we cover our ears at the things we can't bear to hear? I had a sudden vision of Greta shattering into pieces, cracking apart like a woman made of glass. She was so fragile; although she would not admit it, I knew what it cost her simply to dress, simply to come downstairs and eat with us. What if the treatment itself was too brutal? And yet – no other options remained; it was my duty to try it. Amsel had told me I should make the most of my time with her. Ensure she was comfortable. He'd given her twelve months, if luck was on our side. Twelve months. In twelve months, it would be late December again: winter again. In twelve months, the Goethe oak would be spreading its spindly shadow in the frozen heart of Buchenwald, and the latrines in the Little Camp would ice over at night. In twelve months, Karl-Heinz would be only seven years old, and Greta only thirty.

I returned to Doktor Schiedlausky's office under the pretext of discussing the extra food the prisoners received when their blood was taken for the SS. 'One slice of bread and one piece of sausage per inmate soon mount up,' I said. 'Can we reduce that? Are there savings to be made anywhere?'

We were under no obligation to give them anything, said Schiedlausky, but we were tapping up to four hundred cubic centimetres of blood at a time, and if they collapsed it was going to cost us more in terms of lost labour than a bit of bread and sausage.

'Mmm,' I said, nodding. 'Though I understand the weaker ones often volunteer, to get the extra rations or to get out of work. In which case, they likely don't have much work left in them, and it's a waste to give them the bread and sausage at all.'

We talked along these lines a little longer, and then I asked about the medical research being conducted in the camp.

'That's Doktor Ding's department,' he said tightly. 'I just sign certain authorisations when he's away in Berlin, doing whatever it is he does there.'

'I hear his work is highly innovative,' I said.

'You'd have to talk to Doktor Ding,' he said. 'The experiments are nothing to do with me.'

This wasn't strictly true.

My gaze drifted to the shelves, and it was only then I realised they were empty – all the jars of specimens had disappeared.

'I got rid of them,' he said, as if reading my thoughts. 'I don't need Hoven's bad luck dogging me.'

'That sounds rather superstitious for a man of science,' I said. To be honest, though, he wasn't the only one of us distancing himself from those under investigation by Judge Morgen; we were all on edge since the arrests in the Koch affair.

'At any rate,' I went on, 'I've found out more about the machine, the cancer machine. The cure.'

He actually laughed. 'Oh yes?' he said.

'The idea was that it would destroy tumours via electro-magnetic waves, according to the principle of remote sympathy.' I refrained from showing him the paper itself – I didn't want him to know Weber's name, in case he did turn out to be a Jew – but I started to explain the mechanics of the Sympathetic Vitaliser as far as I understood them.

'Sympathy?' he interrupted. 'Sympathy? That's a few hundred years out of date, at least.'

The following day I went to see Doktor Ding in the Hygiene Institute housed in Block 50. I knew him from the administrative side of things, of course, and I sat with him now and then at the officers' club and played a game of skat – but I had no idea about the finer details of his experimental work. No idea at all.

He had a pleasant, open face and seemed very young, and he was happy to show me around his state-of-the-art laboratory. Here was a man, I thought, who had started his career climb early; a man guaranteed to receive a genuine death's-head ring from the Reichsführer. So it seemed to me then, at least – I wasn't to know that in two short years he'd take his own life, hanging himself like a coward from the barred window of a cell and asking his interrogators to tell his wife it was a heart attack. The funny thing is, he tried pills first, and a razor blade – but the blade was too blunt, and the pills made him so drowsy he passed out. Some doctor. Some surgeon. Certainly, though, I envied the way he ran his laboratory, the way he managed to get the numbers right. It was a decent source of revenue, he told me, with pharmaceutical companies and medical institutes paying to conduct their trials inside the camp, where laws around experimental procedures did not apply. I hadn't known that.

The place smelled of stainless steel and bleach, and the sun flashed off the tiles, though we were just a stone's throw from the muck and stench of the Little Camp and the sewage treatment plant I had to visit whenever it malfunctioned.

Ding began to list diseases as we strolled through the gleaming facility: smallpox, yellow fever, paratyphoid A and B, cholera, diphtheria. Any one of them could decimate our troops, he said, but it would be only a matter of time before we developed effective treatments. He was making excellent progress on a typhus vaccine, for instance.

'Should we be wearing masks?' I said. I shouldn't have set foot in the building, I thought. Shouldn't have gone anywhere near. I didn't want Greta risking a cold, let alone something worse.

But Ding said we were quite safe. There were no hosts here, he told me – they stored them over in Block 46.

Block 46: the one with the frosted windows. The one where

they kept the guinea pigs and mice and rabbits, which came out of my budget. 'The animals?' I said.

He shook his head – no, not the animals; he meant the human hosts, and unfortunately they used up five per month, so it wasn't without cost.

You probably don't need to include that.

And I'm not a medical man, of course, so I didn't understand how it all worked.

At any rate, Ding went on, we were making significant progress. That's what they told him. We had the cream of European medical researchers, all working for us.

'Do we have any cancer specialists?' I said.

'Regrettably, no.' He paused. Then he said, 'And how is Frau Hahn?' and fixed me with his kind eyes, and I knew that he knew.

I explained the Sympathetic Vitaliser to him and told him of the promising early results. Again I did not mention Weber's name. Or Greta's.

'There might be something to it,' he said, though perhaps he was just being polite – wanting to give me hope. Then, as if making small-talk, he said, 'I always thought Hahn was a Jewish name.'

'Not our branch,' I said. 'One of those strange corruptions. It's all been checked.'

The smell of bleach stung the inside of my nostrils, and I had the sudden thought that my nose was about to bleed, the way it used to when I was a child. The sensation was the same: a pressure behind my face, the feeling of something awful on its way. An old instinct made me reach for my handkerchief, ready to blot up what I couldn't control – but nothing came.

'Do you think, though, that it could be worth investigating?' I said. I tried to keep my voice steady, but the pressure was shoving against my eyes and nose, forcing a fist up into my forehead. I couldn't understand why this feeling was back, why now.

'You never know,' said Ding.

I could tell he wanted to get on with his work, and certainly I had no desire to bleed all over his spotless rooms. As a boy I had always been embarrassed when it happened in public; I thought I should have been able to wait until we were home.

I rushed back out of the camp and along the path through the forest to Eickeweg. Somewhere in the trees I heard a ticking, a chip-chip-chipping: two branches chafing together in the wind, or a bird sending out a distress call. I was almost at the villa when the bleeding started; I felt it wet on my upper lip. I tugged a handkerchief from my pocket and hurried towards our steps, hoping nobody would see me, but Wolff called out from his front garden, and I had no choice but to stop.

'How is Greta?' he said.

'She's fine,' I said, still holding the handkerchief to my face.

'Only Emmi mentioned she's not been well,' he went on. 'She doesn't have all the details, of course . . . ' He paused, waited for me to elaborate.

'She's fine now,' I said, my voice muffled. I could feel the blood soaking the handkerchief, warm and thick, unstoppable, and I tilted my head. It started to run down the back of my throat.

'You're all right, are you?' said Wolff.

Could he see the blood? Had it soaked right through? I swallowed, nodded again. He'd have loved to know there was something wrong with one of us.

Karl-Heinz came running to me as soon as I was in the door, but I went straight to the downstairs bathroom. 'I'm fine,' I told him through the handkerchief. I stuffed it deep in my pocket and splashed my face with water, then went through to the dining room.

'Are you all right?' said Greta.

'Fine,' I said. I told her she looked nice. She was wearing the yellow dress I'd given her for her birthday, and I kissed her on the side of her neck.

'I'm sorry, we started without you,' she said. 'Karl-Heinz was starving.' A single bread roll sat in front of her, the end broken off. She was fiddling with her silver serviette ring, threading one finger through it, then two, then three, and Karl-Heinz was scooping out the insides of a soft-boiled egg, the yolk splattering on his plate. 'Are you sure you're all right?' she said.

'I'm fine. Honestly,' I said. I started to spoon up the soup Niemand put in front of me, gulping it down hot to get rid of the taste of the blood. I didn't have long, I told her, and this was true; I'd spent over an hour with Ding. Even as I spoke I felt my nasal passages squeeze again, and I sat very still for a second or two, staring at my soup. Then I rushed to the bathroom, catching the blood in my hands.

'Are you sick, Papa?' said Karl-Heinz when I returned to the table.

'No no,' I said.

He wrinkled his nose. 'Don't give it to us,' he said. 'We don't want to get sick too.'

'I'm not sick,' I said. 'Not like that.'

'You'll have to change your shirt,' said Greta, and I followed her gaze to the splash on my chest.

I looked at my watch: I didn't have time. 'Do you know how much I have to get through this afternoon?' I said.

'You can't go out the door like that,' she told me.

I ran upstairs to the bedroom, unbuttoning my shirt as I went, and grabbed a clean one from the wardrobe. Niemand had just finished changing the bedding, and he picked up the discarded shirt on his way out of the room, holding it by its cuffs so he wouldn't have to handle the soiled part. When I came back downstairs Greta was slicing the top off a second egg for Karl-Heinz, fluttering her fingers because it was too hot. She still hadn't finished her roll. Her serviette ring lay balanced on its side, and I noticed a few spots of tarnish.

'Have Niemand clean that,' I said. 'We really shouldn't have to ask.' I looked at my watch again – no more time – and bent to give Karl-Heinz a kiss.

'Yuck,' he said, pulling away from me.

Later, at my office, I noticed a few dried flecks on my boots, and I scraped at them with my thumbnail. My mother had always been so angry with me when my nose bled – as if the blood were something I could command. It seemed to smear itself everywhere: on my clothing, her best tablecloths, our carpets, our worn velvet couch that didn't match the chairs, the plush bear my father said I should have outgrown. The bear had a little button piercing its ear – a tiny dot of steel hidden in the fur, cold and hard and rusted over – and I used to bite on it to see if I could break it, which I never could. It tasted like coins. I can still taste it now, I think, though perhaps I am confusing the taste of the button with the taste of the blood; at this remove, it's hard to be certain. I bled on my schoolbooks, too, soaking through pages of pictureless descriptions of the Thirty Years War, or maps of the great mess of German principalities before the Kaiser created the empire. And I bled on my own work: my long division, my irregular verbs. While my brothers were playing outside, I was stuck at the dining table, rewriting the wrecked pages. My father stood over me, supervising my penmanship; he himself was not an educated man and was determined that I make something of myself. I could smell the drink on his breath as he told me he couldn't decipher a word. I remember he held a handkerchief over my nose one day when it seemed the bleeding would never stop; I know he was trying to help me – he said he was trying to help me – but I couldn't breathe.

Sometimes the bleeding happened in my sleep, seeping through my pillowcase, all the way through to the feathers. I no longer recall how many pillows we had to throw out.

'We can't afford this,' said my mother. 'You do know that, don't you?'

'It's not on purpose,' I said.

A few times, I remember, she slapped me hard across the face to teach me the value of a pillow. And even though she washed the things I bled on – in cold water, because the last thing you wanted was to set the stains – in certain lights, on certain items, I could still make out the shadow of the blood. Once, when I woke in the morning to find it had happened again, I simply changed the pillowcase and hid the soiled one underneath my mattress. That night, though, I could feel the lumps of feathers inside the pillow, hard with dried blood, and I did not sleep. I heard the church clock strike one, and then two, and then three, and I heard my father rise before dawn to go to his job at the bakery, and still the hard little masses in my pillow dug into my skull, as hard as knuckles no matter how I lay. My mother found out, of course, when she stripped my bedding on the next wash-day – I hadn't thought that far ahead. She placed the ruined pillow on the dining table, and when my father returned home from work and handed her a loaf of day-old bread, which was still perfectly fine, and once it was smeared with schmaltz or a little bit of soft cheese you really couldn't tell, she showed it to him. He asked me what had happened to the pillow, his schnapps-breath hot in my face, and then he took his bone-handled pocket knife – a thing I longed to own, but was never allowed to touch – and sliced open the pillow, and we could all see the ugly little lumps that I had tried to hide. My mother nodded at him, and he took off his belt and whipped me across the back of my legs, which was what I deserved, while my mother fed the dirty feathers to the fire. For days the smell of them lingered: in the curtains, the carpets, the back of my throat, in the leaves of the ferns that grew in pots on the sideboard, fluttering in the invisible currents. I thought I could even smell them in my mother's hair when she bent to kiss me goodnight.

'We'll have to do something about you,' she said. 'We'll have to take you to the doctor. Maybe he can chop it off.'

I thought she was joking, but she really did make an appointment. I bled that morning; it happened when I was washing, before I had dressed, so I pinched my nose until it stopped and then rinsed myself clean and didn't tell my mother. I must have missed a bit, though, because in the doctor's waiting room she licked her thumb and scratched something away from the side of my nostril and said, 'Again, Dietrich?' in a disappointed voice.

'No,' I said, but when I shook my head I could feel the clot inside me, blocking the air.

She passed me a handkerchief and said, 'Make sure you're clean for the doctor.'

'I am clean,' I said. 'I am.' I hardly blew my nose at all, but I felt the clot make its way out. It sat wet and red on my mother's handkerchief, an ugly red slug, and she knew that I had lied, but she glanced around the waiting room at the other mothers sitting with their obedient and truthful children, and she took back her handkerchief and crushed it into a ball and pushed it down deep into her bag before anyone could see.

'Silver nitrate,' said the doctor. 'To cauterise the vein.' It was a very simple procedure, and I'd hardly feel a thing. 'Just a little tickle,' he said. 'Just a tiny sting.'

He dipped a thin wooden stick into what looked like water, then passed it up inside my nose. Up and up it went, far further, surely, than was safe. I gripped the edges of the chair. It was the strangest sensation – as if he might reach right up into my thoughts. Then it started to burn.

'Keep still,' he said. 'Just a little tickle. Almost there.' I couldn't see my mother – he was in the way – and perhaps she had left the room, perhaps she had forgotten about me, and perhaps I would have to find my way home on my own.

'Keep still!' the doctor repeated. There was a spot of blood on his white lapel, high up where he couldn't see it himself.

But you didn't ask me about that.

I spread an old newspaper on the scullery table and lined up the brushes and cloths and polish, then gave Karl-Heinz one of my boots.

'This is the servant's job,' he said.

'It's a good thing to know how to do, though,' I said.

The boot still had a splash of blood near the instep, I realised, and he peered at it and asked what it was. Just a bit of blood, I said – just a tiny bit. He drew back. He didn't want to touch it, even when I explained that it was nothing to be afraid of, and that we all had it inside us.

I held his hand up to the light on the wall. 'See?' I said. 'That's your blood.'

'What if it comes out?' he said.

It told him it wouldn't, and passed him a cloth, but he just twisted it into a rope.

'Yours came out,' he said.

'That was just a bleeding nose,' I said.

He wanted to know if I was sick, and I told him I was fine. Then I took another cloth and ground it into the polish. 'Like this,' I said, working on the left boot while he worked on the right. He was making quite a mess of himself, covering his hands and wrists with black smears, and the newspaper too. I tried not to scold him, instead casting my eye over the pages. There was a list of the films and plays on offer down in Weimar – *Cadets* at the Central Palace and *The Brave Little Tailor* at the Nationaltheater – and an article explaining how housewives should store their potatoes so they didn't rot. Someone in Gutenbergstraße wanted to swap a pair of men's ski boots for a League of German Girls jacket, while someone else in Horst-Wessel-Straße was offering a man's wristwatch for a carpet runner. There were notices from people seeking husbands or wives: *Farmer, blond, 35, looks much younger, from good family, would like to get to know educated, thrifty woman with an interest in poultry*. Someone wanted to buy the works of Nietzsche, new or used. And of course, there were the death notices: a sporting and leather goods business mourned the loss of its junior manager; the parents of twenty-year-old Gerhard Heller, awarded the golden Hitler Youth Medal of Honour, requested no visits of condolence.

Karl-Heinz was coating his boot with far too much polish; I knew I'd have to get Niemand to fix it later. 'Don't be so generous,' I told him. 'You'll just make it harder for yourself.' I put the lid on the tin and shifted it out of his reach. 'And now, we buff them until we can see our reflections.' I showed him how to use the brush, making small, quick, side-to-side movements, starting at the toe and working back to the heel, then up and over the calves. 'What do you think?' I said. 'Can you see yourself?'

He peered at the leather. 'I don't know.'

'Look. Here. That's you,' I said. 'And that's me. Do you see?'

'Oh yes,' he said, nodding. He sounded uncertain. We were two dark shapes, the outline of a father and a child – even less than an outline. 'We have a mirror, though,' he said. 'Lots of mirrors. If we want to see ourselves.'

In the leather's sheen I thought I made out a third figure, and Karl-Heinz seemed to see it too. 'Who's that?' he said.

I looked over my shoulder: nobody.

'Perhaps it was Ingo,' he said.

'Ingo is imaginary,' I reminded him.

He was still staring at the leather. 'No, that's not Ingo,' he said. And then, 'Are you really all right, Papa? Are you really not sick?'

'I'm not sick,' I said. 'Not at all.'

On the page underneath the tin of polish, an open letter to our men fighting at the front: *As Josef Goebbels once said, the dead are eternal reminders, the voices of our national conscience that urge us constantly to do our duty.*

I took Karl-Heinz onto my lap and smelled the glorious smell of him. 'You're a good boy,' I said. 'Shall I take you to see the dogs tomorrow? For a special Christmas treat?'

'Yes please!' he said. 'And Mama, too.'

'Mama will probably stay here,' I said. 'It's very cold out.'

'She can wear her fur hat that looks like a hedgehog,' he said.

I told him she didn't really like dogs, and he said she liked Freya, and she had Maxi when she was little, and she used to give her dolls rides on his back. I didn't think it was a good idea, I said. He picked at one of the buttons on my shirt with his dirty fingers and asked if we could see the dogs' special houses.

'Of course,' I said.

'Their bedrooms and their living rooms,' he said.

'Yes,' I said, and he nodded against my chest. Then I told him that some of the dogs – the officers' dogs – ate fresh eggs and drank red wine.

He giggled. 'Dogs don't drink wine. You're being silly.'

'They do,' I said. 'I've seen them. And they eat eggs.'

He said I was telling stories – but the next day, when he and I went to visit the dogs, they ate fresh eggs and drank red wine, and he said he thought he might like to be a dog himself one day. Maybe not a guard dog, though, I said. Maybe a sled dog, running through the snow, crossing frozen lakes. Or a shepherding dog, helping on a farm, making sure the sheep went where they were supposed to.

'But these are shepherds, aren't they?' he said, reaching out to stroke one of the guard dogs.

'Don't!' shouted a handler.

'Sort of,' I said. 'That's what they're called.'

When we came home he drew a picture for Greta: a dog sitting upright at a table, just like a person, holding a glass of wine. She had Niemand pin it to the wall beside the bed.

'Will you stay awake with me?' I asked her on New Year's Eve. 'So we can count down to midnight? Try for another baby, even.'

Of course she would, she said – but she was asleep by seven thirty. I left the stump of the yule candle burning inside the holder with the cut-out hearts, and I saw in 1944 at the officers' club, playing skat with Schiedlausky and Ding. I lost every single game.

First thing Monday morning I telephoned the Holy Spirit Hospital in Frankfurt, where Lenard Weber had conducted his trial. I asked for the director, and his secretary was happy to put me through when I mentioned who I was: Henning Rost, of the Reich Security Head Office. Well, I'm sure he wouldn't have minded, under the circumstances.

Yes, said the director, they'd had some remarkable success with the machine, under his own close supervision, and it was only a pity that the war – the increasing numbers of wounded – had put a stop to further trials.

'And the inventor himself?' I asked. 'Doktor Weber?'

They had to let him go, unfortunately, he said. His ancestry became problematic, once they found out about it.

Weber was a Jew, then, or as good as: a Mischling, Second Degree, which meant he had one Jewish grandparent, though the rest of his family tree was clean. Such persons were even more dangerous than full Jews, in my opinion, since the German portion of their blood could endow them with the intelligence of an Aryan. I didn't want him anywhere near Greta. I remembered the announcements I'd seen in the medical journals when I was searching for his paper – the warnings: *Germans are to be treated by Germans only*. And I remembered the Reichsführer's speech, too: *and along they all come, all the eighty million upright Germans, and each one has his decent Jew*. It was true; we could all point to Herr So-and-so, who used to dry-clean our suits, or Herr What's-his-name, who used to teach our children the violin. Our former neighbour, who was decorated for bravery in the Great War. Our former dentist, who was as gentle as possible, and told jokes to distract us from the tools in our mouths. Yes, we could all name a Jew who had never stepped out of line. *All the others are swine, but here is a first-class Jew*. And I agreed with the Reichsführer, no question: it was easy to be swayed by odd exceptions to the rule, and we mustn't let down our guards, because that was how the disease took hold and spread. Why on earth would I consider bringing a Jew into our lives? There were hardly any of them at Buchenwald by that time – they'd all been sent east, apart from a handful crafty enough to claim they were skilled construction workers who could contribute to our building projects. Here I should mention that the camps in the east were never known to us as extermination camps, and in the transport orders that came from Berlin there was never any information about them. And after the war, I might add, the American prosecutors brought Jew after Jew to the witness chair – Jews who'd been sent to these so-called extermination camps, and yet there they were, as large as life! Because they came back, of course – towards the end, they came flooding back to Buchenwald.

However. What if one decent Jew could cure a hundred Germans? One decent part-Jew? There'd been significant disagreement at the highest levels over exactly what *Mischling* meant; if you poured half a bucket of shit into a bucket of water, to all intents and purposes you still had a bucket of shit. But if you poured *quarter* of a bucket of shit into a bucket of water, didn't you have mostly water? In some cases, I knew, the Führer had pardoned a Mischling – written off a certain amount of Jewish blood to allow that person to join the Wehrmacht, for instance, and fight and die for Germany. And I knew that he'd ensured safe passage to America for the doctor who treated his mother for cancer – even though none of the treatments worked, and the disease took her at the age of forty-seven. But if a particular Mischling *could* cure a hundred Germans, was he not worth saving? If he could cure ten Germans, even. Or even just one, if that German was a mother who could go on to bear more German children. Couldn't I force myself to manage, no matter how it turned my stomach? It made sense. It added up. Decency had nothing to do with it.

That afternoon I rang Henning at the Reich Security Head Office. The operator transferred me to his secretary, who told me he was very busy, and she would have to check whether he could speak to me, and what was my name again?

'Sturmbannführer Dietrich Hahn,' I said. 'I'm one of his oldest friends.'

'One moment,' she said.

I waited and waited, and was just starting to think they had forgotten me, or I had been cut off, when I heard his voice.

'Hahn, you old bastard!' he said. 'How's small-town life? You're at Buchenwald now, I hear.'

'Head of administration,' I said. 'The satellite camps too, including the women's ones. It's expanding by the day. We've our own villa, our own servants—'

'There was a bit of trouble with the Kommandant, wasn't there?' he said.

'Koch, yes,' I said. 'A deeply corrupt individual, unfortunately. But well before my time.'

'And you're under Hermann Pister now?' he said.

I told him Pister was indeed the current Kommandant, but I reported directly to Berlin. I was my own man, more or less.

'Good for you,' he said. 'And how's that incredible wife of yours? Bet you can hardly keep up.'

I was listening for the click that might indicate someone else on the line, and I asked him if we could speak freely.

'How long have we known each other?' he said. 'Of course. Of course.'

So I explained Greta's condition, and the poor . . .

[corrupted]

. . . finished there was silence.

'Henning? Are you still there?'

A long sigh. 'I'm sorry,' he said. 'I don't know what to say. It's terrible luck, just terrible.'

But he could help, I told him. There was a doctor in Frankfurt who invented a revolutionary treatment – an electrical machine. He was a part-Jew, unfortunately, and I didn't mind admitting I couldn't bear the thought of him touching her.

'Sometimes you just have to close your eyes to these things,' said Henning.

'I know. I know,' I said. 'At any rate, if he were to step out of line for some reason – get himself sent to Buchenwald—'

'Consider it done,' he said.

He never was one to waste time: a week later I received a telegram telling me that the package from Frankfurt was on its way.

F rau Starke held the broken doll on her lap. We could see it was a hopeless case: the hair torn out, both arms missing. Better to throw it away.

'There used to be a woman,' she said. 'With a dolls' clinic. I remember she could fix anything. We took my Karolina there when my brother threw her against the wall and she stopped talking.'

'On the Teichgasse,' nodded Frau Jaeger, who had a little shop just around the corner on Kaufstraße.

'That's right, the Teichgasse!'

'She sold stationery too,' said Pastor Rabe. 'Very good quality writing paper.'

'I miss good quality writing paper,' said Herr Proft.

'And she sold jokes,' said Frau Jaeger. 'Snakes that jump out of tins. Severed hands. That sort of thing.'

'Long gone,' said Herr Heller. 'They cleared out the shop in 1938, and then a bit later they sent her away.'

'I was writing a prescription the other day,' said Doktor Lang, 'and my nib tore right through the page. Hopeless.'

Frau Starke peered inside the doll's ugly body, through the holes where the arms used to be. We wished she would put the thing away. 'I promised Eva,' she said. 'She's inconsolable.'

'Could you add a bit of wool . . . ?' said Frau Fleck. She liked to pretend expertise in such matters since she started volunteering with the National Socialist Women's League, though everyone knew she'd only sewn on a few buttons for the Wehrmacht and made a single pair of straw sandals.

'Never mind the doll lady – they've sent all my tenants away,' said Herr Rademacher. 'I'm missing *weeks* of rent. I've written to the police.'

'But who will fix Eva's doll?' said Frau Starke.

Frankfurt am Main, September 1946

The Graf Zeppelin floated above the city like a miracle, and your mother and I waved and waved at it as if the people inside might be able to make us out. But look at the calendar picture taken from the airship, Lotte: the opera house the size of a matchbox. How tiny we must have been.

By May 1943 Frankfurt was all but free of Jews, and they were deporting even those last few who'd been protected. I knew it couldn't be much longer before you and Anna were summoned, and sure enough, the following month they took you to Czechoslovakia – to Theresienstadt – on a blue-skied summer's day.

I have no idea if Baumhauer knew; I certainly didn't mention it at the hospital, and tried to carry on with my work as usual. At Baumhauer's request, I began to write up a case study on Herr Erling for publication – for yes, Lotte, my first miracle was still alive. Alive and thriving. And really, I saw you and Anna no less than I had for the previous three years, but I felt the loss of you more keenly. Though I knew it was illogical, I couldn't shake the feeling that the deportation was my fault.

I don't know what happened to the Vitaliser when I left the Holy Spirit shortly after that – or rather, when I was asked to leave. Towards the end of August 1943, as soon as I'd finished writing the case study on Herr Erling, Baumhauer called me into his office and told me that the hospital could no longer turn a blind eye to my difficult ancestry. Someone had informed him of my Jewish blood, and he'd had to pretend he didn't already know, which was very inconvenient, though he thought he'd been convincing.

'I imagine it's temporary,' he said, as if my Jewishness might somehow respond to treatment.

'It was my understanding that people like me can still practise,' I said. 'Legally speaking. Because of the shortage of doctors.'

'It's complex,' he said. 'If it were up to me . . . well, but it's out of my hands, I'm afraid. Never fear, though – we'll keep your miracle machine safe.' The little red glasses trembled and chimed on his sideboard as he showed me to the door. No schnapps today, then.

'And my case study?' I said. 'On Herr Erling?'

'I'll see to it that the research is published,' he said.

I was ordered to take over the medical care of forced labourers at a shoe factory in Höchst – Russian and Lithuanian women who couldn't speak more than a few words of German. When I asked for an interpreter, the factory director told me I wasn't there to chat, and my only duty was to ensure the women could work. And I have to admit that when the big attack on Frankfurt came in October, and entire streets in the east of the city burned, I was glad you and Anna had left. The bombs fell close to the apartment in Nordend, too, and St. Bernhard's church was badly damaged. The Party called the victims fallen soldiers, and held an ostentatious memorial service on the Opernplatz. I remember sitting in the shelter when all the lights failed, and a little boy next to me started to cry. His mother switched on her torch and drew his name on the wall with its beam: J-E-N-S. The letters glowing on the luminescent paint.

Later in the year I found out that the hospital had tried the Vitaliser – renamed the Baumhauer Machine – on a succession of patients, but all had died. The news made me glad. And ashamed. And around the same time, too, I saw the Erlings in the street. I recognised Frau Erling first, with her pale cheeks and her grey-blond hair set into finger waves. Then I realised that the figure in the wheelchair was her husband. He sat with a thick rug over his knees, his face little more than bone, and I could see he was dying; I could see he was all but dead. I crossed the street.

Baumhauer never did publish the case study.

On the morning of my arrest, I'd been queuing for meat since before dawn. I'd waited two hours outside the butcher's, and my ears and nose stung with the January cold. I hurried home, passing gangs of workers clearing away bomb damage. I'd only just taken off my coat and scarf and put the package of meat on the kitchen table when the doorbell rang. Then rang again.

Two men dressed in civilian suits and Gestapo swagger.

'You must have the wrong house, gentlemen,' I said as they showed me their warrant discs.

'Are you Lenard Weber?'

'Yes.'

One of them had a dark, ragged mole just below his ear; I remember that. I remember looking at it and noticing that it had bled recently, and thinking it was probably cancerous. 'Come with us,' he said.

'Can you tell me why?'

'Because you're under arrest,' he said, and at the same time the other one said, 'You should think more carefully before you tell a joke about the Führer.'

I laughed, which was a mistake. 'I've told no such joke.'

'Put on your coat, Doktor Weber.'

As they led me to the car I said, 'Well, can you tell me the joke?'

'No, we can't tell you the joke!' The cancerous mole flexed. 'It's against the law to repeat such jokes!'

And I shouldn't have said it, Lotte, and I don't know why I did, but somehow my mouth opened and the words rushed out in a silvery cloud: 'There's nothing funny about the Führer.'

His punch caught me right in the kidneys; he was quite the anatomist.

As we drove away I could see his hand straying to his neck, fingertips feeling for the dark little dot. And all I kept thinking about was the package of meat I'd left on the kitchen table, and how long it would keep before it went bad.

I thought they would take me to their headquarters on Lindenstraße, but they drove me out of the city to a railway siding, where a line of cattle cars had stopped and seemed to be waiting just for me. An SS guard ordered me to remove my clothes while another opened one of the cars, and the men inside were naked too, so they could not escape, and it must have been twenty degrees below zero. The guards ordered me to climb in.

I don't know what to tell you about that trip, Lotte. The train had come from the prison at Compiègne, in France, but nobody could say exactly when; my fellow passengers had lost all notion of time. They thought it was three days ago that they had boarded, though perhaps it was four, or two. They licked the moisture from the walls, and then the ice. When three of them were shot for sawing a hole in the floor, the rest of them crammed the bodies into a corner . . . but I think I do not want you to know. And then I think: but perhaps you know anyway. And I wish I could stop myself imagining your train, yours and Anna's, except there is no end to that journey. No end to the shake and gasp of the cattle car looping the track. No water for the dying and no room for the dead to lie down.

Your mother and I spent a day in Weimar when we were on our honeymoon, and we always said we would take you there. It was the loveliest town, with its cobbled streets, its pretty façades, and the river Ilm twisting its way through the park. There was a photograph of her – long since lost – standing in front of the home of Charlotte von Stein, Goethe's cherished companion. I whispered a few lines of one of his Charlotte poems to my new wife as we shaded our eyes against the glare and took in the long, elegant building and wondered who lived there now, and whether we dared knock at the door. *Oh, in distant times lived long ago, you were my sister or my wife. You knew the very essence of my being, could see how the purest nerve rang.* I had committed them to memory with just such a moment in mind, and I could feel the blush that stole across Anna's neck when I pulled her to me, right there on the open street, and spoke them into her ear.

I suppose I should say there *is* a photograph of her; they surface at auction sales and flea markets, those sorts of things, don't they? Perhaps somebody will flip through the pages of our family album, past the portrait of me in my grandfather's feathered helmet, past Anna at Charlotte von Stein's house, and past you, our own little Lotte in your cradle, fingers tight around a silver rattle marked with the pattern of your teeth. (Perhaps the silver rattle will surface too.) I keep trying to remember if Anna added a surname beneath any of the pictures when she labelled them – some piece of information that might return the album to me one day – but she had no reason to; we knew who we were. As far as I recall, all she wrote was *Lenard and Lotte* and *At the Bodensee* and *Christmas 1933*, holding the pages close to her lips and blowing on them so the white ink wouldn't smear against the protective glassine sheets. I used to sit with you on my lap and make a game of guessing what the next picture was before I lifted each crisp translucent leaf; you and I examined the hazy images as if looking at the world through iced-over windows. As if looking at ghosts.

I remember my arrival at the camp like that too: a series of images leached of colour, seen through ice or smoke. The glare when the train door opened. A rush of fresh air, then unstoppable cold. The SS with their pistols and their dogs; the animals already inside the car, snapping at those not quick enough. Our clothing thrown back at us; the grab for any garment, whether it fitted or not. Two women in long fur coats laughing behind their hands. A truck, appearing out of the fog, to collect the dead. Chains of men, arms linked five abreast to make us easier to count, some in shirts too small to button, some in trousers that wouldn't stay up. Snow in my hair. The yelling and the blows if anyone stumbled: *At Buchenwald we don't have any sick. You're either healthy or you go to the crematorium.* The stone eagle and the letters of stone: BUCHENWALD. A place named for a felled forest, for an absence. The double-time dash down the path to the gate on legs that wouldn't work. Whips darting like snakes' tongues. The backwards letters of iron in the gate: *To Each His Due.* And carved into the lintel, holding up the watchtower and its ice-white clock: *My Country, Right or Wrong.* The leap of flame from the great chimney; the smell of singed hair. The guards with their machine guns, watching like gods from high above. Then, rows of barracks stretching down the slope, and a strange police force taking over where the SS left off: prisoners dressed in black, as if we had wandered into a wake. Someone crouching to drink melted snow. The January day dark by mid-afternoon. Every man ordered to strip; every stripped man shorn with blunt clippers. Every stripped man submerged in a solution that stung every cut. We no longer looked like ourselves. Running naked down an underground passage, double time, double time. Ragged clothing that would never keep out the cold, daubed with paint or patched with mismatched strips to give us away if we escaped; wooden shoes that scraped and knocked at tarsal and metatarsal bones. The taking of our details, down to the shape of our ears.

Don't imagine that you've arrived at some sanatorium. Don't harbour any hopes that you'll soon be leaving. Here at Buchenwald a very difficult life awaits you. Here you must work until your arms break – work hard without stopping. Here you have only one right: the right to work hard and without rest.

I would be held in quarantine in the Little Camp – a barbed-wire pen within a barbed-wire pen, the opening guarded by Polish prisoners who marched about in fine leather jackets. We waited in our hundreds in windowless stables built for fifty horses, and yes, the stench was animal, and we stitched our numbers and our triangles to our breasts and our legs and knew that we were no longer greengrocers and architects, solicitors and farmers. My transport all wore the red triangle: the mark of the political prisoner. A Russian who had been there for weeks already said to no one in particular, 'Do you know why they make us stitch them over the heart? So they can see where to aim.' Jabbing at his chest to make sure we understood. Another told us not to drink the water, because it was bad, but some couldn't resist and died a week later. We crammed onto the shelves that were our beds, lying on our sides to make ourselves as small as possible. We opened our shirts for the vaccinations though we had no idea what the syringe contained – nor why they swabbed our chests with cotton wool but never changed the needle. Every day they counted us to make sure no one had escaped. And in that place named for an absence, we listed everything we lacked. We had no soap. We had no handkerchiefs. We had no socks, no toilet paper. We had no spectacles. No coats, no pens, no watches, no towels. No knives or forks. No warm clothes. No toothbrushes. No cups. No underwear. No cigarettes and no money. No combs. No razors. On we went, listing these missing things to distract ourselves from everything else we had lost.

And always, above the stink of our own unwashed bodies, the stink of other bodies: bone and hair and fat, burning.

After four weeks they sent most of my transport to a satellite camp – the cemetery of the French, it was whispered – but they moved me to the Big Camp, where I had to line up for roll call on the mustering ground. The snow sparkled in the beams from the gatehouse tower, transformed itself into silver dust, and we stood until our lips turned blue and our fingers cramped in the cold. Our feet lumps of wood. Supervisors – themselves prisoners, we realised – ran up and down our rows: *Stand up straight! Heads erect! Straighten that line!* When a man gave his jacket to his son, who couldn't have been older than ten, they shouted: *Take it back! Put it back on!* and struck him in the face.

There can be no sympathy here, they said.

And: *If they see you showing any sympathy, they'll punish you.*

And: *If they punish you, roll call will take even longer, and even more of us will freeze to death.*

Every row of men swaying in the electric cold, every man moving to his body's own wild tempo. The dead dragged to the end of their rows. Then, at last, the SS. *Attention!* The dogs strained at their leashes, ready to spring. The block leader's report: *We are so-and-so many; such-and-such a number dead.* The SS started to count. Kicked the corpses just to make sure. Do the numbers tally? If they don't, another count. Up by the gatehouse, a brass band played marching songs. *I hunt the stag in forest green . . . and yet I, a hardened man – I too have felt love.*

In the Big Camp I still had to share a bed, but only with one other man, and we even had a mattress of sorts – a sack filled with wisps of straw that rustled when we moved. A sign on the wall: *One Louse, Your Death*, and the insect vast, bigger than a man's head. Eduard Makovec, my bunkmate, was a professor of mathematics from Prague, so I asked him if he knew anything about Theresienstadt. He shook his head.

'They advertise as spa town,' he said in his broken German.

He was a Jew, though not registered as such; I only knew because on the first day I glimpsed him naked at the wash-basins that spat out the thinnest threads of water. He kept the information to himself, terrified that someone would denounce him to the SS, and when I told him he could trust me not to mention it, he said he didn't know what I was talking about.

Our block senior was a German communist by the name of Voss, an aloof, unsmiling man who was to be obeyed at all times and without question, as were the barracks orderlies who distributed the food. I soon learned to restrict my breakfast to the ersatz coffee they gave us, and to save my portion of bread and margarine until midday – otherwise I'd have to wait four-teen hours until I could eat again. My blockmates were mainly French, with a few Czechs, Russians and Germans who still wore the old striped uniforms. It was your duty to know the rules, they told me, and your duty to keep the rules. If you didn't keep the rules, the SS officer in charge could punish the whole block – and if that happened, the whole block would punish the rule-breaker. That was how it worked. And they said: these are the rules. Do not steal bread. Do not miss roll call. Do not collapse. If you're carrying a tree trunk, do not collapse. If you're carrying a stone that is heavier than yourself, do not col-lapse. If you're carrying corpses, if you're carrying shit, if you're carrying ashes, do not collapse. These are the rules. Do not attempt to look out the window when imprisoned in the Bunker. If you attempt to look out the window when impris-oned in the Bunker, you will receive a lethal injection. Do not speak any language other than German. Do not pause to warm yourself when delivering fuel to the furnace. Do not steal a potato. Do not read the scraps of newspaper issued for use as toilet paper. Do not read the pages of the books and the bibles issued for use as toilet paper. These are the rules. Do not change the words of the songs you are required to sing and sing and sing. Do not attempt to climb out of a ditch of water. Do not tell stories of atrocities in other camps. These are the rules. Do not eat horse fodder. Do not keep your cap on when an officer passes by. If you keep your cap on when an officer passes by, you will receive twenty-five lashes. Do not smile when the loudspeaker says *We retired, for strategic reasons, to previously prepared positions.* Do not leave a single speck of dust. Do not leave the whipping block and the gallows in sight when visitors come to the camp. Do not fail to report to roll call, even if you are dead. Do not make a sound during roll call. Do not smile during roll call. These are the rules. Do not write to your relatives about conditions in the camp. Do not question why your relatives send you empty envelopes, empty parcels. Do not stand up straight if your work requires you to bend. These are the rules. Do not wear paper cement sacks under your clothing to protect yourself. Do not wear a dirty cap. If you wear a dirty cap, a guard will snatch it from your head and throw it past the sentry line for you to run and fetch. If you do not run past the sentry line and fetch it, you will be shot. Do not run and fetch anything that lies past the sentry line. If you run and fetch something that lies past the sentry line, you will be shot for attempting to escape. Do not remember their secrets: their plundering of Red Cross packages, their unauthorised killings, the fact of their venereal diseases. If you remember their secrets, you will be shot. You will be poisoned. You will be injected. You will be strung up.

The day after my release from quarantine into the Big Camp, the voice from the loudspeaker summoned me to the gate. I picked my way across the icy ground, my wooden shoes slipping with every step, and when I grabbed at the iron gate for balance on my way through, the SS man guarding it struck me in the stomach. I doubled over, no air left in me. I could still feel the cold of the gate in my palm. Somewhere nearby, the sound of screams. I was to report immediately to the office of a Sturmbannführer Hahn.

The room smelled of overheated air, and paper and rubber and ink. On Hahn's desk, facing out, a silver-framed photograph of himself shaking hands with Himmler, and in the corner a tall filing cabinet with a single potted plant on top. I removed my cap and stood to attention, training my gaze on the floor.

'I've been reading about you,' he said, unlocking the bottom drawer of his desk.

For a moment I thought he must have some kind of file on me; a record of punishable things I didn't even know I had done – but instead he withdrew an old issue of the *Monthly Journal of the Struggle Against Cancer.*

'Your Sympathetic Vitaliser,' he said. 'Quite remarkable.'

He opened it to my paper and motioned for me to look, and I saw he had circled the section about the two patients who, at the time of writing, appeared to have entered remission. *While further trials are necessary, I believe it is not unreasonable to greet this result as the most promising advance in the field this century* . . .

I shifted my weight; he was watching me, but I could think of nothing to say.

'This is you, isn't it?' He tapped the page with his finger.

'Yes, Herr Sturmbannführer,' I said. 'But that was many years ago.'

'Don't look at me when you address me.'

'Yes, Herr Sturmbannführer.'

'You've had a much more recent success, though. So I hear from the Holy Spirit.'

'A patient appeared to enter spontaneous remission, Herr Sturmbannführer.'

'Appeared? Appeared?' said Hahn. 'I hear the man stood from his bed and walked!'

I opened my mouth to explain I had seen Herr Erling just a few months previously, and it was obvious his cancer had returned and he didn't have long to live – indeed, for all I knew he was dead already – but something made me stop. The shine in Hahn's eyes, the sense of a held breath as he watched me and waited for me to confirm that yes, my machine could cure cancer. Perhaps he was full of the disease himself – or someone close to him was. 'A remarkable case, Herr Sturmbannführer,' I said, and he said, 'Remarkable. *Remarkable*,' and I could feel the need shimmering off him in waves.

'A miracle, by all accounts,' he said.

'A miracle, Herr Sturmbannführer,' I repeated, neither agreeing nor disagreeing.

The calendar on his desk showed the previous day's date, I noticed, and he saw me looking at it and tore it off. Still the sound of screams coming from somewhere close.

'My wife,' he began, and his tone changed. 'I'm told there's nothing more.' He picked up the framed photograph next to the one of Himmler and passed it to me. When I didn't take it, he said, 'It won't bite.' The picture showed a plump-cheeked young woman in a summer dress; she was much younger than Hahn, and had pale wavy hair that hung loose over her shoulders. She stood beside a picnic blanket and smiled, pointing at the camera, her arm around a little boy who was holding a long-haired rabbit. Its eyes were wide, and it had freed one of its hind legs, digging it into the boy's stomach as it prepared to bolt. 'That was less than a year ago,' said Hahn. 'It must have taken root already – so the surgeon told me. You wouldn't know it, would you?'

'Herr Sturmbannführer, if I may ask,' I said, 'what is the nature of your wife's cancer?'

He gave a slow, pained blink. 'It was in the right ovary. One of the most difficult to detect, according to the surgeon. We have only one child.'

I nodded. 'It's certainly unusual in younger patients. And the symptoms are easily overlooked.'

'Overlooked? There *were* no symptoms. If there had been symptoms, don't you think I would have done something?'

Carefully I passed the photograph back to him, and he wiped it with his sleeve. 'She is a wonderful mother,' he said. 'It's very undeserved.'

'You say your wife has had surgery, Herr Sturmbann-führer?'

'One unsuccessful operation. Somebody should be held accountable.'

'And has her surgeon indicated how much longer . . . ?'

Another slow blink. 'Don't look at me when you address me,' he said, without any real conviction. He let out a heavy sigh. 'Twelve months – though that was two months ago, in December. A little more if we're lucky, he said. Lucky.' He rotated the potted plant around so the stunted side faced the light, then took a small brass watering can and dampened the roots. 'But this machine of yours. It can reach things a surgeon can't.'

'That is the theory, Herr Sturmbannführer.'

'And there's no need for the scalpel.'

'The treatment is non-invasive, correct.'

'And . . . ' he said. 'And . . . does it hurt?'

'Not at all, Herr Sturmbannführer. A little pinch – a little sting, at most. A rubber band flicked against the skin. Most people feel nothing.'

'Yes. Yes. And at present the machine is still at the Holy Spirit Hospital in Frankfurt?'

'I believe so, Herr Sturmbannführer. I was let go – I haven't worked there in six months.'

'Mmm. There's a need for consistency in these cases – one of the top Luftwaffe men is a Mischling, for instance.' He peered at my nose and mouth. 'Anyone singled out as Jewish has a much harder time here,' he said. 'Not just from the SS. You've never practised?'

'Do you mean Judaism, Herr Sturmbannführer?'

'Of course, Judaism.'

'No, Herr Sturmbannführer. We're baptised Lutheran. Though we don't attend church.'

'Who is we?'

'I meant my former wife and daughter. My daughter.'

He did remove a file from his drawer then, and ran his finger down a typewritten page. 'Anna Ganz,' he said. 'A full-blooded Jewess. You divorced in . . . 1939. Adultery.'

'Yes, Herr Sturmbannführer.'

'You're an adulterous lot, it seems. So many divorces these days. But all for the best, in your case, given the current circumstances.' He turned the page. 'She remarried a full Jew, and they're all in Theresienstadt.'

'Do you have news of them?' I leaned forward a little, but I was too far away to make anything out.

'Eyes on the floor!' He closed the file again, weighted it under the edge of a carved desk set: a wavy-haired woman sitting between two owls. 'Could you build another machine?'

For all his research on me, he seemed unaware of the most crucial piece of information: the Sympathetic Vitaliser did not work. Again I felt him watching me, waiting for my reply.

'Yes, Herr Sturmbannführer, of course,' I said, 'in theory.' I tried not to sound too confident; I knew what he wanted me to achieve – the miracle he sought.

'There's no theory, surely,' he said. 'You invented the machine. You know how you made it.'

'I'd be working from memory, Herr Sturmbannführer. It's a complex piece of apparatus, built well over a decade ago . . . '

'You built it at the hospital?' he said.

'At my home.'

'Well then, I can arrange for the original – what are they,

plans, blueprints? – to be uplifted from your former home, if they've survived the bombings. Anything you need, I can arrange.'

'Bombings?'

'Very heavy, over the last few weeks.'

I thought of the boxes of notes in the attic, packed away with my father's feathered helmet, and the cracked cheval mirror that used to stand in our bedroom, and your old high-chair, Lotte. The light slanting in on them through the tiny window. 'They're stored at the Holy Spirit, Herr Sturmbannführer,' I said.

'Hmm,' he said. 'Hmm. It's a grey area. You appreciate that a man in my position can't have a non-Aryan – a Jew – touching his wife.'

'Yes, Herr Sturmbannführer.'

'And questions might be asked if someone turned up at the hospital wanting your plans.'

'Yes.'

'And that might be – complicated.'

'Yes.'

He tapped a finger on my file. 'I think, in this case, memory will be safest. Mmm. We'll rely on memory.'

'Very well, Herr Sturmbannführer.'

He seemed to relax a little. 'You understand, of course, that this is essentially a labour camp. Every prisoner is assigned to a particular commando – the records department, the laundry, the armaments works, either here or down in Weimar. Sock-darning. Construction. And some of the commandos are . . . more hazardous than others. The quarry. The gardening squad – they detonate tree roots. Carry endless loads of soil and stones and what have you.' He shook his head. 'I'll make no bones about it: injuries are common. Casualties. It's terribly wasteful. And the infirmary, of course, is full of all kinds of disease, so medical work is out of the question. The same goes for the pathology department. It will be better if nobody knows you have any medical training whatsoever. Do you understand?'

'It's in my file, though, Herr Sturmbannführer. On my card.'

'I'll see to the file and the card. You're not a doctor. We can't have you passing anything on to Frau Hahn.'

'She may well be compromised,' I agreed. 'Any sort of—' But then I stopped; his face had fallen.

'The floor!' he said, and I lowered my gaze again.

'We must be careful, that's all,' he said, turning away from me to look out the window. 'We must be sensible.'

I glanced at the closed file on his desk, held shut by the weight of the carved woman with the owls. It was so close I could have reached out and taken it, checked to see what it said about you and Anna. I could have.

'You'll already have been immunised against typhus and so on,' he continued. 'The vaccine is produced right here, you know. As a result of our experiments.' He sounded proud. 'It's not my area, labour allocation, but I can ensure that you join one of the less taxing commandos. One of the less risky ones. I can see to that. I was thinking the political department – the Gestapo office, where they register the new arrivals. An opening has come up there, processing photographs. What I am communicating to you, Weber, is that you will be kept safe. This is, this is, how shall I put it – this is what I can offer you, should the treatment succeed. Should it fail, however . . . ' He stopped, cleared his throat, turned back to face me. 'Should it prove unsuccessful, I cannot offer the same assurance. Is that clear?'

'Very clear, Herr Sturmbannführer,' I said, my eyes on the floor. And then, because he seemed to be waiting for me to say something else, 'Thank you, Herr Sturmbannführer.'

In my peripheral vision I saw him give the briefest of nods.

'However,' I said. In my ragged suit and my wooden shoes, I knew I was in no position to bargain – but all the same, I found myself saying it: 'However.'

'I beg your pardon?' he said. 'However what?'

'I also have a wife, Herr Sturmbannführer,' I said.

'In fact, you don't.'

For an instant I thought he meant that Anna was dead; he must have seen my fleeting expression, because he added, 'You have a former wife. The woman from whom you are divorced. Remember?'

I pressed my palms against my thighs to stop from shaking. 'She is my daughter's mother, Herr Sturmbannführer,' I said. 'I am concerned for her safety, for my daughter's sake.'

'As I said, they're in Theresienstadt. They have a whole city there, the Jews, built just for them. They should count themselves lucky. I hear they play soccer.'

'All the same, Herr Sturmbannführer,' I said, and took a deep breath, 'I need an assurance that they too will be safe. If I'm to devote myself to your wife's treatment.'

He stared at me, then laughed. 'You do know where you are, don't you? And who I am?'

'Yes, Herr Sturmbannführer. I know where I am. I know who you are. And these are my conditions.'

'Conditions!' He laughed again. 'That's a first.'

I had the feeling that the whole room was humming; that every leaf of paper in every file was starting to shiver. That the windowpanes might break, the carved desk set burst into splinters. I concentrated on it; the golden grain of the wood that rippled through the wooden woman's hair. 'I am the only person who can build you a functioning Sympathetic Vitaliser, Herr Sturmbannführer. I invented the machine, and I know exactly how I made it. Nobody else does.' He opened his mouth to speak, then closed it again. 'And even if you could obtain my notes from the Holy Spirit – even if you could have something resembling my machine made – you wouldn't know the intricacies of its operation. How a course of treatment must be tailored to the individual patient.'

Someone knocked at the door, but Hahn shouted, 'Not now!' When the person had gone away again, he said, 'Your grandfather's blood is showing itself, I see.'

'My grandfather fought at Sedan, Herr Sturmbannführer.'

'Be careful, Weber,' he said. 'We have the Bunker cells for prisoners who aren't careful.' He slid the file back into the bottom drawer of his desk and turned the key. 'How long will you need to build it?'

I thought about the months I had spent selecting the right wood to house the Vitaliser, hand-cutting the dovetailed joints. Coiling the copper, soldering the wires in place – but that was when my patients were still hypothetical, and the only urgency lay in my own ambition. How long did I need to build a machine that did not work? How long? Three months? Perhaps it would be simpler if the Sturmbannführer's wife succumbed before I ever had to start the sham treatment. Except, without her, Hahn had no reason to ensure my protection – and I had no way of ensuring yours, Lotte. 'Two months, I would say, Herr Sturmbannführer.'

'Months! That's far too much time. We don't have that much time.'

'I expect that the scarcity of materials—' I began, but he said, 'Make a list of everything you need. I'll have it delivered to the photo department, and you'll begin construction immediately. You have one week.'

'And if anybody asks, Herr Sturmbannführer . . . ?'

'You're working on a piece of photographic equipment. My secretary will type up something official, with a stamp.'

When I left, the man nearby was still screaming.

In the photo department there were two SS men and a

dozen prisoners. We worked in the same building as the political department, where the Gestapo carried out their interrogations, but our kapo was a decent sort – a German communist, like Voss, who thought we should all be speaking Esperanto. Most of us had little experience with photography, so each man was taught a specific job that he repeated over and over; it ceased to matter whether he was a piano tuner or a carpenter or an insurance agent, or indeed a doctor. Some men processed the negatives, while others printed the images and passed them on once again for development. Only one or two were allowed to take actual photographs – the headshots attached to the prisoners' identity cards, or pictures of the camp required for official reasons. A man by the name of Beltz – a Jehovah's Witness trained in calligraphy – worked on albums for the officers' family photographs, decorating the pages with pretty captions: *The first snowfall* hung with icicles; *Spring on the Ettersberg* threaded with violets.

I was assigned to print development, and for the first week I sat in the darkroom alongside a French prisoner from Châtellerault. I recognised him from my block – a softly spoken young man named Foucher. Apart from the kapo, he was the only one of us with any photographic knowledge. He showed me how to slide the paper into the developer tray in one quick motion so there were no pockets of air, how to rock the tray gently back and forth, and how to judge the right moment to pull the prints out and transfer them to the stop bath. Calm and methodical, he never seemed shocked at what he saw materialise on the paper. He was like a doctor in that respect, I suppose; someone who has learned to maintain the same expression no matter what he has to look at.

And you never could tell what the strips of negatives that came to us might hold – those flimsy scraps of celluloid, as light as leaves. The photo department's collection must have contained thousands upon thousands of images; if a camp building was erected or altered, it had to be recorded, and any special occasions were photographed too. There were pictures of the SS comradeship evenings at the Bismarck Tower, before the drinking veered out of control, and pictures of the Kommandant and his officers showing visiting dignitaries around their model camp: *Here is the cinema, here is the shooting range, this is the mustering ground, this is an example of the inmates' accommodation, see how clean, how decently equipped, look at the windowboxes on the infirmary, blooming with red geraniums, this is the oak tree beneath which Goethe may have written poetry, this is the zoo. Yes, the deer will come right up to you; hold out your hand and pretend to have food.* Also recorded and stored in the collection were any suicides, accidents or executions – though sometimes it was hard to tell which was which – and the physical condition of any patient admitted to the infirmary. And humorous moments, too, were not forgotten: the troops putting on a show, dressed as Jews and women; the tallest prisoner and shortest prisoner photographed together. No matter what I saw, though, said Foucher, I must never attempt to smuggle any pictures out of the camp. The former kapo, Opitz, had tried it – terrible images of terrible things that he thought the world should know about. He'd hidden some negatives behind a framed enlargement of himself, and when an SS man found it and asked him what it was, he said it was a present for his wife. But the SS man broke it apart, and inside he discovered the evidence of the execution – the hanging – hidden behind the portrait, and they shut him in the Bunker. They tortured him and garrotted him. And then, I suppose, they photographed him.

The headshots of the prisoners – front and profile – had to be produced as quickly as possible, so that the camp records were always complete and correct. Sometimes, especially if we had a backlog, a man might die in between having his picture taken and the print being attached to his card, and the SS would yell about the waste of paper and chemicals, not to mention the labour hours. We all just kept our heads down and got on with it; we knew how lucky we were to be working there rather than in the quarry or the gardening commando, where men died every day, or at the satellite camp near the Harz Mountains, where the prisoners laboured underground in the armaments works, and lived and slept down there too, only returning to Buchenwald on the corpse transports when they were as skinny as sticks.

True to his word, Hahn arranged for all the materials for the Vitaliser to be delivered to the photo department: copper contact plates prepared according to my instructions; entire boxes of condensers and triodes, dials and meters. Lengths of beechwood came, and a cake of rosin that smelled like a pine forest. Solder and a soldering iron, and tweezers and pliers that looked like a jeweller's tools, and spools of copper wire, more than I would ever need. I worked on the machine as quickly and discreetly as I could, packing it away at the end of each day and concealing it in a supplies cupboard, but I couldn't stop my hands from shaking when the kapo asked me what I was doing. I showed him the note from Hahn, and he said, 'You're working for the SS?'

'Yes,' I said, and then, seeing his face, 'No.'

He put his head on one side, regarded me in silence. Then he said, 'Do you have a choice?'

'No,' I said.

After that, he asked no more questions.

Foucher, too, refrained from prying. If he wondered why my progress with the photographs was so slow, he never said as much, and he made no comment, either, when I returned to the photo department after evening roll call to continue my frantic work. Within a week I had finished the machine. No dovetailed joints, no brass handles, and the beechwood housing remained unvarnished, the slots to hold the contact plates unsanded, but there it was, my grand experiment, reconstructed from memory. Hahn had me pack it into a carton, and from there a runner delivered it to his office. Once more he summoned me, and when I entered I saw that he had cleared a space on his desk for the Vitaliser. He locked the door and drew the curtains.

'You will test it on me first,' he said, and he took off his tunic and rolled up his sleeves.

'If you wish, Herr Sturmbannführer,' I said. 'However – there is nothing wrong with you.'

'No, there is nothing wrong with me,' he said. 'And?'

'A patient needs to have something wrong with him in order for the machine to work, Herr Sturmbannführer.'

'I want to feel,' he began, his voice low and tight. 'I want to feel if it hurts.'

I nodded. 'If you'd remove your boots and socks, please.'

His feet were smooth and pale and hairless, the malleolus bones pronounced. I attached the contact plates, careful not to pull the straps too tight. When I heard voices outside the office I froze, and so did he – but then he said, 'The door is locked.' I strapped the second set of contact plates to his palms, again ensuring I did not pull too tight, as if he really were a patient who needed gentle handling. He wore no wedding band, but a heavy silver ring glittered on his finger, the death's-head cut deep into the metal. He saw me looking at it.

'Presented by the Reichsführer,' he said, gesturing to the framed photograph of himself and Himmler.

'I'll switch it on now, if you're ready,' I said, and he closed his eyes. The Vitaliser began to hum. 'Do you feel anything?'

'No. Nothing.'

'What about now?'

'No.' He opened his eyes.

'And now?'

'No. Turn it right up.'

'It's at its maximum setting, Herr Sturmbannführer.'

'Shouldn't I feel something?'

'Not necessarily. Some people don't.'

'It is working, though.'

'Oh yes, it's working. You can see the needles moving on the meters. But there are no tumours in its way in your case, Herr Sturmbannführer. Nothing for the electrical flow to confront.' The wrong thing to say.

'So it will hurt *her*, then.'

I shook my head. 'It's unlikely. As I said, a little sting at most. It's your decision, however, Herr Sturmbannführer.'

'Of course it is,' he snapped. 'Of course it's my decision.' He held out his hands for me to remove the contact plates, then pulled the other pair free himself. 'I'll send word if I want you to begin a course of treatment.' And in his bare feet, he saw me to the door.

It was a Monday morning; I remember that, Lotte, because we were overrun with rolls of film that the SS had shot during their weekend. It was the same every Monday, Foucher told me – hundreds of pictures of family outings to the camp zoo, walks along the Ilm, trips to the Goethe House or the Schiller House or the forest around Duchess Anna Amalia's summer palace, easily reached from the camp by following an old hunting trail. Under the darkroom's safelight, I saw all the sights the countryside near Buchenwald had to offer, coaxing them onto the photographic paper and fixing them there – other people's children, friends, sweethearts, other people's memories. In a way these personal pictures unsettled me more than the shots of the dead – smile after smile, metres of teeth.

On this particular Monday I was waiting to hear from Hahn; three days had passed since I demonstrated the Vitaliser to him, and I did not know what would happen to us all if he decided against the treatment. I was developing some pictures of a young woman posing at the spot where the buses from Weimar stopped. She stood beneath the elaborately carved signpost that pointed in two directions: on one side a line of SS men marched towards the casernes, while on the other an SS man with a rifle herded a monk, a pastor and a Jew towards the camp. The young woman leaned back against the post as if waiting for a kiss, her knee bent; then in another shot she held her hands beneath her chin like a film star; then she put one finger to her lips – *don't tell*. As usual, there were a few duds in the roll, where she had moved or blinked. In one of them her hair had blown across her face and she was scowling, trying to push it out of her eyes. In the next shot she had produced a little comb and turned away from the camera to put herself to rights; she probably didn't know she was still being photographed. An SS man appeared in a few pictures too – he must have asked someone else to take those. He and the young woman stood with their arms hooked around each other's waists, their free hands pointing in opposite directions, just like the signpost. I watched the images form, waiting until there was enough detail in the shadows and the skin tones looked right, just as Foucher had shown me, and then I submerged them in the stop bath. There was one picture I couldn't make sense of for a moment, though – a blurry sweep of ridges and hollows, a sandy sea bed at the bottom of my tray. It wasn't until I noticed the three darker lines curving across the middle that I understood: the palm of a hand, the photographer's hand, cupped loosely over the lens. He wouldn't keep that one, I knew, but I developed it all the same; it wasn't up to us to decide what should be discarded. And perhaps the young woman would want the picture – perhaps, after the SS man had thrown it away, she would quietly retrieve it and keep it tucked in a diary or a scented drawer, this strange little close-up, the hand of her love.

I could hear someone shouting just through the wall –

someone furious or drunk, or perhaps both. It wasn't unusual to hear raised voices in the photo department, since we were so close to the Gestapo's interrogation rooms. I paused in my work and tried to make out what the man was saying, but could catch only single words – *pictures*, *lies*, *responsible*. There was a thud against the darkroom door, then the sound of breaking glass, and I ducked. The voice was much closer now.

'Who did it?' he bawled. 'Who is responsible?'

Somehow I knew he was coming for me. I could hear his footsteps, closer and closer. Dumb instinct made me scan the red-lit room for a place to hide, but of course there was nowhere. I wanted to run; I could feel the blood buzzing in my legs, my heart jumping. The last print of the girl at the signpost still lay floating in the developer, changing by the second. Then the door crashed open, and the light crashed in, and someone turned on the overhead lights, too, and I blinked and blinked, and for a moment I couldn't see.

'These are your work, are they?' the voice shouted. I could smell the alcohol on his breath, and when my eyes adjusted I saw it was Wolff, the prison compound commander. He threw a stack of photographs at me, and I held up my hands to catch them even as they pattered to the floor.

'They look like fucking Africans,' he said. 'When you can see them at all.'

I picked them up: shots of three children playing in a snowy garden with their mother, dressed all in white. A little boy in a sailor suit dangled a toy fishing rod into a frozen pond while two older girls, their hair tied with ribbons, stuffed a white cat in a bonnet into a baby carriage. I remembered developing them the previous week; one of the first sets I'd done on my own, without Foucher's help. Even I had been able to see the photographer had no understanding of light.

'I'm terribly sorry, Herr Sturmbannführer,' I said. I didn't know where to put the photographs.

'I don't give a shit if you're sorry,' he slurred, and stumbled against my table. The fluid in the trays shivered.

'What would you like me to do, Herr Sturmbannführer?' I said. I was still holding the unacceptable prints, my eyes on the floor.

'Fix them, of course!' he roared. Some spittle landed on my cheek.

'I'm terribly sorry,' I said again. 'That's the best I could manage. It's the light, Herr Sturmbannführer.'

'Well, fix the light!'

'It's the light at the moment the photographs were taken,' I said quietly, addressing the floor.

'There was nothing wrong with the fucking light. It was the middle of the fucking morning.'

'I apologise, Herr Sturmbannführer. I meant it's where the sun was in relation to the subjects. I can't change that, unfortunately, Herr Sturmbannführer.' I glanced at the pictures of the girl at the signpost. The ones in the stop bath rippled and distorted under the trembling solution. The one still in the developer had turned completely black.

'So it's my fault?' he said.

'Well, Herr Sturmbannführer,' I began, but he waved a wild hand.

'If this was your family and your garden,' he said, 'where would you have put them? Since you seem to know so much about it.'

'Well, Herr Sturmbannführer,' I said, holding on tight to the photographs to stop my hands from shaking. My family. My garden. 'Well, I suppose I would have asked the subjects to turn around, so the sun wasn't behind them.'

'Then how would we see the fucking fish pond?' he shouted. He grabbed a handful of the pictures and held them under my nose. 'I had it built when we came here,' he said, jabbing at it. 'To keep the children happy.'

Your little fingers, Lotte, jabbing at the giant aquarium in the fish market. Trying to catch all the strange and shimmering creatures as they flitted past.

'And I got them the cat,' Wolff was saying. 'The cat and the fish. You'd think it would have eaten them, but it didn't. Something wrong with it. They all died, though. Overfeeding. I kept telling him they don't need much, but he liked seeing them swim up to the surface and guzzle it down.' He flicked through the photographs he'd grabbed until he found one that showed the smaller girl sitting on a stone alligator. 'It was my daughter's birthday,' he said. 'It's not as if we can have it over again so I can get better photos, is it?'

'No, Herr Sturmbannführer,' I said. 'I'm sorry.'

He was quiet for a few seconds, swaying a little. 'But if we could,' he said, steadying himself against the table and taking a few deep breaths, 'if we could have that day again, I'd tell my wife not to buy her that fucking harmonica.'

Before I could reply he started to make a gagging sound, and I thought he was going to vomit. I grabbed an empty tray and held it under his mouth, and he stared at me, stunned. Then he gave a short, hard laugh and flung the tray against the wall, leaving a dent in the wood.

'Who exactly do you think you are?' he said.

'I apologise, Herr Sturmbannführer,' I said.

'There's nothing wrong with me.'

'No, Herr Sturmbannführer.'

'You shouldn't think,' he began, holding a hand to his mouth for a moment, 'you shouldn't think that any prisoner will come out of here alive if we're defeated. Everything is in place. The camp can be destroyed in a matter of hours.' He held a hand to his mouth again, closed his eyes, swallowed a few times. 'It stinks in here,' he said. 'What *is* that? Vinegar?'

'It's the stop bath, Herr Sturmbannführer.'

'Smells like a whore's douche.' He extended his right hand

to me, and for one confused moment I thought he wanted me to shake it. 'The rest of my photographs,' he said.

I passed them back to him, and he tapped their edges on the table, straightening them into a neat pile. 'I think you need some fresh air. It can't be good for your health, shut up in here day after day with those fumes.' Then he staggered out.

The next morning I learned I'd been transferred to the quarry commando. I had seen the injuries from the men who worked there – the dislocations, the crushes, the fractures and the frostbite. The deep wounds dressed with nothing but paper bandages. I had seen the dead, too, carried back to the compound so they could attend roll call before being burned. Foucher caught my eye as he passed me on the mustering ground. The Ettersberg's constant fog masked the hillside, clung to our clothes, but the camp band was playing, their crimson breeches and yellow-piped tunics like something out of a circus, and if we were somewhere else – a boulevard café, for instance, with little round tables and potted palms – everyone would be dancing. The jaunty martial tune boomed across the open space, nothing to stop it but our own bodies. We marched through the gate, passing under the great clock, Foucher to the shelter of the darkroom, and I . . . well, I didn't know, Lotte. Anyone out of step received a blow or two from a rifle butt – or, depending on the mood of the SS, the promise of twenty-five lashes on the punishment block.

Before my first hour at the quarry was up, I thought my arms would break. I had to lift one end of a wooden box filled with gravel, and the partner assigned to me was a much shorter man, which meant the load was always off-balance – it amused the SS to see such mismatched pairs. The plank handles cut into my palms, and the wind bit through my clothes. There must have been hundreds of us down in that pit on the freezing Ettersberg. We had to work at double time, the kapos watching our every move, yelling obscenities and brandishing their cudgels. And, a little further away but no less vigilant, the SS guards, whips and guns at the ready.

'Don't put it down, even for a moment,' my partner told me.

I saw soon enough what happened to those who tried to rest. Bad enough when we stumbled in our loose wooden shoes and the kapo saw; he struck both of us, the blow catching me on my hip. At least we weren't assigned to the carts, like the teams of men whipped and forced to sing as they dragged their cargo of stones, and at least we didn't have to send the filled carts up the slope on their rickety tracks. If they derailed, the loading crew had to haul them back into place with crowbars, but often the carts slipped backwards and overturned, landing on anyone who wasn't quick enough. By the end of the day, a row of bodies lay next to the wooden hut where the kapos went to warm up.

Hours later, as I stood on the mustering ground for roll call, my body did not believe it had set down its load. All through the news broadcast they played for us over the loudspeakers – all through the doubtful stories of *every enemy attack repelled* and *only minor damage sustained* – the weight of the quarry lay in my arms and legs, and when I ate my evening meal, the bread felt as heavy as rocks. My bunkmate Makovec, the mathematics professor from Prague, tried to stay on his side the whole night so I could lie on my back, which hurt a little less, but I woke curled up tight all the same.

When I set off with the quarry commando again the following morning, marching in time to the band, I heard the loudspeaker shouting my number. At Buchenwald it was rarely a good thing to be singled out, and I just kept marching, my heart lurching ahead of the lively beat of the music. A few moments later the loudspeaker called for me again, but the voice was disappearing into the band's brassy booms and flourishes. They'd started a new tune, and I recognised it straight away: 'High on the Yellow Wagon'. Once, Lotte, at the fairground, I put your feet on top of mine and held on to your wrists as we staggered over to Anna at the shooting range. For weeks afterwards you wanted to do it again, and I had to hum the song and manoeuvre you around like my own little marionette. *Onwards the horses keep trotting . . . Gaily the horn sounds its call . . .* But the memory is too heavy; it tugs at my feet, at my hands, pulling me under.

Then the loudspeaker called me by name.

'Hey,' whispered the man next to me. 'Aren't you Weber?'

No. Yes. I shot him a frantic look and kept marching. A crash of cymbals sounded.

'Weber, Lenard! Report immediately to the gate!'

'Hey,' hissed the man again. '*Hey*. You know they'll punish all of us.'

He was right; I knew he was right. Once, Foucher had told me, when an inmate in our block stole some potato peelings meant for the piggery, the entire block went without their evening meal. But Lotte, I can't in all honesty say that was why I owned up – no, it was more that I knew the punished men would in turn take their revenge on me.

I stepped out of my row and made my way back to the gate, where I snatched off my cap, stood to attention and shouted my number to the SS man on duty. They demanded such shows of deference, even the ones clearly new to the job, with their boots still not broken in. I hadn't seen this particular Unterscharführer before, and as I spoke, he pushed a finger inside his collar as if it were half a size too small. I waited for him to say something, to tell me what was going to happen, but he looked me up and down in silence for what felt like a very long time. The band kept up its carnival tune: *Inside, just through the window . . . A lovely, laughing face . . .* Was he deciding how to do away with me? Considering which method would mean the least bother? Finally, he pointed at my chest and said, 'You're going to lose a button.'

I glanced down at my jacket; no buttons were loose, as far as I could tell.

'Hey, Ritter,' he called to another SS man, 'this one's going to lose a button.'

Ritter came over and looked me up and down too. *I'd so love to stay here and rest a while . . . And yet the wagon rolls on.* Your little feet on my feet, Lotte, a dead weight. Anna waving to us from the shooting range – *Over here! Over here!* All the bright prizes lined up behind her: a beer stein painted with the Alps, a celluloid doll with sleepy eyes and one tiny tooth.

'See?' said the first man, and he snatched at my chest, tearing off a button and flicking it away. He looked to Ritter, grinning like a schoolboy who has just fired a catapult at a weakling's back. The band finished their song, and for a moment there was only the drum marking the beat as the commandos marched past.

'And?' said Ritter.

'Well,' said the first man. 'Well, he'll have to sew it back on.'

'And?'

The first man shrugged, and the band started up once more. I could see the button lying a few paces away, snapped threads trailing. Ritter snorted and walked away. 'You'll have to do better than that, Brehm,' he called over his shoulder.

The first man's neck and face flushed red, and he fiddled with his collar again. 'It's the photo department for you,' he said, as if it were a punishment. He squared his shoulders and jutted his chin at me. The music was still booming and blaring, and the other men were still filing past me, keeping time, keeping time.

'What, you don't understand German?' he said, his Adam's apple bulging in his throat.

'Yes, Herr Unterscharführer,' I said. 'The photo department. Thank you, Herr Unterscharführer.'

He frowned at that, and we both stood there for a moment.

I wanted to pick up the button – it was so close, I could have retrieved it in a second.

'Well, at the double!' he yelled, making his voice louder and deeper than it really was. He looked around to see if Ritter had heard him. *'At the double!'* he yelled again, pleased with himself and his new voice.

And I turned and ran back past the other men, trying to catch their eyes – but they all just stared straight ahead of them, at the back of the man in front, or at the ground.

I left the button behind.

In the photo department I went straight to work as if I'd never been away: print after print of new arrivals, each man looking as bemused as the last, and then a suicide tangled in the electrified barbed wire – wrens, we called them; kings of the fence – and then some pictures of a marriage ceremony at the camp's registry office.

'Your Sturmbannführer pulled some strings, eh?' Foucher said, but I simply shrugged.

In the rubbish bin I found the dud picture of the hand cupped over the lens, and I picked it out.

That afternoon, Hahn sent word that I should report to his office. He'd decided to proceed with the treatment, he said, and had arranged a pass for me so I could visit his villa as often as was necessary.

'Obviously not as a doctor,' he said. 'Just to be clear, you understand that things would go very badly for you if anyone found out you were treating an Aryan woman. Treating my wife. Very badly indeed.'

'Yes, Herr Sturmbannführer,' I said. I stood with my hands held straight at my sides, the cuts on my palms smarting whenever I moved.

'And a guard will always accompany you.'

'Yes, Herr Sturmbannführer.'

'What on earth are you wearing?' he said, as if noticing my clothes for the first time. 'That will never do. After we've finished you'll go to the personal effects room and find something tidier. A proper suit, and a decent coat. And some leather shoes. I'll have my secretary give you a note.'

'Yes, Herr Sturmbannführer.'

'Now,' he said, 'it's not unusual for a prisoner to be assigned the job of photographing certain things around the camp. New buildings. Alterations. Isn't that so?'

'Yes, that's right, Herr Sturmbannführer.'

'Well then,' he said, sitting back in his chair, 'you're a photographer.'

'I . . . I work in the photo department,' I said.

'You're a *photographer*,' he said again. 'I want some family portraits taken at our house, and you've been assigned the job. My son and his mother in the garden with the dog; all of us relaxing on the terrace – that sort of thing. You know how to work a camera, don't you?'

'I . . . well, yes.'

'There you are, then. You'll be producing an album for my son. That is what we'll say. An album for the future . . . ' He broke off for a moment. 'I've already had your records altered. You're a photographer. Always have been.'

'I'm a photographer,' I said.

'Correct,' he said.

The following morning I reported to the gate and showed my pass, and a guard walked me to Villa Hahn so I could begin work on my second miracle.

'Cap off!' he shouted as we passed the great stone eagle.

PART FIVE
WONDER WEAPONS

March 1944

In the late afternoon I rested on Karl-Heinz's bed while he played with his model train set. He'd asked me to take him to see the animals in the zoo, but I told him I didn't want to walk that far.

'We can go over the road, then,' he said. 'To the falconer's house. We can visit the birds.'

'They're not there any more,' I said. 'You know that.'

'Yes they are,' he said. 'I can still hear the peacocks.'

'No, darling – they moved them away quite a long time ago. The falconer too.'

I didn't go into detail, but Emmi had told me that they were holding members of the French government in the house, including the former prime minister Léon Blum – and his mistress had chosen to follow him to Buchenwald, and they had married. Imagine that, said Emmi. Loving a man that much.

Karl-Heinz took out his carved animals and flopped onto the bedroom floor. He was wearing a striped jumper that was far too small for him; I should have found something more respectable for him to put on, but I was so tired I couldn't move.

'You look like a poor little orphan,' I said.

'Do I?' He beamed; in his storybooks, stars fell from the sky for orphans and turned into gold coins.

I'd knitted the jumper from odds and ends of wool two winters earlier, before we came to Buchenwald – we had to be seen to be economising for the war.

'I suppose we do,' Dietrich had said, eyeing the garment as it grew from my needles, gaudier by the day.

'Oh,' said the other mothers when they saw Karl-Heinz wearing it. 'How unusual.'

'I knitted it myself,' I told them. 'From odds and ends.'

'Odds and ends?' they said.

'For the war,' I said.

'Oh, the war!' they said. 'Yes, the war. Aren't you thrifty. Aren't you clever.'

And a few weeks later, their children were wearing striped jumpers too.

It had been Karl-Heinz's favourite for many months, but now it was too short in the body and arms, and one of the cuffs was unravelling. I didn't even know why I'd brought it with us. Tomorrow, I thought. Tomorrow I'd put it in the rag bag.

He was loading his wooden animals into the train carriages, trying to squeeze them all inside – Dietrich hadn't yet started the ark. I suspected they'd never fit, but I didn't want to discourage him from trying different solutions; he was a bright boy, and maybe there was some trick I couldn't see. He kept taking them out and starting again: first the monkeys, then the zebras, then the bears . . . no. First the zebras, then the giraffes, then the monkeys . . . no. The elephants first, then the bears, then the tigers . . . One elephant first, then a giraffe, then the two lions . . . Legs and necks poked out at unnatural angles.

'What happens when you come to a tunnel?' I said.

He frowned; he hadn't thought about that.

'I need the boat,' he said. 'When will Papa make me the *boat*?'

'Don't be grumpy, Karl-Heinz. Lots of children don't have any toys to play with at all.'

'That's why Felix's sisters made some,' he said.

'What?'

'For Christmas, their Hitler Youth group made toys and sold them for lots of money.'

'That's nice,' I said.

'Maybe Papa could make some toys to sell. After he's made me the boat.'

'Maybe,' I said, and rested my head on his pillow. 'Would you fetch me some water, darling? Careful with it on the stairs.' Off he ran. He loved feeling important.

Josef came into the room then to put away the clean washing, stepping over the train carriages wedged tight with animals. Karl-Heinz was right: he did need an ark. What good was a train in a flood? I imagined water pushing under the tracks, forcing the bolts to pop, unmooring the sleepers. The carriages uncoupling and surging away, then sinking one by one. Only the fish left to start the world again.

I shouldn't have been thinking such gloomy thoughts, but it was hard not to with Josef in the house, quietly polishing our mirrors and sweeping up our dust, waiting for Judgement Day. Once, when Dietrich was at work – all right, more than once – I asked him about his faith. I'd never seen him happier; it was his duty, he said, to warn non-believers, so they could mend their ways in time.

'Aren't you frightened?' I said to him now. 'Of the end of the world?'

'Not at all, madam,' he said. 'The world is under the control of Satan and his demons, but after the great battle, God will install Jesus Christ as his judge, and he will decide the fate of every human being, and he will resurrect the dead.'

'All of us?' I said, watching him tidy Karl-Heinz's underwear drawer.

'The hour is coming,' he said, 'in which all those in the memorial tombs will hear his voice and come out, those who did good things to a resurrection of life, those who practised vile things to a resurrection of judgement.'

'And what will happen to those ones – the ones who prac-tised vile things?'

'They will be destroyed forever, along with Satan and all his demons.'

Karl-Heinz reappeared then, holding a glass of water with both hands, creeping along so as not to spill a drop. 'Where are the demons?' he said. He set the glass down beside the bed, but I couldn't find the energy to reach for it.

'Nowhere,' I said. 'Thank you, Josef. Would you get his supper ready, please?'

'Yes, madam.'

'Hello?' Dietrich called up the stairs.

'Papa!' Karl-Heinz ran to greet his father, grabbing his hand in the hall and dragging him into the bedroom. 'I made them all fit, but what happens when we come to a tunnel?'

I was glad he was home before Karl-Heinz went to bed; in recent weeks he'd been staying at work later and later – or going to the officers' club. Once he brought back fistfuls of money, and when I asked him if he was gambling he said that there was no harm, and it took his mind off things.

'There's a doctor,' he said now, sitting on the edge of the bed.

'For the animals?' said Karl-Heinz.

'I don't think so, darling,' I said.

'He's had astonishing results with . . . patients in your con-dition. The body is a circuit, you see, and he invented a machine – it's painless, quite painless.'

'Is he a doctor for animals?' said Karl-Heinz.

'I've arranged for him to see you tomorrow.'

I tried to raise myself onto my elbows. 'I'm not sure I can travel . . .'

'He'll come here. He'll come to you. With his machine.' He glanced at Karl-Heinz. 'Who on earth dressed him today? What are you wearing, Karli?'

'Josef said I could,' said Karl-Heinz.

'I hope he hasn't been outside in that,' said Dietrich. 'Come here. Arms up.' He went to strip the jumper off, but it got stuck at Karl-Heinz's head. I could see all my inside-out knitting – all the tails woven in where one colour ended and another began. It was impeccably tidy; no loose ends, just as my mother had taught me, even though nobody would ever see it.

Dietrich was tugging at the jumper.

'Ouch! Mama! I can't breathe!'

'There's a button,' I said, pushing myself up to a sitting position and waiting a moment for the black to clear. 'At the side of his neck.' I unfastened it and pulled the jumper away. Karl-Heinz looked as if he might cry.

'You can't wear this again, Karli,' said Dietrich. 'It's not safe. Do you understand?'

Karl-Heinz nodded.

'Now go and find Niemand and tell him I want to speak to him immediately.'

'Who's Niemand?'

'Josef. Go and find Josef.'

Karl-Heinz nodded again and ran into the hall. 'Josef!' we heard him calling. 'Josef!'

'Not safe?' I said, turning the jumper the right way through. 'What do you mean, not safe? Aside from suffocating him if you don't know where the button is.'

He patted me on the hand. 'So. Tomorrow morning, ten o'clock. We'll see what this new doctor can suggest. But let's keep it to ourselves, yes? I don't want the whole camp knowing our private business.' Then he left the room, and a few minutes later I heard his voice ringing up the stairs. I inched my way to the door and strained to make out the words.

'Nothing with stripes . . . wolfhounds and bloodhounds as well as German shepherds . . . trained to attack . . . limb from limb . . .'

When Karl-Heinz returned, he was shivering.

'Let's find you another jumper,' I said.

That night, after we'd turned out the light, Dietrich lay on his side and began to stroke my hair.

'I think this treatment – I think it's the answer,' he said.

I rolled onto my side too, and I could feel his breath on my neck, and smell the smell of him. And maybe the treatment *was* the answer, and maybe I could be a normal wife again.

'It's all changing,' he said. 'At the Gustloff Works – I really shouldn't mention it – but we're making something very important.'

'Like what?' I said.

'I can't tell you,' he said.

I took hold of his wrist and tried to pin it to the pillow, though he was far too strong for me. 'I think you can. I think you should.'

He laughed his low, throaty laugh. 'Well, Frau Sturmbannführer . . . you must promise not to mention it to anyone.'

'You can trust me,' I said, wriggling closer to him, ignoring the pain that I thought I could feel returning despite my medicine.

'Well . . . ' he said again. 'I understand we're making parts for the new rockets.'

'What new rockets?'

'*The* new rockets. The wonder weapons.'

'Here?' I said. 'Right here?' I let go of his wrist; the pain was beginning to tug at my pelvis, though I don't think he noticed anything was wrong. And how could he, if I didn't mention it? I hadn't mentioned it the last few times we'd slept together, either. I just let him keep going.

Surely this meant the war would turn in our favour, he said; the prisoners were working around the clock. The rockets were the fastest machine ever produced, and even when they began their dive to earth they didn't make a sound, plunging silently from the sky.

'What a sight,' he breathed. 'What a wonder. Thirteen tons of revenge per serve: not a gram less.'

The doctor's name was Weber. He was tall and slender, with yellow-blond hair and long pale fingers he kept trying to retract into his sleeves, and he wore a creased shirt and a suit with a strip of different fabric sewn down the back. In one hand he carried a battered black doctor's bag, and a stethoscope hung limp around his neck. It had a word on it, picked out in white lettering along the length of the cord: INFIRMARY. He was like no doctor I had ever seen.

I hadn't felt well enough to dress that morning, so Dietrich brought a dining chair up to my room and placed it next to the far side of the bed for Weber to sit on. The man didn't shake my hand, and he didn't wonder aloud whether it might yet snow later that day, and he didn't ask about Karl-Heinz, despite the photo of him right there on the wall, next to a picture of a dog he'd drawn for me. He barely looked me in the eye. And stitched to his jacket, a red triangle, and under it a black number – and yes, the same on the seam of his trousers. A prisoner, then. A criminal, right here in my own bedroom.

'You've been experiencing weight loss and significant fatigue, Frau Hahn,' he said. Was it even a question? 'And occasional localised pain. At times you've noticed a heaviness around the sternum, accompanied by nausea.'

'Yes,' said Dietrich. 'That's right.'

'Any abdominal swelling?'

'No,' said Dietrich.

'A little,' I said.

'I'll need to examine her,' he said, and he removed his jacket and folded it carefully over the back of the chair; he was even thinner without it. He rolled up his creased shirt sleeves and washed his hands at the basin in the corner, glancing at himself in the mirror for just a second. What was that I caught in his expression? Concern? Irritation? I couldn't tell. I prayed he wouldn't have to put his fingers inside me – not with Dietrich right there, please God, please God. I pushed back the eiderdown and waited.

Dietrich grimaced as the doctor reached for me, and I wondered what he knew about his crimes that I did not. He felt around my neck first, pressing up underneath my jawbone and behind my ears. 'Tell me if there is any discomfort,' he said. I could smell roses on his skin; traces of my own soap. Dietrich had presented me with a whole case of little pale-pink bars from Paris soon after we came to Buchenwald – enough to last for years – and I'd scattered them through my wardrobe and drawers. Every time I dressed, I closed my eyes and imagined a bright distant garden, bees looping from bloom to bloom.

The doctor listened to my chest next, moving the stethoscope over my nightgown and staring at Karl-Heinz's picture of the dog. His hands, I saw, were covered in cuts. Dietrich was watching his every move now, searching his face for some kind of clue. Weber gave nothing away.

'And I'll need to palpate the abdomen and the pelvis,' he said.

'Oh,' said Dietrich.

'Oh,' I said, and for some silly reason I remembered the water stain on Doktor Lang's ceiling, and how I couldn't tell exactly where it began. 'Should I . . . ?'

'If you wouldn't mind, Frau Hahn,' said the doctor, and I started to take off my underwear while he looked away.

'Is that absolutely necessary?' said Dietrich.

'Well,' he said, 'I suppose I can—'

'We must do as the doctor asks,' I said, and pulled up my nightgown, feeling the gooseflesh creep across my skin. I concentrated on the picture of Hohenschwangau. The golden castle far away.

When he pushed hard into my pelvis, I gasped.

'Does that hurt?'

'No. I'm not sure.' And honestly, I couldn't tell if it was real tenderness, or just the pressure of his fingers as they dug into me.

'And now an internal examination,' he said.

Dietrich's mouth was a hard line, all the blood pressed out of it.

'How long ago did you first notice the symptoms, Frau Hahn?' he asked when he'd finished and once again washed his hands.

'I suppose . . . ' I began. 'I suppose it was . . . It's hard to be sure.' I glanced at Dietrich. 'It was when I was shopping. It must have been last April. I was looking for a present for my husband's birthday, I remember. Not that the birthday has anything to do with it.' I was babbling, I knew, but I felt somehow embarrassed that I hadn't mentioned the pain to Dietrich when it first started. As if I'd done something wrong, and couldn't undo it.

The treatment itself was painless. The doctor brought a large wooden box over to the bedside cabinet, then plugged six long cords into it, each with a copper plate at one end. These he attached to my feet, hands and upper chest by means of canvas straps, saying, 'You must tell me if you feel discomfort at any time, Frau Hahn.' He plugged the machine into the wall and turned it on, and it began to hum. I could feel a faint buzzing against my skin, the way you can when someone leans in close to tell you a secret.

'Well,' said Dietrich after seeing him out. 'That didn't seem to hurt.' He tidied the machine away in a corner of the room, hiding it behind the cheval mirror and covering it up with a folded sheet.

'Another *prisoner*, Dietrich?' I said. 'Is he even a real doctor?'

'Yes, of course. He's from Frankfurt.'

'Why is he here? What's he done?'

'Nothing. Nothing.'

'Then why is he here?'

'You know there are many different reasons.'

'He was wearing a red triangle.'

'Yes. A political prisoner, not a violent criminal. There's nothing to worry about.'

I thought of the doctor washing his thin hands at my basin, glancing at himself in my mirror. Fear. That was the expression I'd seen on his face.

That night, when Dietrich was undressing, I said, 'If he hasn't done anything, there must be some other reason he's here.'

'Who?' said Dietrich. 'What do you mean?'

'The doctor. The prisoner. You said he hasn't done anything.'

'He's a political prisoner.'

'So he's spoken out against the Party. But I saw your face when he touched me. Why couldn't you bear to look?'

Dietrich pulled off his shirt, leaving the arms the wrong way through; a bad habit I'd never been able to cure. Someone else has to turn them back the right way, I used to tell him when we were first married, until I realised it would make no difference – he'd simply shrug and say that's what the maid was for. He came and sat on the chair at the edge of the bed. At forty-five years old – almost forty-six – he was still a handsome man, though he was starting to lose his lovely dark-brown hair, and he'd gained a little weight around his middle after a year at Buchenwald, where he could order any meal he desired and have it delivered right to his plate. When he offered me pork knuckles or beef roulades or schnitzel with anchovies I told him I had to watch my figure, but really I found I'd lost the taste for such food.

'He's a Jew,' he said.

'Oh.'

'Not full-blooded – a half-breed. But still.'

'Maybe he touched me with the German half.'

'Don't joke about it, Greta. It's serious.'

'You mean dangerous?'

'It's a matter of degrees. I believe he has one Jewish grand-parent, but the authorities can't really settle on what that means. What that makes him.'

'It doesn't bother me, if that's what you're worried about.'

'It bothers *me*.'

I knew he must have my best interests at heart. And I knew there was nothing I could say. I just wanted to go to sleep.

'If word got out . . . ' he said. 'Bad enough that people think our name's Jewish.'

'Isn't it?' I said.

'Not our branch.'

'Anyway,' I said, 'you're a Sturmbannführer. You can do what you like.'

'There's a certificate I've applied for,' he said, flicking the clothes-brush over his tunic. 'A pardon from the Führer, to erase the Jewish blood.'

'He can just sign it away?'

'Of course, yes. One of the top Luftwaffe men got one.'

'But how long will that take? Stamps and signatures and so on. And they must be flooded with applications.'

'I suppose so,' said Dietrich. 'I suppose anyone can ask for one, when they discover a patch of rot in the family tree. But I'm hopeful it won't take too long in this case, given who I am. Who we are.'

'A few weeks? Do you think?'

'I don't know. I can't say.'

'Won't the Führer wonder why you're asking?'

'I've said it's to allow important medical research. Which is not untrue.'

'Research?'

'In the meanwhile, we'll carry on with the treatment, as if we already have the Blood Certificate. I'm sure it's just a matter of time. If anyone asks, Weber's a photographer, taking some family portraits for us.'

'And if anyone does find out?'

'Nobody will find out. Nobody but us will know. Not Emmi, not your mother, not anyone.'

'The doctor will know. And so will Josef, surely.'

'They don't count.'

'What if he says something?'

'Why would he do that?'

Through the wall I could hear Karl-Heinz calling out in his sleep.

'The Führer's own mother—' Dietrich began, then stopped.

'It really doesn't bother me, you know,' I said. 'Honestly.'

'Well it should,' he said, climbing into bed.

'One grandparent! It's so silly!'

'Shh,' he said. 'Shhhhh. You'll wear yourself out.'

'I'm not tired,' I snapped, though that was a lie. 'Stop telling me I'm tired all the time.'

We stared at each other in silence. I could see the red line running across his forehead from his cap; sometimes it took hours to fade.

'His hands were covered in cuts,' I said.

Dietrich nodded. 'Some idiot assigned him to the quarry commando. But he was a doctor, *is* a doctor, and he had some extremely promising results at the Holy Spirit in Frankfurt. *Extremely* promising. I don't want to talk of miracles—'

'Then don't,' I said. But already he'd spoken the word, and it hung in the air between us, a shimmering trick of the light.

Dietrich wouldn't name the disease to my face – as if we could pretend I had a stomach ache or a cold that would pass in a few days. A niggling cyst that could be cut away. I knew there were things he wasn't telling me; how bad it was, how long I had. Despite his warning, I did confide in Emmi – I thought I would go mad if I couldn't talk to anyone. I told her about the part-Jewish doctor and his strange machine; how he strapped the contact plates to my hands and feet and chest, how he adjusted the dials and told me it wouldn't hurt any more than a mosquito bite. I asked if she had any inkling of what he might be treating, and she said no, she had no idea, but she supposed it was the cysts. She tilted her head and smiled, and I knew there were things she wasn't telling me too. I shouldn't be so suspicious of my own husband, she said – and anyway, she'd seen Weber coming and going from the house, and didn't I think he was rather striking? And didn't Dietrich mind that this attractive man, this part-Jew with his yellow-blond hair, was visiting me in my bedroom?

I'd noticed his looks, of course – pure Aryan. The kind of man we were supposed to fall in love with.

Emmi started to gossip about Ilse Koch then; about the affair she'd had with Waldemar Hoven, the camp doctor, right under her husband's nose. '*And* she was carrying on with Hermann Florstedt at the same time! You have to admire the nerve.'

'Careful,' I said; Karl-Heinz had just come into the living room. He settled himself on the floor by the couch and began to read, and I reached out my hand and stroked his head. 'Anyway, look where she is now,' I said.

Along with her husband, Frau Koch was in custody down in Weimar – no more baths of Madeira, no more French cognac for breakfast. 'Will there be a trial?' I whispered.

'No one really knows. But there are plenty here who'd happily deal with both of them.' She made a gun of her fingers, took aim at me and fired.

A few days later she talked me into a trip to Weimar with her.

'You can manage that, can't you?' she said. 'Bring Karl-Heinz over to our house, and the servant can look after all of them. I have a few errands to do in town, but then we can get coffee and cake. You'll just have to sit there. All right?'

'Is Scharführer Rehbein driving us, by any chance?' I said.

'Shh!' she said, then whispered, 'We've found the perfect little guesthouse. Very discreet.'

'I don't think you should tell me,' I said. 'Then I won't be able to let anything slip.'

'But you'll come, won't you? Please? People will start to talk otherwise.'

'All right,' I said.

On the way there in the car, I noticed a stain on Arno's shoulder – a ragged red smear. 'Is that blood?' I said.

'What?' said Emmi, and I pointed. 'Arno, is that blood? Are you all right?'

He twisted his head to see the spot and sighed. 'Just my luck.'

'But are you all right?' said Emmi.

'It's not mine,' he said.

'Slaughtering a sheep,' Emmi breathed into my ear. 'Beheading a chicken.'

I had them let me off near Schillerstraße, a wide boulevard lined with shops, though I couldn't think of anything I needed. Halfway along was the Schiller House, and I went inside to buy a postcard to send to my mother; I still hoped she might come for a visit.

I chose a picture of Schiller's study, and when I handed my money to the woman at the counter she said, 'Is anything wrong? Are you feeling all right?'

'I'm fine,' I said. 'I'd like to have a look around, please.'

She studied me for a minute, then said, 'I can show it to you. It's quiet today.'

I followed her through the sprawling house, which was, she assured me, almost exactly the same as when the writer and his family had lived there. 'And certainly the same as when the Führer himself visited just a few years ago,' she added.

'Would you mind going a little slower?' I said as we climbed the stairs, and she said not at all; she understood there was a lot to take in. She reminded me a little of my mother, in fact: around the same age, with pale-blue eyes and fine, flyaway hair. And she must have been going through the change of life, too; every few minutes she pulled a handkerchief from her sleeve and dabbed at her forehead and upper lip.

In Schiller's wife's bedroom the wallpaper was painted to look like folds of cloth, and even though I knew it was an illusion, when I reached out a finger I almost expected to feel cool satin drapery. Was it blue? I think it was blue, or maybe a bluish grey.

'Please don't touch anything, madam,' said the woman.

'I'm sorry,' I said. 'I wasn't thinking.'

She showed me the reception room where Schiller greeted visitors and acquaintances he didn't know well, and then the adjoining room where he entertained friends.

'And this,' she said, pausing for effect when we reached the study, 'is an exact copy of the bed in which he died.'

'A copy?' I said.

'An authentic replica. The original is in storage in the cellar of the Nietzsche Memorial Hall, in case of damage. It'll stay there until the final victory.' She pointed to a notice on the doorframe by way of corroboration.

'It looks real,' I said.

She beamed. 'It's very faithful. His desk and spinet as well, and two chairs. We had them made just up the hill.'

'I'm sorry?'

'You know.' She pointed her head in the direction of Buchenwald and waited for me to reply.

'Oh,' I said. I felt her pale eyes on me, and I wondered if she knew who I was, and I didn't want to give myself away. 'Better to be on the safe side,' I murmured. I was starting to feel a little shaky.

She beamed again. 'Exactly. We couldn't have kept the house open otherwise – can you imagine the effect on morale? If people could no longer see the homes of our most famous citizens?'

'I'm sorry,' I said, 'but I don't feel very—' Legs trembling, I sank onto the bed.

'Oh!' she said. 'Oh, no no no! I can't let you sit there, madam!'

'I'll be all right in a moment.'

'No, but it's Schiller's bed, you see. Here – let me help you.'

She gave me her arm and led me back down the stairs, and then she brought me a glass of water.

I looked at the postcard I'd bought for my mother: the picture of the study with the deathbed and the desk. 'Are these the real ones or the copies?' I said.

'The real ones,' said the woman. 'But look – you can't tell the difference.'

And she was right.

Just after that I received a letter from my mother. Dietrich opened it and took it from the envelope for me, along with a twig of willow catkins she'd sent to mark the arrival of spring. I brushed them across my cheek: soft and fuzzy, like tiny paws. The letter was full of her usual news – her apartment had been chilly over the winter, thanks to the coal rationing, and she was worried about her orchids; my sister's children had been evacuated to the Bavarian alps and were living in a castle. A card fell out of the envelope too: a picture of a saint. Dietrich paid no attention to it; she was always slipping these things into her letters, in the hope I might return to the church. Images of the

Holy Virgin crowned with stars, or a bone-white lamb serene in a field. Sometimes, flimsy little medals. After Dietrich had gone I picked up the card. It showed a man in a monk's habit, the hem drawn back to reveal a wounded shin. And, on the back, a prayer to Saint Peregrine of Forli, whose leg was healed of its tumour when he knelt before a fresco of the crucifixion and prayed. Saint Peregrine: patron saint of cancer patients. And I understood that my mother was telling me what my own husband would not.

In the early days, once we'd got used to the idea, we were excited about the camp – it would remove the harmful elements from our streets and bring new customers to our shops, new patrons to our restaurants and taverns. Herr Noth looked forward to plenty of extra business for his taxi, and indeed, he said, on occasion the camp authorities telephoned him when they released a prisoner and needed him driven to the train station. Certainly, although we had long been a garrison town, it boosted the young women of Weimar to see all the troops who were stationed up on the Ettersberg; no public event was complete without a parade of them in their smart uniforms. Frau Proft said quite a few came to visit the Schiller House, and the Goethe House too. Back then, we all crowded into the Marktplatz to catch a glimpse of the Führer when he stayed at the Hotel Elephant. As one we chanted: *Please dear Führer, don't depart, stay here in our nation's heart! Please dear Führer, hear our plea, step out on the balcony!* And eventually, he'd show himself. He'd had the hotel specially remodelled, with the balcony added just for this purpose, and his own private bathroom installed, too; before that, when he'd needed to use the facilities, he'd had to walk to the end of the corridor, and then word flew around the hotel guests, and when he emerged he had to salute and smile at everyone waiting to see him.

At the very start of the war, we heard they were bringing in trainloads of Poles who had slaughtered ethnic Germans and were responsible for the fighting that had broken out, and we lined both sides of the street outside the station: hundreds of us, waiting for them to arrive. There was an air of anticipation, as if an important dignitary were coming; someone we'd seen in the newspaper and heard on the radio and all wanted to glimpse in real life. Herr Topf remarked that we were lucky the weather was fine, and we agreed that it wouldn't be so easy to stand there waiting if it were pouring with rain – but we would have come anyway. Yes, yes, we said, oh yes – we would have come anyway. Frau Bader said she hoped her washing would be all right until she was home again, and Frau Ungewiss gestured at the clear autumn sky and told her that she shouldn't worry. And even if the sheets and pillowcases were soaked through, she, Frau Ungewiss, would come and help Frau Bader feed them through the mangle again, because it was important to help one another in times like these, important to band together. Yes, we murmured, yes. Our children tugged at our sleeves, wanting to know how much longer they would have to wait to see the Polish pigs, the snipers who had started everything. Not long, we told them, and pressed stones into their hands. Unrelated to anything in particular, Fräulein Eberhardt said, 'What exactly is an Aryan? I looked it up in my Brockhaus and it said they lived in Asia Minor and Persia. But the Eberhardts come from Hottelstedt.' Then we heard a train shriek into the station and shudder to a stop, and one of our lookouts came hurrying to tell us that they were here at last. The news raced along either side of the street, and we readied ourselves, taking in a deep breath and squaring our shoulders.

When they emerged we hesitated for a moment: were these the snipers? The ones who had started it all? Some of them were bleeding from their noses and mouths and didn't even wipe it away. Were these the crack shots, these hunched and scruffy men? But then we saw the SS at their backs, jostling them along with the butts of their rifles, and we saw the furtive and devious look in their eyes, and we knew that these were the ones. We threw our stones at them, the Polish pigs, and showed our children how to take aim, how to put their whole weight behind them.

The camp Kommandant was there too, in his black car, and he shouted at the snipers to put up their hands and sing German songs. Perhaps you can imagine the tuneless result; we felt a pang to hear them butchered in that way. Some of us recalled the degenerate music we'd listened to in little booths at the exhibition in the spring, which wasn't music at all, but a perverse and jarring clash. Herr Topf started to join in with the snipers, raising his mellow tenor above the drone – he'd appeared in several light operas at amateur level, and many thought him worthy of our Nationaltheater itself – but Herr Krieger elbowed him in the ribs and hissed that we shouldn't be aligning ourselves with the Polish pigs, not in any way. Herr Topf muttered that he was just showing them how the words should be delivered; the meaning they held for a proud German. Frau Topf later said he was peevish the rest of the day and even complained about her potato soup – not enough salt, he grumbled, and too gluey, but he finished it all the same. As the snipers marched along, the Kommandant drove through their ranks and shot any who stepped out of line to avoid his car. Pairs of SS men threw the corpses and the almost-corpses onto the backs of trucks, one taking the arms and the other the feet and swinging them once, twice, three times in order to build momentum, the way a pair of friends might throw a third friend into a lake in summertime. We cheered, and so did our children, once we explained to them that this was something to cheer about.

16 October 1954

[tape corrupted in places]

I don't think I was quite clear about the dental gold. It's important to be clear: do you know, in his final plea at the Dachau trial, Prinz zu Waldeck said *please judge me*, but the interpreter translated it as *please sentence me*? And the American prosecution said it made no difference. So, to clarify, it wasn't because of greed that I kept a few little scraps of gold: rather, I wondered at the painstaking work such miniature casts demanded, and how they so perfectly matched the shape of the things they replaced. That was my primary motivation. They were quite beautiful to me, and a reminder of man's ingenuity; that he can fix the body when it fails. I wished I could bring such precision to the animals I made for Karl-Heinz: I imagined a whole procession of creatures fashioned from gold like tiny idols.

One evening, when I was running my fingers through my collection – it relaxed me at the end of a long day – I lifted out a large premolar crown. Something in its bulging fatness made me think of a beetle, its wings raised like blades, and I lifted out another – a molar crown – and found a cat in its contours, sitting with its paws tucked away and its ears pricked, and in another I saw a fish twisting back on itself when it has just been caught. I tipped the whole collection out on the desk and considered each piece, nudging them with the nib of a pen until I discovered the animals they contained. Bees and toads, gorillas and boars, hedgehogs and houseflies and swallows, no two ever the same. It became a kind of memory game: I'd close my eyes, plunge my fingers into the box and choose a piece at random, then see if I could remember which beast I'd assigned to it. I came to know them so well I could call them up at will throughout my working day, their every curve and dip, their hollowed insides. I hadn't shown the collection to Greta – I would have liked to know if she could see what I saw in the little lumps of gold, and perhaps they would have provided a diversion for her too, taken her mind off her illness – but as the months passed, and the box grew heavier, and I still hadn't said anything about it, it seemed better not to mention it at all. She was retreating more and more into herself, spending more and more time in bed, though she told me she wasn't sleeping well.

'I thought perhaps we should have our own rooms,' she said one day.

Her proposal took me by surprise – it was the kind of thing a wife who no longer loves her husband says. The kind of thing a woman having an affair might suggest. I said, 'As if we're not even married?' and her face fell. 'I'm sorry,' I said. 'I didn't mean that. It's just – a change. Something to get used to.'

'Yes,' she said, 'we'll get used to it.'

I offered to move into the spare bedroom, until she was feeling better.

'Until I'm feeling better,' she said.

And in truth, I'd been sleeping poorly too.

Weber was giving her laudanum that I was able to source through my supplies network, though we told Greta it was a vitamin elixir, so she wouldn't be anxious. It was just a small dose, Weber assured me, to keep on top of any discomfort so that the machine could work most effectively – but I worried that it was taking her from me, erasing her. She'd had three of his treatments so far, and seemed no better.

This was exactly what he expected to see, he told me after the third session. She did not develop the condition overnight, and we could not eradicate it overnight either. The therapy worked little by little, cell by cell.

'Then why is she still losing weight?' I said.

'First we need to halt the progression,' he said. 'Then we reverse it.'

It made sense; it did make sense.

He packed the infirmary stethoscope away into the doctor's bag I'd obtained from the personal effects room. It held most of the tools of the trade, and I kept it in the wardrobe in the spare bedroom; I thought it would help Greta to see him carrying it when he visited – to see that he was a real physician. Certainly, he looked decent enough in the clothing I'd organised, and there was nothing of the Jew about him in his physical appearance. I wonder how far I would have gone in my career if I'd had his colouring, instead of my stocky build and dark hair and eyes.

'Sure there's no Jew in there?' Henning used to say, grabbing my ears and shaking my head till I couldn't see straight.

But that's enough about that.

Weber snapped the doctor's bag shut and returned it to me. 'And my daughter?' he said. 'My former wife?'

'They're in good health,' I said. 'I've made some enquiries, and your daughter is attending the school there, and your former wife works as a laundress.'

I made this up, of course; why would a senior officer at Buchenwald be asking after the welfare of some Jewess and her offspring? It was far too risky.

Perhaps leave that part out.

Well, and maybe it was true. It was possible.

Whenever the sirens sounded I took Greta and Karl-Heinz to the shelter in the forest on the other side of Eickeweg, and one evening in late March the Americans attacked Weimar. We could feel the thundering of the flak guns and the explosions of the bombs, close enough to . . .

[corrupted]

. . . wanted to spend as much time as I could with Greta, and I wanted to avoid her, too, so I could pretend she wasn't disappearing before my eyes. Sometimes I could hardly bear to look at her, and I spent many hours at the officers' club, reading the newspaper or joining in the occasional hand of skat, or just smoking a cigar and listening to songs about carousels and kisses and I *know one day there will be a miracle*.

I couldn't concentrate on my work. Schiedlausky, the camp physician, kept waving a survey under my nose: eighty-one per cent of the prisoners in the parent camp were undernourished, and we needed to do something, since it cast us in a very poor light. When I pointed out that the same survey claimed one in ten had tuberculosis, which might account for their substandard condition and was a medical issue, not an administrative one, he lost his patience. I told him I would look into it – but the rations were set by Berlin and checked by the local office in Weimar. While I could manipulate them here and there to save money, so that the camp functioned better overall, you understand, there was nothing I could do to increase them; it was out of my hands. As it was, I was risking my career by requesting heavy labour rations for all prisoners as a matter of principle, regardless of their actual work! This was confirmed by the Americans; this was verified. But unless I went into the individual blocks and gave the food out in person, like some kind of Florence Nightingale, how could I possibly know if it was getting to them, or being diverted by corrupt intermediaries? The actual distribution of meals was Wolff's responsibility, not mine, and there was pilfering on a massive scale, by supply-room prisoners and barracks orderlies and kapos as well as by SS men – at the time I had no idea just how great the difference was between the numbers on my lists and the rations that reached the inmates. Besides, many of them were entitled to receive packages from home, which contained decent food and should have been enough to sustain them.

And weren't ordinary Germans starving too? Every single one of us had to abide by the rationing rules, even our horses and our dogs. Even our carrier pigeons.

'Is this a punishment?' Greta said one day.

'What do you mean?' I said. 'Is what a punishment?'

'My condition,' she said.

I asked her what the punishment might be for, and who might be punishing her, but she stared at me without speaking, then looked out the bedroom window.

'No,' I said. 'No no. The medicine gives you strange ideas. There is no punishment.'

One day Karl-Heinz asked me why his mama was in bed all the time.

'She just needs to rest,' I said. 'It's a big job, being the wife of a Sturmbannführer.'

We were in the living room, and he started kicking the leg of my armchair. 'No it's not,' he said. 'She doesn't even do anything.' Kick. Kick.

'Well, that's not true,' I said. 'She makes sure Papa can go to his office. She sees to it that he always has a clean shirt and a nice breakfast.' I was talking about myself as if I were someone else.

'Josef does that,' he said. Kick. 'I think Mama's lazy. Lazy people are a burden on the rest of us.' Kick.

'Do you even know what *burden* means?' I asked.

He shrugged.

'I don't want to hear you talking like that again,' I said.

'But it's not fair,' he said. Kick. Kick.

I told him to stop, but he kept kicking. I told him he would damage the leg, and we were very lucky to have such a nice house with such lovely things, and lots of boys weren't so lucky. He gave the chair one final kick. What kind of monster were we raising?

'When are you going to make me the boat?' he said.

'What boat?'

'For all my *animals*!' He was almost shouting now. 'They're supposed to have a *boat*!'

'I don't know,' I said. 'When I have time. At the moment I have no time.'

I tried to read the newspaper but couldn't focus, so I took it upstairs and shut myself in the spare bedroom, unlocked the writing desk and lifted out the chocolate box. It was much heavier now than it looked, much heavier than I had realised. I ran my fingers through my pieces of gold, and I became so absorbed in them, comparing a new crown to the older ones and trying to think what it reminded me of, that I didn't hear Niemand open the door. I barely had time to cover the box with my newspaper. The new piece – a piglet? a calf? – clattered to the floor. I slid my foot over it.

Niemand must have seen how flustered I was, because he said, 'I'm sorry, Herr Sturmbannführer. I did knock.'

I don't know how I failed to hear him. The lid of the chocolate box sat at my elbow, and he glanced at it.

'What do you want?' I said.

He told me he was just going to dust.

'There is no dust,' I said.

'No, Herr Sturmbannführer,' he said.

The dropped crown was pressing into my foot like a stone. I looked at the boy for a moment – his smooth, open face, his bright-blue eyes, the fine Nordic nose and chin. His ludicrous religion aside, he was of decent stock; a decent, polite boy. I picked up the crown from the floor and held it out to him on my palm and said, 'Does this remind you of anything?'

'What is it?' he said, peering from the doorway, twisting the duster in his fists. He never dared come too close to me.

'Well, what do you think it is?' I walked over to him.

'A . . . a tooth?'

'Yes, yes a tooth – but what else could it be?'

He frowned. 'Where is it from?'

'It's gold, of course,' I said. 'Real gold, mined from the ground.'

'But I mean,' he said, 'is it yours? Have you lost it?'

I laughed then, and he blushed. 'It's not mine.' I opened my mouth wide and showed him all my teeth. 'You see? Perfect.'

He nodded. I handed him the new crown and said, 'Look closely. Can't you make out a little animal? A piglet, perhaps, or a calf?'

He held it at arm's length, as if I had just spat into his palm. 'Oh yes,' he said. 'A piglet or a calf.'

'Well, which?'

'A . . . a calf,' he said, and I told him that was what I thought too.

'I should get back to my dusting,' he said. 'I need to keep on top of it.' He passed the crown back to me, but I said, 'Keep it. In recognition of your hard work. The house is always spotless.'

'Thank you, Herr Sturmbannführer,' he said, 'but I couldn't—'

'Of course you could,' I said. I was holding it out to him, waiting for him to take it back; I was not surprised he had refused the first time, because that was only polite. 'It's yours,' I insisted, and told him not to say anything about it. Again he refused my gift, even when I pointed out that it was solid gold.

'I don't want it,' he said. He was looking right at me now, jutting his hairless little chin, and I had the sudden thought that I could strike him across it for being so rude. What sort of manners had his parents taught him? He showed not a shred of gratitude – not for my gift, and not for the fact he was allowed to work for a good German family instead of in one of the dangerous commandos, blowing himself up or crushing himself or what have you. I shouldn't even have been talking to the boy; there had been warnings, written warnings about fraternising with prisoner domestics, and here he was throwing my kindness back in my face. I felt the blood rushing to my fingertips – but of course, I restrained myself. I had never struck a prisoner – my job was all paperwork, as you know – and I never would.

'As you wish,' I said, and I tossed the crown into the lid of the box as if it were of no consequence, and then I began to read my newspaper. *The Enemy Faces Fierce Resistance Everywhere. Great Success for the Japanese Navy.*

After he'd gone I looked at it again, but I could no longer see an animal in it. Just a tooth.

I was preparing to leave my office and return home when the Kommandant knocked at my door. An engineer from Weimar was due to come and inspect the sewage treatment plant, he said – you'd think they had nothing better to do – and of course, it was malfunctioning again. Terrible timing, though quite what Pister expected me to do about it, I don't know. The current system was sometimes inadequate to the task, I agreed, pulling on my tunic.

The current system was failing, said Pister. Three thousand cubic metres per day. That's how much sewage it was designed to handle.

Yes, I said. Which was quite a lot, when you thought about it.

Only now, said Pister, we were producing far more than that.

But nobody could have known how fast we'd grow. Weimar . . .

[corrupted]

. . . an epidemic, he said. That's what we were looking at, if we couldn't process it all. And there was every chance it would spread to the SS quarters. Even to the villas.

'On the other hand,' I said, 'the vegetable gardens have never looked better.'

'It's the ashes,' he said.

I didn't want to have to visit the treatment plant before I went home – it was over on the northern edge of the compound, next to the pestilential pen that was the Little Camp, so you can imagine the smell – but Pister was already leading the way.

We followed the guards' path along the ring of watchtowers, the wind blowing grit into my eyes and mouth – it was always windy on that side of the Ettersberg. As we passed the inmates' infirmary I heard someone screaming just over the fence. There was nothing unusual about that – except the person screaming was a woman. 'Are they admitting female patients now?' I said, and Pister laughed.

'It's coming from the brothel,' he said.

I felt myself redden. 'Of course. Of course,' I said, and then, as the screaming continued, 'Sounds like she's enjoying herself. Perhaps she should be paying too.'

In fact, the profits from the brothel were a sore point with me: against my wishes, they had halved the price to one Reichsmark per visit to encourage more prisoners to use it, yet every single prisoner cost us one Reichsmark and thirty-four Pfennigs per day.

By that time, whenever I slept with Greta, I worried I might break her.

Erase that.

'Careful,' said Pister, and I realised I'd almost stepped into a ditch where the prisoners had been blasting out tree roots.

The stench worsened as we neared the treatment plant. I held my hand over my face; I half expected my nose to start bleeding.

Pister stood shading his eyes, regarding the large concrete structure. 'Well, Hahn,' he said, 'what do you suggest?'

'We need to expand it,' I said. 'That's really the only answer.'

'There's no money for an expansion,' said Pister.

He seemed to want me to pull a solution from thin air. The smell was unbearable; I was trying not to breathe. I checked my hand for blood.

'Perhaps,' I began. 'Perhaps if everyone produced a little less shit.'

As soon as the words left my mouth I regretted them, but Pister was nodding, taking me seriously. 'Withhold their rations,' he said. 'Excellent thinking, Hahn.'

I stopped by the personal property room on the way home to pick up a present for Karl-Heinz so he'd stop asking me for the ark; the child prisoners brought all kinds of bits and pieces with them. I poked through a pile of grubby bears and dented tin cars and incomplete board games, and then I found it: a toy butcher's shop with rows of little hooks, and different sorts of meat to hang on them – salamis and sausages and a halved pig – and the butcher in his cheerful striped apron, and even a tiny set of scales. It looked brand new.

Outside the compound I ran into Wolff, and he invited me for a drink at the officers' club.

'I should get back to Greta,' I said.

'And I should get back to Emmi,' he said. 'But they can't begrudge us half an hour.'

Evening roll call was under way, and that night the prisoners had to sing 'The Buchenwald Song' – no longer part of the official repertoire by then, since the chorus mentioned freedom, though some of our men still liked to hear it for nostalgic reasons. *And the forest is black and the heavens red, and we carry in our bags a piece of bread, and in our hearts, in our hearts, sorrow. Oh Buchenwald, I can never forget you, because you are my fate . . .*

Wolff was already holding open the door to the club, and the place was full of life. I could hear music playing, and bursts of laughter clattering against the wooden walls and the coffered ceiling. A fire blazed, the flames red and gold behind the decorative iron runes. If I'm honest, I needed a break from home, a break from the sickroom, where I had to keep my voice low and calm, my footsteps soft – though Greta was often so drowsy I doubted she knew I was there at all. I needed a break from *her*, or at least from her illness. I deserved it.

That seems a terrible thing to admit. Erase that too.

'Twenty minutes,' I said. We took a table near the fire, and I ordered a cognac. 'And for you?' I asked Wolff, but he shook his head and waved the inmate waiter away, then called him back and ordered a coffee.

'Make sure it's scalding,' he said. When the drinks came he opened a silver cigarette case – a heavily ornamented thing engraved with a tangle of initials – and offered it to me.

'No thank you,' I said. I smoked only the occasional cigar; cigarettes made me feel sick, and besides, they were frowned upon by many of the higher-ups.

Albert Schwartz, the labour allocation officer, sat at the next table with the doctors Schiedlausky and Ding. 'From the top!' he said, and they began to sing 'Our Cat Has Just Had Kittens', banging the tabletop in time. *Six of them are dogs – isn't that a scandal? And the tomcat says: I'm not feeding them* . . .

'I saw you had a lunchtime visitor the other day,' remarked Wolff. He flicked the ash from his cigarette and examined its burning tip. 'A prisoner, yes?' he said.

I was ready for this; I knew it had to come, and if not from Wolff then from someone else. All the same, I tightened my fingers around my glass, forced my heart to settle. Wolff knew nothing. I had done nothing. Nothing wrong. 'Yes, the photographer,' I said.

Wolff frowned. 'Was he carrying a camera?' he said. 'I can't remember him carrying anything. I could be mistaken.'

I went to take a sip of cognac and found I had already

finished it, so Wolff motioned to the waiter for another glass. When I asked if he'd join me, he said Emmi wanted him to cut down.

Plenty of men drank to excess at Buchenwald, and at the officers' club they were always trying to fill one another's glasses; it made them suspicious if someone failed to take advantage of all the benefits of the job. Never mind that some of our privileged prisoners included alcoholic SS men, sent to us to dry out on the Reichsführer's orders: the cure was plenty of fruit juice and mineral water, a low-meat diet seasoned with herbs from our gardens, regular outdoor exercise and the writing of essays on approved topics. My father had been a drinker, dead at forty-four from the stuff; I had to hush it up when I applied to join the Party as well as the SS, and when I wanted to marry Greta. It cost me a lot, I can tell you. I'd seen him lying in his own filth, unable even to undress himself or put himself to bed, and I'd seen him strike my mother because she'd used too much coal, and I'd heard him call her a whore because the caretaker had visited to fix a jammed window in his absence. He didn't remember the terrible things he did – he said he didn't remember. He came home with bunches of carnations, or custard tarts glistening with wedges of fruit, and a few days later he did the same terrible things.

I was older than my father by then: a strange thought. And I enjoyed an occasional drink, it's true, but as a matter of principle I preferred to stay in control of myself, and to remember my actions.

I took a gulp from my second cognac.

'Was he carrying a camera?' Wolff said again.

At the next table Schwartz launched into some rowdy story about a ditch that had filled with water over where the gardening commando were excavating tree roots. He did go on.

'Krautwurst bet it would come up to his knees,' he said. 'Ding said his shins – but where's your shin? Up here? Or down here?'

'Between your ankle and your knee, of course!' said Ding.

'Too vague! Too vague!' said Schiedlausky.

'Reimer reckoned his waist, but I bet it'd be over his head,' said Schwartz. 'I mean he was short, but he wasn't a dwarf!'

'It only came up to his balls,' Ding told Schiedlausky, 'but Schwartz got a shovel and gave him a bit of help—'

'Just a nudge!' yelled Schwartz. 'He only needed a nudge!'

'—and then it was up to his neck,' finished Ding.

'Cheat! Cheat!' shouted Schiedlausky, and Ding joined in: 'Cheat, cheat, cheat! Send him to the Bunker!'

'And then I gave him a bit more help,' said Schwartz.

They all roared with laughter.

'I won, fair and square,' he said. 'It *was* over his head.'

'What did you win, though?' said Schiedlausky. 'You said you won. What did you win?'

'Well, the bet,' said Schwartz. 'I won the bet.'

Wolff breathed out a stream of smoke. 'I don't think I've ever seen you have more than one drink,' he said.

'My father was a drinker,' I blurted without even thinking.

'Ah.' He stubbed out his cigarette and lit another. 'You must've kept that quiet.'

My face was beginning to feel uncomfortably hot, and I moved my chair away from the fireplace a little.

'Anyway, the photographer,' he said. 'I thought I recognised him. He developed some of my portraits of Emmi and the children. Completely ruined them. I could have sworn I had him sent to the quarry.'

Someone opened the door then, and I heard singing: they were still going on the mustering ground. At times roll call did take hours, but that was because so many of the prisoners were illiterates who didn't know how to line up in order. By that stage of the night it was just a few Jews left, droning 'The Jewish Song': *Now there is no more stealing, no feasting and no debauchery. It is too late; it is forever too late . . .*

'He was needed back in the photo department,' I said. 'They have to keep up with all the new arrivals – all the identity photographs. You can imagine the chaos if they didn't. How would we know who was who?'

'But why was he visiting your house?' he said.

I took another sip of my drink. 'Greta wants an album made,' I said. 'Something for Karl-Heinz to look back on.'

That shut him up.

Next morning I could still feel his cigarette smoke grating my lungs. I wanted it gone from me – I wanted to push it out in one clean rush of breath – but it scraped at my chest all day.

Karl-Heinz loved his present, though.

And we really would have to have an album made.

What was your question again?

PART SIX
COME, HOPE

Frankfurt am Main, September 1946

A month into my treatment of Frau Hahn, one of my blockmates disappeared – Coslovich, an upholsterer from Trieste. He was a quiet sort who broke his bread into tiny pieces to make it last longer, and called to his dog in his sleep; a kind man. I'd helped him write a postcard home, since they had to be written in German, and once, when I had a sore throat, he boiled me an infusion of coltsfoot picked from the edge of the crematorium. Up until he vanished, he'd been working on maintaining the railway line, and nobody knew what had happened to him. We looked everywhere, frantic to find him; if the numbers didn't tally that evening, we'd be standing in our rows for hours while they hunted for him, the icy wind pushing underneath our clothes, the fog pooling at our feet, and some of us would collapse, and we knew what happened to those who collapsed. When we fell in for roll call, though, the SS man in charge of our block told us we didn't need to worry. 'He'll turn up soon enough,' he said, and cocked his head in the direction of the crematorium.

Nobody reacted. We stood to attention and did not speak a word. In front of us, right where we could see it, the motto on the gate. To our left the jagged flames reaching up from the chimney and into the night, red teeth rising. And metres away, on the edge of the mustering ground, the pathology depart-ment, where prisoners like us prepared skins and skeletons for medical institutes all over the Reich. The voice of the roll-call officer echoed through the loudspeaker: *You jailbirds in the crematorium, show yourselves!* His little joke. And the prisoners who kept the ovens stoked played along, grabbing the corpses and holding them up to the windows. The voice again: *Caps off! Caps on! Caps off! Caps on!* Until the many thousands of us did it fast enough and in perfect unison.

Voss, our block senior, said he would try to find out about Coslovich, and later that night, when we were back in our quarters, he told us he'd drowned.

'Drowned?' I said. 'How could he have drowned up here?'

My earliest memory, Lotte: the Main bursting its banks when the snow and ice melted. Holding tight to my father's hand. Fishermen coming in their boats to ferry people along the drowned streets.

'That's what they told me,' said Voss. 'They said that he went for a swim and he drowned.'

'It doesn't matter anyway,' said my bunkmate Makovec, and I suppose he was right. They would enter his name in the Death Book, choose from a list of causes: *Heart failure* or *Pneumonia* or *Dysentery* or *Sepsis*, or *Shot while attempting to escape*.

Two of our blockmates were already at Coslovich's locker, grabbing his belongings: one snatched the dented bowl and the other the dented cup, but they both went for his comb at the same time and neither would let go. Coslovich had made it himself, carving it from a wooden ruler tooth by tooth. Even though his hair was cropped to bristles he still ran the comb across it morning and night, sometimes for many minutes, and when at last he finished and returned the comb to his locker you could see the lines criss-crossing his skull like a red net. The two men fighting over it – both recent arrivals, and all but bald too – dropped to the floor and kicked and punched and bit each other. The bowl and cup clattered away, and two other men seized them and hid them under their shirts, then started to run to their own lockers to deposit them there, but they didn't get far before half a dozen of their blockmates fell on them. Such brawls often erupted in the barracks – over who had the biggest portion of bread or margarine or cottage cheese or soup, the least rotten potato, the most space on the bunks. The fighting spread like a sickness through the rank air we breathed, it seemed, affecting even the mildest of individuals – men who were chemists and librarians and opticians in their real lives, and never raised their voices, let alone their fists.

The pack attacked the two who had taken the bowl and the cup, and the dull little trophies changed hands by the second. It might have been a Sunday-afternoon film that Anna and I used to see at the Harmonie – the Marx brothers playing it for laughs. And where was I, Lotte, as one by one my blockmates joined in? I wish I could tell you that I watched from a distance. I wish I could tell you that I tried to break it up, made the men apologise to one another and shake hands. That's how I'd like you to think of me. In truth, I made a grab for Coslovich's belongings too – I couldn't even see them by that stage, but they were in there among the scrabble of fingers and feet; I knew they were in there, ready for the taking, and perhaps they were better than the bowl and cup and comb I already had, and perhaps I could trade them for something else. I joined myself to the snarling whirl.

Voss had seen it all before. He'd been at Buchenwald since the beginning; he had helped to build it, that strange little town. Back then, he liked to tell us, under Kommandant Koch, you knew you were a prisoner. The SS made sure you understood that you counted for nothing, and that the only way out was through the chimney. Now they needed us to make them a profit, and the place was a sanatorium. We didn't know how lucky we were. We didn't know we were alive.

He let us fight for a time, and then he stepped in. I felt his hand wrench my shoulder and heard his voice from somewhere far above: *You should be ashamed of yourself.* He would put the bowl and cup aside, he said, for Coslovich's replacement – because there was always a replacement. Even when we lost dozens at once in the transports to the satellite camps, there were always replacements.

Voss separated the pair who had started it all. One of them clutched the comb to his chest, his knuckles white, but our block senior just stood there with his hand out, waiting like a teacher, and finally the man relinquished it. Holding it under the electric light, Voss ran his thumb along the base of the comb, where you could still see the black lines marking off the centimetres and millimetres, as fine as eyelashes. He found the halfway point and snapped it in two, and he gave each man a piece.

Soon afterwards, I was developing some pictures of the SS quarters. There were shots of a broken door handle, a cracked windowpane, a hole in a wall where the plaster had been gouged away. One tile missing in a row of tiles. A chipped toilet bowl. In some of the pictures, if the damage wasn't obvious, an SS man stood pointing at it. He was looking at the camera and smiling in the first shot, but someone must have told him not to; after that his face was expressionless, and he looked only at the damage. A torn blind. A corner of linoleum curling away from its trim. At the end of the roll, the scene shifted; I could see sky appearing as the picture developed, and a group of SS standing around something dark. They were training their gaze on a bundle at their feet, though one of them, pointing at the item of interest, had thrown back his head and was laughing open-mouthed. Slowly the background emerged: the massive roots of an excavated tree, and next to it a ditch filled with water. The last thing to develop was the thing at the centre of the picture: the body of a prisoner, a man, soaked to the skin. I couldn't see his face.

The next time I visited the villa Josef the servant showed me into the living room, where Sturmbannführer Hahn was standing with his back to the fire. The mid-April day was cool, but inside the house the air felt deliciously warm, and I wanted nothing more than to lie down on the couch and drowse, and then to open my eyes and find myself back in our living room in Frankfurt eight years earlier, you kicking your little bare legs on the rug, and Anna playing the piano in the next room, the Moonlight Sonata tiptoeing through the wall – except it could never be eight years earlier, and I didn't know if our living room still existed. In the recent attacks on Frankfurt, even the Holy Spirit had been hit.

'I wanted a word, before you go upstairs,' said Hahn – and he paused. For one terrible moment I thought he was going to tell me that something had happened to you, Lotte – to you and Anna. He rocked on his heels, scratched his chin. 'Is it . . . ' he began. 'Is she . . . '

Usually, when the families of my patients came out with their halting half-questions, I didn't force them to finish. Usually I gave them what they wanted straight away, which was to know, to *know* – but who was I to read the thoughts of Dietrich Hahn?

'Would you say . . . ' he went on. 'I mean, do you think . . . ' The fire spat out a spark, and he leapt away, brushing at the leg of his trousers. He was close to me now, and I saw that his face was shadowed and lined; I wondered how much older he was than his wife. He stood back up, straightened his tunic. 'Well?' he said.

'I beg your pardon, Herr Sturmbannführer?'

I'm not a cruel man, Lotte. Some called me distant when I worked at the Holy Spirit – at times my job demanded it – but never cruel. If a patient's family wanted information, if they wanted to *know* – and some did not – I told them. *His original tumour has metastasised*, I said. *The cancer has spread to her lymph nodes. The cancer is in her bones. He has a year. He has nine months. She has three months.* They may have chosen to disbelieve me, but that wasn't my concern; I had done my duty, given them the truth – the truth as I understood it. Usually they just nodded, as if agreeing to something, and indeed, by that stage often all they could do was agree; there was no more fighting it. Some of them wrote down what I said, in order to remember. They asked me to spell certain words so they could look them up later, try to prove me wrong – *proliferative, squamous, nephrotoxic.* Then, at the next appointment, they returned to my rooms with their miracles: the Spanish woman who was given six months and was still working at her flower stall eight years later; the Belgian man with an abdominal tumour the size of a grapefruit that simply disappeared. 'How do you explain that, Herr Doktor?' they asked. 'Chance,' I told them. It was the kindest reply, and it was also the truth; I had long since parted company with miracles. Yet there in that warm room, with its gilt-framed painting of breaking waves and its model ship sailing along the mantelpiece, its dustless carpets on waxed parquet, its antler chandelier suspended above us like the crown of some vast oak while Hahn stammered his queries, I allowed myself a little cruelty; I couldn't help it.

'I'm afraid I don't understand what you're asking, Sturmbannführer,' I said. I felt the tiniest thrum of power.

He ran a hand through his thinning hair. 'Is there any sign yet,' he said. 'So far, is there any sign the treatment is working?'

'It's still early, Sturmbannführer,' I said. Another spark leapt from the fire and lay glowing on the carpet. Hahn just stared at it. 'Still very early – but I think we can be hopeful, based on my observations to date. Based on the recovery of my last patient.' There I stood, Lotte, all but promising him my second miracle. I thought that surely he must know I was lying; surely he must see right through me. I had to keep reminding myself that he wanted to believe in the machine as much as I did, and if he admitted it was a fraud, there was nothing more for him to do than wait for his wife to die. The spark from the fire glowed brighter. It could take hold, set the whole beautiful room alight. Porcelain vases cracking in the heat. The sails of the model ship swelling with flames.

'Only she seems to be getting worse,' he said.

'This is quite normal,' I said. 'When the Vitaliser begins to break down a tumour, it releases toxins into the system. Gradually the body processes and expels these.'

Hahn's face relaxed a little.

'What we are seeing is an effect not of the disease,' I said, 'but the destruction of the disease.'

'I see,' he said. 'Yes, I see. Well, tell me if there is anything more you need. For the treatments, I mean. It won't be a problem.' He stamped on the spark. 'Too green,' he said as if to himself. 'Full of sap.'

I went to the spare bedroom first, to collect the doctor's bag Hahn had taken from the personal effects room for me. It must have been a few decades old, but it had been well looked after, and though the handle had moulded to the shape of another man's fingers, the black leather was still supple. The clasp opened and closed with barely a sound.

As I crossed the hallway I heard a heavy thud coming from the bathroom, and a cry. Through the door I saw Josef sprawled on the wet tiled floor.

'I'm all right,' he mumbled, but I helped him up and sat him on the edge of the bath. 'I'm all right,' he repeated. I could see a lump already forming on his forehead. A bottle of bubble bath had overturned and was slowly emptying itself down the drain, and when he tried to snatch at it I thought he was going to fall again.

'Just stay sitting down for a minute,' I said. I righted the bottle and checked his pupils as well as the lump on his forehead. 'Do you feel dizzy? Or sick?'

'No.'

'What day is it?'

'What?'

'Do you know where you are?'

He laughed at that. 'Do you?' He watched as I turned on the water and began to rinse away the spill. 'You won't mention anything, will you?' he said.

'Why would I mention anything? What would I say?'

'It's just – plenty of people want this position.'

The bubbles kept frothing under the stream of water, and the whole room smelled like lavender. The bath was a massive affair, big enough for four or five children. It was much more modern than the one we'd had when I was little, with its claw feet and its dark space underneath that my mother liked to check for dust so she could be sure the maid was doing her job. I used to think that it could walk, and that one day it might wrench itself free of its pipes and escape. I remembered how light I felt when I lay with my head on its curving rim and the rest of my body floating: I was driftwood, I was kelp. My mother had been a nurse before she married, and she used to tell me the names of my bones as she washed me. *Lateral malleolus*, she would say, soaping my lower leg. *Medial malleolus. Fibula. Tibia. Patella.* The words sounded like spells; strange and secret names for things we couldn't see. And I remembered reciting them to you too, Lotte, when I washed your little body in our bathroom at home.

'I should go,' I said to Josef, and he placed his hand on my forearm for a moment and said, 'The Lord is nigh unto them that are of a broken heart.'

Frau Hahn was asleep when I entered the room, lying on her side, knees drawn up to her chest. The only sound the ticking of the alarm clock on the bedside cabinet.

'Good morning,' I said, but she did not stir. 'Good *morning*,' I repeated. 'Frau Hahn?' I stood at the side of the bed in my dead man's suit, the jacket too broad across my back, the sleeves and legs too short. This was the only time I saw my reflection at Buchenwald: in the Hahns' many mirrors. 'Are you awake?' I said.

When I used to work late at the Holy Spirit, Lotte, your mother always asked me to wake her when I came home – so she would know I was safe, she said, and then she could sleep. I'd creep into our bedroom, navigating the dark space by memory, by touch. Only when I was in bed would I speak, whispering to her as I settled my body down the length of hers. *Anna. Anna. I'm home.*

I didn't know how I should wake Frau Hahn – it felt far too familiar to touch her hair, her shoulder, her hip. For a moment I stared at the drawing pinned to the wall above her bed: a dog sitting at a table, drinking a glass of something red – well, was it a dog? Why was a dog sitting at a table? Perhaps it was a man. Without warning they came to me then, Lotte: all the pictures you had drawn of the pools and the parks you could not visit. The Italian ice-cream parlour on Frankenallee; the Palmengarten with its yawning grottoes. Little windows to lost places. Did you draw the gardens of Sanssouci, too? Or am I only imagining that you drew them, because of the calendar page I'm writing on? *The Terraced Vineyard of Frederick the Great in Spring.* I can no longer say for sure.

I cleared my throat and was just about to reach out and wake Frau Hahn when she opened her eyes. She blinked at me as if she didn't know who I was.

'Good morning,' I said. 'It's time for your treatment.'

She blinked again, frowned, then said, 'My treatment. Of course. Good morning, Herr Doktor.'

On the eve of the Führer's birthday, Goebbels roared through the loudspeaker: *Never was he so near to us as in the moment of danger, never were we so bound to him as when we felt that he needed us as we needed him.* The next day the camp fluttered with swastika flags, and the band played songs written in Hitler's honour.

More and more often the bombers came, and though they dropped no bombs on us, we could hear the distant blasts. The SS raced for their concrete cellars every time.

Then, in mid-May, there was talk among the prisoners of the catastrophic loss on the Gustav Line in Italy. Those who tuned into hidden radios relayed the information to their trusted circles, who passed it on to their own confidants, and so it spread: the Allies had taken Monte Cassino, and the Poles had raised their flag on the summit. I was in the darkroom when Foucher whispered the news in my ear. The Germans were forced right back to the Hitler Line, he said, leaving the way to Rome all but clear. It seemed possible that Frau Hahn might survive until the war was lost. How much longer could it be? How much longer? My patients and their families had asked me that question so many times over the years, but at Buchenwald I came to understand its urgency.

I'd become friendly with one of the prisoner nurses who worked in the infirmary – a man by the name of Jochen Wirth, also from Frankfurt, and a mechanical draughtsman by trade. He and his brother, who worked in the personal effects room, had arrived at Buchenwald in 1938; they'd been caught with treasonous leaflets, and had only narrowly escaped with their necks.

Few of the infirmary workers had any prior medical knowledge and had to do their best with scant supplies. The prisoner doctors couldn't possibly take care of everyone, so often Wirth found himself treating typhus and typhoid, scarlet fever and tuberculosis as well as fractures and wounds from heavy labour or beatings or bullets – the SS doctors rarely showed their faces. I had seen men near death from dysentery sent back to their blocks with a few charcoal tablets; when they died the same day, or the day after, their lips and teeth were black with the stuff. The infirmary could just as easily kill you as heal you, and even if you survived the treatment, admitting to physical weakness often proved fatal: the SS dispensed with those who couldn't work, those of no value.

Wirth started talking to me one day in the cinema. Yes, for twenty Pfennigs they allowed us to watch films, Lotte: worn-out prints of musical comedies and approved documentaries that they ordered from Berlin. They screened them in the hall where they assembled the transports, and where they stored the whipping block and the gallows when they weren't in use. *Women Are Better Diplomats* was playing on this particular day, and during the scene when Marika Rökk pirouetted across the lawn in a frothy white dress and the orchestra reached a passionate pitch, Wirth leaned over and said, 'Is it true you're a cancer doctor?'

I felt my every nerve turn cold and tight. 'No,' I said. 'I'm a photographer.'

'Are you sure?' he said.

'Of course. I know what I am.'

I thought that was the end of it; he fell silent again, and we watched to the end of the film, when Marika Rökk kissed Willy Fritsch. Later, though, he sought me out in the latrines – where the SS never ventured – for advice on treating a facial tumour.

'You must be looking for someone else,' I said. 'I already told you, I'm a photographer.'

'No,' he said. 'No one else. It was in your file when you arrived, but then they changed it.'

In the stench of the latrines men were smoking low-grade canteen tobacco and swapping bread for cigarette butts, cigarette butts for shoes, or trying to trade the camp coupons the SS awarded for diligence.

'You have the wrong person,' I told him, and headed for the door.

'Wait.' He grabbed my arm, digging in his fingers. 'He's just a child.'

It might surprise you to know that there were children at Buchenwald, Lotte – hundreds of boys, some as young as three. The prisoners did their best to protect them; to keep their names off the transport lists and to register them as workers in the laundry, the tailor shop, the kitchen and so on, increasing their own output to make up for it. According to the records, one three-and-a-half-year-old worked in the watch repair shop, fixing the timepieces of the SS.

'I'll examine him,' I told Wirth. 'But I can't promise anything.'

And so that night, in the half-hour left between evening roll call and the blast of the curfew whistle, I made my way to the Little Camp and diagnosed a prominent haemangioma on the eyelid of a small Russian boy. The lesion was raised and red, like a strawberry, and partially obscured his vision – but there was no need to remove it.

'You can save?' said one of the older prisoners in broken German.

'It's benign,' I said. 'There's no risk.'

'No save?' he said.

I shook my head. '*Benign*,' I said.

He began to shout in Russian, pointing his finger at me, turning the boy's face to show me.

'It's not cancer,' I tried to explain. 'If I removed it, the risk of infection—'

'Not doctor!' yelled the man.

Another Russian prisoner stepped in then and translated, and the man calmed down, but he still kept looking at me as if I had done something terrible.

'Please don't ask me to help again,' I said to Wirth as we left.

Yes, Lotte, I suppose I was a coward – but I could not risk the deal I had struck with Hahn, devil's pact or no.

So much for my plans to save the world.

And I thought of you, and the little birthmark you had on your forehead when you were born, and how it had almost disappeared by the time you left.

And I thought of Anna, helping me choose the brass handles for my machine.

And I thought of my mother, teaching me the names of bones as she washed me in the deep white bathtub.

'What do they look like?' I asked her.

'Like little white branches. Little white sticks.'

'But what are they for?'

'They hold you together. If you had no bones, you couldn't walk. You couldn't even stand up. You'd be all skin – a coat with nobody inside.'

As she spoke I studied my wrists and knuckles, my bumpy knees, as if I could see right through my flesh. And when she had finished, and the water was milky with soap, and it was time for me to climb out, I dragged myself upright and lifted my legs over the edge of the bath, one, two, and I felt it then, the weight of my waterlogged bones, all the little sticks that held me together.

I saw Wirth again a week later. I had just finished the soup they served us on Sundays – it was always a little thicker, with fat white noodles floating in it, and sometimes a thread or two of meat – and I had come to the small grove of trees at the northern end of the Little Camp, down by the infirmary and the brothel. Somewhere in the gatehouse an SS man had lowered the needle on the gramophone, and Zarah Leander was singing: *In the evenings I stood at the seaside, and I hoped . . . for what? I looked for colourful birds. Ah, my fortune shattered like glass!* Through the electrified fence I could see right across the plain to the Kyffhäuser, grey-blue in the spring sunshine, and the Harz Mountains so faint, just a memory of hills. Here and there fields of flowering rapeseed lay like great slabs of butter, and the spire of a village church pointed straight up to the polished sky. The white farmhouses as bright as teeth. A train pulling along a ribbon of white smoke. In the middle distance, a farmer hooked a plough to a pair of draughthorses and followed along behind them, turning over the soil.

'If we can see him, he must be able to see us,' said a voice behind me.

I glanced around at Wirth. 'And smell us,' I said.

'And smell us.' He sat on the warm ground beside me. 'Maybe you stop noticing after a while. Like a . . . like a cracked windowpane that you always mean to fix but never do, until you just don't see it interfering with the view any more.' He offered me half of a small slice of marzipan. 'From my wife,' he said. 'The men in the mail room refrained from helping themselves for once.'

I breathed in the scent of it before I put it in my mouth. At the top of the field the horses turned and began to make their way back down again.

Didn't I walk along Kaiserhofstraße with my father, holding his hand, stopping to look at the stuffed racehorse in the saddler's window?

'How is the little Russian boy?' I said.

'He's gone. He left on a transport.' Wirth's voice was flat and unemotional, as if he were still remarking on hypothetical cracks in imaginary windows – that was the way we all talked about death. 'At least he didn't have cancer.'

'Yes,' I said. 'He didn't have cancer.'

'Do you miss it? Saving lives.'

'I don't think I saved many,' I said. 'I'm not a very good doctor. I'm a much better photographer.'

'I'm not a very good doctor either,' he said, 'but they gave me a white coat, so I look like one.' He lay down, folded his arms behind his head. 'You know how they jab us all in the chest when we arrive? Shall I tell you what I heard?'

I nodded, sucking the sweetness from the scrap of marzipan dissolving on my tongue.

Didn't I used to buy you marzipan mice, Lotte? With black liquorice tails?

'Tell me,' I said.

'I heard that Doktor Ding has no idea what's going on in his fancy laboratory. He put a couple of unspecialised doctors in there, along with a politician, a rubber-factory worker and a pastry chef. A pastry chef! Then this Polish biologist arrives and tells them that what they're making is useless. And they say well, Ding hasn't noticed, shall we just not let on? And he says all right, so they keep making this useless stuff – the marvellous Erwin Ding's marvellous vaccine to protect the German troops.'

'But surely the Wehrmacht must have realised it doesn't work.'

The farmer raised his face towards us then, shading his eyes. One of the horses bucked in its harness. Wirth fell silent.

'He can't hear us, you know,' I said.

Wiping his forehead on his sleeve, the farmer turned back to his plough.

Wirth sat up, moved a little closer to me and lowered his voice. 'After the Polish biologist arrived,' he said, 'they did manage to make a proper vaccine, but only in small quantities. They've kept that for the prisoners who are most exposed, and the troops still get the fake one. The thing is, no vaccine's perfect – some people are always going to get the disease. And if too many do, and Berlin starts asking questions, the lab just sends them some of the good stuff and says this is the batch used on that group of soldiers. And Berlin has it tested, and it's fine.'

'Risky,' I said.

'You didn't hear it from me.'

Wirth had started digging at a stone, prising it out of the

ground with a stick. When he pulled it free he brushed it clean and held it out to me on his palm.

'An ammonite,' he said. 'They're everywhere up here. Once upon a time, the Ettersberg lay beneath the sea.'

We have no water. How could he have drowned up here?

I took the fossil from him and traced my finger around the ridged coil, right to its centre.

That night as I lay in my bunk I listened to the men all around me sighing and shifting in their sleep: muffled whimpers that seemed to come from some distant place, and the rustling of straw mattresses like parched summer grass, and fingernails scratching at flea bites until they bled, and Makovec's breaths so close I could feel them on my heels. I needed to sleep – Voss's whistle woke us well before dawn – but I kept thinking of the people down in the village, the buttery fields of rapeflowers, the farmer with his plough. If they opened their eyes and went to their windows and looked up, would they see the lamps along the fenceline? And every so often the searchlights, sporadic moons attuned to the movement of bodies, and the chimney a great flaring candle. And buried beneath their feet and ours, the fossils from that ancient sea, coiling in on themselves, turned to stone.

In the morning, when the guard took me to the villa to treat Frau Hahn, I found my patient fully dressed and seated on the living-room couch with her son. Sturmbannführer Hahn stood behind her, trying to fasten a string of pearls around her neck.

'I can't see what I'm doing,' he was saying.

'Do we need them?' said Frau Hahn in a voice barely more than a whisper.

'Keep still. Keep still.'

Their Weimaraner dog lay on the couch too, its head in Karl-Heinz's lap. More than once I'd overheard them telling it not to climb up on the furniture.

'We'll have some photographs today, Weber,' said Hahn, and gestured to a camera set up next to the window seat.

Frau Hahn didn't seem well enough to be out of bed; her eyes were glassy, and she kept smoothing her hair with a slow, heavy hand. All the same, when I pointed the camera at her, she sat up and smiled as if nothing were wrong.

'Get the dog to look at the camera too,' said Hahn.

'What's it called, please, Herr Sturmbannführer?' I said.

'Freya. She's called Freya.'

At the sound of her name the dog leapt to her feet, scrambled across Frau Hahn and pushed her muzzle into the Sturmbannführer's chest.

'You're squashing Mama!' said Karl-Heinz.

Without thinking, I took a picture.

'Down!' said Hahn. 'Down!'

'She's torn my dress,' said Frau Hahn, and as they all leaned in to look at the damage, I took another.

'What's wrong with you?' said Hahn. 'Clearly we're not ready. Niemand, get the dog back. Greta, put your hand over the tear. Right then.'

Through the viewfinder they looked so small – as if seen from a great distance; as if they were already a photograph. I thought they might shift their positions in between shots, or change their expressions, at least, but they stayed exactly as they were, all eyes trained on me, including the dog's.

When I finished the film the Sturmbannführer said, 'Now some on the terrace.'

I wondered if I should point out how exhausted his wife looked – recommend she return to bed – but she raised herself from the couch and murmured, 'Yes, the terrace.'

The early June day was mild and clear, and a soft breeze rippled through the trees at the back of the property. The Hahns sat on chairs crafted in rustic style from branches; on the matching table someone had arranged an unopened bottle of Sekt and three glasses, and next to them a bowl of wax fruit.

'Hold up one of the glasses,' said Hahn. 'As if we're toasting something.'

I had to set up the camera right on the edge of the terrace so I could fit them all in the frame, and I glanced behind me once or twice to make sure I didn't lose my footing. Then I started to take the photographs – except Frau Hahn kept blinking.

'It's too bright,' she said. 'I'm sorry.'

'Perhaps if you keep your eyes closed,' I said, 'and I'll tell you when I'm going to take the picture.'

I had meant the advice for Frau Hahn, but all three of them followed it, and it made for a strange sight: a smiling family in their best clothes, eyes shut tight, holding up empty glasses.

'Now,' I said.

'And now.'

'And now.'

And there is Anna, digging in the little patch of garden in our courtyard, eyes squinting against the summer glare. And you only just walking, unsteady on the hot dirt, about to put a stone in your mouth. Now. Now. Now.

Then the Hahns' dog let out a bark and stared beyond me to the trees, and then she barked again and bounded towards them.

'Leave her,' said Hahn. 'She's scented something.'

In the first week of June, word of D-Day flew through the camp from the men who listened to hidden radios. The French prisoners embraced and wept, and we studied the faces of the SS for signs they might be losing heart. Voss reminded us that we were still at their mercy, and that the Allied invasion could make things worse for us, not better – because the SS were scrutinising our faces, too, looking for any signs of glee, any excuse to bring out the cudgel or the whip. All through the official news broadcast about the landings in Normandy, the loudspeaker kept interrupting; it rattled with orders for this or that officer to report to the crematorium or the sewage treatment plant; this or that prisoner to report to the gate. Soon after, they showed us the footage in the camp cinema: American troops decimated by blazing Wehrmacht artillery, and frame after frame of destroyed Allied equipment. The botched invasion paved the way for German victory, the voice said, and already the Reich's wondrous new weapons – pilotless planes packed with explosives – were raining down on London.

But we could read between the lines.

The Hahns' photographs turned out passably well; the only real dud was a shot I'd taken when the dog had run right up to the camera. There it was, the smudge of her eye, and beyond it the skewed garden. Hahn threw it away when he collected the photos, but I retrieved it from the rubbish bin. I had a small selection of images by then that I kept on my work-table – the duds that nobody wanted; the misjudgements and the slips. Hands cupped over the lens. Ghostly double exposures. Blurred ground, accidental sky. I asked Beltz, the calligrapher, to make me a small album from some bindery offcuts.

I never did stop thinking that one day, somehow, you and Anna might materialise in the images I developed. Each one started as a ghost: just a few shadows, at first, and I couldn't even tell if it was a person. Then, however, I made out an eye or a mouth, perhaps the curve of a neck, and the ghost formed as I watched, gathering flesh to its form with every passing second. And although I knew it couldn't be true, sometimes I had the strangest feeling that it was Anna's eye starting to take shape; your mouth; Anna's neck. I held my breath and watched – and they swam up to me in the dark, all the new arrivals to

Buchenwald, and all the suicides and accidents and executions, as wet and slick as newborns.

And then we lost the Barbets – a French father and son who had only just arrived. The son wore a priest's surplice because that was what they issued him with, and one of the older members of our block who had lost his wits knelt before him and asked him to hear his confession. I say we lost them . . . yes, that is still what I say, Lotte. One evening at roll call, we discovered that the father, who was in his sixties, had been sent to the Bunker for deliberately cutting a belt in the Gustloff Works. We knew he was done for; we knew we would never see him again. All night his son railed against the SS: Murderers! Criminals! Soulless devils who deserved to be strung up! He would teach them a lesson. He would take them on with his bare hands, kill as many as he could, starting with our block officer. Voss and the barracks orderlies tried to reason with him, sitting on the edge of his bunk and quietly explaining that if he attacked an SS man, the SS would gun down the whole block. Most of us had lost family members, but we couldn't let our grief endanger everyone else. Surely he must understand the consequences . . . Barbet refused to listen, and in the morning he reiterated his plans for revenge.

And so that day the infirmary sent for him.

Normally, Lotte, you had to have a fever of thirty-nine degrees to be granted a bed – or you had to know the right people. I could have stepped in, warned Barbet of what admission to the infirmary meant. The needle that we all knew was waiting for him.

But I didn't.

And that is how we lost him.

The next time the guard brought me to Eickeweg, Frau Hahn was in bed again. She lay propped against the pillows, her wavy blond hair carefully parted and brushed, a little greasy at the roots. Her colour seemed worse, I thought, and her pulse was listless and faint. A magazine sat open on the eiderdown: *Every dutiful housewife saves bones, but if stored incorrectly they can putrefy and develop maggots*. She was barely awake.

'Do you have a family, Herr Doktor?' she asked.

I flinched; I had not expected her to speak. 'My wife and I have a daughter,' I said.

'And what are their names?'

'Anna and Lotte.'

'And where are they?'

'Still in Theresienstadt. My daughter is at school, and my wife is a laundress. I'm waiting for some news from them.'

She gave a slow, sleepy nod. 'They must come and visit. Now that it's spring.'

I retrieved the Vitaliser from beneath its sheet behind the cheval mirror – Hahn insisted we keep it covered – and I carried it over to the bedside cabinet and set it up next to the alarm clock and the wooden jewellery box that always sat there. The box was carved with oak leaves and runes – and, I noticed, SS lightning bolts. I lifted away the eiderdown and attached the contact plates to Greta Hahn's feet and upper arms. Under her nightgown I thought I could see evidence of abdominal swelling. She raised her head to let me attach the plates to her temples, and I realised I'd forgotten to lie to her; I realised I had called Anna my wife. And perhaps it was just the stillness of the house that day, the stillness of Frau Hahn, the lightning bolts prettily picked out on the jewellery box, but when I switched on the machine I felt my bones begin to buzz.

Karl-Heinz was watching me from his bedroom doorway as I left his mother's room. 'Hello,' he said. 'I mean, Heil Hitler.'

'Hello,' I said. 'I didn't know you were there.'

'I was reading a book. I'm not allowed to disturb Mama.'

'Can you read?'

'Of course.' He held the book up to me and pointed to a page that showed two children dressed as rabbits, walking through the trees with a rabbit family. 'The children went on a lovely picnic and fed the rabbits,' he said, moving his finger over the words.

'Very good,' I said, though he was wrong; they were the wrong words. *Green are the fields and blue are the skies; the world seems so splendid to young bunnies' eyes! Quite splendid, says wise Mama Rabbit, and yet: the hunter is someone you must not forget.*

'Do you want to play with me? Mama's too tired.'

'I don't think I'm allowed to.'

'Yes you are. You're a grown-up.'

'I have to get back to my job.'

He looked as if he might start to cry. 'What's your job?'

'I work in the photo department. In the photographic laboratory.' He frowned at the long words; I had never really known how to talk to children. 'I make pictures,' I said.

'Like drawings?'

'No, photographs. Photos.'

'You took our photo.'

'Yes.'

'Where's your house?'

'I live at Buchenwald. In the camp.'

He had crept closer to me and was looking at my shoes. 'Those aren't very nice.' He poked at the toe. 'And they're too big. Will you grow into them?'

'Perhaps.'

'Why do you come to see Mama?'

'That's my job too.'

'Do you listen to the radio with her?'

'What radio?'

'The secret radio, in the corner. I looked under the sheet one day. Don't tell Papa.'

'It's not a secret radio.'

'That's good, because they shoot people with secret radios. What is it, then?'

'Just something I invented.'

He poked at my shoe again. 'Are you imaginary?'

'Ah . . . I don't think so.'

'The people who live in the camp aren't real people. So you must be imaginary.' He stamped on my foot, and I couldn't help but cry out. 'Does that hurt?' he said.

'A bit, yes.'

'You're not imaginary, then. Where shall we go?'

'Go?'

'On the train.' He sat on the floor and began lining up tin carriages on a set of toy tracks.

'Hmm. Berlin?'

'It doesn't stop at Berlin. I went there once with Mama and Papa and we visited the Rosts and they took me to the zoo. It was a proper zoo, with an elephant. That's how you know it's real.' He reattached a loose section of track. 'Very dangerous,' he said. 'There might be an accident. See?' With the jab of a finger he derailed a carriage; it rolled once, twice, and came to rest on its back like a dead fly. He picked it up, peered inside. 'It's a miracle no one was hurt. Where shall we go? Not Berlin.'

'Frankfurt?'

'No. Where else?'

'I can't think of any other places.'

'Mesopotamia!'

'That's a long way away.'

'The train goes very fast. You can't even see it.'

He sped the locomotive through the air; it flashed like a mirror in his hands and came to rest on the windowsill, next to a long row of carved animals. They sat in pairs, their wooden faces turned to the light.

'Where's the ark?' I said. 'The boat.'

'Papa hasn't built it yet. So I have to put them on the train instead.'

'My little girl has a Noah's ark, I think.'

'What's a Noah?'

'The man who sails the ark. Noah and his wife – they're the ones who sail the ark and save all the animals. And Noah builds it, too.'

'Well, Papa's going to build mine.'

The animals were arranged from biggest to smallest. I hovered a hand over them. 'May I?'

'If you're careful,' he said. 'And put them back where you found them.'

I picked up one of the mice. It was as tiny as my thumbnail, and so light I could barely sense its weight on my palm, but I could make out every whisker, every ridge on its tail. 'Extraordinary,' I said.

'My papa made it.'

'He made all of these?'

'Yes.'

'He's a very clever man, your papa.' I crouched down to return the mouse to the end of the queue, next to its even tinier mate, but without warning my hand started to shake, and I had to steady it on the carpet. I wanted to sink to the floor then and just sit with the animals and the trains. What a pleasant room it was, with its aeroplane wallpaper and its neat little bed. I nudged the mouse back into line with my fingertip, millimetre by millimetre; a hair too far and it would topple the guinea pigs and the guinea pigs would topple the rabbits, and so on and so on, all the way up to the elephants. 'I should go now,' I said. 'The guard is waiting for me.'

'But we haven't been to Mesopotamia.'

'Another time. Goodbye.'

Karl-Heinz scrambled to his feet, held out his hand and shook my own: one firm, decisive movement. 'Goodbye.'

And I cannot remember exactly, but I think it was that same day – in my mind it was that same day – that I found an old theatre ticket in the breast pocket of my suit. A performance of *The Merchant of Venice* at the Burgtheater in Vienna, fifteen years earlier, before all this began.

I suppose it doesn't matter which day I found it.

I tried to write to you, Lotte – one letter and one card per month, officially. A passage of regulations covered much of the space on the paper they gave us, informing recipients that they could send money to their incarcerated loved ones, who could buy whatever they needed in the camp. If I was guilty of some misdemeanour, though, I wasn't allowed to write at all. If my shoes were not polished: no letter. If my shoes were too polished: no letter. If I turned up my collar in bad weather, if I lost a button, if I walked with my hands in my pockets: no letter. When I mentioned this to Hahn, he said he couldn't risk granting me special privileges, otherwise our whole arrangement could falter – including his promise that you and Anna would be safe – so I learned how to say as much as I could in very few words. I hope you read my messages out to your mother, because they were meant for her too, even if I could not say so. I kept waiting for a reply to come. One night I felt something underneath the straw sack: a postcard, written in a childish hand. *Dear Papa . . .* For a moment I thought it was from you, until Makovec snatched it away – his son, he said. I saw how he traced the boy's name with his finger as he spoke, how he tucked it back under the straw sack in the hope that our SS block officer wouldn't find it. We dreaded his surprise inspections, which could come at any hour. He overturned our lockers and scattered our belongings, deciding on the spot which items were permitted and which forbidden, and what the corresponding punishment should be.

Some weeks later, when Makovec wasn't there, I found the

card again and read the message – written in German, according to the rules: *Dear Papa, I am happy and well. It is nice here.* I couldn't read the name at the bottom; Makovec had rubbed it away.

And I could feel myself beginning to disappear too. The bones of my pelvis pushed at my skin, and at night my vertebrae gnawed through my bedding and into the bunk. I had never given much thought to food; it was simply fuel, and I ate until I was satisfied and then stopped. Now, though, I thought about it all the time: my mother's fragrant cinnamon cake heavy with whipped cream, and her rye bread that crumbled against the knife if you cut it too warm. Finger-thick slices of false hare smothered in Anna's dark gravy; the Zeppelin sausages made by a canny Frankfurt butcher to celebrate the wondrous airships; half-wheels of Swiss cheese and hand-made chocolates stacked into pyramids in the shops on the Freßgass; even the gaudy Lebkuchen hearts they sold at the Christmas market, hard enough to break teeth and iced with *You're My Darling* and *I Think Only of You*.

And the white bread and honey you liked to eat, Lotte, when you woke from a nap.

And the raspberry syrup that turned your tongue pink.

And the sip you once took from my glass of apple wine.

And the almonds you once nibbled from the edges of my Bettmännchen biscuit before putting it back on the plate.

In theory we could buy extra food from the camp canteen, but most often the shelves were bare. If we wanted some poor-quality tobacco, we had to buy a second item, marked up to a fantastic price. A kilo of mussels on the turn, or spoiled herrings, or something they called Viking salad: boiled turnips and carrots in whale-oil mayonnaise. Over in Block 46, any prisoners who signed up for the medical experiments received eggs and honey, fruit, real butter, mugs of milk, soup with oats – but everyone knew that the men who entered Block 46 were

for the chimney. Wirth said that those who worked in Block
50, where they made the vaccines for the experiments, sometimes managed to cook up the remains of infected rabbits –
quite safe, once sterilised – except you had to have decent contacts to land a job like that. Once or twice, Voss distributed
onions stolen from the SS, making sure every one of us
received his share. My blockmates and I discussed our
favourite dishes as we squeezed onto the benches and waited
for the barracks orderlies to dole out the cabbage or turnip
soup, and to weigh the bread with a set of crude wooden scales
if there were any disputes. The bread was mostly sawdust, and
the soup tasted more like water than any vegetable, yet it left a
greasy film in our bowls that we could never wash away. There
in the close, musty barracks, we found we could remember
certain meals years after we had consumed them: a wedding
breakfast of calves' breasts in gooseberry sauce, and a birthday
dinner of airy dumplings that seemed to expand to fill the
entire mouth, and duck soup made every Christmas Eve with
the liver and the heart and plenty of pepper. I told them of the
packages my aunt in Dresden used to send my mother to fat-
ten her up after my father died: the pots of schmaltz as thick as
ointment and flecked with pieces of bacon; the coils of sausage
black with blood. We called up this remembered food for each
other in such detail that we swore we could smell it, taste it –
but we knew that hunger was playing its tricks, and eventually
we stopped trying to raise the ghosts of those past meals,
because like all phantoms they left us hungrier than ever.

Instead we described other memories – beach trips and
bicycle rides, a new winter coat, an open-air performance of
Mendelssohn. When it was my turn I told my blockmates
about the exhibition I had seen in Dresden fourteen years earlier: the Transparent Man. The way you could look right
through his flesh to his nerves and his organs; the coiled pink
guts, the fist-sized heart. The filigree of wire twelve kilometres

long. The way he stood on his plinth with his arms raised, begging for something nobody could see. But I did not tell them about the woman I met there.

And in the mornings we were still hungry. And we said: hunger is the eye of the needle and the point of the needle. It is the knot you can't loosen. It is the red light between your fingers when you hold your hand to the sun. It is the vast eye of the needle. Hunger is the sun huge and empty at noon. The thread pulled through your own lips, under and over and under and over. It is the gulping eye of the needle. Hunger is the mouth of the flooded river, too wide to hold itself. It is the stones worn smooth in the gizzard. It is the mouth of the needle. It is the cold throat of the needle. The circling bird, high, high, a hook against the sky. Hunger is the crescent moon, sharp as a broken bone. It is the forest, felled. The knot in the thread and the stitch pulled too tight. The second hand turning on the white face of the watch while the hour hand never moves. Hunger is the gizzard stones grinding themselves to sand. The broken bone caught in your throat. The whittled wood. The bone pecked clean. The swallowed needle, the swallowed river.

If you take your hunger in your arms it will never let you go.

Take your hunger in your arms.

I thought I could hear Greta Hahn speaking very softly as I approached her room. I expected to find someone there with her, but she was quite alone, sitting up in a chair by the door to the balcony. She started when I entered, and slipped something into the pocket of her dressing gown.

'Good morning, Frau Hahn,' I said, ignoring her blush and busying myself with the Vitaliser. Out in the garden, Josef was walking their dog around and around. Around and around.

I think we had a photograph of you, Lotte, pulling along a toy dog, its leash the belt of my dressing gown.

'Good morning, Herr Doktor,' she said. She tried to stand, but sank back into the chair, her face contracting in pain. I guided her over to the bed, then bent and removed her slippers and helped her to lie down.

'Is there any news of your family?' she asked.

'Not really,' I said. 'Not yet.'

'The mail is *very* slow. I suppose all the trains . . . ' She trailed off.

As she placed her arms at her sides and opened her hands for the contact plates, I noticed a pattern on her left palm: a line of dots pressed into the skin at regular intervals. Then she shifted her hips to make herself more comfortable – another little gasp of pain – and a string of beads slipped from her dressing-gown pocket and clattered to the floor. I picked them up for her, and she snatched at them and shoved them into the bedside drawer, and I saw that they were rosary beads.

'Just something my mother sent me,' she said. Another gasp.

'Shall I give you a little of the vitamin elixir, Frau Hahn?'

'Yes. Yes please.'

After she'd drunk it she said, 'I don't believe in them, you know. The beads. I don't use them.'

'It's none of my business, Frau Hahn.'

'You won't . . . ' she began. 'You won't . . . mention them to anyone?'

'Of course not.'

'Thank you.'

She stared out the window at the trees as I attached the plates and turned on the machine. After a time she said, 'My sister and I used to play Confession. We used to make up the most outrageous sins, and then whoever was the priest would forgive them. Just like that.'

'You are a Catholic, Frau Hahn?'

'I was *raised* Catholic,' she said quickly. 'It's frowned upon now, all that. But my mother still sends me these bits and pieces. Rosary beads. Pictures of saints.'

'They can't hurt,' I said.

I had kept the old theatre ticket I'd found in my suit pocket, and my fingers strayed to it as Greta Hahn's eyes closed and her breathing deepened. I didn't know what had happened to the belongings I'd had with me when I came to Buchenwald – my cufflinks and my fountain pen, my wristwatch, my gloves lined with rabbit fur, my wedding ring, my keys. I liked to think they were still in the personal effects room, neatly filed away, and would be returned to me when the war was over. But perhaps not; Wirth, whose brother worked there, said the SS picked over the belongings first and took the best items for themselves, and the less scrupulous kapos and inmates were next in line: suits and shirts and cravats, books and boots, jewellery and watches, accordions and violins, even spectacles, even crutches.

I watched Frau Hahn from the chair next to the bed. There was an intimacy to these moments; as the Vitaliser hummed, my own breaths slowed to match hers, and I felt my neck and jaw and lips and tongue loosen, and more than once I was surprised to find myself wanting to cover her cool hand with mine, or brush the hair from her forehead. Today her eyelids shivered, and she said, 'Saint Peregrine is also a bird. *Falco peregrinus*. It kills other birds in mid-air.' The strange dislodgements of laudanum; the splinters it frees. She fell silent once more, and I unbuckled the contact plates, cleaned them with the chamois cloth and slid them into their slots in the lid, and when I had placed the machine back behind the mirror and covered it with the sheet, I stole from the room and left her to catch the updrafts of sleep.

And after that, week by week, although I couldn't explain it, she started to improve.

June 1944

Y ou look better,' said Emmi, and I could tell that she meant it. People lie to the dying all the time, jollying them along, assuring them that soon they'll be up and around again, back to their old selves. And the dying go along with the lie, because to counter it means letting ⎪death in the sickroom to sit heavy on the bed, to pull the covers so tight you can't breathe. Yes, soon we'll go walking in the hills, soon we'll be waltzing.

And for weeks, for months, Emmi and Dietrich and Doktor Weber, too, had been insisting I looked well when the evidence was right there in front of them in my thin cheeks and my dead eyes, my bloodless lips. I hardly recognised my own face when I allowed myself a glance in the mirror. I drank down the medicine they gave me because it kept the pain in my pelvis and my lower back at bay, though I knew it was no vitamin elixir, and I knew it made me drowsy and dulled. And yet: You're looking better today, they'd say. I can see a bit of colour in your cheeks. Do you feel a bit better? Yes, I would agree, a bit better. *Don't let death in.* You think you can keep it hovering in the hallway, or casting shadows on the windows like trees, like ships, like great swooping birds. *Don't let it in.* But all the while it's already there.

Dietrich didn't mention that Munich had been hit, half the city flattened. I only knew because Josef brought me the card from Mama with the rest of the mail: *Sign of Life*, it said across the top, and *Write clearly*! Then, in my mother's hand, *House completely destroyed. Unhurt. With Tante Adele.*

'But our place is fine,' said Dietrich when I asked him. 'There's nothing to worry about.'

That afternoon I telephoned Emmi and asked her to come over.

'You do look better,' she said, and I said, 'Let's go out.'

'To the garden? Would you like to sit in the garden for a little while? Though the sun's very strong today . . . '

She went to help me up from the couch, but I shook my head. I'd had enough of hiding in the shade like an invalid, a rug tucked over my knees, trying to ignore the prisoners they sent to train the roses and cut the grass. Trying to look through them, as Emmi advised. For the first time in months I felt like putting my hair up, dabbing scent on my wrists, slipping on one of my gowns and going somewhere elegant.

'I want to see the officers' club,' I said. 'Come upstairs and help me choose what to wear.'

We pulled the dresses from my wardrobe – slippery satin gowns of blue and green and silver with tiny hooks and hidden zips and cut-glass buckles that glittered like diamonds. As I slid them over my head I had the feeling I was plunging into water, into cool deep pools; the fabric rushed soft past my ears, and for a moment I could not see, and only my arms broke the surface. Emmi helped me fasten gown after gown, and we stood in front of the cheval mirror and considered my reflection. None of them fitted me any more; they gaped at the bust, sagged at the hips.

'Perhaps a brooch . . . ' said Emmi. 'Or a belt?' She fussed at the fabric, bunching it in her fists, but it made no difference: I looked like a little girl trying on her mother's clothes. Most of the dresses I hadn't worn since Munich, when Dietrich used to take me to a place on Theatinerstraße where they served lobster and oysters on gold-edged plates while cabinets of valuable antique glassware and pottery shimmered against the walls. All the officers took their wives there, and we admired each other's new hats and ate only half of our lobster or oysters before insisting we couldn't manage another bite. When I think about it now, I suppose I never was very plump – only a little in the face, which I hated – but the words of Dietrich's mother had stayed with me: *She'll go to fat; her sort always do.* For years I had eyed the slender waists of the other wives, the fine wrists, the sharp collarbones, and longed to be smaller.

'I've never been so thin,' I said, twisting to see the bumps of my spine. 'One good thing about dying.'

'Greta!' said Emmi, as if I'd slapped her.

'How does saying it make any difference?'

'Anyway, you're not. You're *not*.'

'No,' I said. 'Not any more. I really believe that.' The bottle of Doktor Weber's elixir sat next to the bed; I hadn't used it in weeks.

'But what will happen to your doctor now?'

'Happen . . . ?'

'Well, now that you're cured. You don't need him any longer.'

'I still need him,' I said all in a rush.

'He *is* handsome,' said Emmi, giving me a sly look in the mirror.

'Is he?' I said. I could feel myself blushing.

'And a lot younger than Dietrich.'

'I never think about our age difference.'

'Don't you wonder what it would be like with someone else, though? Honestly . . . the rest of your life with the same man . . . don't you ever want something different?'

'I enjoy his company,' I said.

'The doctor's?'

'Yes.'

'Greta! If I didn't know better, I'd think you'd been pretending to be sick just to see him!' She laughed. 'Telling me off about Arno, when all this time . . . '

'It's not like that,' I said. But maybe it was, a little at least. I thought of his hands on me, feeling for my pulse, listening to my heart, fixing me. Don't we all fall in love with those who rescue us? 'He's a good man. He has a wife and child in Theresienstadt.'

Emmi waved a hand. 'That's one problem solved, then.'

'What do you mean?'

'Greta, you can't be that naïve.'

'They have a whole village there. It's like a spa town. They play soccer.'

'If that's what you want to believe.'

'Anyway,' I said, 'Dietrich will reward him.'

'A nice trip east.'

'No. He'll release him. Send him home. He deserves it.'

'Greta, he's an enemy of the Reich.' She glanced behind her, though we were alone, then lowered her voice. 'A part-*Jewish* enemy of the Reich. He can't go home.'

'The Führer's own mother was treated by a Jew,' I said. 'Did you know that?'

'I don't believe you. He'd never allow such a thing.'

'It's true. He'd been their family doctor for years.'

'It didn't work, though. She died.'

'Yes. She died. But he was merciful – the Führer was merciful. He let the man emigrate to America.'

'I wonder what he would have done if she'd survived. That would have been difficult.'

'There's a certificate you can get,' I said. 'A pardon. Dietrich applied for one for Doktor Weber, but we haven't heard anything yet.'

'A certificate? What can a certificate do?'

'Well, it cancels the Jewishness. Removes it.'

Emmi laughed. 'Miraculous! Whatever next! Perhaps they have one for idiocy. I could apply on Otto's behalf.'

'A top Luftwaffe man got one.'

Emmi squeezed my shoulder. 'It *is* a miracle, what your doctor's done,' she said, unzipping me. 'I thought I was going to lose you.'

I took off the baggy dress and tossed it on the bed with all the others I'd discarded like bad decisions. Then I changed back into my skirt and blouse, pushed open the balcony door and stepped outside. I leaned over the balustrade, closing my eyes and breathing the summer air into my lungs. It almost stung. I was alive.

'Come away,' said Emmi. 'You're too close to the edge.'

'No,' I said.

'It's smoky out there today. You're letting it inside. Can't you smell it?'

Now that she mentioned it, I could smell something – but it didn't bother me. I was alive. Alive. I could breathe the thickest smoke, catch a bullet in my hand. I could climb into the bear pit.

'Come next door,' she said, dragging me back in. 'You can borrow one of my dresses. We're the same size now.'

She offered me her arm to help me downstairs, but I laughed and ran down on my own. My limbs were so light; I could have just kept running, out the door and along Eickeweg, until my feet left the ground and I flew.

I grabbed my purse, but it was empty apart from a few coins.

'I don't have any money,' I said. 'I was sure I did.'

'Don't worry about that. We won't have to pay for anything.'

Emmi's wardrobe was three times the size of mine, the clothes packed in so tightly it was hard to tell what they looked like. She plucked out little samples of cloth, now and then tugging free a dress for me to try. Up close, the gowns smelled sour and unaired, and inside them, around the neck, I could make out lines of grease where they'd rubbed against bare skin; sometimes the faintest of marks around the armpits, too.

And maybe it was just the way they fitted me so much better than my own clothes, or maybe it was the different room, the different mirrors that showed me my profile and my back, but I no longer felt like myself. Emmi stood behind me and twisted my hair in her hands, pinning it up the way she wore hers. I thought of the game my sister and I used to play, when we'd sit at our mother's dressing table, Helena behind me on the tapestry stool. I'd clasp my hands behind my back, and Helena would reach her arms around in front of me and we'd pretend they were mine. We called her Frau Fischer, this figure in the mirror who was not quite my sister and not quite me. She was getting ready to go out – to the theatre or the shops or church – and she powdered her face with great clumsy swipes, and buttoned up my mother's blouses in the wrong holes, and screwed her earrings on crooked, and pinned her hats on askew. And we'd laugh and laugh at poor Frau Fischer, who couldn't see everything that was wrong with her. She couldn't even manage her own hair without making a mess of it, brushing it over her face, over her nose, bump-bump, dividing it into wonky braids that she tried to pin to her head, only they wouldn't stay in place. *Yes*, she'd say as they drooped down over her ears or her eyes, *yes, that looks lovely.*

Our mother had a tiny comb just for her eyebrows, to make sure they behaved. Was it bone? I think it was carved from bone; certainly in my memory it's as fine and sharp as only bone can be. One day my sister snatched it up from the dressing table and said, 'They look like caterpillars!' – something our mother used to mutter as she set her eyebrows to rights, frowning at herself all the while. Helena grasped my chin and turned it to the left and then to the right. From somewhere behind my head she said, 'This will never do. Not for afternoon tea with the marchioness.' She combed one of my brows, too hard, and I winced as the fine little teeth scraped at my skin. 'A bit of suffering never hurt anyone,' she said, one hand still gripping my chin so I couldn't wriggle away. Then she reached over and aimed the comb at my other brow – at where she thought my other brow should be – and I could see it right in front of me, those little bone teeth coming straight for my eye (yes, they were bone, I'm sure of it), and in the mirror I could see it too, as if it were happening twice over, once to me and once to Frau Fischer. I'm not sure if my sister misjudged where my eyebrow was or if I flinched out of the way – for years after we argued about it – but I felt the comb dig into my eye, and I screamed, knocking Helena's jaw with the back of my skull. She screamed too, and when our mother appeared we were each crying and pointing at the other, and our dog Maxi was standing in the bedroom doorway and barking.

'She made me bite my tongue!' Helena said.

'She poked my eye out!' I said.

Helena spat a tiny thread of blood into her hand. 'Look! Look!'

I cupped my hand over my eye and said, 'I can't see!'

Mama made a glass of warm salt water for Helena to rinse her mouth with, and she bathed my eye with salt water too. 'Can you see now?' she asked.

'I'm not sure,' I said, which was untrue.

She lay me down on her bed and lifted up my eyelid and checked for damage, and her hands were soft and warm, and I could have stayed there forever.

'I think you'll live,' she said, but she cut a square of gauze for my eye all the same, fixing it in place with a long white bandage that she wound around my head so it looked as if something terrible had happened. And when I stood up and walked about and peered at the world through just one eye, I found I couldn't quite tell how close and how distant things were, and even my own hands held up in front of me looked different.

'Why does she get the bandage?' said Helena. 'She's just pretending. There's no blood.' She glared at me across the supper table, but her mood improved when Mama brought her mashed potato and stewed apple to eat, because of her bitten tongue, and fed her like a little baby, blowing on each tiny serving. She used one of her special apostle teaspoons: Saint Peter, Helena's favourite.

'Now then,' Mama said after supper, 'you've both been very wicked and you'll have to go to confession tomorrow. And no more Frau Fischer – you'll only hurt yourselves. Understood?'

We nodded.

'Hold out your hands,' said Mama, so we did. And she took her wooden spoon and smacked us both as hard as she could. And we never played Frau Fischer again.

Emmi opened a separate wardrobe that held only furs. 'Choose one,' she said.

'Where on earth did you get so many?'

She shrugged. 'Here and there. I don't know.'

They were impossibly soft, almost nothing against my fingertips, but when Emmi lifted them from their hangers and laid them across my shoulders and around my neck I felt their animal weight. 'I can't decide,' I said, and she laughed.

'Wear them all!'

She was behind me, and I couldn't see her any more, just her hands spreading one fur on top of another, mink on fox on chinchilla on wolf, until I thought I might disappear under the pile of pelts. In the mirror a great hunched beast looked out at me with my own face.

We made our way along the path through the forest and across the road, and soon enough we came to the high wall – the Isolation Barracks, where they kept special prisoners.

'They have a princess behind there, you know,' said Emmi.

'A real one?' I was concentrating on my feet so I didn't trip; Emmi's dress was too long on me, and it brushed the ground.

'Oh yes, a real one. An Italian beauty – Mafalda von Hessen. She brought all her silk underwear with her, and a case full of jewels, so I heard.'

'But what did she do? Why did they arrest her?'

'Who knows? Maybe she used the wrong fork for the fish course. Wore blue with green.'

'Maybe she had a love affair with a handsome farmer,' I said, and Emmi looked at me sharply.

'What's that supposed to mean?'

'Just . . . be careful. You'll get him sent to the front.'

She snatched at the tip of a spruce branch, snapped it off. 'I haven't done anything wrong. Not really.'

We'd hardly set foot in the club before a pair of officers invited us to join them at their table. Reimer and Dunst were their names, and it was clear Emmi already knew them.

'This is Greta,' she said. 'She doesn't want to hear any of your colourful stories.'

'Maybe I do,' I said, but Reimer nodded and said, 'Understood.'

'This is cause for celebration,' said Dunst. 'Two women! Schnapps or Sekt? Sekt, I think,' and he ordered a bottle.

'Do you think that's wise?' Emmi whispered in my ear.

'I'm back from the dead,' I said, more loudly than I intended, and clinked my glass to hers.

'Are we drinking with a ghost?' said Dunst.

'Do I look like a ghost?'

'Well, I am haunted by you.'

Reimer groaned. 'I apologise for my friend.'

'Prove to us that you're human,' said Dunst.

I said, 'Can ghosts drink?' I took a sip of the Sekt, and the bubbles sparked against my tongue and throat, dozens of little shocks.

'Perhaps,' said Dunst. 'I don't know – I've never met a ghost.'

I took another swallow of Sekt, and another.

'We have plenty of time,' murmured Emmi.

'If you are a ghost,' said Dunst, draining his own glass, 'who were you before you died?'

'I don't remember. Nobody.'

'So you *are*—' he began, but Reimer nudged him and said, 'She was the wife of Sturmbannführer Hahn. She *is* his wife.'

Dunst blushed from his collar to the roots of his hair. 'Excuse me, Frau Sturmbannführer,' he managed to say. 'I hadn't realised.'

Did the whole place know of my disease, then? I felt my thinness at that moment, my missing flesh – I was wristbones hard against the tabletop, a spine hard against the chair. I was ribs held together by a satin belt.

A great cheer sounded from the other side of the room, and I saw a man stand and stuff his pockets with banknotes. Dietrich; it was Dietrich. And he was coming our way.

'Another hand!' one of his companions called after him. 'Show some mercy!'

'Tomorrow, perhaps,' he replied. Then he noticed us. He stopped, frowned, as if he couldn't believe what he was seeing. 'Greta?' he said, though of course it was me; I was just wearing a different dress.

Reimer and Dunst studied their drinks. It was Emmi who spoke.

'Will you have a glass of Sekt?'

A fifty-Reichsmark note slipped from Dietrich's pocket, and we watched it flutter to the floor. 'Why not?' he said. 'A small glass.' He insisted on paying.

22 October 1954

[tape corrupted in places]

To begin with it was just a distraction, something to do with my hands – if I sat at the officers' club with ten playing cards to fan out in front of me, sorting them into suits and calculating their value, deciding how much to bid, I didn't dwell on Greta's illness and whether she had guessed its name, and I didn't try to decide whether she looked better or worse. I could stop thinking for a little while, too, about Weber's mongrel hands on her, and how many months had passed since I'd applied for the German Blood Certificate. I was known to be a careful man, a man who took few risks, so when I started suggesting we play skat for money, nobody cared: I presented little threat. The more my companions drank, though, the worse they played, and by the middle of 1944, when the Allies had landed in Normandy and the Americans had taken Rome, and the Red Army was pushing us back all along the eastern front, and the air-raid warnings kept coming – by then they were drinking a lot. And it wasn't just the officers – the troops, the guard battalion, were getting through huge quantities of beer; every month we had to increase our order. And yes, perhaps the men administered a few unautho-rised beatings when they'd had too much to drink, but only when the inmates violated the rules. Stole vegetables from the gardens and what have you. Besides, the way I understood it, such a beating was actually in a prisoner's best interests: any *official* punishment had to be recorded in his file, and therefore could delay his release date, not to mention the fact that it was likely to be harsher. In the trial at Dachau the defence made a half-hearted attempt to argue this point – unsuccessfully, of course, as the Americans had already made their minds up. They resorted to all sorts of charades to incriminate; a prisoner who swore black and blue that I beat a Russian in the piggery couldn't even identify me in the dock, despite peering at all thirty-one of us for minutes on end. Number 21! No, Number 19! Oh, Hahn didn't wear glasses at the time – let's make them all face the wall, remove any glasses, then turn back to the witness like some kind of theatre act! And this will make you laugh: one cripple testified that when he was at Buchenwald an unknown man struck him on the head with a stick, or maybe it was a riding crop, or maybe it was a dog whip, and then later on other prisoners told him I was that man. That's the kind of evidence the prosecution presented. Hearsay. Staged photographs. Goodness me, they allowed written testimony, which ruled out cross-examination, and they paid witnesses for their time!

Certainly, though, most inmate deaths weren't due to mistreatment on the part of our men but the result of disputes amongst themselves, or the diseases they brought with them into the camp, or indeed the scheming by the illegal communist underground to do away with undesirables. *To Each His Due* and *My Country, Right or Wrong* and *Long Live Stalin*. Oh yes, there were some losses in the prisoners' infirmary, but again, many of these can be attributed to the ludicrous politics of the German communists who ran the place: doctors were bourgeois, but male nurses were comrades, and therefore when it came to treatment, the opinions of the male nurses – who had no medical training – took precedence. Looking back on it now, I can't quite believe we allowed them so much power. Perhaps that was a mistake. I do know that we didn't have enough men of our own to run the parent camp and all the satellite camps – so why not make use of the resource on our very doorstep? Why not delegate? Except there they were, sneaking about, forming secret resistance cells. Stealing grenades and carbines and storing them under the geraniums. And the scheming didn't stop after the end of the war. If you read the trial transcripts carefully, you'll see one or two witnesses who mention they were threatened by the communists – if they made any favourable statements about the SS, they'd lose their welfare benefits. An absolute scandal. Nobody gave it much attention, but I'm confident you'll be able to make up your own mind.

On the day we received word that the Soviets had reached the remains of the camp at Lublin, the bar at the officers' mess ran out of schnapps and I won a hundred Reichsmarks in less than two hours. I kept upping the stakes, waiting for my luck to run out too, and hand after hand it held.

'He's unkillable,' said Hans Schmidt, throwing down his cards and stumbling away from the table. 'Don't go near him.'

I seemed to have a knack for winning, and then a taste for it – and more than that, I thought if I could attract enough luck at the skat table, then that luck would follow me home, and Greta would improve. I know how that sounds. But she *did* improve; when I saw her at the club I felt I was looking into the past, at the girl I'd met when I was almost thirty-seven and she just twenty-one. She'd borrowed one of Emmi Wolff's dresses and had pinned her hair up like Emmi too, and she wore a little bit of makeup, but nothing whorish. I had won over four hundred Reichsmarks that evening; my winnings filled my hands, and there she was, my own best prize, returned to me. I even felt generous towards Weber; when he asked me why he hadn't heard from his daughter, I did him a favour and told him that she and her mother were both in good health and that I'd seen to it they were receiving decent rations. Of course, I was not a man in possession of such power, not a man with the influence of someone like Henning.

But Weber was so clearly relieved at the news, so grateful for it, and that was a kind of power.

And then, after that, I couldn't stop playing skat, because if I stopped the luck would leave us and Greta would worsen again. And yes, I know how *that* sounds. As it was, she'd begun to fill out where she'd been so thin, her face regaining its plumpness, and I knew that the machine was working; it really was working. I funded the games with my winnings, and sometimes with cash from our bank account – I still had my box of gold, after all, which weighed almost two kilograms by that stage. And for a time I kept winning more than I lost, and all through my working day, all through the meetings and the paperwork and the decisions, I found myself longing to return to the club, and to feel the slip and skim of the cards.

I remember one meeting in Pister's office that I thought would never end. The Kommandant and I, along with Schwartz, the labour allocation officer, were negotiating with a factory director – a Herr Ringleb, who was in charge of the munitions plant at Allendorf. We had already travelled there earlier in June to meet with him, and I thought the matter had been settled, but he was still unhappy with the terms of the arrangement. He'd given us his word he would hire our prisoners, and we'd pressed him to use females from the satellite camps as well as males – they could fill the bombs and grenades, or work in the laundry, for instance. We'd charge him just three Reichsmarks per unskilled worker per day, rising to five for those with more experience. This was very reasonable, said Schwartz, very fair: he'd supplied thousands of workers to businesses across the Reich, and he could assure Herr Ringleb that the factory's profits would cover the cost of the labour many times over. He'd been a savings-bank inspector at one time, he said, puffing out his chest: he understood money.

Ringleb made more calculations on a sheet of paper already

covered with his neat little sums, and I glanced at the clock and laced my fingers together to hold myself still; I could feel my blood fizzing, my nerves as taut as wire.

'They call them lemons,' said Schwartz, looking around at us as if we should know what he was talking about. 'The women who fill the bombs. All the saltpetre turns them yellow.'

Ringleb returned to his sums. I stared at the far wall, and the elaborate wooden chest that had belonged to Karl Koch, with a quote from Goethe – I believe it was Goethe – carved into the lid: *The man who has self-control and exercises it achieves the hardest and greatest of feats.* I dug my nails into my palms.

'A worker is a worker,' Ringleb said at last. 'The tasks are not complex. I don't need so many five-Reichsmark ones.'

'I'd be careful about cutting corners, Herr Direktor,' I said. I considered telling him about the railway link to Weimar, which had run for precisely one day before the foundations collapsed – but then, how would that make us look? Instead I said, 'Of course, you're welcome to source your labour elsewhere,' and began tidying away my papers.

'Hold on, hold on,' he said. 'Let's not be hasty.'

Hasty!

Schwartz came with me to the club, and I wasted no time in finding another man to join us for a hand of skat – Herr Große, factory director of the Gustloff Works. He was something of a figure of fun to us, if I'm honest; a travelling sewing-machine salesman desperate to fit in. It was said he wore his Party pin even on his nightshirt. 'We play for money here,' I told him, and he almost choked with excitement. But he was a decent enough companion, and soon my agitation settled. I enjoyed the logic of the game – the complex calculation of points, and also the decisions it demanded: bidding for the right to play alone, or forming an alliance. Declaring a Null game, and then trying to lose every trick. Over the next few hours I won ten Reichsmarks and lost twenty-five, won thirty and lost fifteen, and I would have kept playing, but Schwartz – so self-important, so full of advice nobody wanted – told me I'd be wise to stop at that point.

'Men unwind in different ways,' I said. 'Just one more hand.' And for the first time in my life I heard my father's voice in my own, and he could have been there in the club with us: *Just one more glass.* Well, it wasn't any of Schwartz's . . .

[corrupted]

. . . following night, Wolff must have seen me looking around for a table – I was trying to avoid Schwartz – and he waved me over. He was already quite drunk, and he and Schiedlausky were polishing off plates of pork with apple sauce, carrots and red cabbage, all produced from our own piggery and vegetable gardens.

'I hope you've had a better day than we have, Hahn,' said Wolff. 'Idiots and imbeciles. That's what we're dealing with.'

Near one of the villages, he told me, a Pole had been accused of defiling a German woman, so they'd arrested him and rounded up a dozen other Poles from Buchenwald for good measure. It fell to our men to go and carry out the appropriate punishment in the forest where the crime had taken place; there was never any shortage of volunteers for these things.

'Bit of an excursion,' he said. 'Chance to stretch their legs. And some necks!' He laughed at his own joke, took a long swallow of beer. 'Eh, Schiedlausky?' he said. 'Some necks!'

The doctor nodded.

They were due in the forest at ten, Wolff went on, and he'd allowed plenty of time to drive over and set it all up – here he slopped his drink on the tablecloth, attempted to slide a serviette underneath it and spilled even more. 'Damn,' he yelled. 'Waiter! What was I saying?'

'You'd allowed plenty of time,' I said.

Yes, plenty, he said. *Plenty*. But by quarter to they hadn't even left Buchenwald. Idiots! They couldn't figure out how to load it onto the truck. Couldn't make it fit. And they were just as bad unloading it and bolting it together. He started on a fresh glass of beer.

Schiedlausky was turning his coaster around and around. There was a huge crowd, he said. All the Polish workers had to come and watch, and there were people from the villages too, and from Weimar. Jostling for a place. Getting impatient.

'It was what, half past twelve by the time we'd finished hanging them?' said Wolff.

'Twelve fifty-three,' said Schiedlausky. 'That was the final time of death.'

'Far too late. Such a waste,' said Wolff.

I produced my deck of cards, and both men watched as I slid them from their box and tapped them on the table. I watched my hands too, cutting the cards again and again, cutting and shuffling, cutting and shuffling, and I blocked out the noise of the other tables of men talking and laughing, and listened only to the shushing of the cards.

Wolff took a few more gulps of beer and said, 'Deal them, then. It's been a long day. Look at the state of poor Schiedlausky.' He jabbed a finger at him. 'He'll have to go and talk to his hypnotist again.'

'He's a respected physician,' said Schiedlausky.

'He's a Jew,' said Wolff.

'Well, a Catholic Jew.'

'Even worse.'

I kept my eyes on my cards. I had a decent hand: jack of spades, jack of hearts . . .

'Do you ever have bad dreams, Hahn?' said Wolff.

'Not that I remember,' I said.

'Schiedlausky here has bad dreams,' he said, 'so he scuttles off and tells them to one of the inmates, would you believe.'

'He's a respected physician,' Schiedlausky repeated. 'Chief doctor in the Little Camp.'

'I know the one you mean,' I said. 'He's always trying to get more supplies.'

'Yes, exactly,' said Schiedlausky. 'He takes pride in his work – treats patients according to their racial value. And he has his own room. A three-piece suit.'

'He's still a Jew,' said Wolff.

'I suffer from insomnia, Hahn, that's all,' said Schiedlausky. 'This man – a very experienced psychiatrist who can count Sigmund Freud among his associates—'

'Another Jew,' said Wolff, who was slurring his words by now. 'God, my cards are shit. What do you have, Hahn?' He leaned across the table and tried to see my hand, but I pulled it in close.

'This Doktor Katzen-Ellenbogen—' Schiedlausky began again.

'Stupid fucking Jew name,' said Wolff. 'Like Hahn. Eh, boys?'

'This Doktor Katzen-Ellenbogen has been able to help me sleep,' said Schiedlausky. 'Quite a few of the officers have seen him. Gestapo as well as SS.' He lowered his voice. 'I heard that Dombeck went to him after punishing a prisoner for eating a carrot from the vegetable gardens. He'd just kept jumping on his chest until the ribs gave way, and he couldn't stop dreaming about it. Very unpleasant for him.'

'But he's Jewish?' I said. 'And treating Aryans?'

'Exactly,' said Wolff. 'It's a fucking disgrace, if you ask me. We should report them.'

'The man who has self-control and exercises it achieves the hardest and greatest of feats,' I said, but Wolff was busy draining his glass in one swallow. The Jews were a particular sore point for him since they'd started arriving in their thousands from Auschwitz – Hungarians and Poles, mostly. Mind you, the French and Belgians and Dutch were streaming in too, and it made no difference to my books whether they were Jews or not – it was still my duty to feed them, and as a matter of principle I didn't discriminate in terms of rations. That's important to put on the record. If they chose to refuse perfectly decent food because it wasn't kosher, well, they had only themselves to blame. Due to the summer heat many died on their way to us, unfortunately, and in order to identify the dead we even went to the trouble of having them photographed, and showing the pictures to their fellow transportees. Such examples of special care simply were not mentioned in the American trial, and nor was the fact that countless transports arrived at Buchenwald without any notice whatsoever. Most of them didn't stay long – we sent them on to work at the satellite camps, all with sufficient clothing as well as the correct rations for the trip, though of course delays due to Allied terror attacks were out of our control – but during the transit periods the Little Camp was bursting with them. Whenever possible, I put coffee and food at their disposal – whenever possible. Under the circumstances, I think you'll agree I did all I could to provide the necessities. I even bought . . .

[corrupted]

' . . . find your Jew doctor?' Schiedlausky asked me. 'With the – what was it? The miracle machine?'

Shut up, I thought. Shut *up*. I glanced at Wolff, who had let his cards drop to the table and was staring into the middle distance.

'No,' I said. 'I never did.'

It was almost one o'clock when I made my way home through the forest, the moon a scoop of light. Owls hooted from the shadows, and the trunks of the beeches were smooth grey columns, as sturdy as the stone holding up a church. I made sure I looked in on Greta; she opened her eyes when I kissed her forehead, though I had not meant to disturb her. But surely, wasn't it time I moved back into the master bedroom? Time we started trying for another child, now that she was better?

'I lost,' I said.

'Lost?' she murmured. 'Lost?'

'Nothing. Just a game.'

I went to the kitchen – I was hungry for something, though I couldn't say what. On the dresser the measuring cups shaped like geese stretched their necks towards the south, and the little iron weights sat in a pile on the scales. I spread some schmaltz on a slice of bread and ate it in the dark. *There now*, I heard my mother say. *That'll fill a hole.*

We all heard about what happened in the forest; some of us went there for a look, though they tried to keep us away. It was hard to secure a good spot with so many people from the villages there too. Frau Dornig pushed her way to the front, which was only right given the circumstances, and when the men told her it wasn't a sight for women she just went around the back and pushed her way through again. We had to admire her determination to see him get what he deserved. Shameful, she said, that such a thing should happen on our doorstep, and we knew that she meant the rape and not the hangings. That's what she insisted on calling it: a rape, and her niece a poor innocent girl, hardly more than a child. We didn't have the heart to take issue with her; she had no children of her own, and had always been close to Irma. You should have seen what they did to her, she said. In broad daylight on the village square, in front of everyone! Her beautiful hair . . . She didn't mention the sign they'd hung around her niece's neck, and we were too polite to bring it up, but we all knew what it said: *I Have Defiled My Race*. Poor Frau Dornig. People will forget about it in time, we told her, though privately we knew that such a stain on the family name was permanent. *I Have Defiled My Race*. Nobody was going to forget that.

Frankfurt am Main, September 1946

Though my work in the photo department saved no lives, still it offered a kind of comfort: one day, I thought, when the war was over, even if there were no prisoners left to speak, the thousands of pictures we'd developed would tell the story of what happened at Buchenwald. It amazed me, the way the SS documented their crimes – the executions, the experiments. The men burned to the bone with phosphorus to see how they reacted to treatment. The men deliberately infected with typhus, serving as hosts to keep the germs alive. The men fed poisoned food to determine the fatal dose. The men shot while attempting to escape. The men hung by their wrists until their tendons tore, the men twisted on the electrified fence. As if these crimes were not crimes at all. And always, ringing through the walls of our building, the men being interrogated by the Gestapo.

One day in June, Foucher managed to get his hands on a rudimentary camera. He stole two rolls of film from the stock that the SS bought for their weekend snaps, and on a Sunday afternoon a small group of us went for a walk around the compound. Although we were permitted to speak only German in the presence of the SS, on Sundays you could hear half a dozen different languages within a few paces: Spanish, Italian, French, Hungarian, Russian, Polish. We passed one of the most powerful prisoners in the camp, who sported a beautifully cut suit and an unshorn head and led a Doberman on a leash. We passed a man wearing a target painted on his chest.

I saw our colleague Beltz from the photo department too – the calligrapher who decorated albums for the SS. He was walking with Josef, the Hahns' servant, and two more Jehovah's Witnesses, murmuring about the Day of Vengeance, when God would destroy all human governments. The radio shouted at us through the loudspeaker – Goebbels, I think, making sure we knew that victory was at hand. Then an aria started up: 'Come, Hope', from Beethoven's *Fidelio*, the gentle call of the horns announcing the soprano, and I wanted it to be Lotte Lehmann, the same as my old gramophone record, though I knew it wasn't possible: they had banned her. Foucher wrapped the camera in newspaper and tore a small hole for the lens, and he took eight shots of the camp while we kept lookout, and then eight more. Apart from the guards in the watchtowers, there were no SS around on a Sunday – but plenty of prisoners were only too eager to do their duty, reporting offences in exchange for a few cigarettes or a bit of bread, a pat of margarine. Foucher took pictures of the mustering ground, the brothel, the Little Camp infirmary, the latrines, the prisoners lying on the sunny strip of grass opposite the smoking crematorium, the Goethe oak – parched and leafless even in June – and if we noticed anyone looking at him too closely, we started an argument among ourselves to detract attention. Now and then a chilly breeze caught at us, despite the sun.

We didn't dare develop the film; Foucher hid the rolls in a tin that he kept under the floorboards of our block. I glimpsed other photographs in there too, and when I asked him what they were he studied my face for a few seconds.

'Duplicates,' he said at last. 'I printed an extra copy, for after the war.' A Russian with a bullet in his head. A barrowload of the naked dead, numbers already inked on their foreheads to speed things up at the crematorium.

'Put them away. Put them away!' I said.

Foucher thought I'd heard someone coming, and he

scrambled to hide the tin – but in fact, Lotte, I just didn't want to see it – didn't want to know about it. I remembered what he'd told me about Opitz, the former kapo: how the SS had found the execution negatives hidden behind the portrait he'd framed for his wife. For weeks afterwards I avoided crossing that section of the floor; I couldn't shake the feeling that the boards would collapse under me.

And then I was discovered. Beltz, the calligrapher, had made me an album for my dud photographs – just scraps tied together with string, and no need for his hand-lettered captions. I kept it on my work-table, this little book of mistakes, of moments that nobody wanted, and when I was alone I liked to look through its pages. I was busy mounting my latest picture in it – the corner of a ceiling – when one of the SS overseers appeared.

'What do you have there?' he said.

Before I could answer, he grabbed it from me and flicked through it, snorting. 'Not much of a family album.' He stopped at a photograph of a blurry booted foot. 'Who is this?' he said.

'I . . . I don't know, Herr Scharführer.'

'But it's clearly an SS man.'

'I don't know who it is, Herr Scharführer.'

'It's a very strange thing, to keep a picture of an SS man's foot. And all these others. What are they for?'

'They're just mistakes, Herr Scharführer.'

'Mistakes? Mistakes?'

'They're nothing. I don't know.'

'There's a cell in the Bunker for those who steal the property of the Reich,' he said. 'A death sentence, if you're lucky.'

He was shouting now, and I closed my eyes and waited for what was coming – and then I heard Foucher's voice.

'It's a sort of training manual, Herr Scharführer. Just something we put together so we can all become better at our jobs.'

The SS man turned to look at him.

'May I?' said Foucher. 'You see, Herr Scharführer, the one with the boot is underexposed – there's no detail in the shadows – while here it's the opposite problem, and the whites are burnt out. In this one the developer needed replacing, so the headshot appears very muddy, with no contrast. And here the negatives mustn't have dried evenly, so you can see water streaks—'

'Yes yes, all right,' he said. 'Get back to work, the pair of you.'

'What were you thinking?' hissed Foucher after he had gone. 'We could have been done for – Beltz too.'

'I didn't know I was doing anything wrong. They were just duds.'

'You still don't understand how this place works, do you?' he said.

In July, after we heard of Claus von Stauffenberg's attempt on Hitler's life, the men in my block could hardly contain themselves. His own officers, turning on him! Makovec, my bunkmate, produced some food he'd received from home and invited a dozen of us to sit down to a feast. I was grateful to be included; I knew – everyone knew – that Makovec had chosen the others because of their potential value to him. Our block senior Voss, of course. The barracks orderlies who served our meals and could ensure their favourites got the thickest portion of soup, taken from the bottom of the kettle, and a share of any surplus. An Austrian man who worked in the labour administration office – useful if Makovec's name ever turned up on a transport list. I pass no judgement on such strategy, Lotte, and while other thin men looked on from the shadows, we feasted on one slice of black bread, one spoon of jam and one piece of cheese each. Perhaps Hitler was dead, we said – perhaps they were simply withholding the truth as long as they could – but just as with the D-Day landings, Voss warned us not to let our guard down. And then the SS played it over the loudspeaker so we could hear it for ourselves: the Führer assuring Germany he had survived. His voice filled the mustering ground, forced itself inside the barracks; it set the barbed wire singing. The man could not die, it seemed.

On I went, developing pictures for the SS. A woman stroking a dog. A girl with a bow in her hair, sitting on her father's lap. Portions of tattooed skin, excised and tanned into parchment. A prisoner shot through the back of the head. A cake beneath a banner that read *Good Luck, Gabriela!* Men dressed as sailors and men dressed as women, dancing on a stage. Another prisoner shot through the back of the head. Men swimming at some unknowable beach, having a grand time, pushing each other under. One day, Foucher murmured, these will be their undoing. And I nodded.

And yet. Somewhere in the ruins of the Holy Spirit, I imagined – perhaps still in my former office, if it hadn't been destroyed, or in an unburned carton in the cellar – was a collection of other images: X-rays of cancerous bones, of tumours lodged in lungs, documented before I began the trial of the Vitaliser and then three months, six months and twelve months after, if the patients lived that long. Photographs, too, of distended abdomens and growths on necks and fingers and legs – and yes, post-mortem shots of diseased livers, bowels and brains. Some patients were part of the control group – have I mentioned the control group? The ones who received no treatment with the machine at all, just like the untreated geraniums? Every proper experiment demands such a cohort, and at the time it wasn't difficult for me to separate the patients out; if I was treating a metastatic adenocarcinoma, I simply matched it as best I could with a similar example in a subject of similar age, and that subject received no treatment with the Vitaliser. However, I failed to correct for belief – the control group should have received treatment from a dummy machine, so that all patients thought they had the same chance of cure. I don't know why I overlooked this; in my rush to prove the

Vitaliser's worth, I ignored the accepted conventions of science. I ignored my duty. It was an embarrassing error, and something my detractors delighted in pointing out. *Was it not possible*, they bellowed, *that sheer faith in Doktor Weber's ridiculous wooden box might explain the two survivors? That sometimes, in persons of a gullible disposition, faith can trump a tumour?* I can still quote those lines from memory, while others are lost to me – the daily conversations I had with Anna about the books we were reading, or the holidays we might take, or the school you would attend, Lotte. Only shadows remain; the broadest of shapes. Most of the words have fluttered from me like moths, gone, gone. Now why is that?

Perhaps, if the machine really had worked, I might have felt something more than a passing regret for those who received no treatment, but disregarding the two who survived for a time – and we must, since they are statistically insignificant – both groups died at the same rate. You could see the tumours spreading on the films, flakes of ash in the lungs, holes in the bones, mistakes I could not fix. I filed them away when I knew there would be no second trial of my machine. I didn't want to look at them – not because they showed how quickly death can grow inside a person, how little control we have, but because they showed the failure of my grand idea. That was a kind of death too – so I thought at the time. Now I would give anything to be that gloomy young man again, climbing the stairs to the attic to pack my machine away, Anna standing at the bottom and calling to me – what did she say? Something comforting, I think. *This is a small setback.* No, that doesn't sound like her; the voice is more mine than hers. *Never mind, Lenard – you'll have other brilliant ideas.* Perhaps. Perhaps she said something like that.

Or perhaps she simply told me to be careful not to bump my head.

One day I developed some pictures taken in a forest clearing: a group of SS men assembling a piece of wooden equipment, surrounded by spindly pines. They set up two posts first, as if they might be about to play a game of soccer. Then they fixed a crossbeam in place, and then, at one end, a flight of wooden steps – and I saw it was a gallows. Next came the condemned men in their striped uniforms, hands roped behind their backs, and one man in a dirty overcoat. Past the bones of the trees they walked, past the SS who stood chatting and looking at their watches. One prisoner stared straight at the camera with a puzzled frown. I could make out the weave of his jacket, the P for Pole on his breast, the stubble on his jaw, as if I were right there with him in the dappled clearing, close enough to touch his face. And in the background an audience of Polish workers, and an SS man watching them, his back to the camera, and other people peering through the trees, people in ordinary clothes. I'd heard about this action – twelve Polish inmates pulled from the camp, though they'd done nothing wrong. Hanged one by one, and then the final hanging of a Polish worker who'd gone for a walk in the forest with a German woman. They strung him up slowly; I heard he took six minutes to die. And yes, here were the pictures, the documentation. The camp doctor feeling for a pulse. I smelled the sap in the air, felt the dead needles slipping underfoot. And were my hands tied behind my back, the rope cutting off the blood? Or was I standing to one side, glancing at my watch, wondering if we'd be back in time for lunch? Or looking through the trees, jostling for a place?

I plucked the pictures from the developer and slid them into the stop bath and the fixer, then washed them and hung them up to dry, and then I began on the next set of negatives, and the next, and so the days passed. I took some more photographs of the Hahns – Karl-Heinz digging in the garden while his mother rested on a seagrass chair; Karl-Heinz playing with a toy butcher's shop; the whole family pretending to eat a wedding-anniversary cake – and Beltz began to decorate an album for them: *Our Time at Buchenwald*, the hand-painted lettering garlanded with beech twigs. I went to a concert in the cinema hall and listened to groups of prisoners singing Bavarian folksongs and Yugoslavian folksongs, and the orchestra performed forbidden works under false names, and the SS clapped and clapped. I went to illegal concerts in the blocks, too, on Sunday afternoons, when prisoners read from books of poetry, or played tunes on instruments conjured from thin air. In the canteen I saw a performance of *Twelfth Night*, the prisoner actors wearing costumes made from dyed bedsheets and Auschwitz rags, and wigs made from shorn hair. And every two weeks I put on the jacket of the man who had seen *The Merchant of Venice* at the Burgtheater in Vienna, and then I reported to the gate with my pass, clicked my heels and yelled my number at the regulation distance of three metres, and a guard walked me over to the villas on Eickeweg so I could treat Greta Hahn. I told myself I wasn't harming her – not *harming* her, as such; not neglecting my duty. The treatment wouldn't make her condition any worse; it wouldn't cause her to die any faster. I pretended I didn't see the rosary beads she scrambled to put away when I entered the bedroom, and I gave her the elixir to help her feel better, and then I started the machine. I was simply offering her a little hope – a little comfort. We find them where we can.

And it began to seem to me, Lotte, there in that unreal place, that there might be something to the Vitaliser after all. Perhaps it was not a coincidence, simple random chance, that Frau Hahn was improving. Her lumbar and pelvic pain had disappeared – and more astonishing, so had the growth on her remaining ovary. Hadn't it? When I palpated the area I thought I could not feel anything, and I found no evidence of abdominal swelling. This wasn't the course her particular cancer usually took; it placed her well outside the norm, beyond the bell curve, in the white uncharted space of miracles. And that is how I began to think of Greta Hahn: as a miracle, my second miracle.

Naturally, the only way to check the disease hadn't spread to her bones was with X-rays, but I wasn't about to risk something that might prove my treatment a failure – you can understand that, can't you? And if she survived – if she really was my second miracle – then mightn't another trial be possible? A bigger one, with several machines, and a whole team of specially trained operators at my disposal? And Anna waiting for me every night when I came home, and you, Lotte, just down the hallway in the parlour, playing my father's piano? I could teach you how to swim and how to waltz. These were the thoughts I had, in my more hopeful moments – but there were other moments, too. If Frau Hahn survived, her husband would have no further use for me; no reason to keep me alive, or you and Anna. He told me that you were both still in Theresienstadt and both still very well, and he made sure you received decent rations. But once his wife was cured, why would he bother any more? And why would he risk saving a part-Jew who might let slip he had treated his wife? I knew the war was on the turn – from the men who listened to the secret radios, the news circulated through the compound: the Allies had captured Florence, Paris could not hold, the Soviets had liberated the camp at Lublin, the SS had tried to destroy it before they fled but the gas chambers wouldn't burn. How much longer? How much longer? In our blocks we talked about it as much as we once had talked about food, though we could never answer it; the question was as vast as our hunger, the rumours metastatic. And while we longed for the end, we also feared it: when the Allies were close enough, we believed, the SS would raze the camp, wipe the Ettersberg clean of their crimes.

On the day the bombers came, then, that was my first thought: *The Germans are destroying the place.* I had just finished treating Frau Hahn with the Vitaliser, and I told her I was pleased with the way she was responding.

'We need to keep up the regimen for a while longer yet, though,' I said.

'But I'm feeling so well. Whatever it was – a cyst, or something else –' she glanced at me '– it's gone.'

'All the same, I need to be cautious,' I said, and held her gaze. 'Given my situation. You understand.'

Something in her expression changed, and she said yes, yes of course she understood.

When I'd packed away the machine she said she would accompany me downstairs, and as we passed Karl-Heinz's room I could see him playing with his trains: *takataka, takataka.* His carved animals lay in a pile at the side of the tracks, and he picked them up one by one and said, 'You can come, and you. But not you. You've been too naughty.' Then the front door opened and Hahn called, 'Hello hello! Where's my best boy? Are you home?' and Karl-Heinz raced past us and down the stairs to his father, yelling, 'Papa! Papa's back!'

You used to greet me like that, Lotte – anyone would have thought I'd been gone for months, the way you flung yourself at me, wrapping your arms around my legs and refusing to let go. Anna said it wasn't fair that she was the one who stayed home with you every day, reading books to you, dressing and undressing your dolls, wiping the stewed apple from your hands and your hair, yet I was always the hero.

'She loves you too,' I told her. 'She adores you. Look how she copies everything you do.'

Perhaps even then, Lotte, you could see how you mirrored your mother; you had her soft dark curls, her big dark eyes. Sometimes, when I watched you scolding our cat or trying to buckle your shoes, covering your ears when we told you they were on the wrong feet, I had the feeling I was seeing Anna as a child. And I could pretend that we'd always known each other, your mother and I; that our time together reached back further than memory. And that, I now know, was a kind of miracle too.

Downstairs, Hahn was saying, 'Show me your hands,' and Karl-Heinz was holding up his palms for inspection. 'Absolutely filthy!' said Hahn. 'Mama, have you seen these hands?' He took him away to wash them – and then the sirens sounded.

PART SEVEN
THE FRUITS ARE RIPE, DIPPED IN FIRE

It got to the point that the population up on the hill threatened to outnumber the population down in Weimar. We thought the camp would keep the prisoners contained, but more and more often we couldn't go about our business without having to watch them labouring on our roads and on our building sites, shovelling our snow, clearing away the debris after the attack on our armaments works and our train station, not to mention arriving dead-eyed and stinking at our freight depot. And although we'd been told that the camp would re-educate them, mould them into useful members of society, we began to realise that most weren't even German. Over on Cranachstraße a team of them dismantled our wrecked aeroplanes; it was impossible to see anything from the street, but Fräulein Gräber refused to walk past the place. We understood her reasons: she had taken up with a very nice man who'd begun his training up the hill, but after only a few weeks he'd requested an immediate transfer to the Luftwaffe. He had to get away, he said.

Some of us employed in the factories were forced to sit alongside them, and although we kept ourselves to ourselves as much as humanly possible, it was easy to see they took no pride in their allotted tasks. Herr Forst, who supervised hundreds of them at the armaments works, making sure they carried out their duties to an acceptable standard and did not try to commit acts of sabotage, said you just had to get used to it; we were at war. And besides, he'd arranged for some of the prisoners to make him a toy wheelbarrow for his son, and an electric hot-plate for his wife – it was just the thing for frying his sausages.

'I hope you're not buying your meat from Geier's,' said Frau Kappel, and we laughed; the SS had reprimanded the butchery for selling spoiled wurst to the camp.

'What else was I supposed to do with it?' said Herr Geier. 'I let them have it for half-price. It was perfectly good enough for criminals.'

'The SS?' said Herr Forst.

'The *inmates*,' said Herr Geier.

In preparation for his supervisory role, Herr Forst had taken part in a group tour of the Gustloff Works up the hill. He'd seen the efficiency reports: the details of each prisoner's output expressed as a percentage of that of a regular worker, and any transgressions noted, such as conversing on the job or failing to perform errands at double time. He'd even met a civilian overseer – a man from Hottelstedt who saluted the group as if he were a general. And after the tour, he said, the director offered them a look inside the fence, and he telephoned the Kommandant, and the Kommandant met them at the gate. 'He asked us what we wanted to see first in his model camp, and to a man we said the crematorium. I thought we might find evidence of gassings – you hear of such things – but there was nothing of that nature there, nothing at all.'

'Nothing?' said Frau Andrecht.

'Nothing,' said Herr Forst. The Kommandant led them past the prisoners' barracks, and they were allowed to go inside if they wished, and it was clean and decent with neatly made bunks, just like the barracks from Herr Forst's soldier days. They could speak to the prisoners, and most of them were there because they were communists or conscientious objectors. Only a few of them wore the green triangle of the true criminal.

'They knew you were coming, of course,' said Herr Bittermann.

'I know what I saw,' said Herr Forst.

'Well, I refuse to drive there any more,' said Herr Noth. 'On principle.' The place was a source of irritation for him; too often lately he'd been summoned to drive this or that SS personage into Weimar in his taxi, only to find that they'd made their own way down the hill before he arrived.

'And the kitchens!' Herr Forst went on. Spotless and sparkling, and a canteen full of healthy, sustaining goods that the inmates could buy. Hungarian salami, sardines in oil, cheese, ham . . . goods that were hard to come by in Weimar, unless you had the right contacts. They finished their tour in the Kommandant's headquarters with a glass of French cognac each, he said, and they all remarked on the scandalous discrepancy between the enemy propaganda and the facts.

Herr Bittermann snorted, but Herr Gräber also confirmed the decency of the camp; he had visited several times to check the sewerage system, because we didn't want a repeat of the 1939 epidemic.

'The place looked all right to me,' said Fräulein Fleischer, who'd had a perfect view of it when she took her pupils to a farm on the plain to hunt for potato beetles. 'Horrible creatures,' she shuddered, 'but the children were proud to do their duty.'

And Herr Kolbe, whose delivery company, we knew, transported coal and straw and noodles and all manner of goods up the hill, said he couldn't complain; he'd rented some Russians to help with the loading and unloading of his trucks, now that so many of our own men were away. They cost only two Reichsmarks per prisoner per day, which was a cheaper rate than the camp charged for other nationalities, on account of their poorer condition; we often saw them limping along with their frostbite and their rags.

'I wondered,' began Frau Dreher. 'I wondered . . . whether we might not give them some warmer clothes. Some better shoes.'

There was silence for a moment, and then we agreed that such an action would not be tolerated. Hadn't they sent Herr Anders up the hill for less? And the elderly Herr Behr, too, following the attempt on the Führer's life, because he was a Social Democrat?

'We all do our duty,' said Herr Lenz. 'We need to look after our own.' And certainly, he set an example with his generosity – the previous Christmas his firm had donated a great quantity of wood to our Hitler Youth girls so they could make toys for less fortunate children. The little dolls' cradles painted with edelweiss! And the Messerschmitts looking so real! How proud we had been to see our daughters' work on show in the house of Charlotte von Stein.

'Still,' continued Frau Dreher, who had the kindest nature but sometimes missed the point, 'a few of them displayed quite severe wounds – one had a gash on his leg that by rights needed stitches, for instance.'

We reassured her that this was simply proof they were unruly criminals, Bolshevik sub-humans who couldn't resist violent dust-ups amongst themselves. It was proof they were in the right place.

'Weimar?' said Frau Dreher.

'The camp,' we said.

'They're sitting pretty, really,' said Herr Forst. 'Food and shelter, and a job to keep them busy. It's more than they deserve.'

'There's nothing to the rumours, then?' said Frau Dreher.

'Rumours?' we said.

'The beatings and the torture. The starvation. The executions.'

'Well,' we said, 'is there ever anything in the newspaper about that?'

'No,' she said.

'And I saw no evidence of gassings, did I?' said Herr Forst.

'No,' she said.

'There you are then, you see?'

Herr Wieck pointed out that the camp doctor was a frequent visitor to his restaurant – they shared a love of the Schwarzwald mountains, they'd discovered, and often chatted about trips they had made to that part of the Reich.

And Herr Krell, who supplied the camp with potatoes – he made two deliveries a day in the autumn and winter months – said they were perfectly pleasant to him, and business had never been so good.

'I always stop for a drink with them when I deliver their beer,' said Herr Nadler.

'They're very nice to me too,' piped up Fräulein Staub, who worked as a secretary to one of the officers up the hill, within sight of the compound itself. 'Just ordinary people.'

We knew that neither she nor Herr Nadler nor Herr Krell nor Herr Wieck could say much more than that, but we were grateful to them for dispelling Frau Dreher's rumours before they gathered momentum.

When the bombers came in August we thought they were coming for us, but soon enough we realised it was the camp they wanted – the factories next to the camp. At first we were relieved, until Herr Forst pointed out that they might destroy the electrified fence – blow the whole thing open. That would be far more serious than the occasional escapee we saw the authorities rounding up. With nothing to contain them, the prisoners would flood out to rob us and rape us. We knew we would not sleep that night.

FROM THE IMAGINARY DIARY OF FRAU GRETA HAHN

August 1944

We didn't expect the attack – there were plenty of alarms, yes, but the planes were always heading somewhere else. Karl-Heinz and I both hated the shelter that burrowed under the forest on the other side of Eickeweg, built specially for the SS families. Narrow and white and cold, and wet with condensed breaths, the walls of the T-shaped passageway curved like the inside of a bone. Sometimes we didn't bother leaving the villa, we just took shelter in the cellar – and when the sirens sounded that day I was sure it would be another false alarm. It was shortly past twelve – a beautiful, clear afternoon – and I had just finished my appointment with Doktor Weber. He was pleased with my progress, I could tell, and I said I imagined we'd be able to stop the treatment soon, but he explained that it was important to keep it up for some time yet by way of maintenance. He needed to be careful, he said, and I think he meant for his own sake as much as mine.

I was seeing him to the door, and Josef was bringing lunch to the dining table, and Dietrich and Karl-Heinz were washing their hands – don't forget your thumbs, I could hear Dietrich saying – when the sirens started screaming. We thought we had plenty of time. I said to Josef that he should cover the food to keep it hot, and I told Karl-Heinz to find a book to take with him. We would all go across the road to the shelter, Dietrich said, and Doktor Weber and the guard would return to the camp. But in a matter of moments we heard the planes approaching, coming closer and closer, and Doktor Weber was hesitating by the front door, looking out at the sky, and I said, 'What is it?' And then I looked out too, and I saw them: the planes flying in perfect formation, and a puff of smoke descending like a single cloud in the blue sky. I said, 'Dietrich, do we have time?' but he didn't reply.

'You'll have to come down to the cellar with us,' I said to Doktor Weber.

'What's that?' said Dietrich.

'I said Doktor Weber will have to come downstairs with us.'

'I did my thumbs too,' said Karl-Heinz. 'See, Mama?'

'That's against the rules,' said Dietrich. 'He must return to the camp. The guard will take him.'

'Mama,' said Karl-Heinz, louder now, 'I didn't forget my thumbs. They're nice and clean.'

'Good, good,' I said. I knew there were no shelters for the prisoners inside the fence. Up until now it hadn't mattered, but the planes were right above us; I'd never seen anything like it, not so close to home. I had to shout over the noise. 'And what happens . . . ' I started to ask, but I saw Karl-Heinz staring out the front door, his eyes huge and white, his fingers in his ears.

I pulled the door shut, then strode over to Dietrich and said right in his ear, 'And what happens if my doctor is killed?'

'They'll never bomb the camp,' he said.

'They're right overhead, Dietrich,' I hissed. Why could he not understand that? Could he not hear how close they were? And besides, Doktor Weber had been treating me in secret for months, right here in our house: the rules were well and truly broken.

'I'm very pleased you remembered your thumbs,' I said to Karl-Heinz, and I ushered him down the cellar stairs with Josef. 'Herr Doktor?'

He and the guard paused for a moment, glanced at Dietrich, then came down the stairs too.

In the cellar all the preserves were rattling, shifting on their shelves. A jar of cherries inched its way to the edge, and I could see it happening, and I could see what was about to happen, but I didn't lift my arm to point, didn't bother to say anything. What did it matter if it fell? We must have had dozens of jars; we'd never eat them all. *The fruits are ripe, dipped in fire . . .* They caught the light like stained glass in some dark church, and I saw Doktor Weber run his eye over them, taking in the story they told, and the cherries crept closer to the edge, closer and closer, and when they fell, as I knew they must, I was the only one who didn't jump.

'Is there a ghost?' said Karl-Heinz in a small voice.

'Don't be silly,' said Dietrich. 'It's the aeroplanes. The vibrations.'

And I felt something in me shaking, shifting closer to an edge. I closed my eyes, breathed in and out, in and out. I could smell the cherries, tart and sweet at the same time, and the dirt that clung to the carrots and potatoes, and I was wearing a filmy summer dress and sitting on the terrace, and Erna, our maid from home, brought me a plate of cherries with whipped cream, and I wanted to ask her if everything was all right in Munich, if everything was still there waiting for us under the dust sheets, our couches and our beds and our mirrors, our crystal chandelier – but she was already gone. I ate the cherries one by one with a little silver spoon, its handle cast in the shape of an apostle, though I couldn't tell which. Peter, with his key? Or John, with his cup of sorrow? I squashed each cherry against the roof of my mouth; I hardly needed to chew. The Ettersberg sloped away at my feet, falling all the way to Weimar. Where was the church, with its carved confessionals full of whispers, its women to replace the dead flowers? Where was the rose window, its bright heart shining with the holy face of Jesus? I was too far away.

'Not too close,' someone said. 'It could all come down on top of you.' Dietrich; it was Dietrich.

Karl-Heinz was over by the wall of preserves, crouching down to look at the smashed cherries. Behind him the jars were juddering. 'Just the aeroplanes?' he said.

'Of course,' said Dietrich.

'Maybe it's Ingo,' I said. I don't know why; the name just popped into my mind.

'It could be!' said Karl-Heinz. 'He likes playing down here.'

'I don't think we want Ingo back, do we?' said Dietrich, but it was too late – he was there in the cellar with us, this other little boy, hiding in the shadows, shaking the shelves. Breaking things.

'Come over here,' I said. 'You'll cut yourself.' I wanted to go and guide him away from the glass, but all of a sudden I felt too tired to stand; I didn't have the breath for it. 'You'll cut yourself,' I said again.

'Then Doktor Weber can fix me,' said Karl-Heinz.

'Come over here. Sit with me.' I patted the empty seat. 'Now, what does Ingo look like?'

Karl-Heinz settled into my side. 'He's a bit like me,' he said, 'but smaller. He doesn't eat his carrots. He doesn't wash his thumbs.'

We heard a great whistling, loud enough to mask the sound of the engines, and it jangled my teeth and my bones, and then the explosions started. And they were very close.

26 October 1954

[tape corrupted in places]

I'd begun taking cash from Greta's purse. That sounds like a confession, but I wasn't stealing – I'd earned the money myself, after all, and it was just something I did now and then, so I had enough to see me through my evenings at the skat table. Greta was in the habit of leaving her handbag downstairs in the entranceway, and it was easy for me to borrow five Reichsmarks, ten Reichsmarks; I replaced the money once I'd won it back, most of the time, and she never knew. But the rubbish women keep! I found myself sorting through all the pockets and pleats in her bag, all the dark compartments zipped shut, pushing aside old cinema tickets, crumpled handkerchiefs, receipts from Weimar coffee houses, a hat pin that scratched across my knuckle, a small white pebble veined with grey, the stub of a pencil, a folding comb, a broken shoe buckle, an unwrapped sweet, a tiny mirror with an embroidered back. No value to any of it.

I remember that the day before the attack I'd meant to visit the bank, only I ran out of time, so I slipped two five-Reichsmark notes from Greta's purse. I think Niemand saw me, but I didn't care: I was in my own house. And in any case, over the course of the evening I won almost five hundred Reichsmarks; I could do no wrong. Never mind the mopers slouched over their drinks at the prospect of Paris falling, and never mind the arrival into protective custody of dozens of Allied secret agents as well as over a hundred enemy airmen – we'd worry about what to do with them later. On my way back to the villa I lingered on the forest path. It was a calm, clear summer night, and I was not far from home, and my wife, my lovely Greta, who no longer showed any sign of the disease, waited for me just through the trees. I filled my lungs with the scent of moss and leaves and cool dark earth. I could make out the dead branches tidied into stacks, ready to be taken away and burned. I would have to return to my carving, I thought; it had been too long since I had felt the simple shape of the thing held within the wood. Perhaps I would make Karl-Heinz his ark, and I'd arrange something special for Greta too: a bangle, perhaps, like the one she often admired on Emmi Wolff's wrist. Goodness knows, I had the gold for a hundred bangles.

There's something else I remember clearly about that night: I was just about to resume my walk home when I noticed, on the path ahead of me, one of the fat snails you find on the Ettersberg, bigger than any I'd seen in our windowboxes in Munich. Those I used to peel from the geraniums and pitch down into the courtyard so I could hear them smash on the cobblestones, and I'd taught Karl-Heinz to do the same. I picked it up and held it on my palm, felt its damp muscular foot working against my skin. A miracle I hadn't stepped on it. The stalks of its eyes shifted in my direction, and I wondered if it could see me. When I tapped a finger to them they shrank from my touch, and then it tucked its head away too. I traced the coil of the shell: such a pretty thing, patterned light and dark, like the grain of some exotic fruitwood. I carried it a little way into the trees and placed it in the shelter of some roots.

After the attack, as soon as the all-clear sounded, I told everyone to wait in the cellar while I checked the house. I didn't know how bad it was, but I knew there must be some damage.

'What do you think has happened?' said Greta.

'Nothing, nothing,' I said. 'I'll just make sure.'

I thought I could smell burning, though everything seemed fine as far as I could see. The picture of the breaking waves hung crooked, and two dining chairs had backed away from the table where our lunch still waited for us – nothing more. Upstairs, also, appeared all but untouched. In the spare bedroom, only my hairbrush had fallen to the floor, too many strands of my hair caught in its bristles, and my chocolate box was still in place in the writing desk. Karl-Heinz had cleared his trains from the tracks, I noticed, and replaced them with his carved animals. He'd set them marching along like carriages, nose to tail, all the way up to the bend, and there he'd built some of the smaller animals into a bridge so the bigger ones could walk across their backs. I was pleased he was having fun with them.

As I made my way to the master bedroom the smell of burning grew stronger and stronger, but again, I could find no damage. The doors to the balcony were open, and the air beyond them hazy with smoke – and when I stepped outside I couldn't even see the forest. My eyes and throat stung, and shouts came from the direction of the Wolffs' villa next door. I ran downstairs and into the garden, where silvery strips of foil covered the ground, eddying around my feet as I checked our villa from every side. More shouts from next door, filtering through the trees and the smoke. I knew I should go and see if I could help, and I would, I would, just as soon as I'd made sure our own house was all right. Sparks glided through the air like fireflies, and ashy fragments drifted past, alighting on my arms and legs before fluttering away again. I heard a window explode next door, and then another – yes, definitely the Wolffs' windows and not ours. It seemed we had been spared. And then, rounding the corner, I saw that our roof had a hole in it – an area where the tiles were missing, perhaps only two metres square, but directly above our bed. Far too close.

I ran back inside and checked the ceiling: nothing had

caught, nothing had found its way inside. You couldn't tell anything was wrong. Then I headed next door.

The Wolffs' villa was listing like a sinking ship, the roof torn off, the front wall blown to splinters, and the whole upper storey on fire. For a moment I stood on the cratered street, blinking as if I had just risen from our bed. The smoke scraped at the back of my throat. I felt a terrible heat rush against my face, and I remembered visiting my father at the bakery when I was a boy, and the shove of hot air when he opened the ovens.

I heard Wolff calling for me: 'Hahn! Hahn! Come here!'

He crouched in the remains of their dining room, coughing, trying to shift a pile of shattered planks, and when I ran up their front steps I saw Emmi lying face down in the wreckage, her hair and her arms and the exposed back of her neck white with plaster dust. The shorn-off timber covered her lower half, and a joint of meat sat next to her, slipped from its platter, the juices soaking into the carpet. I don't know why I remember that. Wolff and I grabbed at the pieces of wood and threw them aside, and he kept shouting at me even though I was right beside him. A bump like a plum had formed above his eye, and his temple was bleeding. He'd told Emmi to go to the shelter, he said, but they never listened, did they?

'Where are the children?' I said. He didn't answer me. I blinked against the smoke, tried not to take it in.

'We're meant to be going to the theatre tonight. Her idea,' he shouted.

In the storey above us, something collapsed.

'Wolff, the children?' I asked again. 'Are they all right?'

Again he didn't answer me, and when I grabbed his arm and spoke to him once more, he frowned at the movement of my lips.

'What?' he yelled in my face. 'What are you saying?'

'The *children*,' I mouthed.

'Frau Schmidt took them over to the shelter,' he shouted.

Somewhere nearby another window exploded. Wolff touched his fingers to the cut on his temple and stared at the blood and did not move. I had to push him towards the steps. Then I lifted Emmi and carried her out to Eickeweg and laid her down, gently, gently. But she was already dead.

'What's happened?' said Greta when I returned to the cellar. 'Why were you gone so long?'

'Not here,' I said, cocking my head at Karl-Heinz.

She asked if our house was all right, and I told her it was fine: just a few tiles missing from the roof. I could still feel the weight of Emmi Wolff, the dead swing of her arms, and I brushed the plaster dust from my chest.

'Oh, thank God,' she said. I'd been gone such a long time, and she'd been so worried, and it had all sounded so near.

She leaned on me to climb the stairs and had to stop halfway to catch her breath. It was just the shock, she said. She'd be all right. Weber was behind us, and I noticed him holding out his hands, as if she might fall. When he saw me . . .

[corrupted]

. . . to the camp. The guard had gone on ahead, and I walked with Weber; the place was in such chaos that nobody gave us a second glance. Debris littered Eickeweg: broken timber, burnt-out cars, whole uprooted trees, bits of garden furniture and bedsteads and things I couldn't identify. There were thousands of pieces of the silver foil, too, dropped by the enemy to throw off our radar, and pamphlets fluttered along the pavement and clogged the front gardens. I picked one up: Generalfeldmarschall Paulus was calling for an end to hostilities, citing our defeat at Stalingrad as proof we should give up. Well, he had shown his true colours when he surrendered to the Soviets and didn't even have the decency to commit suicide. No real German would listen to such a man.

The smoke turned the afternoon to dusk, and for a moment

I wondered how much time had passed. How long had we stayed in the cellar? We walked past the shattered SS garages, where flipped vehicles lay helpless on their backs, and came to the Gustloff Works, where hardly two bricks were left standing. All the machinery wrecked, forced into great twisted messes of steel, and mixed up with bodies and parts of bodies; I doubted anything could be salvaged. Even the stone eagle at the train station was broken, its beak shorn off. My building was mostly intact, but many in the camp command area were gone, including the political department where Weber worked on the photographs. Two secretaries, their faces smudged with soot and their hairpins falling out, sat crying in the rubble. Another woman dashed past with a stack of envelopes. Weber said nothing, but I felt the glee rippling off him.

We entered the camp through the eastern gate, and the men were still at their posts in the watchtowers, machine guns aimed. 'There you are,' I said to Weber. 'Business as usual.' That side of the compound was the worst affected, with the laundry and disinfection buildings on fire, and the wind spreading the flames to the tailor shop and shoe repair. Already I was adding up sums in my head, calculating how much it would cost to replace all the lost supplies: the soap, the blankets, the clothing, the towels, the delousing solution. And who knew what else had been lost? I had no idea how I would balance the books. A group of our men stood guard as prisoners dismantled the burning ruins so the fire would not spread. They worked with their bare hands, and I noticed two of them exchange a smile as they pulled down the slumped walls. I should have had them shot – I'm speaking figuratively – but up ahead we saw a great fiery mass, and at first we did not understand what it was, and then Weber said, 'The Goethe oak. They have hit the Goethe oak.' Even though it was burning in front of us, I could not believe it. Even when we went and stood so close that we could feel the flames and hear the fizzing of the sap; even when the smoke poured over us and into our eyes and mouths. No, I said. *No.* I would not allow it.

Later I returned home to find Felix Wolff playing marbles with Karl-Heinz.

'Now, Felix,' Greta said, 'you can have anything you like for supper. Josef will make you anything at all.'

He said he didn't know what he felt like.

'Anything,' said Greta.

He said he didn't know.

'You must be able to think of something,' she said. 'Pancakes. Fried potatoes.' Her voice began to catch.

'It doesn't matter,' I said. 'Niemand always makes delicious suppers.'

Greta wouldn't eat a single bite herself. She sat the boys down at the table by the window seat and watched them wolf down their slabs of ham and sausage, and didn't bother to remind them not to talk with their mouths full. 'I don't believe it. I just don't believe it,' she kept murmuring. Above us the antler chandelier cast its bony shadow on the ceiling. Felix was going to sleep at our house, Karl-Heinz told me, rolling a slice of cheese into a telescope and studying me through it. In fact, he said, maybe he could live with us forever, now that his mother was dead.

'They took her to the hospital,' said Felix. 'That's where they take sick people.'

'Oh, poor Emmi, poor poor Emmi,' Greta burst out.

'Darling,' I said sharply, and she collected herself and said, 'Pyjamas and teeth. Off you go.'

After the boys had disappeared she asked if I thought Emmi's death had been instant.

'Definitely,' I said.

I realised I was tapping my heels beneath the dining table, left then right, left then right. I couldn't stop, couldn't sit still.

Greta went to tuck the boys in, and then she went to bed herself; she was wrung out, she said.

I had to check on a few matters, I told her. See if anyone needed help.

There were only a few men at the officers' club, and no music played. I couldn't find anyone to join me in a hand of skat, but I shuffled the deck anyway, until I could hardly feel my thumbs, then drew random cards and tried to guess at them. I was wrong every time. Again my heels were tapping under the table: left, right, left, right. I ordered a schnapps and gulped it back. I could still taste smoke in my throat.

'Terrible thing,' said Schwartz, pulling up a chair. I didn't feel like talking to him, but already he was ordering me another schnapps and asking if my family was all right.

I said I thought they were, or at least they would be.

He nodded. 'Terrible thing,' he repeated, 'about Emmi. Do you know, do we know, if Wolff will stay on?'

'I imagine he will,' I said.

Schwartz seemed surprised. Wolff had his sympathy, really he did, but a loss like that was not to be underestimated.

'Didn't he call you an arsehole the other week?' I said.

He waved a hand: water under the bridge! But perhaps, he said, someone should mention to Wolff that it was his duty now to stand aside for a man better equipped to deal with the strains of the position.

I said I imagined Kommandant Pister would discuss it with him.

'Did you hear that his own wife and daughter were injured?' said Schwartz. 'Not badly,' he added. 'Still, though . . . it makes you think.'

Jack of clubs, I thought, and turned over a card. But I was wrong.

For days the attack was all anyone could talk about. I tried not to raise it at home, so as not to upset Greta, but the truth was, it had me rattled. Even the monkeys in the zoo had gone quiet, and Martin the bear hid in his concrete cave. I kept stumbling over bits of deformed and melted glass and rubber and metal, impossible to tell what they once had been. And the water supply was causing me more problems: the pipes had been hit in so many places that we had to lay an emergency line and bring in water in trucks, which I could ill afford. The Isolation Barracks just through the forest, which housed our most prominent prisoners, were totally destroyed and would have to be rebuilt at considerable expense. Rudolf Breitscheid, the Social Democrat, was killed outright, as was Ernst Thälmann, the leader of the German Communist Party – an unfortunate accident, but I can assure you that's all it was. The Italian princess, Mafalda von Hessen, who ran for the nearby shrapnel trench, was buried up to her neck in dirt; only her head remained free. It sat on the earth as if severed from her body and cried for help, and they had to dig her out and carry her to the brothel, because the SS hospital was already full, and the inmates' infirmary was overflowing with SS and prisoners alike. Schiedlausky amputated her wounded arm; the brothel whores had tended to it, and – little wonder – an infection set in. She died two days later, whether from blood loss or infection or clumsy surgery I do not know. Whichever, it was sure to reflect badly on us.

More importantly, though, the factories had suffered – not just the Gustloff Works but also the SS's own German Equipment Works; both would have to cease production, perhaps permanently. The raid on them sounded almost comical: prisoners running about in circles, skin alight, hair alight, trying to dodge the firebombs while trying to stay inside the sentry line as well. Those who did flee across it were shot by the guards – Ukrainian idiots who also shot at the German SS taking shelter in the forest with the prisoners. So much for our model camp. I should have been pleased, I suppose, that most of the bombs meant for the SS quarters hit the quarry instead; although several hundred head of prisoners were wasted, at least I wouldn't have to replace too many supplies in the casernes. Still, it affected morale; the men thought they were safe here, protected by the presence of the prisoners. Now everyone was on edge, running for the shrapnel trenches at the merest hint of a raid. And poor old Scharführer Rehbein was dragging himself about the place, and at the funeral of Emmi Wolff he could barely stand for weeping. It was indecent. He lost all ability to do his job, and quite frankly turned so soft that I judged him no longer worthy of his uniform. Soon afterwards, he was called up to the eastern front.

Then there was the question of Weber's job. We lost the entire photo department, and I knew I would have to think of some other position for him – something indoors, with little risk of injury or death. The storage warehouse? Darning socks? The solution came to me when I heard Schwartz saying that the inmates' index in the political department had gone up in flames too and would have to be reproduced card by card from their files. They'd need a whole team of prisoners, working day shifts and night shifts.

'I have just the man,' I said. 'A German. Very methodical. Very careful.'

That night I dreamt about the lost photo department; about all the valuable pictures fluttering into ashes. The feasts at the Bismarck Tower, the solstice bonfires, the amusing shows the men put on, when they dressed as women or Jews. The opening of the railway, when Reichsführer Himmler came to Buchenwald. After I woke I still couldn't quite believe they were gone; the loss felt too big to hold. I was grateful, at least, that I'd had the foresight to order a print of myself with the Reichsführer following his visit. He was shaking my hand, looking me in the eye and smiling, and although he'd moved on to the next man within seconds, you couldn't tell that from the picture; the photographer did well to catch it. There is another print – *was* another print – the very next one on the roll – in which the Reichsführer had turned away from me but I was still talking; I wasn't sorry that one burned. I was asking him how long he would stay in Weimar, as if I were a common barber or chauffeur making meaningless small-talk. Stupid. Stupid. I should have mentioned the savings the camp had made because I'd managed to keep to the sixty-Pfennig daily food allowance per prisoner – unchanged since 1938. I should have explained my plans for further economising. That's what I should have done. At any rate, in the picture I had framed for my office, it appeared that we were old friends, old comrades, even; that we were about to share a cognac and tell each other about our children – first steps, first words, family resemblances. What miracles they are! How radiant! What fine grandchildren they will produce! We'd ask after the happiness and health of spouses – Greta is expecting our fifth child, I'd say, and is very involved in the National Socialist Women's League – and we'd reminisce about the early years of the struggle. We'd toast the future; we'd toast the past. We'd put the world to rights. Hahn? I'd laugh. Jewish? Just one of those strange corruptions, my friend.

Do you know what I heard? I don't imagine it matters now, and perhaps you have heard it too: they said that he baulked at the sight of blood. That he did not have the stomach for the camps; that he turned as pale as a ghost when watching an Einsatzgruppe action in Minsk. Something splashed on his coat, and he started to retch and sway, and would have fallen into the pit had someone not led him away from the edge. But I cannot believe it; perhaps he had just eaten something too rich. There's always an innocent explanation. He was once a chicken farmer, after all – he would have seen his share of blood, and must have wrung many necks, in the early years at least, before he had others to do it for him. And in the end, didn't he slip the hangman's noose by biting down on poison? That shows the substance of the man, even though I do not approve of those who took the easy way out. After the bombardment, I wondered if he might return to Buchenwald to inspect the damage, bolster morale. I could have secured plenty of photographs then. *This was the Gustloff Works, Herr Reichsführer – already we have plans in place to rebuild it on an even bigger scale.* Schwartz had scoffed when I had the photograph of myself shaking hands with him framed, but I imagine he was sorry after the photo department burned; he could talk all he liked about the day he met the Reichsführer, who not only shook his hand but also clapped him on the upper arm, but if there was no evidence of that moment, then who was to say it ever happened?

FROM LETTERS WRITTEN BY DOKTOR LENARD WEBER
TO HIS DAUGHTER

Frankfurt am Main, September 1946

The afternoon of the bombing, since the photo department was gone, I made my way to the prisoners' infirmary. I passed a man, I remember, who was carrying an armful of unexploded incendiary bombs with a dazed look on his face. Another man began shouting at him in Polish, and finally he lowered them to the ground; he'd thought they were firewood. At the infirmary Wirth directed me to the most urgent cases, and in the confusion nobody thought to ask why a photographer was removing shrapnel and stitching wounds and setting shattered bones. Ambulances from Weimar delivered limited medical supplies, and I had to do the best I could with little clean water and not nearly enough bandages and dressings. The injured arrived on stretchers, planks of wood, doors blown off their hinges, and the dead were taken away by horse and cart. There would have been far fewer casualties if the men in the armaments works had been allowed to evacuate to the compound while the bombs fell. Hundreds of corpses littered the place, along with severed limbs and torsos and heads; we were lucky, I suppose, that a bomb that landed in the crematorium courtyard failed to explode. Lucky, too, that the Americans had spared the camp itself, by and large, and there was almost no damage to the prisoners' barracks. But how much longer? How much longer?

The SS were frantic to save their own – those who had suffered wounds and those still pinned beneath the wreckage, trapped in the cellars of the ruined buildings, slowly running out of air. They spoke to us courteously, fed us meat so that we could work fast enough to rescue them. A Jewish physician summoned to the infirmary told me that one of the guards, his foot caught under a fallen girder, had called to him as he passed: *Comrade! Help me, Comrade! God bless you!*

That night in our block I could smell the burning Goethe oak, and the smoke lay its soft fingers over that other smoke peculiar to Buchenwald, covered it up for a few quiet hours. In the dark the tree released all it had held in its branches for hundreds of years: indigo summer evenings when you think night will never truly fall, and wildflowers gathered by lovers and made into chains and crowns, and birds calling and falling silent in the forest, and the weight of snow, the weight of it, and the roots shrugging up through the soil, and all the other trees cut into barracks and bunks.

It burned until morning.

And because it had not burned enough already, the SS ordered it chopped down for firewood. Some of us took a sliver of it, to keep as a souvenir; I myself broke off a thin black finger, small enough to hide. I still keep it close.

Adamczyk, Antoni: that was the name on the first index card I filled out, though I don't know why I remember that one in particular. They set us up at tables in the storage warehouse, in a room full of empty suitcases. It smelled of mothballs and shoes and damp wool, and each day we saw the new arrivals thronging in to surrender their belongings and collect their camp-issue clothes. What a beggars' parade they made: one man in a giant's coat and a tram conductor's cap, the next in a pair of knickerbockers, the next in a woman's blouse. The warehouse couldn't hold all the personal effects, and outside they piled up and up, guarded by a snarling German shepherd. One day a little boy with a whistle ran up to it and started stroking its ears; he can't have been more than four. The dog licked his face.

To begin with I worked slowly, making each new card as neat as possible, checking it line by line against the original file. Name, date and place of birth, marital status, children, address, religion, nationality. Reason for arrest, previous convictions. Height, build, face, eyes, nose, mouth, ears, teeth, hair, language, distinguishing marks, characteristics . . .

'You'll be here for centuries if you keep that up,' the man sitting next to me whispered. 'Do you know how many thousand we have to get through?'

Haider was his name – a hotel porter from Innsbruck. He looked to be in his sixties, but perhaps he was younger; it could be hard to tell a person's age at Buchenwald. He was frail and hunched, and had lost his left thumb in an accident at the Gustloff Works just before the bombing. Through the paper bandage, the wound looked infected.

He must have seen me staring at it, because when the kapo was out of earshot he said, 'You should have seen the civilian foreman when it happened. He turned so pale – not because of the blood, but because he thought they'd blame him. They made me sign a statement: *This accident was my own fault, as I failed to pay proper attention to my work.*'

'Quiet!' yelled the kapo.

I could have offered to examine it for him. He disappeared soon afterwards. I don't know; I just got on with my copying, grateful they hadn't put me on the night shift, and on Sunday afternoons I went to the edge of the little grove of trees and looked at the view of the plain, or attended one of the cultural events the prisoners organised: a concert of forbidden jazz, a talk on Rimbaud. Once, with Wirth, I listened to the string quartet rehearsing in the pathology department, where the plaster death masks watched us from the walls. And soon I could produce a dozen index cards per hour, Lotte: I learned to copy the names and numbers so quickly that I hardly read them at all, hardly took them in.

FROM THE IMAGINARY DIARY OF FRAU GRETA HAHN

September 1944

I hardly recognised Eickeweg; the bombs had come so close. The Schmidts' villa lost its roof, and Kommandant Pister's wife and his little daughter were hurt, and oh, poor Emmi, poor poor Emmi. The SS victims were buried as heroes in the main cemetery in Weimar, and I lost track of all the names, all the graves piled with greenery, including the graves of children, and it could have been us, it could so easily have been us. The damage to our place was only superficial, Dietrich said. It wasn't structural; it wasn't going to fall down around our ears. We were quite safe. But I could feel the pain returning, chipping its way up my spine and into my chest. I wanted Emmi back. I wanted my mother, and she would not come. In her absence I read the prayer card she'd sent, with its picture of Saint Peregrine drawing aside his robe to show the tumour on his leg. Every year, it said, thousands of pilgrims went to the church in Forli to see his body, which had never decayed.

After they bombed us, I had a terrible thought, a shameful thought: destroy the place. Blast a hole in the hill and bury it. Then we could all go home, couldn't we? I think I said this aloud one day, to Doktor Weber. We could all go home, I said. He just carried on buckling the contact plates to my back.

'But you'd have to come to Munich to treat me,' I said. 'Would you? If you no longer had to?'

'Of course, Frau Hahn,' he said, and I chose to believe him.

Dietrich spoke of the Buchenwald villa as home now, and so did Karl-Heinz, as if they no longer remembered our home in Munich, our real home. I longed for our apartment in the city, with its radiators that creaked and ticked, and the chandelier that chimed when Erna dusted it, and yes, even Dietrich's mother living one floor below and rapping on her ceiling when we were too noisy. I missed the iron door key that smelled like coins and was too big for my favourite purse. I missed our lovely kitchen where I sat drinking tea with my friends on dark afternoons, the flame under the teapot shifting in the currents of our conversation, and the narrow window that looked down to the courtyard where the maids beat the carpets. Sometimes I used to watch when Erna beat ours, the dust rising into the air around her, all the dust and the dirt that worked its way into the pile under our feet without our even noticing. It always surprised me, how much there was. But were the cobblestones in the courtyard rounded or flat? And what was the precise colour of the building's stucco façade? When I tried to recall these things, all I could see were the quarry-stone paths in our garden at Buchenwald, the wooden walls of our house at Buchenwald.

'It's a yellowish cream,' said Dietrich. 'Like parchment.'

'I've never seen parchment.'

'Like old ivory, then. Like the handles of my mother's knives.'

'I can't remember them either.'

'It doesn't matter,' he said. 'It's still there. All of it is still there waiting for us.'

But I was not sure I believed him.

2 November 1954

[tape corrupted in places]

I found myself terribly upset at the loss of the Goethe oak.
There'd been no water to spare to extinguish it, even if it
had once sheltered the great poet.

Is this relevant? Shall I go on?

It burned until morning; at times you could hardly make
out the tree, just a furious scribble of flame. And no less dreadful once the flames were out: black branches, black trunk, as if
crammed with poison sap. It had been the living centre of
Buchenwald once, that oak – the heart, spared when the forest
around it was cleared to make way for the camp. A reminder
of the Germany we were fighting for. Back then, they'd encircled it with a little iron fence to protect it, and the inmates
called it Buchenwald's first prisoner. It was true that in recent
times, because of the water problems, I suppose, it had begun
to dry up, and its bark had fallen off. But on the days when
trainload after trainload swarmed the mustering ground and it
seemed we would never process them all, let alone feed them,
and on the days when the drains blocked and the deterrents
failed and the quotas were not met and the sewage treatment
plant broke down and the stench of the place lodged in my
throat and I could not balance the books and my secretary
brought me more and more papers to sign – on those days the
tree had always cheered me. Even just the thought of the tree.
I am not a man of letters, but after it burned I felt moved to
look for some fitting lines in Greta's volume of Goethe so that
I would have something to say about the loss.

I asked her where it was, and she pointed to the bookshelves from her spot on the couch. Her strength was leaving her again, it seemed – but I told myself it was just the shock of the terror attack, and of Emmi's death, and nothing more sinister. Nothing . . .

[corrupted]

 . . . because of me.

I stood with Hans Schmidt beneath the charred limbs. It would have to come down, he said. It could collapse. Kill someone.

'*Is it one living creature, which has split within itself?*' I said, and waited, but the adjutant just glanced at me sideways, and I knew he did not recognise the lines; his tastes, after all, extended only to adventure novels and pulp crime, which he borrowed in their dozens each month from the prisoners' library.

He said, 'They'll need an axe and a saw. Will you see to it?'

Then he returned to the crematorium.

After the tree had been felled I went to look at it before they cut it up for firewood, but I wish I hadn't. It lay on its side like the remains of some extinct beast, the flesh of which has long since rotted away. I'd heard that the prisoners took pieces of it as souvenirs, and this should have pleased me: the thought that in such a criminal rabble there lay some reverence for German ideals. I ran my hand over the stump, searching for a spot where I could chisel away a piece to take for myself, and my skin snagged on the jagged wood, and I felt a splinter shoot into my fingertip. I bit the inside of my cheek so as not to cry out. I must have brushed against the burnt branches without noticing, because when I returned home to see whether Greta had eaten any lunch, she remarked that I smelled like ashes. She was sitting on the couch, her meal unfinished on the end table, the volume of Goethe on her lap. And when I sat down next to her I left black smudges on the cushions, and I realised the back of my uniform was filthy with soot, and I had to have it cleaned.

I couldn't get the splinter out; though I tried and tried I was unable to dislodge it myself. I thought it would work its way free of its own accord, but my whole fingertip was swollen and red and hot to the touch, and I knew it had turned septic. Greta said I should have it seen to – Doktor Weber could fix it for me quite easily.

'And have him treating both of us?' I said. 'When we don't have the Blood Certificate yet?'

She asked if the certificate really mattered any more.

Of course it mattered, I told her.

But the splinter seemed such a tiny thing, almost embarrassing to mention, when other men had lost their wives and children. And also, and also – this is hard to explain, and perhaps not in line with your question – I wanted to keep part of the tree with me, this tiny sliver that had taken root in my own flesh and blood. For weeks I kept visiting the stump of the oak, coming up with reasons to enter the compound when most of the men did their best to stay away. *My Country, Right or Wrong.* I needed to assess the damage to the laundry and the disinfection room, I said; check whether we might not be able to improve the water supply as part of the repairs. And in fact, the water supply *was* improved – but only because the wrecked armaments works had stopped draining it. I knew there was no saving the oak, but since the attack, since it had been chopped down, I found myself searching the thin air where it had stood, looking for a mass of green flourishing in the drab camp the way it hadn't for years; a great green miracle. I refused over and over to believe in that emptiness – and then over and over, as I came closer, my gaze fell to the cracked and blackened stump. I wondered whether it might not sprout again; you see that sometimes, don't you? New leaves growing from a stump? But whenever I checked, it was as lifeless as ever.

And I wasn't sleeping, and when I did sleep I dreamt of the burning tree, and lost photographs hung from its branches, all the stubble-headed pebble-eyed men as thin as paper, and they burned too. There were thousands on the latest transports, and although we split them up on arrival, sending the women and children to Ravensbrück with the usual generous rations, we were obliged to receive hundreds of children into the parent camp as well. Most were too young to work, and I had no idea how to manage this new drain on supplies. Let me tell you, they represented a dangerous and unstable element: when one of them decided he recognised the prisoner who denounced his father to the Gestapo, he began to pelt him with stones. Other minors saw what was happening and joined in, and then the adults came too, and soon enough the job was done. But men like Henning, enthroned in their lavish Berlin offices, paid no attention to how many head they sent our way, nor the quality of the transports. They clattered across the compound in their wooden shoes like some vast herd of goats, and I couldn't stop adding up the numbers, trying to make them work, even in my bed. I remembered Schiedlausky's recommendation: the doctor in the Little Camp who had helped him sleep. The Jew doctor. And despite what I'd said to Greta about the Blood Certificate, and despite what I knew about Jews, I started to wonder whether he might not be able to help me relax at night too. *We should report them* – that's what Wolff had said. But my broken sleep was affecting my work, and my skat games as well – I had made a few costly mistakes, when I'd chosen a high-risk, high-reward strategy, announcing that I'd win every trick. I couldn't afford to make many more.

To reach him I had to enter the Little Camp over on the northern edge of the compound, with its stinking stables full of Jews and lice and its piles of corpses. He had a private bedroom, though, and as he showed me in he made no attempt to hide the butter, meat, eggs and medicines he had finagled from Danish Red Cross packages. He wore a decent suit, the waistcoat buttoned up across his stout middle, and his head was unshaven, his grey hair coarse and plentiful. On his bedside table, a fine fur hat.

'You are a full Jew?' I said, though I could tell it just to look at him – his thick lips and heavy face, his eyes dark and stealthy and hooded by bushy black brows.

'I do not recognise that aspect of my ancestry,' he said in a deep and confident baritone, leaning back comfortably in his chair and motioning for me to sit on the bed. 'I am a eugenicist.'

I had heard of his work concerning the classification of prisoners; how he had discovered Aryan blood amongst some of the Polish children; how he had identified the French communists, with their Mediterranean and African blood, as the prime carriers of scarlet fever and diphtheria and other diseases of the throat. How he treated those patients who deserved treatment and withheld treatment from those who did not.

'You are a prisoner,' I said.

He smiled. He could only help me, he said, if I forgot that he was the prisoner and I the SS officer.

I shifted my weight, and the bed squeaked. 'When you hypnotise a man,' I said, 'what happens to him?'

It was like a deep relaxation, he said. Most people felt very refreshed afterwards.

'But there is no . . . loss of control?' I asked.

'This is not a vaudeville routine, Herr Sturmbannführer,' he said. 'It is a recognised therapy to relieve psychological distress.'

Oh, he was pleased with himself. The funny thing is, a few years later he'd stand trial alongside me at Dachau – and how he'd play to the gallery! *You have placed the stigma of Cain on my forehead. I shall not plead any extenuating circumstances. If in your opinion I am guilty, then I am more guilty than any of these other accused.*

I asked him if he'd used the technique on my colleagues without any ill effects, and he said he'd helped a lot of men at Buchenwald to feel more comfortable about what they did. Then he told me to close my eyes and imagine I was walking down a dark staircase, and with every step my body felt heavier and heavier. And yet I still remember his questions.

'Now,' he said, 'what is troubling you?'

There had been so much damage, I said. So many losses.

What was the nature of the damage? The loss?

We thought we were safe, because of the camp. If I'd known, if I'd really known, I never would have brought my family to that kind of place. They didn't deserve it.

What did they deserve?

Something other than Buchenwald.

What kind of place was Buchenwald?

I kept thinking about it, I told him. Dreaming about it.

Tell me the dreams, he said.

The tree was on fire, the oak tree. And the photographs, too – thousands of faces going up in flames. I couldn't breathe.

Whose faces?

I didn't know them, I said. I couldn't tell them apart.

Why did it matter? The loss of a tree? The loss of some pictures of strangers?

It took us by surprise. It was so close. Our neighbours' house was firewood.

He asked if I was speaking of the air raid.

Yes, I said. The terror attack.

And these faces. Did I know them?

No. But it would be expensive. The whole card file had to be copied. The cost of the cards alone – I had not budgeted for it. I didn't know how I'd pay for it.

And I was still speaking of the air raid?

Yes, I said.

And only the air raid?

I opened my eyes. 'Of course, yes.'

'Close your eyes, Herr Sturmbannführer,' he said.

I don't know what I was thinking, going to see a Jew. Slippery customers who use slippery tricks. He used them at the Dachau trial, too. *If I supposedly committed those crimes, I ask for only one grace – that the full measure for my alleged crimes should be applied. Because if a doctor, a former member of the Harvard Post Graduate Medical teaching staff, has committed such crimes, then die he shall and die he must.* He was out by 1953.

I kept my eyes open.

He asked if there was anything else I wanted to disclose – some of the men had found it very liberating to talk in detail about their work.

I hadn't come to talk in detail about my work, I said.

'It seems to me,' he said, examining the label on a tin of herring, 'that you are deeply troubled by a burden you cannot discuss.'

'Of course there are things I cannot discuss with someone like you,' I told him.

'In that case, Sturmbannführer,' he said, 'my treatment will be of no value to you.'

Small mercies – right after that, Kommandant Pister recognised that we could no longer accommodate such large numbers of inmate minors. The very young ones had attached themselves to the adult prisoners like sons to fathers, and I knew for a fact that some of the kapos had made pets of them, organising extra food and dressing them in fine clothes, cosseting them to within an inch of their lives – it was quite unhealthy. I even came across a three-year-old Jew spoiled not only by inmates but also by SS men, who fed it fruits and candies. The inmates kept it in the storage building, which was under my jurisdiction, and when I stopped in there one afternoon to visit the office of my finance clerk I found the minor running up and down the corridors, making a terrible racket with a whistle. This was a place of work; naturally it was my duty, as a matter of principle, to take charge and order it removed. That was all I said. All I suggested. The transport lists were not my area, as you know, despite how hard the Americans pressed my finance clerk to admit otherwise. And anyway, later I found out that a prisoner nurse gave it an injection to cause a fever so it was unfit to travel – so you see, sometimes the injections *saved* lives. And then the communists who worked in the labour administration office took the minor off the list and added a different one in its place – a Gypsy or some other Jew, I expect. There were plenty to choose from, gaily chewing their way through my supplies, refusing to pull their own weight. I have no idea what was so special about the first one, though. It was a strange episode, because let me tell you, the communists who these days bray so long and loud about equality and brotherhood had little time for the Jews at Buchenwald. Oh yes. Ask yourself why they – the communists – look so well fed and well shod in the photographs.

I should say that though I had mentioned the unworkable numbers of minors to the Kommandant, I had not suggested any solution; it was his own decision to remove a decent quantity of them to Auschwitz.

Frankfurt am Main, September 1946

For weeks following the August air raid, Eickeweg was busy with teams of prisoners clearing away the debris. The SS stood guard, as usual, but their hearts weren't in it; they didn't bawl at the men to work faster, or come up with reasons to kick and beat them, or tell lewd jokes among themselves about Polish women and German shepherd dogs. Rather, they simply watched as the prisoners gathered up broken glass and dented radiators, jagged pipes and china tiles blown to pieces. I suppose I should have been pleased to see the damage – my blockmates couldn't stop talking about the bombing, crowing over the loss of the Gustloff Works, agreeing that this was a real turning point. But how much longer? We'd heard that a group of Allied airmen had been brought to the Little Camp – evacuated from prison in Paris right before its liberation. According to them, the war would last only a month more. Just a month.

I kept thinking, though, about what would have happened if the Hahns' house had taken a direct hit. Otto Wolff's villa next door to theirs slumped to one side, its legs kicked out from under it, and his wife was among the dead. Shards of window glass still jutted from the front garden, as if the Wolffs were growing knives. When I was passing by on my way to treat Frau Hahn I saw a little pile of salvaged possessions by the front steps: a jigsaw puzzle in its box, a hand mirror, a framed print of a donkey in a straw hat. I slowed to look, but the guard chaperoning me prodded me on to the Hahns'.

Surely he knew by then – surely *everyone* knew – that my visits had nothing to do with producing an album of photographs . . . ? And yet nobody said a word.

The Hahns' house was intact – just a tarpaulin patching a small section of the roof – but I realised with a shiver that it was right above the master bedroom. Too close; much too close. I'd spent so long worrying that cancer would kill Frau Hahn I had never considered that something else could. What if there was nobody for me to save?

The Sturmbannführer was waiting in the bedroom when I arrived. He gave me the briefest of nods, and I had the feeling that he wanted to say something. I waited for him to speak, but he simply cleared his throat and then, after a moment or two, gestured to the Vitaliser and said, 'We don't have all day.'

She appeared a little weaker, paler, no colour in her lips or her fingernails, though she sat fully dressed on the edge of the bed.

'You seem well this morning, Frau Hahn,' I said, and she gave a listless nod. I held my fingers to her wrist and felt for her pulse: faint and slow, barely there at all. She sounded short of breath. 'Good,' I said. 'Very good.'

A breakfast tray sat next to the bed, untouched – warm white rolls, slices of salami and cheese, little dishes of jam and butter. I could have grabbed it and finished it in a moment; I could have shoved my mouth straight into the food and eaten it like a dog.

'Are you not hungry?' I said.

'I can't face it.'

'Well, it's been an unsettled time, with the air raid, and the damage to the house. But you must keep your strength up.'

'It makes me feel sick.'

'She won't listen,' said Hahn. 'I've tried everything.' He came and stood beside me, lowered his voice. 'I mean – we can't force-feed her.'

'It's the shock,' I said. 'It will pass.'

Hahn looked tired, and I noticed he was cradling one hand in the other – but when he saw me glance at it, he dropped it to his side.

'Well,' he said, 'I should get to work.'

'Dietrich,' said Frau Hahn. 'Just ask him.'

'No need,' he said.

'*Dietrich*,' she repeated. She coughed, then paused to catch her breath.

I busied myself carrying the Vitaliser over to the bedside cabinet.

'My husband has a splinter,' she said as I began to uncoil the cords. 'He needs you to remove it.'

The desire to laugh seized me, so I bowed my head. 'Of course, Herr Sturmbannführer. May I?'

He showed me his hand then, staring past me as if he held something neither of us wanted to acknowledge. The tip of his finger was swollen and red, and he flinched as I examined it. I pressed harder. 'Hmm,' I said, and frowned. 'When did this happen?'

'A month ago.'

'A *month*?'

'Perhaps a little longer. It was the Goethe oak.'

'Terrible. Terrible,' I said.

There was a pause. 'The tree? Or my finger?'

I squeezed, raising a ridge of his flesh between my thumb-nails. 'It's difficult to find the entry point, this long after the event. It's already begun to heal. Have you tried to remove it yourself?'

'Of course, yes, but I only have two hands, and the splinter is in one of them.'

'He just wanted a souvenir,' said Frau Hahn.

'A dreadful thing,' I said. 'The tree.' I opened my doctor's bag and withdrew a needle and a scalpel, though I doubted I would need the scalpel. 'I'll try to make this as quick as possible,' I said. 'Do you need some ice?'

'Ice?'

'To numb the area.'

'Josef can fetch you some ice, darling,' said Frau Hahn. Another cough. 'It might be a good idea.'

'I don't need ice,' he said.

'If you'd just rest your hand on the windowsill, then,' I said. 'So I can see properly. And please try not to move. That's very important.'

Frau Hahn let out a sudden gasp.

'Are you all right?' Hahn and I spoke in unison.

'I'm all right,' she said.

I took hold of his finger. 'Hmm,' I said again. 'It's unfortunate you didn't see a doctor straight away. I fear you've only driven it in deeper.'

'He's very busy,' said Frau Hahn.

I broke the surface of his skin with the needle and felt him wince, the tiniest shock jolting from his hand to mine. He was looking out the window at the trees in their garden, the leaves already on the turn, and beyond them the devastated SS garages.

'It may not be as bad as it appears,' I said. I began to probe with the needle; how easily it entered his flesh! Another little jolt. 'It's just as well you mentioned this today,' I went on. 'It's not unusual, in such situations, for sepsis to develop.' Jolt. 'Which can be fatal.'

'Fatal?' murmured Frau Hahn.

'No no,' Hahn said over his shoulder. 'Everything is fine.'

'Yes,' I said. 'Everything is fine.' I took up the scalpel.

A Year of German Composers – except in my pile of torn-off calendars, Lotte, I can find only Beethoven, Mozart, Wagner and Bach to write on. No sign of Mendelssohn. No sign of Meyerbeer.

I remember a concert in the camp one night – an orchestra of prisoners, conducted by a man who had performed for royalty. We closed our eyes and listened to 'Tales from the Vienna Woods' and 'Jesu, Joy of Man's Desiring', and the notes lifted into the evening air and drifted and dissolved.

'Do you know,' Wirth said to me, 'that in Frankfurt, an aerial mine blasted Goethe off his pedestal? And tore off his arm and head?'

And it must have been around that same time that they hanged a man in front of us all. Usually they confined the hangings to the basement of the crematorium, stringing them up on hooks like sides of meat. We all knew about it; the prisoners entered the red brick building and disappeared, exiting only as smoke. I'd seen Pister's adjutant Hans Schmidt returning home to Eickeweg after one such chore, picking up his youngest child and stroking him on the head.

And I want to tell you these things, Lotte, and I do not want you to know these things.

Filing into the mustering ground for roll call that evening, we felt the frost in the autumn air. As we made our way to our places, our minds already on the cold that was coming, we passed the wooden platform. *What's that for?* we murmured, but we knew, we knew. In the pitiless lights our bodies cast strange shadows, and the band played a gavotte.

The SS rushed the headcount so they could get to the main event. As soon as they had tallied us up, an announcement came over the loudspeaker: 'Prisoner Number Such-and-such, who escaped from the camp, has been captured. He has been sentenced to die by the rope as punishment for his act, by order of Reichsführer-SS Himmler.' Not the Kommandant but the Reichsführer. Not the officers lined up in front of the gate but the Reichsführer. Not the SS who were marching the prisoner to the gallows, who were ordering him to climb on the three-legged stool, who were placing the noose around his neck and the other end of the rope around the hook. Not the man who kicked away the stool. Not the metal voice from the loudspeaker that warned us not to speak and not to look away. Not any of them, but the Reichsführer.

Corpse carriers to the gate.

Only a few days later, well before my next scheduled appointment with Frau Hahn, the Sturmbannführer sent word that I was to report to their villa immediately. He was in the bedroom when I arrived, sitting next to the bed and holding his sleeping wife's hand, but he let it go and rose to his feet as soon as I entered, as if he didn't want me to witness their small intimacy.

'It's stopped working,' he said.

'How much did you give her?'

'Not the elixir, the machine. The machine's stopped working.'

That's the trouble with miracles, you see, Lotte: sometimes they don't stick.

I came to the edge of the bed and felt my chest lurch. 'Good morning, Frau Hahn,' I started to say. He cut me off.

'Look at her. Would you say it's working?'

She lay with her eyes closed, as thin as a child. Her skin was greyish, her breathing shallow, though as I watched she gave a deep and shuddering sigh, the way Anna sometimes did in her sleep.

'It can be deceptive,' I said. 'Some patients, in my experience, do get a little worse – do appear to get a little worse – before they get better again.'

Frau Hahn gave another sigh and seemed on the verge of waking.

'Worse? Worse?' he said, as if he didn't understand the meaning. 'She's dying. I know what death looks like.'

Yes, I thought. 'No,' I said. 'Let me explain.' I didn't know what to say, how to contradict what was right in front of us – but even then, even by that stage, I could tell he was waiting for me to do just that. I felt it buzzing like a charge in the close air of the bedroom, his wish for me to say that he was mistaken, that she was not dying. I looked to the window, where I could see the trees in the garden turning red and gold. The sky was low, full of rain; a storm was coming, and it wasn't far away. Frau Hahn had settled again, and to gain a little time I took her pulse, pressing my fingers to her cool wrist as he watched and waited. I hoped he wouldn't see how I shook. I could hear a breeze picking up, starting to buffet the house. For a moment – it can't have been longer than a second – I felt no pulse; nothing more than the pliant stems of her bones. I shifted my fingers a millimetre, shifted them again – she couldn't have died just now; I would have noticed, we would have noticed. The end wasn't that close – not yet. Was it? Was it? And yes, there, flicking back against my fingertips: the insistent beat of the blood. *Here*, it said. *Here . . . here . . . here*. Outside the wind shook a flurry of leaves loose.

'The reason she seems to be slipping is simply the treatment taking greater effect,' I said. 'The waves pass through healthy cells as well as through the growths, and while they don't damage them, they disrupt things for a time. Like the wind shaking the leaves of a tree.'

'Is this common?' he said. 'In such cases?'

'Very common,' I said. 'At this stage.'

'You never mentioned it. Never warned us.'

'It's what I would expect to see, Herr Sturmbannführer. It's a good sign.' I was looking him right in the eye.

'A good sign,' he repeated.

It had begun to rain now, to pour, and a pale yellow leaf splattered against the window and stuck there like a little hand. I didn't think Frau Hahn had heard us talking, but when I folded back her eiderdown and began to attach the contact plates, her eyes fluttered open and she turned her head to look at me.

'How long?' she whispered. Under her nightgown, her swollen stomach.

'I'll just roll up your sleeve now, Frau Hahn, if I may,' I said.

'How long?' she repeated, beginning to cough. 'Until the wind stops?'

'What did she say?' asked Hahn.

'Something about the wind.'

'Is it too noisy, Gretalein?' he said. He strode over to the window and glared out at the bad weather. As if he could command it to be still.

'How long?' she said again.

'Not long,' I said.

That night the storm pushed at our block, louder than the rasping breaths of those not far from death, and I thought it might wrench it from its foundations and send it sailing through the camp like a ship. And perhaps the other blocks as well – all of us set afloat on a sea of mud, taking the tangled fences with us, and the rocks and tree roots too, gliding down the slopes of the Ettersberg towards the houses below. And what would they say, the people down there, when we arrived in their midst? A skinny flotilla of strangers from a place they swore they did not know.

I clutched at the scrap of wood I'd saved from the Goethe oak. I wondered whether I could die – whether the records could show that I had died. Wirth had told me of such cases: word might reach them that this or that prisoner was to be hanged or shot or sent to one of the death camps, and so they swapped his name with the name of a dead man. You had to have a contact, a comrade, who worked in the right place – and sometimes, yes, a man on an undesirable list was swapped with a living prisoner rather than a dead one. Wirth said that in these cases they chose only the real criminals, or those who would die soon anyway, in order to save men vital to the underground resistance – men of greater value. I still don't know what I think about that. You could survive for years after such a swap, though, submerged, pretending to be someone else, and perhaps, after a time, you would begin to believe you were this other person, and you wouldn't have to pretend.

I imagined disappearing. No longer having to make believe I could cure a dying woman.

'Perhaps we should enlist,' I said to Wirth that Sunday. We were on our way to our usual spot behind the infirmary, to rest for a while and look at the view of the village, and the church, and the hills that seemed to float untethered in the foggy white distance. In a corner of the mustering ground half a dozen Russians were dancing in their spotless tunics and gleaming boots, each trying to outdo the other with his acrobatics, and down by the storage warehouse a group of Czechs practised a choral work, the minor-key song full of the promise of winter.

'Take ourselves off to the front?' said Wirth.

'It might be safer than here.'

Himmler had written to every German political prisoner at Buchenwald that autumn, urging us all to volunteer to fight for our country, but Kommandant Pister hadn't encouraged us to take up the offer; he needed the Germans to run the camp – to keep the hordes of men under control – so he and his SS didn't have to. Only a hundred or so had presented themselves.

And anyway, Lotte, if I enlisted, or took another man's name, Hahn would have no reason to ensure your safety.

We passed one of the placards they put up around the place: *There is one path to freedom. Its milestones are obedience, diligence, sincerity, order, cleanliness, sobriety, truthfulness, willingness to sacrifice, and love of the fatherland.*

'Are you in trouble, Weber?' said Wirth.

I waved my hand. 'It was just a thought.'

Nearby, the Little Camp with its fenced-off tents for the thousands who wouldn't fit anywhere else, and the infected wounds and the dysentery and the illegal water supply that flowed only on Sunday mornings. The corpses sprawled like sea wrack. The Jews who gathered in small groups to whisper their forbidden prayers. And the shelves of Muselmänner: the skeletal prisoners caught in their death-trances, unable even to blink away the flies, too far gone.

But what could I have done?

October 1944

When a woman in our parish was dying of cancer, she was in so much pain that she couldn't speak. What was her name? Frau Fritzsche . . . Frau Fischer . . . She kept attending Mass for as long as she could, and we watched her creep up the aisle to receive communion from Pfarrer Tremmel, her skinny hands grasping the end of each pew as she passed. Helena and I jostled with one another; neither of us wanted to sit on the end, where she might touch us with her sick fingers. When she stopped coming, the whole parish prayed for her at Mass. I don't remember if we prayed to Saint Peregrine, but I have been praying to him. I'd like to visit his church in Forlì, if Dietrich would let me go. Dietrich, who didn't believe the bombs would come even when we saw the planes right above us. But Mama could take me to Forlì. Together we could kneel before Saint Peregrine's incorrupt body and ask him to bless me, to bless us. Then she could hold my hand as we made our way to our pew to sing the 'Dies irae', and Pfarrer Tremmel would invite us all to pray for the woman who couldn't walk for pain. And there at the front of the church, between the wavering candles, my grandfather in his linen shroud, his body as hard as three-day-old bread, and if you touched him he would turn to crumbs.

PART EIGHT
NULL GAME

4 November 1954

[tape corrupted in places]

He was very credible, you see. That was the problem. The wind shaking the leaves of a tree: that was what he said. Disrupting the healthy cells, just for a time. It was a good sign. And didn't things work like that? Didn't things often deteriorate before they improved again? Hadn't Goebbels only just said the same thing, essentially? *We are, despite it all, on the right path. The future will prove that.* I started serving Greta the elixir in pretty glasses etched with dragonflies so it wouldn't seem like medicine.

One evening I was sitting with Karl-Heinz in the living room, playing Happy Families with the deck I'd bought him.

'Do you have the Führer who is friends with children?' he said.

I handed it over.

'Do you have the Führer who is friends with animals?'

I gave him that card too.

'Do you have the Führer who is friends with nature?'

I told him no, and he asked if I was sure, because sometimes people didn't say what cards they had. They just wanted to win. Like Felix. Karl-Heinz had asked him if he had Rommel, and Felix lied and said no, but he did have him, and then he won.

'Well,' I said, 'we must be kind to Felix at the moment.' I didn't tell him that Rommel had died – succumbed to serious head wounds, according to the papers.

He made a face and picked up a card.

'Do you have Hindenburg?' I said.

He didn't, so I took a card too, and saw that the one underneath wasn't part of the deck – it wasn't even a playing card. 'What's this?' I said.

There was a picture of a black-robed saint on the front, displaying a wounded leg, and on the back an Italian church that held his remains. There was a prayer, too: a prayer to Saint Peregrine, patron saint of cancer sufferers.

I asked Karl-Heinz where it had come from.

'I found it,' he said.

Again I asked him where.

'Under your bed,' he said. 'Under Mama's bed.'

Elisabeth must have sent it. Elisabeth, with her absurd superstitions. Her medals and her holy water. Elisabeth, who would not visit, who sent prayers in her place. She should have been proud of her daughter's position in the world; how far she had come from her beginnings.

I told him I wasn't angry, and he scrutinised my expression as if to make sure. Then he said that the new card was meant to be instead of Rudolf Hess, because we couldn't have Hess any more, because he was a traitor.

So he was, I said. Good boy.

A deranged traitor, he said.

Yes, I said, yes. But we couldn't have the new card either. It didn't belong. It ruined the game.

He pointed out that if we did away with Hess, we wouldn't have enough cards.

Well, I said, one family could make do with three people.

You should have heard him: that wasn't fair! Every family had to have four!

Perhaps one family had an imaginary person, I said.

No! That was stupid!

'Shh,' I said, and pointed at the ceiling. 'Mama is right above us.' I waited until he had calmed down, and then I said,

'I know what we'll do. We'll paste a picture of someone else over the top of Hess. All right?'

'All right,' he said.

After we'd finished our game – a draw, we decided, because of the missing card – I called Niemand to give Karl-Heinz a bath and put him to bed. The living room was very quiet then. In the past I might have worked on a piece of carving, but I had lost the ability to sit with just the knife and the wood, and the idea of the finished object, and the thoughts that came in the silence. I turned on the radio, but I didn't want to hear about the Red Army pushing into East Prussia and massacring German civilians and raping German women. My nerves jumped and buzzed and my blood hurtled to my fingertips, and I knew I had to play a game of skat. I had to. *Don't don't don't don't* . . . but already my feet were leading me to the mirror in the entranceway, and I watched my hands button up my coat and pat the pockets for money. I admit that it was a hunger . . .

[corrupted]

. . . birthday, and he insisted on schnapps. I must have had five, maybe six large glasses; after that I said no, but Schmidt told me I shouldn't have set the prices in the club so low if I didn't want people to buy the food and drink. Schiedlausky was entertaining us with stories of a Danish doctor, Værnet, who was trying to cure homosexuality through surgical intervention.

'I don't perform the procedures myself,' said Schiedlausky. 'I just observe them.'

Schmidt said that sounded reasonable to him, because you wouldn't want to get too close – you wouldn't want to catch it.

I stared at my cards and tried to calculate their value, but I kept losing my place. What should I bid? What were they worth? I lost trick after trick, and Schiedlausky said I should have declared a Null game.

'I wonder what Værnet does with them once he's cut them off,' said Schmidt, fanning out his hand. 'Hahn, you're looking a bit pale there. Shall we order you something to eat? A nice big plate of meatballs?'

He was the very last one the Americans hanged, and he deserved everything he got.

Though more than five thousand came to his funeral.

Then they started talking about Waldemar Hoven – the man who had faked his medical dissertation, the man who had carried on a lengthy affair with Koch's wife. Since his arrest by Judge Morgen they'd held him in Weimar, but now he was back at Buchenwald – locked in a basement cell of an SS caserne damaged in the bombing, and still charged with murder by lethal injection.

'I mean, how stupid do you have to be?' Schmidt was saying.

When I tried to focus on my cards they wavered and blurred, the king trembling on his throne. All these years later, I don't remember whether I won or lost in the end.

On the way back to the villa I felt everything coming up. I had time to step off the path and into the trees, at least, so nobody would see it the next day. I crouched down, the forest spinning around me, toadstools as big as saucers pushing up through the damp leaves.

At home I lay on the living-room couch, but the walls slipped and tilted and the antler chandelier whirled like a strange carousel. I thought I might be sick again. I sat up, grasped the edge of the end table – and there was Elisabeth's prayer to Saint Peregrine. I wanted to tear the thing to pieces. Rip off his head, his hands, his cancerous leg. At Buchenwald, with a wound like that, he wouldn't have lasted a week. The clock in the entranceway struck two. I hadn't realised it was so late. My stomach lurched, and I swallowed hard, once, twice. Then I went to the telephone and dialled Elisabeth's number.

Her voice was thin and distant when she answered.

'Who gave you permission—' I started to say, but she interrupted me.

'What's the matter?' she demanded. 'Has something happened?'

'Why would you send her this?' I said, and I remember brandishing the prayer card.

She didn't know what I was talking about, of course. Send her what? Was everything all right?

'Who knows?' I said. 'Now that you've given the game away.'

There was a pause, and then she asked what I meant.

I heard myself starting to shout. If Greta didn't know, she might not give in to the disease! There had been studies, respected studies . . . Then I heard a noise in the hallway: Karl-Heinz in his pyjamas, holding a finger to his lips.

'This is private,' I said, but when I waved him away I lost my balance and dropped the receiver.

I could hear Elisabeth's tiny voice coming from somewhere near my stomach. 'Dietrich? Dietrich? Hello? Are you there?'

I picked up the receiver again and leaned against the wall.

'Dietrich,' she said. 'Have you been drinking? How serious is it?'

Not serious at all, I said; Greta was improving. But we didn't need any spells. Any prayers to dead Italians.

She started to tell me that faith could heal – that she personally had seen it heal.

I hung up the telephone and stood there for a moment, listening to the clock tick. In the conservatory Freya whimpered in her sleep, twitching on the excellent horsehair mattress I'd had made for her. My eyes fell on the table beneath the mirror; there was a little note, a little card, weighted under an empty vase. Carefully, very carefully, so as not to lose my balance, I pulled it free: a photograph of myself, hacked from one of Weber's shots, and pasted onto the Hess playing card.

I put it back.

Then I went to Greta's room and put the prayer card back too.

I was shocked at how little we had left. How quickly our balance had dwindled.

'There must be a mistake,' I said, but the woman at the bank checked and double-checked and said she was very sorry; there was no mistake.

The solution was quite simple, of course: more cutbacks. If an inmate could survive on two hundred grams of horse meat per week, then why not one hundred and eighty? And if one hundred and eighty, then why not one hundred and fifty? I can see you understand the logic. It wouldn't mean much of a difference per prisoner – hardly noticeable, I imagined, and no one important need know – and yet the cumulative savings would be considerable. And then, we could raise the prices in the prisoners' canteen, too. Charge them a fraction more for their luxuries: their tobacco and their war beer and their seafood paste. And as the man responsible for those savings, those extra profits, via which we could improve the general situation, I deserved a small percentage. That was only fair.

Frankfurt am Main, September 1946

Frau Hahn was more lucid the next time I visited, though she looked no stronger. Josef was arranging a hot-water bottle at her back but couldn't get it right, and finally she pushed the thing to the floor and dismissed him.

'We should have brought Erna with us from Munich,' she said. 'I did tell him . . . but once he gets an idea, you can't change his mind.'

'Is your back giving you some trouble, Frau Hahn?' I said.

'I must have pulled something. Too much gardening.' She gave a half-smile. 'My mother grows rare orchids – too beautiful to cut. Their little faces. Their little mouths.'

'I can give you some more of the elixir,' I said. 'For your back. And the Vitaliser will help.' I dripped the laudanum into a glass patterned with dragonflies and added some water.

'I don't remember the last treatment,' she said. 'I've been having strange thoughts . . . saying strange things. And then I forget the things I've thought and said, and all I know is . . . ' a pause, while she caught her breath ' . . . all I know is they were not normal, but everyone pretends that they were. That there's nothing wrong.'

'The elixir can have that effect,' I said. 'It's quite common.'

'I don't like it. I'm drifting away from myself. Further and further away . . . And it's upsetting for Karl-Heinz.' She gasped and closed her eyes as the pain pinched. When I held out the glass of laudanum, she shook her head. 'Is the mind a circuit too?' she said. 'Like the body?'

'There are circuits in the brain,' I said.

'Thoughts are just electricity, then.'

'In a way.'

'Does that mean they leave a trace of themselves? A physical trace?'

'I . . . well, I don't know.'

'Maybe one day we'll have a machine to record them and keep them.'

'Imagine the size of it, though,' I said.

And we both agreed that a machine like that, even for one person, would take up too much room. Still, we said. What a thing.

'Will you have the elixir now, Frau Hahn?'

'What will happen if I don't?'

'It's your choice, of course,' I said, 'but I wouldn't advise withdrawing that strand of the treatment. The elixir complements the work the Vitaliser does. It . . . it attunes the blood, so the waves can travel unimpeded throughout the body.'

I was making it up on the spot, but she was starting to nod, to agree. 'I suppose so,' she said.

'And if it means Karl-Heinz hears his mama say a few funny things – well, that's a small price to pay for her cure, isn't it?'

'Her cure,' she repeated. 'Yes. Yes.'

'Will you have a little, then? Just a little? For your back?'

With a jolt I realised that this was the voice Anna used when she was trying to get you to eat your lambs' brains, Lotte, or your mashed carrots. *Just one more bite. It'll make you big and strong. It'll make you see in the dark.* The lies we tell – but you believed them too. I held the laudanum to Frau Hahn's lips, and she began to drink it down. In the cheval mirror I saw myself tipping the glass with the dragonflies on it so she took every drop. The shadows in my hollow cheeks. The jut of the bones. I carried the machine over to the bedside cabinet and began uncoiling its cords, attaching the contact plates to her body.

'I probably shouldn't mention this,' she said, her voice drowsier now, 'but I've been praying.' My hands were on her chest as she spoke, my fingers close to her throat, and I felt the words as much as I heard them. 'We're not supposed to pray any more, are we? We're not allowed. Don't say anything.'

I wasn't sure what she intended by that last remark, so I continued my work without replying, but she placed her hand on mine – more firmly than I would have thought possible, given her condition – and said, 'You won't talk about it, will you?'

'Of course not, Frau Hahn.' She was still holding my hand, and I didn't draw away, though I listened for footsteps in the hallway.

'It's only the rosary,' she said. 'Where's the harm? No harm, surely.'

'No,' I said. 'No harm.' She was rubbing her thumb and forefinger together, and I remembered the line of indentations I had seen on her palm, and the tiny rosary beads. I attached the last pair of contact plates and switched on the machine.

'Mmm,' she murmured, echoing its hum. She turned her head to the side, watched me make my adjustments. 'Do you pray, Herr Doktor?'

The question took me by surprise; my hand slipped on one of the dials, and the needle shook like a stalk of grass.

'I don't believe in God,' I said.

'But you're a Jew.'

'No.'

'No? You're not a Jew? Has there been a mistake?'

'I'm told I'm part Jewish.'

She gave a long, slow blink. 'A mistake would make things much easier. He wouldn't have to bother about the certificate.'

Before I could ask her what she meant, she began to cough. The contact plates on her chest loosened and slipped, and she held a hand to her mouth. She tried to take a breath but the coughing wouldn't let her go; her whole body shook with it, and when she finally stopped and drew her hand away I saw that there was blood on her palm. I refused to believe it at first – ovarian cancer did not spread to the lungs, typically, but to the pleura that lined the chest. The build-up of fluid could cause shortness of breath and coughing, but I'd never observed blood. And yet, there it was, streaked across her pale palm. It must have been due to the sheer force.

'How long have you been experiencing such a bad cough, Frau Hahn?' I asked, keeping my voice calm, level, as if I were asking after a mutual acquaintance – though of course, there could be no such person. I began to open drawers, looking for a handkerchief, but the first three I tried contained only under-wear: corsets and garter belts, slips trimmed with lace, all cut from the palest silk and shimmering like the inside of a shell.

'No,' she said, 'no. There.' She pointed to her dressing table, and in my haste to shove the other drawers shut I caught a pinch of blush-pink silk in one. I opened the drawer again and pushed the garment back into place, and it was so light, so soft, it felt like bare skin.

A tiny framed photograph sat among the bottles of scent on the dressing table: Karl-Heinz as a baby, I assumed, held in the arms of his father, who could not stop smiling. I found the handkerchiefs – also nothing more than little wisps of fabric – and I soaked one with water at the washbasin in the corner, then wiped her hand clean. I was relieved I couldn't see any blood on her nightdress or her bedding, though I discovered a spot on her bedside cabinet. I wiped that clean too. 'Frau Hahn?' I said. 'How long have you been coughing like this?'

'I don't know. I can't remember.' Her voice a whisper.

If it had spread to the pleura, how much time did we have left? And what would happen when Hahn realised? I looked at the streaks on the wet handkerchief, the way their edges blurred and feathered. They would wash out, surely they would wash out, and Hahn might not notice the coughing for a time, and perhaps, with a little luck – all right, a miracle – the war would be lost when he did. Hadn't the Americans crossed the Moselle? Hadn't the Red Army liberated Belgrade? So we heard. Over and over I rinsed the handkerchief in the basin, tilting it to the light to scrutinise it the way Anna used to when she washed your baby things, Lotte. If she could just hold on.

'Josef will take care of that,' said Frau Hahn. 'You mustn't, Herr Doktor. Please.' She sounded embarrassed.

'I don't mind,' I said, and wrung it out again. I had no reason to mistrust Josef, but the less he knew about the severity of Frau Hahn's condition, the better. I spread the handkerchief out. I was afraid of scrubbing it too hard; I had the feeling it might pull apart, simply dissolve – but it seemed clean. I'd caught it in time; the blood hadn't set. Still, I couldn't look at myself in the mirror.

I returned to Frau Hahn's bedside and found myself taking her hand once more and holding it tight. 'It's all right,' I told her. 'Everything is all right.'

She nodded and closed her eyes. 'An act of grace,' she said. 'A pardon. That's what he's waiting for. Then he'll feel better. But if it's in the blood . . . ' She fell silent.

I attached the contact plates again and resumed the treatment, and her breathing settled into a normal, easy rhythm. I thought she was asleep, but when I finished she opened her eyes and said, 'Thank you, Herr Doktor. I feel much better.'

I lugged the Vitaliser back into its corner behind the mirror and covered it up; it was heavier every time.

'Before you go, Herr Doktor,' she said, and paused. 'Before you go . . . I wonder . . . I wanted to ask . . . '

'Yes, Frau Hahn?' I was expecting a question about her condition; perhaps the day had come – the day I knew must come – when she would admit she knew its name.

Instead she said, 'Would you do me a favour?'

An even more difficult question to answer. 'If I can, Frau Hahn,' I said, but something in her voice made me want to run.

'Would you bring me a book?'

A book. Just a book. I exhaled. 'Of course,' I said, looking around the room for it. She had some volumes of poetry she read sometimes, I knew. 'Where is it?' I had no desire to start opening drawers again.

'No,' she said. 'It's not here.'

'Is it downstairs?'

'No.'

A bubble of dread began to expand in me. 'Where is it?'

'I don't have one. It's not . . . it's not approved material.'

'Oh,' I said. 'Yes. No.'

'But I heard that there are books like that in the camp. Confiscated books. I thought you might be able to find one for me. Without telling anyone.'

'What is the book, Frau Hahn?'

'A bible. I'd like a small bible.'

'Oh,' I said again, because I didn't know what else to say. Had she any idea what she was asking?

'We used to read it,' she said, her eyes drifting to the ceiling. 'My sister and my mother, every Sunday night after supper. We'd take turns reading out our favourite verses. *Jesus said unto him, If thou canst believe, all things are possible to him that believeth. And straightway the father of the child cried out . . .*' She faltered. 'You see, I can't remember it. Do you know it?'

'No, Frau Hahn,' I said. 'I'm sorry. I'm very sorry.' And I felt I was apologising for something else, something much bigger.

'I had to give it all up, of course. Dietrich was very clear about that, right from the start. Which was fair. Don't you think?'

She shifted her gaze to me, though it seemed unfocused, as if she were looking through me to someone else. All the same, I nodded and said, 'Yes. That was fair.'

She smiled. 'I was in love. And it wasn't a hardship, it really wasn't. I'd already stopped going to church – stopped believing. My poor mother. Though she liked him . . . she liked Dietrich, at first.'

'I'm sorry, Frau Hahn,' I repeated. She started to cough, and I rushed to pour her a sip of water, but she managed to stop of her own accord.

'Nothing,' she said, waving me away. 'Nothing.'

'I should go now. Is there anything else?'

'He was so small in his coffin,' she said. 'Wrapped up like a loaf of bread. Mama let me carry them. As tiny as sesame seeds.'

'Yes,' I said, smoothing the eiderdown for her. Perhaps she wouldn't remember asking me the favour; it wasn't unusual for a patient on opiates to lose entire conversations. As I was creeping from her room, however, she called after me: 'Just a small one. You won't forget, will you?'

In cold weather, small stoves burned in the blocks at Buchenwald, but they didn't send their heat any great distance; the ice spread across the inside of the windows like white mould. During my first winter in the camp, a Frenchman who had been on my transport hadn't been able to stop shivering at night. He moved his straw pallet to the floor, first a few metres from the fire, and then every night closer and closer, until finally – despite Voss's warnings – he was sleeping right in front of it. The problem was the shock of the cold in the morning when we had to fall in on the mustering ground; he wasn't strong enough to withstand the sudden change, and he collapsed, and they took him away.

What the rest of us understood, Lotte, as we remained in our icy bunks, was that it did not pay to become in any way comfortable at Buchenwald.

And I was becoming comfortable with Greta Hahn.

We had access to books in the compound – in Block 5 there was a library of close to sixteen thousand approved titles, and when dignitaries visited they marvelled at this generous facility and agreed that Buchenwald was indeed a model camp. On the shelves sat *Diseases of Fruit Trees* and the speeches of Göring and *The Führer's Struggle for World Peace*; manuals on the rearing of cattle, *The Riddle of the Russian Soul*, *Fundamentals of Internal Medicine*, almanacs by which to navigate the stars and, in English, *The Girls' Own Book* and *The Happy Prince*. We could read Kierkegaard and Nietzsche, Schopenhauer and Hegel. We could read Darwin. We could read *Hunger Fighters* and *Life Begins at Forty* and the *Nibelungenlied*. We could read *Don Carlos* and *Danton's Death*, and we did, aloud, when we were sure nobody could hear. There were animal stories and travel stories: *My Hunt for the Unicorn*, *Mysterious China*. There were novels: *Bleak House*, *The Black Knight*, *The Man without Qualities*, *My Company in Poland*. And there were Plato's *Dialogues* and Goethe's *Faust* and Rilke's *The Book of Hours* and Kassner's *Melancholia* and sixty unthumbed copies of *Mein Kampf*, behind which a family of mice had built their nest – but no bibles. Those we saw only in fragments, along with sections of other confiscated volumes in the bales of waste paper collected by thrifty and war-conscious Germans. Someone must have realised they could be put to good use – Sturmbannführer Hahn, or someone like him – and so we prisoners wiped our backsides with the story of creation; we cleaned our raw behinds with Marx and Mehring, blotted up our dysentery with psalms. The only place I might find an intact bible, I knew, was the personal effects room, where all newcomers deposited their belongings on arrival, and where Wirth's brother worked. The personal effects room, in the storage warehouse, where I was making the new index cards.

Of course, I could have said no to Frau Hahn. What would she have done? Reported me to her husband? She already had more than her due, this officer's wife in her villa, dying on clean sheets. I was powerless to help my fellow inmates – apart from the lack of supplies, I was a photographer, officially, not a doctor, and the best I could do was bind their dog bites and their sores with dirty rags, shove back their dislocated limbs while the loudspeaker blared its relentless speeches and songs and *Corpse carriers to the gate*, and at roll call the searchlights lit us up like a cast of thousands in some doomed epic. In the Little Camp, I knew, the block seniors earmarked the weakest newcomers, and the only way out was the corpse cart. Why should I do anything to comfort Greta Hahn? And yet, and yet. It's strange to admit, to put into words, but I had grown fond of her – close to her, even. Something in me couldn't bear the thought that this particular person would vanish – this particular body it had taken thirty years to make. I knew it so well by then: the grey eyes with the tiniest flecks of green, the pale high arches of her feet, the single coppery mole on the back of her right hand. The particular pattern of her veins – parallel lines on one wrist, Y-shaped on the other. The long and spatulate fingers, the cramped toes, the downy swell of her earlobes. I wanted her to live, Lotte – not just because our own lives were tied to hers; I wanted *her* to live. I'm sorry if that shocks you. I remembered the words of my old professor: *They are not people – they are diseases. You are of most value to them if you approach them as such.* And that was the tactic I'd used in the real world. I'd kept my distance from my patients, never allowed myself to consider them anything more than *invasive ductal carcinoma of the breast* or *osteosarcoma of the proximal tibia*. Here at Buchenwald, though, here in this unreal place, where death came every day, such tactics did not work. And perhaps – this is hard to say – perhaps, in a way, Frau Hahn had taken your mother's place. Taken *your* place. I don't mean I loved her; no, not that. But I could try to treat her, to help her. I could try to save her.

I asked Wirth if he thought his brother Franz might help me. I didn't explain why I needed a bible, and by that stage Wirth knew better than to ask: he just looked at me. 'Give the devil your little finger, and he'll take your whole hand,' he said.

Franz was ready when I came to collect it. He checked that nobody was watching, then lay a black suit across the counter and opened the jacket, and inside was a very heavy bible with a tooled leather cover and an elaborate clasp. Powdery gold clung to the edges of the pages, and I could make out a duller streak through their shimmer, like unpolished brass; the place where someone's thumb rested while he or she leafed through, looking for the right verse. I found pressed flowers near the back: a stem of foxgloves, their petals as light as the wings of moths. Gently I lifted them free, traced my finger over the indentations they left behind, the tea-coloured speckles. A woman must have placed them there, I thought; women were the ones who pressed flowers. Anna had kept a rosebud from her wedding bouquet, dried to a hard little nub in the back of a photograph album – but I didn't want to remember that. Instead, I skimmed the verses between which this unknown woman had placed her stem of foxgloves. *Herein is our love made perfect, that we may have boldness in the day of judgement: because as he is, so are we in this world.* Someone had picked the foxgloves for her, I decided – on a walk in the countryside, when everything was still and heavy and jammed with colour and heat. He'd let go of her arm for a moment and bent and picked them for her, and she'd carried them all the way home. *There is no fear in love; but perfect love casteth out fear: because fear hath torment. He that feareth is not made perfect in love.* It had to mean something. It had to. But of course I couldn't know her, this lost woman, couldn't raise her from the page. I could just as much make the petals mauve again, the leaves green. Who knew what had become of her? And perhaps the verses meant nothing after all; perhaps she had chosen that spot near the back simply because the weight of all the pages above would best preserve the flowers. She was someone logical, sensible, I decided. And that told a story too, didn't it?

'Well?' said Franz, and I shook my head. It was too big for me to smuggle out, and far too big for Frau Hahn to hide in her bedroom.

'This isn't a department store, you know.' He sighed. 'Wait here.'

The sacks of clothing stretched away into the distance, hanging on their hooks; there was no end to them.

When Franz returned he produced a much smaller bible with a plain black cover. Inside, an inscription: *To Peter, on the occasion of your confirmation, 22.5.19, from your loving parents.* And then, written in a different hand, a family tree, starting in the 1740s with a Johann Vogel and his wife Maria, née Roth, and descending through seven cramped generations, the names growing smaller and smaller as the writer realised he was running out of space. Peter Vogel, born in 1905, appeared near the bottom of the page, next to his wife Ottilie, née Böhm, but they'd had no children – or at least, no names were recorded. I slipped the little volume beneath my shirt, where it rested against my ribs like a cool hand, and I was about to go when I noticed I'd left the foxgloves lying on the counter. I knew that sooner or later the bible I'd found them in would probably be pulled apart, the pages torn from the spine and dropped into the toilets and latrines, all the epistles and the gospels smeared with shit, the songs and the psalms, the lamentations, the miracles, but I slipped the pressed flowers back into place anyway, matching the leaves and petals as best I could to the shape they had left behind, and then I closed the book and fastened the clasp.

That night I dreamt of the Transparent Man. He lowered his arms and opened my shirt, peering at my chest with his transparent eyes, touching my flesh with his transparent hands. When he spoke, his throat shone, and his voice was water over river stones; it was melted glass. *Will you turn off the bulbs? Shut out the crowds? Bring me something to eat?*

The day of my next appointment with Frau Hahn I hid the small black bible inside my suit, and for hours I could feel it pressing at me as I bent over the prisoners' files, copying their details onto the new index cards. I was eager to see her – not just because of the danger of being discovered with the bible, I realised, but because I knew it would make her happy. As the guard accompanied me to the villa I felt almost buoyant, as if I'd been shopping on the Zeil in Frankfurt and found the perfect present. Along Carachoweg we passed a gang of prisoners hauling along a cart, delivering loads of cement to the Little Camp. Urged along at double time by SS whips, they sang 'Thuringia, Lovely Land'. *O freshest forest green, soft bloom on rosy cheeks; from every window a welcoming smile.* I looked away. But do you remember your mama's green leather gloves, Lotte, with the diamond pattern around the wrists? I bought them for her on the Zeil, before you were born; as soon as I saw them I knew they were exactly right, and I couldn't wait for her to try them on. She laughed when she unwrapped them, and asked me how I'd chosen exactly the thing she would have chosen for herself. You only had to look at them, she said – the fine, fine grain of the leather, the tiny stitches – to know that they would last forever, and that she'd never need another pair.

The early November morning was cold and still, no breeze to shift the constant smoke that clung to the Ettersberg like bad weather, but someone had placed a vase of greenhouse roses on the table just inside the Hahns' front door, and their scent filled the entranceway and followed me up the stairs. Frau Hahn was saying the rosary to herself again when I entered the room, and I sat beside the window and waited for her to finish. She knelt at the edge of the bed, reciting the Hail Marys, and then the Our Father. Her eyes were open, and she stared into the corner of the room, where I hid the machine behind the mirror. As if she were praying to the beechwood box. She took a breath after every few words, so the prayers were all broken and strange, and slowly her fingers worked their way around the loop of beads until they found themselves back at the beginning, and near the very end she turned her head and looked straight at me: *forgive us our trespasses, as we forgive those who trespass against us.*

When she'd finished, in the quiet of the bedroom I said, 'What does faith feel like?'

She sat on the edge of the bed and thought for a second or two. 'Like a vibration,' she said. 'A shaking that moves through your blood and your bones.'

'Like love.'

'Yes. Like love.'

I checked that Josef was downstairs, and then I took the bible from my pocket and placed it on her lap.

'What's this?'

'You asked me to bring you a bible, Frau Hahn. I have brought you a bible.'

'A bible,' she said. 'A bible.' She coughed, then caught her breath and opened the black book, running a finger over the names written in the front. 'Who are they?'

'I don't know.'

'We used to read it,' she said, tapping the page as if she meant this particular bible. 'On Sundays, after supper. Helena had the best reading voice. You have to go slower than you think – that's the trick.' Her finger paused under one of the names. 'There's a Dietrich.' She looked up at me. 'He can't know about it. He can't find it.'

'No,' I said.

'Will you help me?'

That's the trouble if you say yes to one favour: more will follow. 'Help you?'

'To hide it.' She reached over to her bedside cabinet, on top of which sat the wooden box carved with oak leaves and runes and lightning bolts. I had always thought it was for jewellery, but when she lifted the lid I saw it contained a book. 'Presented to us on our wedding day,' she said, pulling the marbled volume from its slipcover. The spine said *Mein Kampf* in gold letters, and the front was stamped with Munich's coat of arms. 'We'll keep in it here,' she said, and I thought: no. No, *you'll* keep it in there.

'In plain sight?' I said.

'Nobody ever reads it.'

'But what will you do with . . . with the original book?' I said. I couldn't speak its name.

She opened it and showed me the first page. *To the newly-wed couple. The capital city of the movement extends its best wishes for a happy marriage.* Dated and signed by the mayor of Munich.

'I was so young,' she said.

'You still are young, Frau Hahn.'

'Everything is happening too fast. There's not enough time.'

No, there wasn't enough time – and yet, at Buchenwald, every day was longer than the last. Over and over we filed to the mustering ground for roll call, waiting in the floodlit glare while they counted us to make sure we were all still present, standing to attention on our deadening feet. *Corpse carriers to the gate. Corpse carriers to the gate.* In our barracks we discussed the different ways the SS might destroy the camp before the Allies could take it – perhaps they would set fire to the place, or shoot us one by one, or bomb it from above, blasting us from the face of the Ettersberg, leaving behind only dirt, the white roots of shattered trees. And still the prisoners poured in, wretches from places even worse than Buchenwald, their skulls too big for their bodies. When I realised some of them had spent time in Theresienstadt I asked them if they knew Anna and Lotte Weber from Frankfurt, or Anna and Lotte Hirsch. A small-boned, pretty woman, I said, with a high forehead and a narrow chin and long black hair, and dark eyes that were almost black too, and a little girl who looked just like her, who would be – here I had to think, Lotte – who would be eight years old. Oh yes, they said, there were plenty who fitted that description, though they didn't recognise the names. But then, they said, the names were always changing at Theresienstadt as more prisoners arrived and more were sent further east. Not all, though, I said. Not all were sent further east. No, they said. Not if you were lucky. I took in their bony frames, their scabbed skin. They were weak from the trip in the cattle cars, delirious. That was what I told myself.

Greta Hahn's fingers pattered against the mayor's signature, picking out some old song. When she stopped the page lifted, enough for me to see the portrait of Hitler hazy beneath its sheet of tissue, and I remembered you sitting on my lap, Lotte, and pretending to guess at the next photograph in the album. Do you remember? I don't suppose you do; you were not yet three. The shape of my parents and my grandparents rising up through the blur of the thin white pages. The shape of myself as a child. Anna in a beach basket at the Bodensee, Anna on skis, Anna as a bride, Anna as a bride, Anna as a bride. Eventually you knew the pictures from memory, but we still played the guessing game, and I invented family events that had never happened: Oma Weber when she dined with the Kaiser, you on the back of an elephant, myself as a concert violinist. And then I lifted the sheet of glassine, and it was an ordinary photograph at the beach or the park after all. Oh, that's right, I said. Oma was never a trapeze artist. Opa never fought bulls.

Frau Hahn was positioning the bible over the title page,

checking its size. Then she took a pencil from her bedside cabinet and traced around the edges.

'What are you doing?' I said, though I had guessed already.

'I need a sharp knife,' she said. 'In the kitchen. The second drawer.'

Downstairs, Freya the Weimaraner was waiting by the front door, and she lifted her head and swished her tail across the floor when she saw me. Josef was in the kitchen, slicing bread. He pushed the loaf through the machine, the circular blade cutting it to the exact thickness the Hahn family required. He stood right in front of the knife drawer.

'Frau Hahn would like some of the cherries from the cellar,' I said. How easily I lied. When Josef nodded and went to fetch them, I grabbed two slices of the bread, as well as some cheese and a piece of sausage, and stowed them in my pockets for Foucher and Makovec. Real Emmental! And real liver sausage, not the half-rotten substitute stuffed with ground fishbones that they fed us. Then I opened the drawer and considered the knives. Something small, something sharp – I tested a few of them against the pad of my finger. Already I could hear Josef returning from the cellar, so I snatched up a paring knife with a hooked blade and hid it up my sleeve like a villain.

'Shall I take them to her?' I said, holding out my hand as Josef spooned the cherries into a pretty little bowl and set them on a tray, but he said no, it wasn't my place to wait on Frau Hahn.

'Of course,' I said. 'Just as you wish.'

I made sure to address him loudly on our way upstairs. 'I think she's getting her appetite back. She said she felt like cherries – it's a very good sign.' As we passed Karl-Heinz's room I saw that the train tracks no longer looped across the floor in their endless figure eight; someone had pulled them apart and put them back together in one long line that stretched from wall to wall, disappearing into the dark space under the bed.

By the time we reached Frau Hahn's room the bible had vanished and she was dozing – or pretending to doze; I couldn't tell.

'Josef has brought you your cherries,' I said, and a flicker of confusion passed over her face, but only for a moment.

'Thank you,' she said, taking two slow, deep breaths. 'How lovely.'

'There are plenty more, madam,' said Josef, placing the tray on Frau Hahn's lap and waiting for her to lift the spoon.

'Thank you, Josef,' she said. Then, when the boy did not leave, she added, 'That will be all.'

'Yes, madam,' said Josef, and he straightened the bed and tidied away a dressing gown and then, at last, went back downstairs.

Frau Hahn dipped the spoon into the fruit and turned the bowl on the tray, considering the cherries. I knew she wouldn't eat them.

'Did I want these?' she said.

'No,' I said. 'I had to get him out of the kitchen so I could find a knife.'

'You'll have to eat them then,' she said, pushing the tray away and producing the bible from underneath her pillow. 'Where is it?'

I withdrew the paring knife from my sleeve and gave it to her, and I took the tray onto my lap, and as I ate the cherries, each soft little globe bursting on my tongue like a miracle, she began to cut the outline of the bible from the pages of *Mein Kampf*. She left only the mayor's signature and the portrait of Hitler intact, and soon enough she'd sliced through to Chapter One: *Today it seems to me providential that Fate should have chosen Braunau am Inn as my birthplace*. Sometimes she cut through two layers at a time, sometimes three, pulling them free and discarding them on the eiderdown, and she was so preoccupied with her work that when I finished eating the cherries, and only a pool of juice remained, I lifted the bowl to my lips and drank every last drop.

'I did that at the dinner table once,' she said, removing another page. 'My mother called me a filthy little animal, and that night she made me eat my supper without a knife and fork. She wouldn't even let me use my hands.'

I thought: that doesn't sound like much of a punishment. But I said, 'I apologise, Frau Hahn. I didn't want to let it go to waste. In these times of shortages—'

'My sister made a noise like a pig, right there at the table, so Mama took her cutlery away too. Or perhaps it was a dog.' Another page, and another. Her breaths audible. 'She and Papa sat and watched us eat our supper like dogs, making sure we finished it all. They didn't say a word. My sister cried, but I didn't. I didn't cry.' She had stopped cutting, and the paring knife had slipped from her hand.

'We'd better start your treatment,' I said. 'It's getting late.'

She blinked a few times, as if just waking up. 'Do we have to?'

'Why ever not?'

'I have so much work to do.' She gestured at the mutilated book on the bed.

'Frau Hahn, you can't possibly finish that today.'

Some of the pages slipped to the floor. 'But where can I keep the bible?' She was holding it to her chest now, as if I might take it from her. I thought she was going to cry.

'What about under the mattress?'

She shook her head. 'That's the first place anyone would look.'

'Why would they look? Who's looking?'

'I think Josef pokes around.'

'Not under the mattress. Not with you right there on top of it.'

'I don't know what he does when I'm asleep. The elixir makes me sleep so deeply . . . Anything could be going on, and I wouldn't have a clue.' She started to gather up the removed pages. 'Will you burn these?'

'I – I'm not sure where I—'

'Just throw them into the living-room fire when you leave.'

She made it sound so simple. *There were very few Jews in Linz*, read the uppermost page. *Over the course of the centuries their outward appearance had become Europeanised and had taken on a human look; in fact, I even took them for Germans.* 'Very well,' I said.

'Do I have to keep taking it? The elixir?'

'Yes, Frau Hahn.'

'I don't know what it's meant to do. I can't remember.'

'It's helping you.'

I will abstain from all intentional wrong-doing and harm: that was the oath I had sworn. My duty as a doctor.

But I wasn't harming her; I wasn't.

And besides, I was no longer a doctor.

She handed me the bible. 'You'll have to take it with you, and bring it back next time.'

I grabbed her by her thin wrist then and leaned in close; so close I could feel her breath on my face. 'Do you know what would happen to me if they found it? What a risk I took in bringing it to you?'

She stared at me, the whites of her eyes huge. 'What would happen?' she whispered. The alarm clock ticked beside the bed, marking off the seconds. She said, 'You're hurting me.'

I let go of her wrist. I could see the white marks of my fingers on her skin. 'I'm sorry. I'm sorry,' I said. 'I wasn't thinking. I know what we'll do.' I slid the bible and the knife into the slipcover and shut them away in the carved box, leaving *Mein Kampf* lying on top. 'If anyone notices, they'll just think you're reading it.'

She grimaced, and a small cry escaped her lips.

'I'm sorry,' I repeated. 'It's the best I can—'

She cried out again, a guttural, animal sound, and clutched her side. And when I realised she was in pain, my first thought was not how I could relieve it, but what it meant for my own survival – mine and Anna's and yours, Lotte. No, I was no longer a doctor. I poured her a dose of the laudanum, which she drank without question, and then, even though I knew the Sympathetic Vitaliser was a fraud, a lie, I applied the contact plates to her shins and temples and flicked the switch. The low drone filled the room, *hm, hmm, hmmm,* as if someone unseen were trying to reach a decision.

'You need me, don't you?' she murmured as I was packing the machine away again. 'For your family.'

'Yes,' I said. 'I need you.'

She nodded. 'I won't tell him. About the pain.' Then she said, 'Will you call me Greta?'

When I left her she was already falling into her drugged sleep. Josef was upstairs, cleaning the windows – they filmed over so quickly there – and I slipped into the living room and threw the excised pages into the open fire. They took quickly, flaring into tall bright flames that reached as high as the chimney's mouth, and I felt a sudden surge of heat against my face. Then they were nothing.

I listened for a few moments, and when I was sure I was quite alone, I withdrew the bread and cheese and sausage from my pockets and stuffed it into my mouth.

December 1944

The wind shaking the leaves, he said, but I am bare branches, I am a trunk clogged with knots. I am invaded. Something is wrong, and I know it and have known it. The powdery light. The ash in the air. Where would we go, Karl-Heinz and I?

To my mother, my mother. To sit in her lap, to feel the thrum of her blood.

My rings loose on my fingers. Loose enough to slip off and disappear into some crack, down some drain.

Thoughts are just electricity. Sparks in the dark skull. I said, do they leave a trace of themselves? A machine to record them and keep them long after we're gone. Imagine the size of it. Still. What a thing.

The ash in the air. The smoke. Breathe.

Yes, I was feeling stronger. No, I had no pain. Yes, I would come downstairs, drink some mulled wine. I was turning a corner, I knew it, and we had Lenard – Doktor Weber – to thank.

But look at me, playing Confession.

The air-raid warnings were coming every other day, and we didn't know what to do with ourselves. Frau Proft said things must be bad, because one night the authorities shifted the coffins of Goethe and Schiller to Jena. When they converted the old tunnel system under the park into an air-raid shelter for us, we felt safer there than in our cellars – we were twelve metres deep – but then we realised they were letting prisoners in.

'Shut away with spies and murderers and rapists,' said Frau Starke.

'It's a step too far,' said Herr Heller, who'd had a poem published in the local newspaper and felt he could talk with some authority. 'An insult to all our young men away at the front. *O steely light to crown them bright! O Iron Cross to cherish! Though they may fall, so say we all: Never shall they perish!*'

'I'm certain they're responsible for the break-in,' said Frau Jaeger, whose garden allotment had been vandalised the previous week. Someone had cut her wire fences, stolen clean washing and a pair of binoculars, and let out her chickens and rabbits.

'Yes, it must have been them,' said Doktor Lang.

'And if they're all wiped out in an attack?' said Frau Andrecht. 'Who else will clear away the debris? Check for duds?'

'And how else will we build the Gauforum?' said Frau Proft.

The massive complex on Platz Adolf Hitlers made our houses look so small; the Gauleiter broke the ground for it in 1936, and it was still under construction. The Hall of the People would hold twenty thousand of us, and its bell tower was to be the tallest building in Weimar, taller than all of our church spires, and just as fine as anything in Berlin. We had to sacrifice a few of our oldest little streets, but they built us a smart new one to make up for it, and called it X-Straße: when the war was won we'd choose a new hero to name it after. For years the teams of prisoners had been coming to mix the cement and lay the stones for the Gauforum, though recently things had slowed down.

'I heard they're inviting the Führer to open it when it's finished,' said Pastor Bachmann.

'If it's finished,' said Frau Dreher.

'It must be costing a fortune to feed them all, though,' said Frau Ungewiss. 'And they'll be getting the heavy labour rations too, while here we are having to make do.'

'You should see the loot in Kohlstraße,' said Herr Gräber. He'd had reason to glimpse the sorting room at the customs office one day, and he couldn't believe his eyes. Piles and piles of Red Cross packages; mountains of parcels sent from private homes across Europe. The SS were tearing into them like animals, snatching at the coffee and jam, the cigarettes and eggs, wolfing down jars of peaches and pears and little cakes of chocolate without even trying to hide it, pocketing the hand-knitted socks and scarves, the bars of soap, the vitamins, the toothbrushes. It was shameful; they knew full well it was their duty to divert such items to the Reich.

'But there is a price to be paid,' said Frau Dreher. 'For taking such things.'

'Only if you're caught,' said Frau Rademacher.

Frau Proft said, 'Like Herr Beiter, you mean.' For years everyone had known that Beiter the tobacconist would sell you as many cigarettes as you could smoke provided you brought him some eggs or bacon. When he was found out they fined him and put him in prison, and his wife took her own life. One or two of us went to visit him and did what we could to provide sympathy, but we didn't say what we were all thinking: that he deserved it.

'I heard,' said Frau Bäumler, 'that the SS don't notify the family when a prisoner dies, so the Red Cross still sends packages.'

'It's not just the SS helping themselves,' said Herr Auer. 'I know of certain larders that are very well-stocked. Tins of cocoa. Preserved peas, green beans. Slices of bacon. Strings of sausages.'

And it was all very well to have the ration coupons, said Frau Rademacher, but making sure you followed the rules was another matter: *Just as in the 69th allocation period, in the 70th allocation period only potato-starch products may be purchased using coupon numbers 21 and 22 from the pink groceries cards as well as numbers 9 and 10 from the blue groceries cards . . .*

'Well,' said Herr Donnert, 'why should those criminals up on the hill be eating sausages and bacon when we have to make do with potatoes and cabbage? When there's not a joint of beef to be had in all of Weimar? Not so much as a rabbit left in the forest?'

'He's right,' said Frau Häusler. 'I've managed to come by the odd bit of bacon myself, the odd tin of this and that, and I don't care who knows. It's nothing more than I'm due. I have four children to feed.'

And so an argument flared, and we couldn't agree just who had the right to the goods in the packages, and some of us shouted that the SS should open the sorting room to the public and let us help ourselves, and others insisted that there had to be a system of distribution so the goods were allocated according to need. And some of us remained silent and did not speak at all.

9 November 1954

[tape corrupted in places]

T his hasn't happened in years – I don't know why it's
started up again. I just need to put my head back and
pinch my nose for a moment . . .

So yes, word came that our neighbourhood in Munich had
been hit; as far as I could ascertain, our building was still
untouched, though many others were craters. I could have
kept the news from Greta, the way I had kept her illness a
secret – but I told her, because it was proof that we were right
to come to Buchenwald. We should have brought our wedding
china, she murmured. And the prisoners in the quarry kept
chipping out the stone, breaking up the Ettersberg a little
more every day, and the prisoners in the gardening squad kept
clawing out the frozen tree roots, and at the new camp at Berga
they started blasting tunnels, and I began to think that the
whole of Germany might collapse into a hole in the ground.

We could not cope with the masses of prisoners they were
sending to us – all the scrap from the cleared camps. Adjutant
Schmidt tried to keep on top of the ones the Gestapo brought
to the basement of the crematorium – and here I must make it
clear that despite the stories you might have heard, no inmates
of Buchenwald were executed there: only criminals who'd
received a fair and legal sentence. And the witnesses who said
they saw me in that place clearly confused me with Schmidt,
or with Schiedlausky – why would the head of administration attend such events, for goodness' sake? Nothing was
proved. So yes, Schmidt tried to keep on top of those ones,

and happily accepted the bonus cigarettes, liquor and meat awarded for such work, but my budget couldn't cover the upkeep of the rest of them; the sums did not work, the books would not balance. I tried to do what I could as a matter of principle – earlier in the year, for instance, I'd ensured we had eighty thousand pairs of woollen socks available for the coming winter, but we lost them in the August terror attack. Such events were quite out of my control. Believe you me, I . . .

[corrupted]

. . . that stage they were even sending us members of the Wehrmacht, members of the SS, who were guilty of desertion: decent German men at heart, some of them still in uniform. We were forced to dispose of the ashes in the sinkholes on the southern slope of the Ettersberg – the Devil's Pits, where Karl-Heinz liked to ride his sleigh. Still, despite the ballooning numbers, I continued to take into account the well-being of the prisoners – I engaged a Weimar firm to supply us with hernia trusses, for instance, which allowed many of them to continue to work. And we never resorted to gas: that must go on the record. At Buchenwald itself, we never gassed anyone. Though it would have made my life much easier.

The trial of Karl and Ilse Koch was playing out too, finally, and I had to give evidence about the spoils we found when we raided their villa. Judge Morgen had stockpiled a ferocious amount of evidence, and the prosecutors called on prisoners as well as colleagues, presenting ledgers from the camp, personal bank statements and even private correspondence between the Kochs. Ilse once again was distancing herself from her husband, claiming that she'd known nothing about his crimes, and that she'd grown frightened when she happened on his bankbook one day and saw the huge sums. It was quite disgraceful, the way she flirted with the authorities. I didn't disclose any of this to Greta; it would only have worried her. Certainly, I didn't mention that they were charging Koch not just with embezzlement of funds but with incitement to murder too. He'd caught syphilis on a trip to Norway, it seemed, and two medical orderlies from the camp treated him in secret, and he had them done away with – shot while attempting to escape – in case they talked. And that was where he tied himself up in knots – the *unauthorised* killings. Greta didn't need to know about such things.

As if that weren't enough, Weber was becoming impossible. He kept asking me for proof that his family was safe in Theresienstadt; he'd heard stories from some of the new arrivals, he said. That it was a transit camp. That the prisoners were sent on to Auschwitz. I told him I would look into it – but how could I? What would you have done, in my position? Bad enough that I had summoned him in the first place, and even worse that he was treating Greta. And still no word on the certificate to eliminate his Jewishness. Impossible.

The simplest thing would be to dismiss him – to threaten to dismiss him. Despite his insistence that only he could administer the treatment, perhaps the magic lay in the machine and not in its maker; perhaps he didn't have to apply the contact plates and turn the dials himself. But I wasn't willing to take the risk. I saw how he bent in close to the beechwood box when he was operating it – checking for the tiniest of signals, it seemed, like a safe cracker listening for the click of a lock about to yield. I doubted he could teach that to someone else – or I doubted he could teach it in time. Twelve months, the surgeon had said, and that was twelve months ago. I was all too aware that December was here again; there was a savage bite in the air. But she had improved, hadn't she? Overall, thanks to Weber, she had. This was a temporary setback; she would improve again. She herself insisted the treatment was working. And in the end, even if it was unsuccessful, at least I would know I had tried my very best. At least I would have peace of mind. If nothing else.

It was Schwartz, the labour allocation officer, who told me about the inspection at Theresienstadt. The Danes had been poking around, he said – wanting to make sure their resettled citizens were safe in this model town, this place built on the Führer's orders for the Jews of Europe. The Danish king had arranged to send a party from the Red Cross to look it over.

'Can you imagine?' said Schwartz. We were passing the gatehouse, and we watched the new arrivals crowding into the mustering ground to be shorn and disinfected – a thousand head had been delivered that morning alone, give or take. Schwartz seemed in a contemplative mood, and for once he didn't bother to wave his pistol around when the inmates failed to salute him as they marched by. He would oversee the selection of the usable ones, sending them for a medical examination and then off to work at one of the satellite camps. All very well for Schwartz, but it meant that at the parent camp we were left with the malingerers who were of little use as workers and were therefore more expensive to keep. The number of amputations from frostbite alone! I can't tell you how many prosthetics and crutches I had to find the money to buy. The American prosecution failed to understand why the inmates wore clogs even in winter, when we still had a decent supply of leather shoes in the warehouse; they offered this up as evidence of an evil common design. In fact, the reason was perfectly innocent: if we issued the leather shoes to prisoners to wear in the camp, what would they put on when they were released?

I asked Schwartz how much notice they'd had at Theresienstadt.

Quite some weeks, he said – but you'd want months, wouldn't you? Years. Where would you even begin? He looked through to the compound as if trying to answer his own question.

'There,' I said, nodding at the crematorium.

He shook his head. 'Best to burn the whole camp down and start again.'

Perhaps the bombing was still too fresh in my mind, but I could see it as he spoke: the wooden barracks on fire, and the wooden gallows, and our wooden villa, and the stump of the Goethe oak too. It wouldn't take much to set it alight. Turn everything to ashes.

A cat stole up to us then and threaded itself around our legs. Two such animals had been approved for the prisoners' library after rodents gnawed their way into several valuable copies of Rosenberg and *Mein Kampf*, and this one in particular seemed determined to deposit as much hair as possible on my uniform. I shook it off and attempted to brush the hair away.

'Nobody's been asking about this place, have they?' said Schwartz, bending to scratch the creature between the ears.

'Not as far as I know,' I told him.

That was just it, though, he said. You wouldn't know, until you found out. And then you'd have a matter of weeks to put everything to rights.

In front of us the backwards motto on the gate: *To Each His Due*. That wouldn't burn.

The business with Koch was the last thing we needed, I said, and he agreed. Exactly the wrong sort of attention.

We both fell silent. The trial had finished, and while Ilse was released for lack of adequate proof, Koch himself had received a death sentence. Two death sentences, in fact. Everyone was wondering when the execution would be carried out, and where, and by whom. Himmler wanted to hang him in front of everyone at Buchenwald, including the prisoners, I heard. I thought of my box of gold locked away in the writing desk – but that was nothing in comparison to what Koch had stolen. I had taken only my due, only what I deserved – a tooth here and a tooth there – nothing, really, in the scheme of things. Certainly, I hadn't . . .

[corrupted]

' . . . they believed it?' I asked. 'The Danes. The Red Cross.'

Schwartz nodded. They were led along a set route, he said, so they could see all the flowers that the prisoners – the residents – had planted, and the freshly painted housing blocks, and the carousel for the boys and girls, and the shops and coffee houses that looked like real shops and real coffee houses in a real town. Bread and baked goods filled the shelves in the bakery, and jars of sweets glittered in the sweet-shop window. There was even a mayor, who also seemed real, and nobody thought to ask why his face was bruised. They'd thinned out the numbers by a few thousand head beforehand, so it didn't look too crowded, and placed the more presentable prisoners – residents – at certain points along the route, telling them what to say if the Danes asked any questions, and to say nothing if they asked the wrong ones. Eichmann himself had come, and various officials from Berlin, to make sure it all ran according to plan. A group of children performed a little opera about talking animals or some such rubbish, and a choir, led by a famous conductor, sang Verdi's *Requiem*. 'Crazy Jews,' someone heard Eichmann say, 'singing their own requiem.' And Schwartz and I laughed, because it *was* crazy, if you thought about it. Then I . . .

[corrupted]

. . . and told Weber that his family was fine, and that it was common for mail not to get through, what with all the disruptions to the railway lines. 'I've checked,' I said. 'They're perfectly well. And besides, the Red Cross inspected the place. Is that proof enough for you?'

He nodded, and I thought that was the end of it – but then he said, 'All the same, I would like a letter from my daughter.'

I was watching Karl-Heinz practise his handwriting when I had the idea. He was copying a paragraph from one of his schoolbooks into his exercise book for homework: *The flames shine brightly on all the boys and girls. They raise their hands and sing a song. Kurt thinks of the sun. His father said the fire comes from the sun.*

'Very good. Very neat and tidy,' I told him. He didn't need to press so hard, though – he was ruining the next page.

The sun is the mother of the fire, he wrote, his thumbnail white with pressure – and on the last word, the tip of his pencil snapped.

'I can't do it! It's all wrong!' he yelled, and started to cry.

'No no,' I said, taking out my whittling knife. 'You're almost finished. Look, we'll just sharpen the pencil.'

The next day I went to the mail room and told them I needed to sort through the incoming letters. There must have been thousands of them, sent to the inmates from all over Europe – and yes, some sent from other camps. I shuffled through them until I found what I wanted: a card from Theresienstadt, written in pencil. I could hear the radio in the gatehouse playing songs through the loudspeaker.

When I returned to the villa Greta was in the living room, listening to the same broadcast. A Magda Hain song started: 'Seagull, You Fly to the Homeland'. I sat at the table by the window seat, where the light was best, and erased the message on the card as well as the recipient, careful not to tear the surface. Then, with the tip of my whittling knife, I blurred the date. Niemand was running the carpet sweeper over the rugs, I remember, and when I blew the little grey eraser scraps off the table he rushed to sweep them away.

'Karl-Heinz,' I said, 'I have an important job for you.' I gave him a pencil and the cleaned card and said, 'I need you to write a note. I'll tell you the words.'

'All right,' he said. 'Who is it for?'

'Dear Papa,' I began, and waited as he formed the letters.

'Is it for you? Why am I writing to you?' he asked.

I motioned for him to keep going. 'How are you? I am fine,' I said.

Niemand was by the doorway now, still busy with the carpet sweeper, jolting it over the edge of the rug so it dumped a thick rope of dust and dirt at his feet. He was starting to get on my nerves, and I really didn't need him listening in. Watching. I dismissed him for the day.

'That's better,' I said to Karl-Heinz, who asked me if he should write anything else.

'We have plenty to eat,' I said. 'P-L-E-N-T-Y. That's right.' Then I had to tell him not to write *that's right*. 'Mama is well too,' I said. 'Write that.'

'*Are* you well too, Mama?' he asked.

Of course, I said.

Of course, said Greta from the couch.

He wanted to know if he could go and play, and I said, 'Second-to-last line. Lots of love. L-O-V-E.'

No one likes to be alone in the night time, sang the radio.

'Last line,' I said. 'Your Lotte. L-O-T-T-E. Good.' I had to tell him not to write *good*. I pointed to the space for the name and number and address and wrote Weber's details on a slip of paper for Karl-Heinz to copy.

It wasn't until a few days later that I noticed the damage to the table: he had pressed so hard that I could read the whole message dug into the wood, and the name, prisoner number and address all jumbled in with it too.

FROM LETTERS WRITTEN BY DOKTOR LENARD WEBER
TO HIS DAUGHTER

Frankfurt am Main, September 1946

I thought I was seeing things at first,' said Wirth.
It was a Sunday afternoon in December, the last day of
1944: too cold for us to sit looking at the view of the plain,
and too foggy to see very far anyway. Instead we walked
around the mustering ground, stamping our feet to keep
warm.

'What things?' I said.

'A whole column of them, walking up the hill like ghosts.
Blue and white, white and blue. I stood at the infirmary window and rubbed my eyes. Hundreds of women and children
stumbling up the slope. Heading for Buchenwald.'

'Women?' I said. 'And children?'

He nodded. 'Prisoners from somewhere or other. I could
hear the dogs and the gunshots. They came as far as the gate,
and then they stopped. And they waited there in the snow for
I don't know how long. And then they left.'

That night, a show for New Year's Eve: a painted grandfather clock that opened on the stroke of twelve to release a
child. He wore a Soviet uniform and the number 1945.

I heard, Lotte, that one of the prisoners managed to salvage
a section of the Goethe oak; a block from the trunk, charred
down one side. He was an artist, this man, an accomplished
painter and a master carver – he had made all the decorative
signposts around Buchenwald, and the officers used to call on
him to produce special pieces: sculptures of their children,

portraits of their dogs. He received nothing in return for this illegal work, but he and the other artists and craftsmen didn't complain, since it meant fewer men to make cartridge cases and aircraft parts, and fewer raw materials for the war. They even used to suggest items they could produce: might the commander of the guard battalion like a costly desk set of marble and bronze, similar to one made for the Reichsführer SS? Might the prison compound commander's wife welcome some wrought-iron window bars on their villa, particularly on the ground floor? Books bound with brass and copper, decorative silver photograph frames, vast chandeliers, fireplace tools, ashtrays, letter openers, cradles, chests carved with mottoes and runes, tables inlaid with shell and bone, intricate models of sailing ships . . . anything the officers or their wives requested, the prisoners made.

The block of oak from Goethe's tree, however, wouldn't decorate an SS home. The artist concealed it in the pathology department, where he was working by that time, and from it he carved a wasted face, a death mask. For his models he used the plaster casts taken from prisoners who had died, copying the hollows and contours of their cheeks, the plum-stone swell of their closed eyes, to make a face that contained them all. A group of men stood guard for him as he shaped it, sweeping up the slivers of wood as they fell, ready to hide the tools if the SS came. We knew what would happen to him if he was caught, but when he finished the carving he showed it to anyone who asked, unwinding it from a piece of sackcloth and displaying it like some starved and holy icon. The face rested snug in the sac of oak, its back charred from the fire. He let us cradle it in our dirty arms, kiss the cool wooden brow. I myself sat with its weight in my lap for quite some time, Lotte, unwilling to let go, aware that other men were waiting their turn even as they kept watch.

The face could not stay; the kapo charged with buying

groceries for the SS smuggled it out of the camp and into the safekeeping of a family in Apolda.

I wish that I could see it again.

I kept my own little piece of the tree hidden under my straw mattress. Sometimes, when I couldn't sleep, I imagined I could feel it beneath my head, pressing at my skull to remind me of something. The carved face came to me then, the bony mouth forever open, swallowing the frozen night, and I knew that it was hidden at the heart of the tree all along.

And it began to follow me into my waking hours, that face, and wouldn't leave me. It made me think of other faces, too, even though I didn't want to think of them: Anna watching me in the mirror as she brushed her hair, lips parted, eyes as dark as berries. The black curls flexing down her back with every stroke, alive in the shimmer of the bedside lamp. And your face, my Lottelein, when you put your favourite doll to bed on the radiator, and its head melted and collapsed; all winter we couldn't get rid of the smell. And Hahn's face when we watched the Goethe oak burn. His open mouth, his mouth empty of any words that might make sense of the blazing branches. The all-clear had sounded: we were safe. That's what I told him.

Each time I visited Greta Hahn she had carved away a little more of the book, and in between our treatment sessions she hid the cut pages inside it along with the knife, then gave them to me to burn. The hole in *Mein Kampf* grew deeper and deeper, like an escape tunnel, until one day she sliced free the final page: *A State which, in this age of racial poisoning, devotes itself to the care of its best racial stock, must one day become master of the Earth*. I started to congratulate her on her work – and then I saw that she was crying.

'Have I brought this on myself?' she said.

'What do you mean?'

'This . . . this condition. This place. I was fine before we came here. Before I agreed to come here.'

'That's a strange notion.'

'But it's true. In Munich I hardly had a cold, even when Karl-Heinz was sick. Dietrich used to say don't kiss him, keep your distance, but I paid no attention.' Her eyes drifted to the windows. 'I know what goes on out there,' she said, beginning to cough. 'Just past the gate.' She waved a tired hand. 'We're so close.'

I wanted to say that I doubted she did know what went on in the camp. The cudgel blows and the rifle shots, the lethal injections, the floggings. The men hung on hooks until they suffocated. The skin-covered skeletons that haunted the Little Camp; the lice that retreated from their bodies just after death. And I'd heard that we were to have a gas chamber, too, but a small group of prisoners with the right contacts kept delaying its construction. How much longer? Instead I said to her, 'Patients in your condition can have all kinds of troubling thoughts, Greta. Your treatment will be more effective if you do not dwell on them.' I uncovered the Vitaliser and lifted it onto her bedside cabinet.

'Is that true?' she said.

'In my experience.'

She sighed, nodded. 'I'm sorry, though,' she said in a low voice.

'What are you sorry for?'

She waved her hand again, then withdrew a card from her bible and passed it to me: a picture of a saint in a black robe, displaying a wounded leg.

'What's this?'

'My mother sent it. It's Saint Peregrine. Like the bird.'

'The bird?'

'The peregrine falcon. *Falco peregrinus*.'

I had seen such cards before, I recalled, in the wards at the

Holy Spirit. Pinned to the walls, tucked under pillows. The things we hold close; the totems and the charms.

'He's the patron saint of cancer patients,' she said.

The word drifted in the space between us. I could feel her scrutinising my face.

'Is he?'

'Yes.'

I studied the picture of the saint. 'Why would your mother send you that?'

'I suppose she thought it might help.'

I kept my gaze on the card. 'And what do you think?'

She looked away. 'They have his body,' she said. 'In a church in Forli, in Italy. All laid out in a glass box, and dressed in his monk's robes. People go there, they go there . . . '

I began collecting up the last excised pages from *Mein Kampf*. Slowly Greta's eyes closed.

'He had a tumour on his leg . . . they were going to amputate. But he prayed . . . he saw Christ descend from the cross and touch the tumour, and it was healed.'

'A miracle,' I said.

'Mmm.' Her eyes flickered open. 'If I were well enough, I'd travel to Italy to visit his shrine. You can see him there – you can see his body in its glass case, and it has never decayed. Perhaps when I'm better.'

'When you're better, you won't need to travel to Forli.'

'There have been miracles,' she said. She closed her eyes once more, and I set about attaching the paddles, then turned on the Vitaliser. 'Remember all the candles?' she said as it started to hum. 'We drank tea in the piazza . . . under the shade of the lemon trees. You told me that green was my colour . . . you bought me a paper cone of candied almonds . . . the air smelled hot . . . hot cobblestones and sugar . . . '

I slipped the card back into the bible and the bible into the hole she had made in *Mein Kampf*. It was a perfect fit, and once the cover was closed you couldn't tell it was there at all.

'I'm sorry,' she murmured again.

And I understood that she was not sorry for the things beyond her window, not sorry for Buchenwald, but sorry because she was dying. Though she'd pulled the covers high, I could tell her stomach was swollen, full of fluid from the spreading disease.

'Will you pray with me?' she said. 'The rosary?'

'I don't know the words.'

'Yes you do.'

And when she began, I realised she was right: I had heard her saying them often enough by then that they'd made a home in me, those prayers to a mother and a father. And as we recited them, her fingers moving along the row of beads, holding each one as lightly as a seed to be pressed into the ground, I knew that I was praying for her life as fervently as one who believes. Once I thought I heard footsteps in the hallway, someone pausing and listening outside the door – but nobody knocked and nobody entered.

And perhaps I prayed your card into being, Lotte; it came for me that day. There wasn't much to it, and I kept checking it to make sure I hadn't missed anything. And I kept repeating the words I had prayed with Greta Hahn: *Deliver us from evil. Deliver us from evil. Deliver us from evil. Amen.*

FROM THE IMAGINARY DIARY OF FRAU GRETA HAHN

January 1945

I left the picture of the Führer intact, and the page with the mayor's *best wishes for a happy marriage* – but underneath it is a hole. Not a word remains, only the white edges.

Plenty of room to swallow the bible.

He almost found it once. He wanted to tidy my hair for me, and he lifted the latest issue of *NS-Frauen-Warte* from the top of the carved box, looking for the comb. *Adopting a Child: many young war orphans are waiting to be welcomed into a new family.*

'Try the dressing table,' I said.

He couldn't find the comb there either, and I said it didn't matter, but he came and sat on the edge of the bed and began working his fingers through my hair, pausing when he reached a knot and calmly untangling it.

We took down the Christmas tree, unclipping the little candle holders and chipping away the wax, laying the swastika baubles in their cotton-wool beds. Where was the holy family? The set of carved figures from my mother? Ah, but they were not allowed, and I hadn't seen them for years.

'Are you well enough for this?' he asked, and I straightened and said yes, I was feeling much better.

My bible inside the cut book inside the slipcover inside the dark box. Its red ribbon hanging like a slumped tongue.

The first time Dietrich took me out, I was still a Catholic. You'll have to give it up, he said, and I said yes, yes of course, and he said Hitler and Himmler were both raised Catholic, so it was no obstacle as long as I renounced it, and my legs felt feather-light. We went to see the film about the Olympics, I remember – but no, we can't have, because the Olympics hadn't happened then. *Triumph of the Will* – wasn't that it? With the Führer descending from the clouds? As we sat there in the dark I was aware of the nearness of him, of his elbow resting against mine, his thigh close enough to touch. His shoulder pressing into me as he whispered certain facts: do you know that Leni Riefenstahl shot over sixty hours of film? Do you know she had pits dug in front of the speakers' platform so she could get the right angles? Afterwards we went to Café Luitpold, and he admitted he'd researched the information beforehand so he would have something to say, which made me like him all the more. But he could have said anything in that dark cinema and I would have nodded and murmured and shifted a little bit closer. He could have said anything at all. His breath on my neck. The scent of him.

Yes. Yes. And later, the first time we went out after Karl-Heinz was born – let me have a turn with him, said Dietrich's mother, who hadn't liked me at first, and oh, what a clever girl you are, Greta, and I could do no wrong – that's when we saw the film about the Olympics. The divers impossibly slow against the sky. I could feel the music shuddering in the soles of my feet, rushing up through my legs, and for a moment I was weightless. Filled with the future.

PART NINE
THE TRANSPARENT MAN

12 November 1954

[tape corrupted in places]

At the start of 1945 the parent camp alone numbered thirty-six thousand head, and with the Soviets bearing down on Auschwitz, thousands more were on their way. We did our best with them; even those dead on arrival received their own number. They were debited against Buchenwald, too, when they weren't our dead at all, which helps to explain the figure trotted out as gospel in the Dachau trial: five thousand deaths per month in the final stages. This assumption was not in accordance with the truth, but how the Americans loved the sound of their own voices! *We are unfortunately unable to comply with the request of counsel with respect to furnishing the whereabouts of the victims. They were last seen, may it please the court, being carted into the crematories and from there they went up the chimney in smoke and all the power of the United States and all the documents in Augsburg and elsewhere cannot tell which way they went.*

I heard that the SS set fire to the clothing warehouses at Birkenau before they fled, and blew up the last crematorium. Some of us believed that the Allies might part ways – that the Americans and the British might unite with Germany to fight the Soviets – but Warsaw had fallen, and Kraków had fallen, and every day the news grew worse. Berlin told us we could no longer send sick prisoners to recuperate at Bergen-Belsen – and let me just say that at the time we believed it was a convalescent camp – so we would have to take care of the swarms of extra invalids ourselves. I requested additional clothing – in writing and by telephone, more than once – but nothing came. There will be documentation somewhere to prove this. Later on the persons responsible were tried and sentenced at Nuremberg, and rightly so, but at the time I didn't have the supplies to feed and clothe thirty-six thousand *healthy* men! And Schiedlausky, in his wisdom, approved extra alcohol rations for the SS men supervising corpse retrieval from the transports – easy enough for him to sign off on it, since it all came out of my budget. Here I should clarify that it was also Schiedlausky who decided how best to sort and process those arrivals – that was well beyond the scope of my duties. The crematorium worked non-stop, smoking all through the night – you can imagine how much of my budget it consumed – and then we started to run out of fuel. The Reichsführer authorised emergency burials because the rats were attacking the stacks of bodies; we had to restrict cremation to German citizens only. And yet, despite the increasingly desperate situation on the Ettersberg – or because of it, I suppose – my colleagues still found time to nurse their petty concerns. Schwartz came to me for no other reason than to complain about an undelivered package from his wife. She'd sent him a box of her baking from home, but it had never arrived; in its place he received an anonymous note, postmarked in Weimar: *The contents of your parcel were delicious – but nothing to smoke?*

'Some disgusting thief,' he hissed, 'ate my poppyseed log. My special fruit loaf. My little chocolate mushrooms with the hazelnuts on top. Some filthy criminal put his hands all over the card Johanna made to wish me a happy 1945.'

'They'll find him and deal with him,' I said, and they did – a Dutch guest worker at the post office in town – but even then Schwartz was not satisfied.

'Johanna is heartbroken,' he said. 'She spent hours chopping the dried fruit and nuts. It's not good enough.'

My secretary brought me a pile of papers to sign then, so I

was able to get rid of him. After that I trimmed the dead parts from my potted plant – had I overwatered it? Underwatered it? – and tried to clear my mind, but by that time the only thing that calmed me was the cards. I was playing for money almost every night, after Greta had gone to sleep, and it no longer mattered whether I won or lost; the gamble was the thing. I started to make bets with myself away from the skat table, too – small, private predictions to see if I could guess the immediate future. Whether the temperature would fall below minus five. The colour of the smoke from the crematorium; its prevailing direction. The number of times that Freya would turn around before settling onto her mattress, flattening remembered reeds and rushes from the days when dogs were wolves.

And Weber was still pestering me for news of his family; apparently an actual card from his daughter wasn't enough. In the end I telephoned Henning again, though I hated to ask him for any more favours.

He could make some enquiries, he said, and paused. How was my family? How was Greta?

'We thought we'd turned the corner,' I said. 'But lately . . . I don't know.'

He asked what her doctor thought, and I told him that according to Weber she was improving. The machine disrupted healthy cells as well as diseased ones. The weakness would pass.

'And Greta?' he asked. 'What does she think?'

'That she's feeling better,' I said.

'Well then,' he said. 'You see?'

I kept up my bets with myself: *Today, Greta will finish her breakfast.* Wrong. *Today, in the cattle cars that arrive from the east, there will be corpses frozen solid, stuck to the metal floors.* Right.

Two weeks later a letter arrived from Henning – a Christmas

card, in fact, though it was well past Christmas by then. *Saving paper*, he scrawled on the front, which showed a bird singing in the snow. He sent it to my home address, and inside, beneath the greetings for *A joyous yuletide and a prosperous 1945*, he listed the details about Weber's family that he'd obtained from Theresienstadt. The names and the dates, so we could be sure we had the right individuals: Anna Hirsch and . . .

[corrupted]

. . . the beautification for the Red Cross inspection at Theresienstadt, they also shot a documentary film there. *Something to calm your doctor down?* he wrote.

When I was next in Kommandant Pister's office, I asked him if he knew of the film.

'I heard about it,' he said. 'Singing children. Games of soccer. Contented workers.'

Then he told me that once again the authorities in Weimar had requested an inspection of the camp's sewerage system. They were concerned about some cases of typhus nearby and wanted to check it wasn't coming from us.

'Should we agree to the inspection?' I said, and he said no, we should not agree.

Not my decision.

He stood up from his desk, ran a hand over the chest carved with the Goethe quote. Had I heard, he said, that at Groß-Rosen the prisoners had started backing the SS? Standing alongside them, armed and waiting for the enemy?

'Armed?' I said.

'It would never work at Buchenwald,' he said.

As soon as I returned to the matter of the documentary film he said, 'It's far too late to do anything like that here, Hahn, if that's what you're getting at. And what would it prove?'

'All the same, I'd be interested in seeing it,' I said.

'What would it prove?' he repeated.

Exactly what I needed it to: that Theresienstadt was not a

death camp. *Pigeon-grey*, I thought as I left Pister's office, but when I stepped outside and looked over to the crematorium, the smoke was almost black.

I began to notice that Greta was losing the weight she had gained back, and her skin was dry and chalky, her breath sour. One night I found her engagement ring glittering in the drain of the bedroom washbasin. It looked for all the world as if she'd tried to wash it away.

When I told my grandmother I was going to propose, I remember, she gave me a few bits and pieces to sell, to put towards the ring. I knew they were nothing special – nothing of particular value – but I wanted to buy Greta the best diamond I could; given the difference in our ages, I wasn't sure she would say yes. I went to a pawn shop and waited while the owner, a sly little man, rummaged through the necklaces and brooches, holding them up to an eyeglass and finding flaws that were invisible to any normal person. He offered the glass to me to prove he wasn't lying, showing me how to fit it into my eye socket – it was still warm from his own, which I found rather disgusting, but I wanted to see. I wanted proof. I squinted at the marcasites and garnets and faceted jet: all the scratches and abrasions I never knew were there. All the dirt. The bits of lint. The single hair – human? Fox fur? – caught under a claw. And I could see my own skin, too; the tips of my fingers magnified many times over. How pitted they were. How rough. He asked me what figure I had in mind, and then counted out a quarter of that amount.

'Forget about him,' Henning said when I told him. 'Just you wait – he'll get what he deserves.'

And three years later, when Greta and I were married and Karl-Heinz was walking and talking, I strolled past the place where the pawn shop used to be; the front window was boarded up, and painted warnings splattered the brickwork.

I don't know how she could have failed to notice that the ring had slipped from her finger and into the washbasin. In any case, after I retrieved it from the drain and dried it on a hand towel, I heard her calling me from the bath. I was shocked when I saw her – all the flesh had withered from her arms and legs, whittled clean away, but her stomach was swollen as if she really were with child.

'Will you help me get out?' she said.

As the war neared its end, I found myself thinking more and more of the past. When I first met Greta I had already begun to make my mark at Dachau, and she understood the long hours I needed to devote to my work, and didn't nag and complain the way many women do. My efforts were not going unnoticed, I assured her, and they would not go unrewarded. When I was offered the position at Buchenwald I knew what it would mean not only for my career, but also for my family. Yes, there would be difficult aspects to the job – no position of authority is without them – but I was confident that after the war those who had shouldered such difficulties would receive their due. By 1945, though ... by 1945 I was beginning to wonder why we ever went there. Greta never had a day sick in Munich; never a cold, never an ache or pain. Perhaps she was right; perhaps it *was* the place that had made her ill. My hair was falling out by the handful, and Karl-Heinz was not the same boy, either. 'Look at your model train set,' I told him. 'Look at your rocking horse and your marbles and your books. Your beautiful butcher's shop! Imagine if you lived in Hamburg or Dresden, or down in Weimar, for that matter, where lots of boys don't even have a house. Goodness me, you have a zoo right on your doorstep! Bears! Monkeys! What do you say about that?' Nothing.

And then, I heard somebody crying when I came in the front door one afternoon in February: somewhere nearby, sobbing. 'I'm sorry, I'm sorry,' he was saying. 'Please stop. I don't know. I'm sorry.'

I followed the sound to the kitchen, where I found Niemand and Karl-Heinz. They didn't notice me at first, and from the hallway I saw that Niemand's sleeve was rolled up, and that Karl-Heinz was pinching the inside of his arm – pinching and twisting.

I said, 'What are you doing?'

They both started, and Niemand's hand flew to his sleeve to roll it down.

'A game, Herr Sturmbannführer,' he said. 'We're playing a silly game.'

'Karl-Heinz, is that true?' I asked, and the boy nodded. I looked from one to the other. 'It didn't sound like a game,' I said. 'Why was Niemand crying?'

The servant stared at the floor. They were just pretending, he said – but I made him show me his arm.

Bruises covered it, all the way up from his wrist, some as dark as thunderclouds, and others yellowing, almost healed – and there were bright-red patches, only just made, too fresh to have bruised yet. Around those I could make out the marks of little crescent-moon nails, and in places the skin had been broken.

'What kind of game is this?' I asked.

Neither of them answered. I grasped Karl-Heinz by the shoulders and waited for him to look me in the eye. 'If you hurt Niemand's arm,' I said, 'he won't be able to make you hot chocolate. He won't be able to sweep the floors and scrub the bath and wash the clothes. Then what will we do?'

'Get another one,' he said.

Over the following days I tried to draw out the truth from them, both separately and together. Had Niemand done something that only Karl-Heinz knew about? Did he need to be disciplined? But I could discover nothing more; it seemed there was no reason for this game of theirs. I decided not to trouble Greta with it, though I would have welcomed her thoughts, especially regarding the correct punishment for Karl-Heinz. Should I withdraw all desserts for a month? Forbid him to play with Felix? Should I take to him with my belt, as my own father had done to me? I could still remember the crack of the leather on my bare legs, though I could no longer recall many of my crimes. And Karl-Heinz appeared to be waiting for his punishment, wanting me to reach a decision. All I could think was: *Today, the loudspeaker will play 'Women Are No Angels'.* Wrong. *Today, I'll see a fox in the forest.* Wrong. *Today, Martin the bear will rise up on his hind legs as I pass.* Right. *Today, the smoke will blow east.* Wrong. *Today, they will bomb Leipzig.* Right.

A few days later, after a final unsuccessful discussion with Karl-Heinz, I said to him, 'Which is your favourite pair of animals in the ark?'

'You haven't done the ark yet,' he said. 'It's imaginary.'

'I've been working very hard,' I said.

He wanted to know if I'd been working very hard making the ark.

'My proper work,' I said. 'My duty.'

In a sulky tone he told me I hadn't done the people yet either. I hadn't done the ark, *and* I hadn't done the people.

It was evening, nearly time for him to go to bed, and Niemand had brought his pyjamas down to warm them in front of the fire.

'It's late,' I said. 'Tell me which pair of animals is your favourite.'

'The tigers,' he said, and he clawed at the air and roared.

'Show me,' I said.

He ran out of the living room, still roaring – 'Quietly! Mama is sleeping!' I called – and he returned with the carved tigers.

'Now choose your favourite,' I said, and held out my hand. He passed me one of them; it was warm from his fist, and I ran my finger over the sharp points of its ears. Extraordinary that they had survived, the ears; I expected they would have long since chipped off, because I knew how rough little boys could be, but clearly he had looked after the animals. 'And now,' I said, 'throw the other one into the fire.'

'What?' he said, so I told him again – throw the other one into the fire.

He wouldn't do it. 'Why, Papa? No, no!'

'Shall we throw this one in, then?' I said. 'Your favourite?' I aimed it at the flames, and he began to cry.

One of them had to go, I insisted. He'd been very wicked; it was a matter of principle.

He pretended not to know the reason, so I told him he knew very well – Niemand's arm.

When he started to protest I said, 'You've had plenty of chances to explain yourself. Now throw it in.'

He knelt down in front of the fire, looked back at me once more, and I nodded. He tossed the tiger into the grate. It made a little puff of sparks, and he gave a final sob and fell silent, and we watched and waited, and then the dry wood flared as the flames took hold. The tiger's ears were on fire, its face was on fire, and for one wondrous moment it seemed to quiver and rise hissing to its feet.

Then we heard a voice. 'What's going on?'

We both turned to see Greta at the living-room door, leaning against the frame, impossibly small in her nightgown.

I told her she shouldn't be downstairs, she should be in bed, but she said she'd heard Karl-Heinz crying.

'What's going on?' she asked again.

'Nothing, nothing,' I said. 'You need to rest.'

She turned to Karl-Heinz. 'Is something going on?' she said.

The boy looked at his mother, then at me. 'Nothing, Mama,' he whispered.

I told her we'd help her back upstairs. I took one of her arms, and Karl-Heinz took the other, and as I watched him grasp on to her I thought of the marks on Niemand's skin. And as I was thinking of them, those dark little twists, Greta winced, and Karl-Heinz said, 'I'm sorry. I'm sorry.'

We tried to guide her into bed, but she pushed our hands away. 'I can do it myself,' she snapped, and again Karl-Heinz said, 'I'm sorry.'

As she manoeuvred herself onto the mattress I stood aside and clasped my hands behind my back to refrain from helping her. She took a long time to find a comfortable position, and when finally she lay back she kept smoothing the lace on the bed linen until it lay flat and straight. Karl-Heinz was over by the machine, I noticed, standing next to it with his head on one side. He reached out a hand and lifted the corner of the sheet, bending to peer underneath.

'Don't touch,' I said.

When we came back downstairs to the fire, the tiger had disappeared.

It is true that hundreds of prisoners employed in Weimar were wounded during the dreadful February bombing – the Kromsdorfer Straße armaments works and its barracks were badly hit – and it is true that we did not let them into our hospital and clinics. This was a purely logical decision on the part of our German Red Cross: there were only so many beds available, and only so many bandages, and we needed those beds and bandages for our own people. They stood a better chance of recovery, after all, than the skinny men who watched us with hollow eyes, who reached for us with spider hands. Those men we sent back to the parent camp; they had their own hospital up there on the hill, we reminded ourselves.

Other prisoners, who hadn't been wounded and therefore could still make themselves useful, were sent to tidy away the debris after the raid, and to check for dud bombs that might still go off, and to dismantle the teetering façades that might fall and kill someone. We were terrified the bombers would return, and the authorities warned that we must be ready at all times and always know where our gas masks were: they would protect not only our throats, but also our eyes. If we could no longer see, we were doomed.

We lost so much: our beautiful old buildings on the northern side of the Marktplatz; everything but the façade of the Nationaltheater. Bombs hit the houses of Goethe and Schiller, and Anna Amalia's palace, and the St. Peter and Paul church, where Herder and Luther once preached, and the Herz-Jesu church as well. The poor Bittermanns lost their chemist's shop, and a whole gang of prisoners came to clear away the mess; Herr Bittermann said he could hardly bear to look at them sorting through the ruins. And hundreds of our citizens died in the attack – thirty-seven in the German Mortgage Bank on Coudraystraße alone, which Doktor Amsel missed by minutes; almost all the children in the National Socialist Kindergarten on Richard-Strauss-Straße, their little lungs burst – so the prisoners dug mass graves, too. They must have realised the urgency, but often we saw them leaning on their shovels, eyes closed despite the watchful guards, and Frau Rabe said she spotted one man sprawled fast asleep on the ground. I wanted to jab him with the toes of my boots, she said, and remind him of his duty. They asked for bread and water, these criminals digging the graves, but we remarked that they were not there to eat lunch. Still, the occasional citizen gave them a little something: we saw Frau Lang handing out thin slices of bread, and Frau Hertz brought several flasks of substitute coffee. All the less for their own families, we murmured.

We had to draw the line at Frau Dreher's behaviour, though. One of the bombs had damaged her house, so a team of prisoners came to fix it – Frenchmen, mostly. Herr Ziegler, who lived next door, said she not only invited them inside, but she also spread her kitchen table with a pretty cloth and allowed them to sit there and eat!

'What did you feed them?' we asked.

'They were no trouble,' she said.

'But what did you feed them?'

'They were skin and bone.'

'What did you feed them?'

'I unwrapped a few biscuits. A bit of dried fruit.'

'From a Red Cross package?'

'I suppose so.'

'A Red Cross package labelled in French?'

'It might have been.'

'And what did they say, the French prisoners, when they saw this Red Cross package labelled in French, and the French biscuits and the French dried fruit?'

'Thank you. They said thank you.'

And that was not all. Herr Ziegler said he overheard the prisoners asking Frau Dreher what LSR meant – they had seen it painted everywhere. And before she told them the truth – that it stood for Luftschutzraum, or air-raid shelter – she said, 'It means *Lass Stalin 'rein*. Let Stalin in!' And she laughed a deranged laugh.

We had no choice but to report her.

At the cemetery, a beautiful statue to honour the fallen employees who lost their lives in the service of the German Mortgage Bank. A stone woman mourning in her stone robes.

Frankfurt am Main, September 1946

One day in February, when the guard escorted me to
the Hahns' villa, the Sturmbannführer himself
opened the door. For a split second I thought something terrible had happened, and I froze on the threshold and
said, 'Is she all right?'

'Your daughter is safe,' he said, glancing over my shoulder
to make sure the guard was out of earshot.

'I meant Frau Hahn,' I said.

'For goodness' sake, come inside.'

He shut the door behind me and by instinct began to help
me off with my coat, as if I were a guest, then shook his head
and stepped away. By instinct, too, I flinched from his hands.

'Safe?' I said. 'What does that mean? Has she been released
from the camp?'

He sighed. 'Town,' he said. 'Not camp.' He started to climb
the stairs to his wife's room, gesturing for me to follow.

'Herr Sturmbannführer? Is she no longer in the camp?
And . . . and her mother?'

'In your position, Weber,' he said, still making his way up
the stairs, 'I wouldn't ask too many questions.'

I swallowed, willed my chest to stop shaking. 'And in your
position, Herr Sturmbannführer,' I said, 'I wouldn't antago-
nise the man who can save your wife.'

He stopped, turned. Looming above me on the staircase,
he seemed twice his usual size. Under his chin I could see a
tiny patch of stubble the razor had missed. We regarded each

other for a moment. The clock ticked in the entranceway below.

'You are not in my position,' he said quietly.

'Am I not?'

The clock began to chime then, marking the three-quarter hour with its unfinished tune.

He turned away and climbed to the top of the stairs. 'They have made a film,' he said. 'A documentary.'

'What do you mean, a documentary?' I hurried to catch up with him.

'Just that. It documents life in Theresienstadt.'

'Life?'

'Of course, life. Daily life in the camp. In the town. I myself haven't seen it, but that is what I'm told. A bakery. A coffee house. A choir. So you see, they will be quite safe.' He paused outside the bedroom door. 'She's been coming out with some troubling things. She's not herself – you'll see what I mean. The doctor is here, Greta,' he said as we entered the bedroom.

She turned her head towards us, smiled. 'I went yesterday,' she said. 'I saw him in his glass box . . . undecayed . . . He could have opened his eyes and sat up and started to speak.'

'You see?' said Hahn. I wanted to press him for more information about the documentary, but he collapsed into a chair and held his head in his hands.

'Not a sign of corruption,' said Greta. 'Not a single sign of decay.'

'Is that so?' I said.

'Oh yes. It's a miracle.'

The Sturmbannführer was still slumped in the chair, so I set about washing my hands, scrubbing them clean with the pale-pink soap. In the mirror I could see Greta lifting an arm to reach out for something that wasn't there, but by the time I had dried my hands, removed the sheet from the Vitaliser and carried it over to the bed, she had settled. Hahn rose from his chair and bent to kiss his wife's forehead. Then he left the room, and a moment later I heard the front door close.

Greta had shut her eyes and lay very still. So still, in fact, that my fingers raced to her wrist to feel for her pulse – and there it was, as soft as the flick of a feather, though she did not move. The progression of her disease frightened me; it was clear she was taking more and more laudanum, and I knew it couldn't be long before Hahn realised what I already knew: the Vitaliser did not work, never had worked. Perhaps Frau Hahn's faith in it had granted her a little longer than statistically expected, but now the cancer was bolting through her and there was no stopping it. I switched on the machine, took up the contact plates, then paused. Would it matter, I thought, if I did not treat her at all that day? If I just let her rest? Who would know? The Vitaliser was humming its low hum, ready to begin, but I put down the plates and sat in the chair beside the bed and watched Greta. She was so young – much younger than Hahn. I recalled a patient of mine who had died of oesophageal cancer at thirty-eight; she was fifteen years younger than her husband. 'We always imagined I'd be the one left behind,' she'd told me. 'Emil won't know what to do with himself.'

I looked at the swell of her stomach: a different treatment today, perhaps. I opened the doctor's bag and withdrew one of the large syringes, then went down to the kitchen to find a candle and matches. When I returned Frau Hahn had woken, and she smiled and said in a sleepy voice, 'I thought I heard you. When is Mama coming?'

'Soon,' I said. I lit the candle and held the needle in the flame to sterilise it.

'Then she'll see what it's really like. She doesn't believe me, you know. Although lately I've been having my suspicions too.'

'I just need to do a little procedure,' I said. 'It won't hurt. Not very much. All right?'

She nodded, and I lifted her nightgown and inserted the needle into her stomach to draw off the fluid. I emptied it into the washbasin, then drew off more, and repeated the procedure for the fluid on her chest. 'This will help with the swelling,' I said. 'It'll help you to breathe.'

'Thank you, Herr Doktor.'

When I folded her nightgown back down she leaned over to the carved box beside her bed and withdrew the bible from the shell of *Mein Kampf*. 'I've marked it,' she said, passing it to me, and I realised she wanted me to read to her.

The book seemed to fall open of its own accord, the pages parting to the place where the ribbon marker lay. The verses were underlined with pencil. 'Praise ye the Lord,' I began, 'for it is good to sing praises unto our God; for it is pleasant; and praise is comely.' When I paused I could hear the Vitaliser still humming at my side, louder with each passing moment. 'The Lord doth build up Jerusalem,' I read, 'he gathereth together the outcasts of Israel.'

'Switch it off,' said Frau Hahn.

I looked at her. 'The Vitaliser? Are you sure?'

She nodded. And that was when I knew that she knew I could not save her. And I switched it off, my miracle machine, and the room fell as silent as a cave.

'He healeth the broken in heart, and bindeth up their wounds,' I continued.

As I was leaving I saw Josef kneeling on the bathroom floor, scrubbing the bath. A few of Karl-Heinz's wooden animals sat along its tiled edge, I noticed, lined up in a precise row, one animal per tile. Josef paused in his work and bent further into the bath. He was pulling at something that didn't want to come loose, and when he straightened I thought he was holding a dead rat by the tail. I must have let out a sound, because he turned to see me watching from the doorway.

'I'm sorry,' I said. 'I didn't mean to frighten you.'

He smiled. 'You didn't frighten me.'

The rat swung between his fingers, sodden and squashed – and I realised it wasn't a rat at all, but a clump of hair pulled from the plug hole.

'Disgusting, aren't they?' he said. 'They wondered why the water wasn't draining properly. Couldn't work it out.'

'Shh!' I said, and I looked over my shoulder, up and down the hallway.

'Oh, there's nobody around to hear. Just poor Frau Hahn, and she doesn't know what day it is.' As he flicked the hair into the washbasin I caught sight of his inner arm; it was dotted with little cuts and bruises.

'What happened to you?' I said. He was already pulling his sleeve down, but I snatched at his hand, turning his damaged skin to the light. 'Who did this?' He winced and pulled away, held the arm to his chest. He wouldn't look at me, but I could see his face in the mirrored medicine cabinet. 'Josef, who did this?'

'Karl-Heinz,' he whispered into the mirror. He turned on the tap to wash his hands, and the thing he'd pulled from the drain twitched and flexed as the water caught at its tail.

'Have you reported him?'

'Of course not.'

'But you must say something – otherwise he'll never stop.'

'It's not that bad. I think he's tired of it now.'

'And what will he do next?'

He shrugged.

'When did it start?'

'I don't know – a few months ago.'

'Months?'

'He asked me about—' he hesitated. 'He asked me about the end of the world. He said his father told him that's why I'm a prisoner, because I believe that the world will end, and that only believers will be saved.' He was still washing his hands, scrubbing and rinsing, scrubbing and rinsing, though the skin was cracked and raw. 'He wanted to know what it will be like, and I said it wasn't something children needed to worry about, but he kept asking me. So I told him that yes, we are in the last days: God has thrown all the demons from heaven, and they are here with us on earth. Where? he asked. Where are all the demons? What does a demon look like? And I said they look just like us; just like a normal person. So how can you tell they're demons? he said. By what they do, I said. And will everyone die, at the end of the world? he said. No, I said, not everyone: those who believe will not die, and a few very special people will go to heaven, to rule over the earth with Jesus, and others will be chosen to stay here forever, in a paradise on earth, and they will never get sick and never die. Never die? he said. Never die, I said. And who chooses them? Does the Führer choose? God chooses, I said, and he only chooses the people who have shown that they deserve it. And God will bring the dead back to life, too, and they will have the chance to save themselves, but if they fail then God will destroy them forever, as well as the people who don't deserve to stay. They will be gone, they will be nothing, and can never come back. Never? he said. Never, I said. And then he went very quiet, and hardly spoke to me for a few days, and I thought that was that. But then he started asking me *when* it would happen, *when* the world would end. And I said I didn't know, only that it *would* end, and soon, and he got very angry and said that I was keeping secrets, and it was wrong to keep secrets, and I had to tell him when the world would end so he could make sure his father did something about it. And I laughed. And that's when he grabbed my arm.'

I turned off the tap, took a towel and dried Josef's hands for him, careful to pat rather than rub. 'You know they'd let you go, if you renounced your faith,' I said.

'I know.'

'Would it be so terrible? Just to say the words, without believing them?'

He shook his head. 'All we have is the Word. No. No. They'll get what they deserve – you'll see.'

'To each his due?'

That made him smile. 'To each his due.'

'And what about me? Is there any hope for someone like me, at the end of the world?'

He studied our reflections in the medicine cabinet before speaking. 'You seem like a good man, Doktor Weber,' he said at last. 'But that's not enough.'

'I didn't think so.' I gestured at Karl-Heinz's animals queuing on the edge of the bath. 'The water will damage them,' I said.

'He's been playing at floods,' said Josef.

'Is that how it will come?'

'No.'

I handed him the towel, and he scooped up the mass of hair and rolled it into a bundle, then began to scour the washbasin.

'Your patient,' he said, 'how long does she have?'

I knew he meant Frau Hahn, but I said, 'Who?' The word echoed around the tiled space, hit against the window and the mirror, the hollow shell of the bath.

'You don't have to pretend,' he said. 'I know she's dying. How could I not know? You only have to look at her.'

'No,' I shook my head. 'No no. We're making progress. Sometimes, in such cases, it can seem the end is approaching, but I can assure you . . . my machine is . . . any day now . . . '

'Your miracle machine,' said Josef.

'I've never called it that.'

'But they do. I've heard them.'

'That's nothing to do with me.'

Josef kept scouring the basin and didn't reply.

'I've given them hope,' I said. 'What's wrong with that? You understand hope.'

Still he didn't reply.

'You don't know what's at stake,' I said.

'You seem like a good man, Doktor Weber,' he repeated, 'but you are not doing a good thing. It makes me uneasy.'

'What does that mean? Josef? What do you mean, it makes you uneasy?'

'You don't even believe in the machine yourself, do you?'

'Well,' I said. 'Well, the early trials indicated—'

'But now. *Now.*'

I sighed. 'I did believe in it. At one time, I did. I was going to save the world.'

'He believes it might still work. I've heard him say it. Don't you think it's time you told them?'

'I can't.'

'Well, someone should.'

I felt a terrible heaviness in my bones. 'Josef,' I said, and I grabbed at his arm. 'You mustn't say anything.' His breath was on my wrist, and I forced him to look at me. 'Please. Please promise.'

'Let go,' he said.

When the guard was marching me back to the compound, Hahn came hurrying out of the administration building. 'I need a word with the prisoner,' he said.

In his office he sat down at his desk, surrounded by untidy stacks of paper. 'These things she's been coming out with. You heard her.'

'It's the elixir, Herr Sturmbannführer,' I said. 'Quite normal. It complements the work the Vitaliser does. Attunes the blood, so the waves can travel unimpeded throughout the body. This film—'

'But what does she mean?'

'Nothing. Nothing. It's just a harmless side effect.'

'Harmless,' he said.

'Yes.'

'I thought it might be a sign that the disease is advancing.'

'It's a side effect of the treatment. Not the disease.'

'One thing I've been wondering,' he said. 'Why doesn't everyone know about your machine?'

'The war,' I said.

'Yes, but before the war.'

I thought of my conversations with Baumhauer; how I had convinced him to approve the trial. 'Other researchers were starting to follow suit. A clinic in Gallspach. The University Hospital in Vienna.'

'Vienna?'

'Oh yes. The University Hospital. There were serious flaws in their design, of course. Perhaps, after the war is won . . . '

'Yes, after the war is won.' He pulled some documents towards him and began lifting the corners of them with his thumb, signing his name without reading.

'This film,' I said. 'I want to see it. The film about Theresienstadt.'

'Impossible.'

'You're a powerful man, Herr Sturmbannführer. You can ask for anything you like, and it'll be there by morning. Hey presto.'

He went to shift a stack of paper out of the way but could find nowhere else to put it. 'You've heard of Kommandant Koch?' he said.

'Of course.'

'So you know what happens to those who abuse their power. And anyway, the film hasn't even been finished,' he added, signing his name over and over.

'There must be footage, though. Hours of it.'

He shrugged. His pen scratched out another signature.

'You tell them you've heard of the film,' I pressed on, 'and are considering a similar project at Buchenwald.'

'You're giving the orders now, are you, Weber?' He laughed. 'At any rate, it seems very late in the piece to be making films. Even imaginary films.'

'You'd like to view what they have so far, to see how it's done. Otherwise . . . ' – I took a deep breath – 'otherwise I'm not sure how long I can continue with Frau Hahn's treatment.'

He was looking up at me now, still holding the pen to one of the documents, his signature incomplete. The ink had started to pool, leaking across his half-written name. Covering it up. One of the piles of paper toppled across his carved desk set – the girl with the owls – and he pushed the pages clear but didn't bother to straighten them. Then he said, 'I can't make any promises.'

Neither could I.

Of course, I knew that the machine couldn't save Frau Hahn, couldn't save you or Anna or me. I also knew, however, that the Red Army had reached the Oder, and the Germans had failed to push back the Allies at Ardennes. How much longer? I thought of Frau Hahn's listless gaze, her pallid lips disappearing into her pallid face. How much longer?

Before curfew that night, Wirth came to find me in the latrines. I hadn't spoken to him in a few weeks; it was far too cold for our Sunday strolls. Although he tried to make a joke about the stink of the place – 'New cologne, Weber?' – he had a different look in his eyes: hunted, haunted. He'd been transferred to work in the Little Camp, he said. Sometimes he assisted the chief SS medical orderly, and sometimes it was his duty to deliver the treatment himself.

'Do you think—' he began. 'Do you think they know what the needle means?'

'Who?' I said.

'The ones in Block 61.'

The death block; we'd all heard about it. About the lethal injections that waited behind a door marked *Dispensary*.

'I mean,' he said, 'most of them are already so far gone. It's probably a release. Don't you think?'

'I imagine so,' I said.

He lit a canteen-tobacco cigarette and inhaled.

'Is it true they're hiding Jewish children over there?' I asked.

'Hundreds of them,' he said. 'In Block 66. They know the SS will never set foot in the place.'

Such things were possible then, Lotte. Such miracles.

March 1945

I missed Dietrich. I know I was the one who asked him to move into the spare room, but I missed the smell of him against my sheets, the weight of him next to me. I pushed myself over to the edge of the mattress and stood, grasping the bedside cabinet for balance, then made my way around the edge of the room, holding onto the wall. The ticking of the alarm clock. The trees still bare outside the windows. Hohenschwangau high up in the forest. The start of the rain.

How long did it take me to reach the door? To cross the hallway? Freya whimpering at my bare feet all the way, her ears as soft as the gills of a mushroom. *Let me out. Let me out.* Karl-Heinz's trains packed with the contents of his butcher's shop. The swans on the Bodensee. And then, yes, the smell of Dietrich. His dressing gown. His hairbrush. His folded socks and vests. At the back of a drawer a Christmas card from Henning: a bird in the snow, singing, and inside a note about Doktor Weber's family. I hadn't realised the Rosts knew the Webers. Though didn't we all holiday in Rügen that summer? And climb to the top of the Königsstuhl? The white chalk too bright in the sun. I couldn't look. Such sad news; I put it in my pocket.

And a chocolate box locked away too, far heavier than it should be, and I lifted the lid and the pain came, punching at my pelvis and my chest, and it was too heavy for me to hold. Hail on the floor.

'Come along,' said Josef. 'I'll help you back to bed.'

I don't know how long my mother had been waiting.

'I was asleep,' I said.

She said, 'Let me open the window.'

The ice, blasted into my lungs. The smoke.

'I know why you're here,' I said.

'Why am I here?'

'Because it's nearly the end.'

'That's not true.'

'Can't you smell it?'

My younger self carved in oak, watching Dietrich as he worked. She was quite cold.

I opened Henning's Christmas card. The bird in the snow, singing; the news of Doktor Weber's family. I took out my bible – though it was never mine. I turned to the family tree at the front and read the rows of names and dates, from Johann Vogel and his wife Maria, née Roth, all the way down to Peter Vogel and his wife Ottilie, née Böhm, who had no children. Then I took a pen, and at the very bottom of the page, in tiny letters, because there was hardly any room, I added us. The Webers as well as the Hahns.

16 November 1954

[tape corrupted in places]

If I'm honest, truly honest, I suppose I suspected she was slipping, but I couldn't help remembering how she had improved the previous summer, how the disease seemed to lift from her not too long after Weber began his treatments. And I was running out of choices.

Henning was reluctant to help with the film at first. 'Once you let someone like that get the upper hand . . . ' I remember him saying.

'He doesn't have the upper hand,' I said. '*He* is the prisoner.'

'Mmm,' he said. Then he asked how Greta was.

I told him she was coming along well. As well as could be expected. 'Do you know, they were trying a similar machine in Vienna?' I said. 'At the University Hospital.'

'Vienna?' he said. 'Another Jewish idea, then. I suppose you have to give them credit for something.' He asked me where I would screen the film. The camp cinema?

But that was too public. I said I could borrow a small projector from the office – so I'd need a copy in the correct format.

'Mmm,' he said again. 'Do you really think it will help, though? At this stage?'

'If it was your wife,' I said, 'if it was Susannah, wouldn't you try anything?'

He sighed and said he'd ask.

A week went by, then another. We were halfway through

March, and the Americans had swept across the Rhine at
Remagen, and thanks to the frantic clearances further east, I
was now the chief administrative officer of the largest camp in
the Reich: just as I'd always wanted. The Isolation Barracks
even contained some Stauffenbergs. When the enemy
squadrons passed overhead – on their way somewhere else, I
told myself – the whole place shook. I felt it in my teeth, in my
stomach. And then the bombs, juddering in the distance.
Schiedlausky told me questions were being asked about the
state of the prisoners sent to work on external construction
projects; how could they be so emaciated when they were
receiving the heavy labour supplements? Was this evidence of
some kind of administrative corruption, perhaps? I did not
like what he was implying, and I told him . . .

[corrupted]

. . . but according to the rations, it was impossible for a
prisoner to starve to death under my administration. Hadn't I
once purchased an entire carload of smoked tuna fish for the
camp, since it wasn't rationed? This is the kind of extra care I
took, above and beyond what duty required of me. You're welcome to check the surviving documents. As for the construction command, I want to make it very clear that they themselves were responsible for their prisoners, so any irregularities
were not my fault.

Still, it was a deeply unpleasant state of affairs. I was gambling every night, losing massive sums, and hot sand filled my
head, and I had to keep playing, I had to, and always, always I
tried to guess what was coming. *Today, Karl-Heinz will kiss me
on my cheek when he leaves for school.* Wrong. *Today, I'll need
six hundred steps to walk through the forest to my office.*
Wrong. *Today, a new transport will arrive from the east that
nobody has warned me about.* Right. *Today, the enemy will
reach as far as Frankfurt.* Right. *Today, the enemy will reach as
far as Hanau.* Right. I couldn't stop, even when I lay in bed and

listened to the rain and waited for sleep. Right or wrong, right or wrong; my country, right or wrong.

And the Führer wanted us to liquidate all remaining Jews, because they shouldn't be permitted to rejoice in Germany's defeat, and the Reichsführer ordered that we spare them and ensure they had sufficient food and medical care.

Impossible.

The film reached me at the end of the month.

Frankfurt am Main, September 1946

One Sunday morning, on the way to the Hahns' villa, a small grey-brown feather blew across my path, almost invisible against the wet ground. It whirled in the sudden breeze, spiralling up towards my fingers, and the guard at my side didn't notice as I caught it and put it in my pocket.

Karl-Heinz was in his bedroom, laying out cards in sets of four. 'Hitler, Hindenburg, Göring and Hess,' he said. 'Hitler who is friends with children, Hitler who is friends with animals, Hitler who is friends with nature, Hitler who is friends with the arts.'

In the spare bedroom the Sturmbannführer was locking something away in a desk, and he came to say goodbye to his wife before he returned to work. I went through the motions of setting up the Vitaliser, attaching the contact plates to Frau Hahn, who wearily held out her hands for them. I treated her for less than five minutes, just until the Sturmbannführer had gone, and then I lifted the machine back into its corner, covered it up like a songbird for the night.

'Will you read to me?' said Greta.

I took the bible from its hiding place, opened it to the underlined psalms and began. 'Why standeth thou afar off, O Lord? Why hidest thou thyself in times of trouble? The wicked in his pride doth persecute the poor: let them be taken in the devices that they have imagined.' When I looked up, I saw Karl-Heinz at the door, and Josef too.

'Are you reading her a story?' said Karl-Heinz.

'A kind of story, yes,' I said.

They stayed and listened for a while, Karl-Heinz resting his head against Josef. What a strange little family we made.

'In the Lord I put my trust: how say ye to my soul, Flee as a bird to your mountain?' I read. 'For, lo, the wicked bend their bow, they make ready their arrow upon the string, that they may privily shoot at the upright in heart.'

Josef said, 'It's time for your bath, Karl-Heinz.'

We heard the water running, filling the tub, and outside the rain began to plummet down.

'Keep going,' said Greta.

'If the foundations be destroyed, what can the righteous do? The Lord is in his holy temple, the Lord's throne is in heaven: his eyes behold, his eyelids try, the children of men.'

Drowsy now, Greta said, 'We climbed to the top of the Königsstuhl, do you remember? On the island. On Rügen.'

'Yes,' I said. 'I remember.'

'Where were your daughters? Lotte and . . . Anna? Is it Anna?'

'Lotte is my daughter. Anna is my wife.'

'Henning sent the news in a Christmas card. A bird in the snow, singing. Your two girls, Lotte and Anna.'

'Yes,' I said. 'Lotte and Anna.'

'We always wanted two. They must have stayed behind in the church. Praying to the bones.' Her lips were dry, and she licked them.

'Would you like some water?'

'Yes. Yes, water.'

I filled one of the dragonfly glasses and held it to her mouth, and she sipped. Then she said, 'I need to pack. We'll miss the train to Forli. We'll miss Saint Peregrine.'

'Everything is all right,' I said.

'When does it leave?'

'Not for a little while.'

She watched me close the bible, but before I could return it to the hollowed-out book she said, 'Will you take it? Please take it.'

I wasn't sure if she meant it to be a gift or if she wanted to keep Hahn from finding it. When I slipped it into the pocket of my jacket my fingers brushed something soft.

'I nearly forgot,' I said. 'I brought you this.' I took out the little grey-brown feather, which had curled in on itself so that it looked like nothing more than the spine of a dead leaf. I smoothed it back into shape in my palm and presented it to her. 'From a peregrine,' I said. And perhaps it was, too; just across the road from the Hahns' villa was the old falconry, where they used to keep birds of prey and now kept special prisoners.

She took it between her thumb and forefinger, ran it across the blue-white skin at the base of her throat. 'The fastest bird in the world,' she murmured. 'Faster than any living thing.' Her gaze drifted to the windowpane, and the white sky. 'Look at the tree,' she said, and when I did not reply, she repeated it: 'Look at the tree. Look at it.'

She was starting to sound distressed, which was not uncommon at that stage. I knelt next to the bed and pressed her hand; from that vantage point, I could see no trees, only the fog and the rain. But I followed her gaze and said, 'Yes. The tree. Yes.'

At the start of April, it was clear to me that the end was very close. I think Hahn knew it too. We could hear the rumble of artillery, and an air raid came every day, the planes flying in V formation like flocks of silver geese. On Easter Sunday Hahn ushered me into their dining room, then lowered the blackout blinds and set up the projector on a table, pointing it at a wall hung with photographs.

'Take those down,' he told me.

I was surprised to see some of my own work there – the

family portrait I had taken of the three of them sitting on the couch with their dog; another of them out on the terrace, holding up their wine glasses. The rest showed his son – Karl-Heinz in a sailor suit; Karl-Heinz on his first day of school, with a cone of sweets almost as tall as himself. There was one of an elegant young woman in a satin evening gown – Greta, I realised, though her face was fuller than I had ever seen it, and her eyes bright. The backdrop suggested opulence: swagged velvet, a lush palm, three ruined stone columns. I looked at the dress she was wearing – didn't Anna have a dress like that? Hadn't she worn it to a dance we attended at the Palmengarten, years before you were born, Lotte? Some function for the hospital staff, before her Jewishness came to the director's attention. It must have been Christmas; the ballroom was filled with fir trees strung with tinsel and lit with candles, and we could feel the heat as we passed, and I told Anna not to dance too close to them. I thought I remembered the feel of the gown's little glass beads under my palm, as hard as grains of sugar – and yes, surely Anna had worn a belt like that, with a buckle made of rhinestones, and surely she too had parted her hair low on the side and pulled it back to the nape of her neck?

'We don't have all day,' said Hahn. How long had I been standing there holding the portrait of his wife? He took it from me and placed it face down on the sideboard, gently, very gently, and I unhooked the rest of the photographs. Outside, heavy rain began to fall.

We both jumped when Josef entered the room.

'What is it?' said Hahn.

'I just came to see if you'd like some coffee, Herr Sturmbannführer,' he said, peering at the projector.

Hahn shook his head, waved him away.

'And for you, Herr Doktor?'

'He's not a guest!'

'No, Herr Sturmbannführer.'

'Just keep the door shut,' he said. 'I'm not here.'

He turned on the projector, and it cast a window of light on the place where the pictures had hung. Then he started the film.

A choir performed Mendelssohn's *Elijah* for a well-dressed audience. On a café terrace dotted with sun umbrellas, waitresses served refreshments. People exercised in the open air, read books, sketched, knitted and played chess. *When the sun is shining*, said a voice, *everyone likes to enjoy a few hours of free time in the parks of the old fortress*. Groups of singing men and women set off for work, spades and rakes over their shoulders. Customers browsed in a menswear shop, and a married couple collected a parcel from the post office. Children played on swings and rocking horses, built sand castles, splashed about in a paddling pool. I recognised no one. Then, a children's opera. From what I could gather, a boy and a girl needed to buy milk for their sick mother. They tried to raise the money by singing in the village square, and when an evil organ grinder chased them away, a cat, a dog and a bird came to their rescue, bringing a whole chorus of children to help them sing. I watched them file onto the stage in their Sunday best: a girl with a ribbon in her curled hair; two boys wearing striped shirts. And then, Lotte, a girl in a white dress, and there was something about the profile of her chin, the line of her arm . . . I moved closer to try to make her out as she turned and stared at the camera for a second – but another child took his place in front of her. Karl-Heinz ran into the living room then. He laughed when he saw the children singing on the wall; he pointed at the boy with his face painted like a dog, and he began to bark. The beam snatched at his shadow and projected it, twice his size, covering up the singers, blotting out the girl in the white dress.

'You're in the way!' I said, and his face fell.

'I wanted to be a dog.'

'Don't speak to my son like that,' said Hahn, but I didn't reply – I was busy with the projector. I didn't even think to ask Hahn's permission, and he didn't think to reprimand me.

'Go and find Niemand,' he told Karl-Heinz. 'He will make you a hot chocolate.'

I rewound the film to the start of the chorus and searched the images again and again. The girl with the ribbon in her hair, the boys in the striped shirts . . . and there, right there, the girl in the white dress, just for a second, until another boy stood in front of her. Each time I willed him to move out of the way, to move, move, *move*, even just a few centimetres – but of course, he never did.

At some point I realised that Hahn was scrutinising the footage too; I could make him out in my peripheral vision, leaning forward in his chair.

'What is it? What do you see?' he said.

'I don't know. Nothing.'

'It can't be nothing, if you keep going back over it.'

'I can't tell.'

Rewind, start again. Rewind, start again. It made no difference. The children finished singing, the audience applauded, the curtains closed. The tail of the film flicked free of the reel and clattered in the quiet dining room, a dead leaf skittering along a pavement, just out of reach. I stared at the empty block of light on the wall, the hooks for the Hahns' photographs. We sat there in the dark for a time, the two of us, listening to the rain. In the kitchen Josef began chopping something on a wooden board.

Hahn said, 'Is there nothing else you could try?'

I said, 'I suppose I'll have to take your word for it, that she's all right. That they're all right.'

'No,' he said. 'I mean with Greta. A different frequency? Longer treatments? There must be something.'

Nothing. There was nothing. No way to stop what was coming. The rain pelted down, and in our blocks we wondered how they would liquidate us: a mass shooting? Poison in our food? Flamethrowers from the watchtowers? Perhaps, we said, the SS would just evacuate us all, marching us off to be gassed, or to some distant destination that we would never reach, waiting until the last one of us stumbled and fell. We heard that Pister was considering surrender; he even allowed a prisoner to sing for us over the loudspeaker, as if one tiny kindness might wipe away everything else. For a little while, a French chanson drifted across the compound: *Ménilmontant, mais oui, madame, c'est là que j'ai laissé mon coeur* . . . But it was not over yet. And I kept thinking, Lotte, about the girl in the white dress. In my dreams I climbed through that bright blank window on the Hahns' dining-room wall, and there I found you both, you and Anna, and we chased the skittering leaves along the pavement until we came to our own front door, quite out of breath.

PART TEN
TO EACH HIS DUE

April 1945

The music woke me. Somewhere a choir was singing; somewhere in the house. How could that be? But I had stopped asking questions nobody would answer: are the cries of peacocks always the cries of peacocks? Why are the doctor's hands covered in cuts? What is the smell in the smoke? How much time is left?

I walked across the hallway and down the stairs, and the music grew louder and clearer, and I knew I had heard it before but I couldn't remember its name. *Help, Lord! Help, Lord! Help, Lord! Wilt thou quite destroy us?* If I could find them I would ask them, the people who were singing somewhere in my house, and surely they were very close by; their mournful voices rose around me like water, slowing my steps, pulling me under.

There. There, beyond the conservatory, the door to the garden. Oh, the weeds! Choking the few tulips left from the bulbs I'd planted with Karl-Heinz. *The harvest now is over . . .* When I pulled at one of them it just kept coming; an endless unspooling of green. I wound it around my wrists like something saved for the war effort. All along the beds of pansies I followed it, and across the stone pathways that scraped at the soles of my feet, and past the arch of climbing roses that in summertime smell like apples. I stopped and buried my nose in the sharp little buds, but all I could detect was this place, the smell of this place. And on and on the choir sang, and still I hadn't found the roots of the weed. *Will then the Lord be no more*

God in Zion? I kept pulling it free, winding it around my wrists, until I reached the stone wall at the far end of the garden and could go no further. It must have come from the forest, this rampant weed, or from the place just over the brow of the hill, on the chilly northern slope. I snapped it off at the base of the wall, though I knew there was no killing it.

Something rustled behind me; I'd thought I was alone in the garden, but when I turned I saw a bird landing on the pathway, displacing the dust with the draught from her great wings. And the bird was a bird of prey: a peregrine falcon, her beak a grey hook, her feathers stippled like a dark road when the rain has just begun. Those on her head gave the impression of a hood, and she watched me, unblinking. I could see myself reflected in her eye, my body distorted and strange and not my own, and when the pain came – because it always came; because despite what I told Dietrich, it always came, and nothing could make me comfortable – when the pain came I saw myself hunch and shake, and I saw my mouth make the shape of a prayer. *Will then the Lord be no more God . . .* what were the words? And the bird turned and lowered herself to the ground, and small and tight with pain I crawled onto her back and lay along her soft length and felt the thrum of her blood. As we rose above the garden I heard the last notes of the choir falling away, and I remembered a concert hall lit with chandeliers, and a gown of oyster satin made for the occasion, and Dietrich's hand at my elbow and his voice in my ear. As the bird climbed higher and higher my hair flattened against my skull, lying as flat as feathers now, and the air cleared, and I opened my mouth and let it rush inside me, this clean, clear air. How strange it was to see our house from above – to see all the officers' houses from above, lined up along Eickeweg with their terraces and their gardens and their neat stone paths. We were climbing so quickly my eyes started to stream, and I blinked and looked away, and when I looked back I could no longer tell which house was ours.

The bird's wings sounded in my ears like a long, low sigh as she took me even higher, and in a moment or two we were gliding above a great pit gouged from the hillside. I could see tiny men loading tiny rocks onto carts and sending them up the sides of the pit, and sometimes the carts reached the top, and sometimes they overbalanced and bumped all the way back to the bottom. The tiny men leapt clear when that happened, but if they weren't quick enough the rocks or the cart knocked them flat. And then there were fewer tiny men to reload the cart and send it to the top of the pit, and so the cart fell, hitting more of the tiny men, and then there were fewer men still. I was too remote to make out their faces, too remote to hear any cries, and it didn't seem real, this silent little scene – but I looked back towards our street, and there were the rows of houses on Eickeweg, and there were the walls and terraces and paths built from quarry stones. Eickeweg, named for the man who had recognised what Dietrich could become: when we first came here Dietrich said that one day, if he played his cards right, he might have a street named after him too. I used to imagine the ceremony: a brass band playing merry marches, and Karl-Heinz holding my hand, so proud of his papa, and all the men in their dress uniforms, chests tinkling with medals, and the women in fabulous hats. There'd be a wide ribbon strung across the street, secured around the trunks of trees that were still only saplings – because this was a brand new street, not one with some unsuitable old name the locals would persist in using; not one with a history. After the speeches I'd take a pair of enormous scissors – I'd need both hands to hold them, which would make everyone smile – and I would cut the ribbon. And then we'd all walk down Hahnstraße and admire its smart apartments and cafés, and someone thoughtful – perhaps even the mayor – would unknot the ribbon from the tree trunks and give it to Karl-Heinz to take home.

That is what I used to imagine.

The peregrine flew still higher, and I could see not just the southern slope of the Ettersberg but the northern slope too: row upon row of rectangular huts, and the ring of watchtowers, and the zoo just outside the electrified fence with its every buzzing barb – was that a tiny bear, standing on its hind legs to roar at us from its pit? I was too distant; I could not hear, I could not say. We hovered above the vast empty space where they lined the prisoners up each day to count them. Was that a toy gallows, its hooks hung with loops of wool? Again I was too distant. And the gate opened and the men began to file in to take their places, hundreds of them, thousands, some carrying . . . well, what were they carrying? Sacks of feed? Bundles of rags? I couldn't tell. The peregrine swooped a little closer, a little lower, but still I couldn't be sure what I was seeing, and I screwed up my eyes for a moment against the pain that jolted through me. The bird folded her wings flat against her body then, made a bullet of her body and launched into a dive, and as we shot head first towards the ground, faster than any living thing, I pressed myself close to her feathers, grabbed at them with my fists, the spines bending in my grip like tiny bones. And my pain roared in my ears, and the camp hurtled up to us, closer and closer, and I felt the pull of the electrified fence, the waves of its high-tension song, *wilt thou quite destroy us*, and the endless men pouring through the gate were not carrying sacks of feed, not carrying bundles of rags, but other men, dead men, because they had to be counted too; counted and accounted for. I took a breath, held it and held it . . . And the bird opened her wings, and we skimmed the air just above the prisoners, and one or two of them glanced up to see the source of this strange sudden breeze, but we were already gone. Towards the south we flew, towards the forest, dark and soft and still, the shadows collecting in the crooks of the trees.

'I want to go back,' I said, but I was not sure I meant Eickeweg; not at all sure. And Dietrich knew how to put Karl-

Heinz to bed; how to tell him a story; he knew, he knew. On we flew, through one day and another, surely, the forest below us blurring to a dark ribbon, and at last the sky darkening too. I thought of Lenard Weber's machine – not the Sympathetic Vitaliser, but the machine he and I imagined that morning when the powdery light washed across my bed. The enormous machine that could catch our thoughts and keep them. I knew it was just an idea, this machine, just a thought itself, but I liked to call it to mind now and then. All the little sparks.

'Where are we going?' I said. 'Are you taking me to Forli?' In the beat of her wings I heard it: *home, home, home.*

They were sending all the horrors of Europe to us. It hardly seemed fair. Those filthy creatures descended on Weimar in their legions; criminals full of lice and disease and guilty of who knew what. They stank to high heaven – Frau Andrecht saw one soiling himself in public, displaying himself without a shred of shame, not caring that a decent German woman on her way to buy bread should have to witness such things, which tells you all you need to know. For months we hadn't dared go walking in the hills; they had taken that small pleasure from us. We needed to keep our distance. And who was to say they wouldn't overthrow their guards and invade us, smashing our windows and stealing our valuables, all the things we had hidden and buried? There were too many of them, far too many. You could see at a glance that they would waste no time in setting fire to our houses and slitting our throats, stringing us up like pigs – and worse for the women, said Frau Andrecht; much worse.

In the first week of April, thousands more arrived on foot. We had heard that they were coming, marched here from Ohrdruf; Frau Pauli's sister had seen them pass through her village and had shot one of them herself, and Frau Pauli's nephew – just thirteen – had shot three. An outstanding example to the rest of his Hitler Youth group, she said; she was sure there would be some kind of ribbon awarded, some kind of badge. Herr Gräber, though, said now was not the time for heroics, and we must think about the consequences: Frau

Pauli's sister and nephew might have done the shooting, but once the Americans came we would all pay the price. And so when they dragged themselves down our rainy streets, past our very windows, we did not interfere.

And then, no sooner had the SS packed the camp tight than they started to empty it: an endless procession of criminals stealing past our front doors, on the lookout for whatever they could pilfer. We were not safe in our own homes.

23 November 1954

[tape corrupted in places]

I never met Karl Koch in person, but goodness knows I had my work cut out for me, trying to fix all his imbalances in the books, trying to get the numbers right. For twenty months they held him in a cell in Weimar, and then they brought him back to Buchenwald, to the shooting range next to the German Equipment Works, so he could receive his due. None of the prisoners would be able to see the execution, but they knew it was coming; everyone knew. The information crackled and buzzed through the camp, shoved at the doors along Eickeweg.

I kept looking out the windows of my building, waiting for them to drive him along Carachoweg. *In the next fifteen minutes, he will pass by.* Wrong. *In the next ten minutes, he will pass by.* Wrong. *In the next minute, he will pass by.* Wrong. The day was smokeless and still, and I breathed the fresh air deep into my lungs and tried to hold it there, and perhaps when I returned home Greta would rise from her bed and comb her hair, put on her sky-blue dress and come and drink coffee with me on the terrace. We would look out at the rain-washed garden, watch Karl-Heinz playing with Freya and remark on the mild spring weather. And perhaps the Americans had not yet taken Kassel and Gotha, and the French had not yet taken Karlsruhe, and Germany was still Germany – but I kept checking out the window for enemy tanks, too; I knew they could not be far away. I could *hear* the front drawing closer and closer. And more and more prisoners were coming – thousands from the satellite camp at Ohrdruf alone, which was the first one the Americans reached. It was clear the place had been terribly mismanaged, despite my signing off on it in the best of faith. Where should I have found supplies for them? At the American trial the prosecution kept returning to all the equipment left in our casernes when the troops evacuated, but as I explained under oath, very clearly and patiently, this was the property of a different department. It was even marked differently: *Waffen-SS* instead of *KLBu*. If it had been marked *KLBu*, the camp could have used it, but it wasn't marked *KLBu*. At any rate, quite apart from equipment, there was not enough food, not nearly enough, and not enough water, though rain was drenching the place, and I heard reports of cannibalism in the Little Camp, *cannibalism*, which only goes to show. Everything was changing, by the hour it was changing, impossible to predict. They'd let Waldemar Hoven out of his cell – he was working down in Weimar, reinstated as an SS doctor for the police, as if he'd never committed a crime. And Wolff was throwing parties each night at his villa, drinking whatever he could find, consorting with the worst kinds of women, and Pister had met with the prisoner leaders to discuss surrendering the camp, and the day was smokeless because there was no more fuel for the crematorium, the SS could not burn the bodies, they piled up and up, the numbers no longer mattered, the rats were everywhere underfoot. As a last resort the SS had begun to bury the corpses in mass graves on the southern slope of the Ettersberg, down by the Bismarck Tower.

I finished the letter I'd been drafting all day: a declaration from Doktor Lenard Weber, confirming that I had behaved decently in every respect, and that he personally could confirm my good character. I asked my secretary to type it up for me. Then I returned to the window.

Schwartz was making his way down the corridor with a

stack of files. 'You've missed him, you know,' he called. 'He's already here. But you can see him tomorrow.'

I asked if he was going to attend.

'Are you?' he said.

I said I thought it was the right thing to do.

'Yes,' he agreed. 'The decent thing.' He balanced the files on the windowsill to get a better grip; really, he'd overloaded himself. 'Shouldn't you be sorting through yours?' he said. 'While there's still time?'

And I looked around me, and the corridor was full of men and their secretaries clearing away files, as many as they could carry.

I asked Schwartz if he'd heard that they'd put out a call for weapons.

'Who?' he said.

'The prisoners. On a secret transmitter,' I said.

Later that day, Pister tried to round up all the Jews for evacuation, but they were too wily to report to the mustering ground, and hid themselves in the barracks and tore off their badges and would not be drawn out into the open despite the briskest of efforts. The next morning, again the SS ordered all Jews to step forward. When only a fraction of them obeyed, the men began searching the rows, singling out any prisoner with suspicious features.

And I could have betrayed Weber. Here is a part-Jew, I could have said, a man who obtained a sham divorce from his Jewish wife in order to save his own skin. Despite how he looks, this man is a Jew through and through. But I did not. Instead I returned home and waited for the guard to bring him to the villa.

He signed my letter, by the way, just before we went upstairs to Greta – and without any hesitation. Make sure you include that.

I looked out at the farms that spread from the foot of the Ettersberg all the way to the Harz Mountains, the Brocken hidden somewhere in the haze. The air was cold and damp, and I buttoned my coat right up to the collar; winter was a long time leaving. All reports indicated that the Americans were advancing along the plain, straight for us. I hurried to the shooting range.

When I saw Koch, I won't pretend the sight of him did not shock me. Unshaven, dishevelled, a lot thinner than in the photographs taken when he was stuffing himself with roast duck and cognac at the camp's expense. It looked as if he'd been beaten, too. I think that I'd been expecting him to carry himself like an officer; that he would stride into position as if he had essential business at that particular spot, as if he himself had commanded the firing squad to line up before him. Infallible, untouchable. But he could have been any vagrant without so much as a belt to hold up his trousers. He could have been any prisoner. Adjutant Schmidt offered him a blindfold, which he refused. Then they bound him to the stake.

'You should have heard him in the Bunker last night,' Woolf said into my ear. 'Screaming and crying like a child.'

'That information should . . .'

[corrupted]

. . . positioned myself a decent distance from Koch and trained my eyes on the space just behind him, and the men took their places – men who had seen him every day; men who had taken orders from him. I tried not to dwell on that. Do you know why such sentences are carried out by a squad, and not a single shooter? I can see that you don't; I can see you've never really thought about these things. It's not in case the bullet misses its mark, but rather so that no one man will have to carry the knowledge that his shot was the fatal one. That is the reason. That is the theory. As the line of men readied themselves, though, I saw the way their eyes glittered, the way they licked their lips. They would be telling this story for years. Koch stared up at the sky as if checking for rain, but he must have been able to make out the figures pushing at the base of his vision, the raised arms, the cocked rifles. 'Shoot well, boys,' he said. That's all. Shoot well, boys. Then Schmidt gave the command. And when they fired I saw him slump before I heard the shots, and even though I had witnessed other shootings, and even though I knew that this was just the way things worked – that the air slowed the bullets' vibrations, that our eyes are quicker than our ears – it seemed that the world was not behaving as it should, that something had gone very wrong. The men were shaking one another's hands, slapping one another on the back, and Koch hung collapsed at the stake, a hole in his forehead, definitely dead, but all I could think about was that tiny moment, that splinter of a second when his head was already falling to his chest though nobody had heard the shots. As if they were not real; as if he were pretending, or ducking just in time, and would not die after all.

I wondered what Ilse Koch would make of her husband's death; I'd heard that she'd gone to live with his sister in Ludwigsburg, where she drank to excess and brought home a different man every night. At the Dachau trial, only two years widowed, she'd take the stand visibly pregnant. *These are the most vulgar lies . . . I was a housewife and a mother. I had nothing to do with concentration camps. My husband never told me about it, and I never saw nor heard of any of these things that are being talked about here.*

When I returned home, the villa was so quiet that I knew. I knew as soon as I closed the door behind me. I knew as soon as I took off my cap and lay it down in its usual spot on the table beneath the mirror. I knew as soon as I saw my own reflection, as soon as I looked myself in the eye. I knew as soon as I heard myself, a splinter of a second later, call her name.

I began to bolt up the stairs, but the weight of the air in the house slowed my legs; the leaden quiet. Where was Niemand? Where was Karl-Heinz? Shouldn't he be home for lunch, chattering about peculiar dogs with dachshund legs and pinscher ears, and how many Easter eggs he still had left, and goodness knows what else? I heard Freya's claws ticking across the floor somewhere nearby, then silence again. I knew but did not know. One of Karl-Heinz's carved tigers stood at the top of the stairs, front paws poised on the edge of the tread. Ready to escape, or jump. We had told him so many times: someone could trip. Someone could fall to their death. I picked the tiger up as I passed. Was it the male or the female? Karl-Heinz had never let me sand one of them down to make it smaller, so I couldn't tell. I felt the lines I had cut into its side; little channels that cast their own shadow so they appeared as black stripes against the oak. And I recalled that I had burnt its mate, which might have been the male or the female; thrown it into the fire to punish Karl-Heinz. I knew but did not know.

Weber knelt next to her, his back to me. I could not see her face. Slowly I walked to the other side of the bed, and she looked just as she'd looked when I left her in his care so I could attend the execution: eyes closed, hair brushed smooth, hands resting on the lace decorating the bed linen. He would try a longer treatment, he'd told me as he set up the machine. And a different frequency, too, just as I'd instructed. I touched her chest and it was warm, as warm as usual, surely, and I knew but did not know.

And yet.

'I'm sorry,' said Weber, still on his knees.

I held up my hand to silence him.

If he did not speak, then he could not say it.

I touched Greta's shoulder, and it was also warm. Warm enough.

Weber's eyes were on me, huge with fright. I touched Greta's fingertips. Cool; cooling. But hadn't she always complained of cold hands and feet? When we were newly married, hadn't she pressed them to me in bed if she wanted me to fetch her a cup of tea or one of her magazines? Her secret weapon, she said.

And yet.

What was I waiting for? The sound of shots? She had been dying for so long, hadn't she? I knew that; I knew it. All through those last months, the proof was right there in front of me; I had seen her falling a little more every day.

Weber rose to his feet. He started to talk, but I cut him off. I wanted to know why he hadn't sent for me.

'It happened so quickly, Herr Sturmbannführer,' he said. 'There was no time.'

I asked if she'd spoken, and he said no, it was very peaceful.

'Peaceful,' I said.

'Very peaceful,' he repeated.

Behind him sat his machine, the dials dead, the contact plates hanging like hands. He turned and began to dismantle it, tidying it away as he did at the end of every treatment session, putting it all back in its proper place. I walked around the bed and stood next to him, watching him wind the cords into neat little skeins. I was close enough to catch the scent of Greta's soap rising from him as he went about his business. I have never been a violent man, but he would not stop fussing with the Vitaliser, wiping the contact plates clean with their special cloth, slotting them into the lid. The last two cords were kinked and tangled, and he worried away at them, only his hands started to shake, and he was simply making it worse. As I said, I have never been a violent man, but it seemed he would never be done, that I would never be done with him. And at the same time, I did not want him to finish. I did not want him to go. Now why is that?

In the end he wound the tangled cords together and stuffed them into the lid, and then he lifted the thing, working his fingers underneath its solid body and easing it off the bedside cabinet. Really, some sort of trolley would be a better arrangement, I thought. I should see if I could find . . . but of course not. Of course not. I watched as he took the weight of the box and began to move it towards the mirror in the corner of the room. In the distance, the sounds of battle. I said, 'They died in their first year at Theresienstadt. Pneumonia, I think it was. Or maybe tuberculosis? Something like that.' I saw his face turn ashen, his hands begin to slip. 'Nothing to say, Weber?' I asked. 'I find that hard to believe. You've been talking for months. You've done nothing but talk. The waves of healing energy, the miraculous vibrations, blah blah blah.'

'My wife?' he whispered. 'My daughter?' The beechwood box had slipped to his fingertips now, and he staggered under its weight.

I shrugged. 'Long gone.'

'But she wrote to me,' he said. 'Lotte wrote to me.'

'No she didn't,' I laughed.

He tried to set the box down, but it fell from his grasp and crashed to the floor, breaking open at our feet. We both leapt back. The glass etched with dragonflies chimed against the bottle of elixir; someone singing in a distant room. Rain began to pelt the windowpanes. I looked down at the wrecked machine, and all I could see was broken beechwood. The unvarnished corners darkened from handling. I nudged at the remains with the toe of my boot. A bit of coiled copper, a soldered wire, a condenser. Some smashed glass, sugary underfoot. I felt a rush of air, a cold current pushing at my face, the space around me displaced by some great wing.

'Is this all it ever was?' I said, more to myself than to him.

He cleared his throat. 'Herr Sturmbannführer,' he began, 'just as the body is a circuit—'

I had no wish to hear any more. 'You are to report to the Bunker in one hour,' I said. 'Now get out.'

A little while later I heard the front door open, and then Josef's voice: 'You'll need to wash your hands first.' I caught Karl-Heinz as he ran up to the bedroom, and I sat him down on the top stair, underneath the print of the swans on the Bodensee. I could smell the rain on him.

'Mama was very sick,' I said, 'and now she has gone.'

'To Italy? To visit the bones?' he said.

I didn't know what he was talking about. 'No, not to Italy,' I said.

He buried his face in my neck, nestled in close, then flinched away from me again.

I had felt it too; a hard lump against my chest. I reached into my pocket, and my fingers closed around it: the carved tiger.

'Why do you have him in your pocket?' he asked.

I told him I found it on the stairs, and he said he was sorry.

'You know what could happen,' I said.

'Someone could break their neck,' he said. Then he started to shout – it was because he had nowhere to keep them! If I made him the ark, they could all live in that!

I did not tell him to lower his voice. 'You're quite right,' I agreed. 'I should have made you the ark.'

He could help me, he said.

We'd have to see, I said.

He walked the tiger along my arm, roaring softly.

Weber failed to report to the Bunker, of course. I summoned him over the loudspeaker and even had his block searched, but the whole place was in uproar, with nine thousand head arriving from the satellite camps, and Pister making frantic telephone calls to secure enough trains to evacuate the Ettersberg in time, and the prisoners devising all sorts of sly tricks to delay evacuation. The Gestapo had come up with a list of forty-six prisoners – ringleaders in the communist resistance, they maintained – and they summoned them over the loudspeaker too, but the lot of them had gone to ground, and despite rigorous searches they could not be located. And Weber also had hidden himself away; slunk into some hole, some sewer. I never saw him again.

'You'll have her sent home, of course,' said Greta's mother when I telephoned. 'Pfarrer Brunner will say the Mass.'

The woman had no idea. 'Apart from anything else,' I said, 'travel is impossible at the moment. You must know that.'

'Well then,' she said, 'what's the name of the Catholic church in Weimar? And who is the parish priest?'

I said I'd see to it that the service was befitting of a Sturmbannführer's wife – though to be honest, up to that point I had not thought about a funeral. I had not thought about a coffin or a wreath or a hole in the ground.

Elisabeth began to sob. 'This is your fault,' she said. 'This is on your conscience.'

'I can't hear you,' I said, and hung up.

We buried Greta in Weimar, but no one came; they were too busy getting rid of paperwork and grabbing civilian clothing from the personal effects room so they could disguise themselves. Pister dithered like a fool, unable to decide whether or not to clear the camp, so Prinz zu Waldeck had to whip him into line. Both of them must have known it was too late to cover their tracks either way – far too late, despite the Americans stalling at Gotha. I stopped tearing the days off my desk calendar, but that wasn't going to change anything. The air-raid warnings were coming so frequently that even when the sirens fell silent I could still hear the ringing in my ears. In the sky a pair of American planes circling low and lower, like flies that won't leave a piece of spoiled meat. The number of inmates approached fifty thousand – and then the camp began emptying block by block; the SS marched them down the hill in their droves and sent them on to Dachau and Flossenbürg and Theresienstadt, by train or on foot, it didn't matter which, as long as they weren't there for the Americans to find. On our way to Greta's interment – it was no funeral – the side of the road was thick with corpses soaked by the rain. I tried to hold my hands over Karl-Heinz's eyes, but he looked all the same. On the way home I didn't bother.

From the Ettersberg I could see little explosions all along the horizon, and blazing air raids lit up the plain at night. On the tenth of April, the rumble of cannons as close as Erfurt. Then, on the morning of the eleventh, machine-gun fire from the forest. More American planes overhead, so close I could have reached up and touched the white stars. The blasting of artillery shaking the ground beneath my feet; the terrible wail of a siren unheard until then: the enemy alarm. And finally, an announcement over the loudspeaker: *All members of the SS are to leave the camp immediately*. The men began throwing their knapsacks from the windows of the casernes to hasten their getaway, grabbing motorcycles or bicycles, whatever they could find.

I ran back to the house, Wolff close behind me on the path through the trees. We had to go, and straight away, he said; soon enough, the prisoners would make for their caches of hidden weapons.

'You'll see,' he called, stumbling over the roots of a tree. He was very drunk. 'They've been stockpiling them for months, I know they have,' he spat. 'Stole them part by part from the Gustloff Works – and when the Americans bombed us. Bastard criminals. Maybe I'll disguise myself as a woman.' He began to laugh and could not stop. All bets were off.

Later, after our arrests, they would chain the two of us together naked and lock us in a windowless room. Beat us with whips, shove us against electric heaters. Half a slice of bread and half a cup of water per day. So that tells you something about justice.

I changed into an ordinary suit, almost tripping myself up as I rushed to pull on the trousers, my hand flailing behind me for the armhole in the jacket. 'Karl-Heinz!' I yelled. 'Put on your coat and boots!' For once I didn't bother to hang up my uniform; I left it where it fell, crouched on the bedroom floor, slowly deflating. I seized my wallet and my keys, a clean hand-kerchief, a comb – and the gold? Could I take my box of gold? Or bury it in the garden, so I could dig it up later? Under the . . .

[corrupted]

. . . was no time, no time, and I hurried to Greta's room. For a few seconds I hesitated in the doorway. What should I choose? What could I carry with me? I grabbed her rings and her fountain pen and the photograph of Karl-Heinz as a baby in my arms. What else? What else? The wreckage of Weber's machine lay piled in the corner where I had shoved it, only half covered by its sheet, and I could see the gouges in the floor where he'd dropped it. Too deep to sand away. I searched Greta's bedside cabinet for something meaningful, a small memento, but there was only the rubbish her mother had sent – prayer cards, saints' medals, rosary beads, a bottle of Lourdes water. On top of the cabinet, the carved box pre-sented to us on our wedding day. I didn't remember if I had even looked inside it since then, though like everyone else I pretended I had read *Mein Kampf* from cover to cover. I opened the lid and lifted out our copy, and it was so light, so insubstantial in my hands, and I knew something was wrong. Inside the front cover the signature of the mayor of Munich, and his best wishes for a happy marriage, and then the portrait of Hitler looking off to the side, beyond the edges of the book – how many times had I stood in front of the mirror and copied his famous eyes? I rested my fingers on the picture – and the whole thing puckered and collapsed, and I saw that the book was hollow behind it, that someone had taken to it with a blade and carved an empty space. A space to hide things.

It must have been Weber, sneaking around in my very own house, spiriting away stolen valuables – items that belonged to us. Answering the urge of his dirty blood. And then, when he knew Greta was nearing the end, he must have taken his hoard with him. Certainly, there was nothing left now. My toes knocked against something under the bedside cabinet, and when I knelt down to look I found a copper coil from inside the machine. The core of the thing, its humming heart.

I checked my reflection in the cheval mirror, pulling at the lapels and waistband of my suit, trying to make it fit a little better. It was too small for me – I'd put on weight at Buchenwald – but still, I looked ordinary enough, I thought. I smoothed my hair into place, and the ring on my hand caught the light – the silver death's-head band from Greta. I'd worn it for so long it had become part of me, the silver mellowing to a soft sheen from all the thousands of scratches invisible to the naked eye. I no longer worried that it wasn't an official one, that I never would be awarded an official one; it was so close to the real thing that nobody could tell the difference. I realised I'd have to leave it behind too; what point was there in dressing like a civilian if my hand gave me away? But when I went to take it off, it wouldn't budge. I tugged at it, tried to wriggle it from side to side, tried to force my nails underneath – I felt the joint straining, as if it might break. I was only making things worse; around the ring my flesh reddened and swelled. I didn't know what to do, and I had to leave, I had to get away. A piece of soap lay on the washbasin in the corner, smoothed to a pale pebble. It must have been over two years since I'd given Greta the box of soaps from Paris, and there were still whole untouched cakes of the stuff tucked away, I knew, scenting her clothes. I didn't want to think of all the dresses hanging empty in the wardrobe, the jumpers folded flat and airless in the drawers. I turned on the cold water and held my hand under it for a few moments to make the blood recede, then lathered around the ring. Not far away, I knew, the SS were destroying the water pumps that I had babied for so long. Soon Buchenwald would fill to the brim with shit; there would be no stopping it. I worked as quickly as I could, but the more I tried to ease the ring free, the more my fingers kept slipping. 'Niemand!' I yelled. No answer. He had probably fled, along with all the other cowards, and this was why we'd lose the war. There was no loyalty any more, no sense of duty, of working together for the common good; everybody wanted to save his own skin, and to hell with the rest of the country. Even Himmler had turned tail – the Führer's Loyal Heinrich, who had never presented me with a proper ring, sneaking off to try to negotiate with the Allies. Well, he would get what he deserved.

I rinsed and dried my hands, and then I opened Greta's chest of drawers. It didn't take me long to find one of the unused cakes of soap, and I slipped it into my pocket. Then I picked up the copper coil from Weber's machine, dropped it inside the gutted book, slid the book into its slipcover and returned it to its box, and shut the lid.

My hands still smelled like her.

Karl-Heinz was waiting for me at the bottom of the stairs, boots on, coat on. I tied his laces for him.

Then I hurried down to the cellar and found the first-aid kit, and I wound a bandage around my left hand, covering up the immovable ring. It looked convincing, I thought, as if I really had hurt myself – digging a child from the rubble, perhaps, or helping an elderly person put out a fire.

Then we made our way to Weimar and blended in.

The Americans trumpeted to the world that they liberated the camp, but most of the SS had fled before they
arrived with their tans and their teeth. The prisoners,
too, tried to take credit for the liberation: they had stormed the
gatehouse tower, they said, overpowered the guards. On the
day that it happened – however it happened – we weren't at all
sure of events up on the Ettersberg. In the early evening, our
police president telephoned the camp to issue an order to take
care of all remaining inmates. He asked to speak to the
Kommandant, but the voice on the other end told him the
Kommandant wasn't available. And when Fräulein Eberhardt
at the telephone exchange answered a call from the camp, she
asked how things were looking up the hill. Well, the voice said,
fifty-fifty. She said, 'Have you killed all the inmates? Don't let
any out.' And the voice reassured her none had been let out.
Then it started: the Americans arrested our mayor and
appointed Herr Gräber to act in his place, and at the same
time they looted our homes; Frau Haack tried to snatch back
her best linen supper-cloth – she had embroidered it herself –
but it tore in two. Frau Fleck remarked that they took more
than supper-cloths, and then refused to say any more. When
the Americans told Herr Gräber that we had to come and look
at that place up on the Ettersberg, he said the camp was nothing to do with us, and we'd known nothing of what had gone
on there. Such a tour would be humiliating, he said, and he
pointed out that if Hitler had done evil things, it should be

acknowledged he had done good things too. But the Americans were having none of that.

We put on our suits and ties, our best blouses and our pearl earrings, and we gathered all along Paulinenstraße to walk up the hill together, arm in arm, chattering in the spring air. Were those violets we could see at the edge of the beeches? When would the rations improve? Oh, for some real coffee! Some whipped cream! We patted at our hair, pinched blood into our cheeks, and Fräulein von Schirach, who used to be a famous opera singer, sang a sad little song. Those of us wearing winter coats were already beginning to regret it. The Americans drove unsmiling alongside us, as if we might try to escape.

Frau Häusler said she hoped it wouldn't take too long, because she still had six broken windows to board up; she'd had to leave them covered with cardboard, and anyone could punch it free and climb inside. Fräulein Fleischer said she wished she could offer to help with the windows, only she'd sprained her wrist, and had to rest it for two weeks. She held it up so we could see, and yes, it was wrapped with a bandage; she'd secured the end with a pretty cut-glass brooch because she couldn't find a safety pin. Frau Nickel said she would help with the windows, which was kind of her, because she was already looking after her sister's boys, poor little mites. At one point Herr Gräber cocked his head at the Americans flanking us. 'I think they're taking our pictures,' he whispered. 'I think they're filming us.'

We passed the blackened remains of the Gustloff Works, where they made parts for the secret weapons that should have won the war. Herr Bittermann said he'd heard that the Americans had found whole boxes of gold and watches and precious stones hidden in a cave in the quarry: whole *boxes*, he said. As we drew closer we could smell the place – excrement and sweat and the stench of meat gone bad. And we looked at one another. Hadn't we been smelling it for years? Every so often, in our own back yards, when the wind blew from the northwest? Or when we'd forgotten to wash the fruit we picked from our trees? Or when we'd gone walking on the Ettersberg, or when we'd brought our children to visit the falconry in order to distract them? But we didn't have our children with us today, and we weren't here to feed the deer and to see the raptors tear at the dead mice offered them by their keepers. We took our handkerchiefs from our pockets – folded and ironed; we had not let standards slip – and we held them to our noses and mouths and did not want to breathe. We read the inscription above the entrance to the camp: *My Country, Right or Wrong*. And we read the backwards iron words on the iron gate: *To Each His Due*. Well, what did that even mean? It was very unclear, murmured Fräulein Eberhardt.

Then the tour began, and we were astonished that some of them addressed us in German.

'What a thing,' whispered Herr Kolbe.

'They must be traitors,' said Frau Starke.

As the German-speaking Americans talked they pointed to a table, and then we saw what was on it. No, we said. No. This was not real. Because we could not believe our eyes. Pieces of skin tattooed with angels and cowboys. A pair of lungs like wrinkled wings, suspended in a jar. A bottled heart. Two shrunken heads, their hair as luxuriant as a lapdog's. A lampshade made from human skin – that's what our guides told us, at least. But where were the eyewitnesses? The prisoners who had themselves seen the skin stripped and processed?

And then the filthy living quarters and the squalid hospital. The stench of blood and faeces and decay; the bony figures who stared somewhere past us and did not seem to care that we were there at all. One prisoner said, 'Have you brought us your children to eat?' Another's feet were half rotted away. The laboratory with its death masks, its halved head which must have been a model but looked real enough. Then the crematorium, and yes, there were ashes and bones in the ovens, which proved nothing in particular. But something must have gone very wrong in the last frenzied days of the war: in the courtyard the bodies were piled high, not even buried or burned, not even covered with a sheet. We had the feeling the ones with open eyes were watching us. And prisoners peered over the fence, some of them children – we had not known there were children – and they watched from the roofs, too, and the Americans kept pointing their fingers. But we could see for ourselves how thin the corpses were – piles of pipe cleaners, we thought; piles of kindling – and not a scrap of clothing between them. Herr Wille, who had come with his unmarried daughter, said it wasn't proper. We held up our hands for shade, as if the dead glared stronger than the sun, as if it hurt to look. And when Fräulein Eberhardt closed her eyes, an American – a black American, no less – jabbed her in the back and told her to open them again. 'I heard it was typhus,' said Frau Kappel, and Herr Noth said, 'Don't touch anything! It's very contagious.'

Frau Krieger fainted clean away, and nobody managed to catch her. They sent two men to carry her clear of the group for some fresh air: prisoners, if you please, who hauled her like a corpse, the hairpins slipping from her pretty crocheted snood. Without warning Fräulein Gräber vomited on Frau Dornig's best suede shoes: had she caught something already? Frau Dornig was very good about it, and said it didn't matter, though we all knew how difficult suede was to clean. But then, who would wear suede to a place like this? So perhaps Frau Dornig herself was to blame. Herr Bittermann gave her his handkerchief to wipe the shoes with, but afterwards she didn't know what to do with it; she couldn't give it back to him – he made it clear he did not want it – and she hesitated to put it in her own pocket. Finally she crumpled it into a ball and carried it in her fist for the rest of the outing.

Were we right or were we wrong? The Americans pointed at the piles of bodies and said they died of hunger. They died of dysentery. They died of the cold; they died by lethal injection. They drowned in the stinking latrines, their nostrils and throats stopped with shit. They fell to their deaths in the quarry – they hardly needed a push – or they were crushed by the stones they carried, or by the carts that carried the stones up the slopes of the pit. They ran across the sentry line and knew they would be shot and they were shot. They died of their wounds from the whip or the cudgel; they died when they were strung up by their wrists for hours. They died when they hung from hooks in the blood-spattered basement; see their heel-dents in the walls? They died of typhus. They died when they were injected with typhus to see if typhus could be cured. They died when their blood was taken for wounded soldiers (though not Jewish blood, so Jews had to die in other ways). They died when the SS judged their beds were not neatly made. They died when they could no longer stand.

We did not believe them, these German-speaking traitors. This was not real. The figure swinging from the gallows was a dummy filled with straw. Those were animal bones in the ovens. And there must have been an epidemic; something that had spread so quickly it couldn't be contained. Dreadful, of course, but nobody's fault.

They kept us up there for hours in the hot sun with not a bite to eat. At one point Frau Fleck just sat down on the ground, right there on the dirt. We started to wonder whether they'd ever let us out, or whether they'd release the prisoners and lock us up instead. Fräulein Fleischer complained that her wrist was hurting. Fräulein Gräber insisted Frau Dornig let her take the suede shoes home to clean them; she felt terrible, she said.

On the way back down the hill, Herr Wieck made a joke – just a silly remark about his hair, most of which he'd lost. 'I should have asked them how to shrink my head,' he said, 'so what I have left looks thicker!' We all laughed – goodness knows, we needed to laugh – but one of our armed escorts heard us. He marched us up the hill and made us tour the camp again.

Later, they will order us to bury hundreds of corpses. They'll delay this as long as possible, despite the heat and the stench, so all the journalists can see them. Perverse, we'll say; leaving the dead unburied to make some kind of point – but these are the sorts of people we're dealing with. Prisoners will show up at our doors, demanding we feed them, and we'll have no choice. Frau Hennicke will fry a bit of cabbage and ham for one of them while he sits at her kitchen table, and she will discover that he was a car dealer just like her husband. From the villages that supply us with our food they will requisition thousands of litres of milk per day; hundreds of kilograms of butter; fifty tons of potatoes. They will eat better than we eat, all the former prisoners who need to be sent back where they came from; they will eat us out of house and home. Some of them will eat so much that they will keep on dying. And we'll be forced to carry away their shit from their overflowing sewage treatment plant, and the shit will be on everything and in everything, and clearly the treatment plant never was big enough. And Herr Gräber, our acting mayor, will complain to the authorities – the new authorities – that only the real Nazis should be assigned such work, not the citizens who simply had contact with the Nazis, but the authorities will tell him that the punishment is deserved. Then they will replace our acting mayor with the elderly Herr Behr: a prisoner; a former prisoner. And for weeks and weeks, after all the shit has been cleared away, they will make the women of Weimar keep coming up the hill to peel the tons of potatoes, and during the short lunch break, former prisoners will make speeches about the terrible things the Nazis did at the women's camps.

When the child prisoners leave at last for France, they will chalk the side of their train carriage with broken German for us to see: *Wher are our parrents? You murdrers.* And a little later the Soviets will give the camp another name and fill it with different prisoners, and then later, too, when they dismantle it, we'll come and take the gallows wood to rebuild our homes, and help ourselves to the zinc that lined the corpse carts.

Later still, you will speak of Weimar as an idea, a dream. The place where German democracy might have taken root and flowered, if it weren't for that Austrian. You will visit the houses of the poets – how small the rooms, for such vast hearts, you will think – and we'll watch you through the lace curtains of our own small-roomed houses as you point and pose and say it's not what you were expecting. And the camp will be an idea for you too; a place you might try to build with your own guilty conscience, piecing it together from pictures and stories of our camp and of other camps, because it's hard to tell what happened where, and the map in the brochure isn't much help – and in the end you will say you can't imagine. And you will shake your head to collapse your imagined camp, send it skittering away. But you did not have to live at the foot of that hill, nor breathe the smell of it for years, nor wash it from your clothes and skin and hair, only it never really left you. Yes, it was our camp; ours. This is what we cannot explain.

Frankfurt am Main, September 1946

I realised that Greta was nearing the end when I saw how she began to pluck at the bed linen. I had observed this action in many patients in their final days and hours, when they were closer to death than to life, and under normal circumstances I would have made sure the family knew there was little time left. Even in this case, so far from normal, I still could have sent for Sturmbannführer Hahn; I still could have allowed him those last moments with his wife. But I did not. I knelt beside her bed, and I took her hand and closed my eyes, and her hand could have been a different hand, a more familiar hand, as long as I didn't look. 'It's all right,' I said. 'Everything is all right. You don't need to be afraid. Soon it will be over.'

Even then, I knew she wanted to believe me. Even then, when the beechwood box sat dead in the corner and I was not the man she had married, I felt her belief flutter through her, fly along every nerve till it rattled in her throat.

And perhaps she too had called up somebody else. Perhaps she imagined that Hahn knelt at her side; that the hand she held was the hand of her husband. Did it matter? When he told me about you and Anna, I was glad I hadn't summoned him. Glad I had taken his place.

I saw Josef when I was leaving the villa for the last time. He was standing on a step-ladder in the living room, dusting the prongs of the antler chandelier.

'It's almost here,' he called as I hurried past the doorway.

I stopped. 'The end of the world?' I could hear Hahn in the bedroom above, shoving something across the wooden floor: the remains of the Vitaliser.

'Yes,' said Josef, letting go of the chandelier to refold his cloth, the spiky branches swaying overhead.

'Frau Hahn has died,' I said, and he nodded. 'Goodbye, Josef.'

'Goodbye, Doktor Weber.'

Voss arranged for me to go to a tuberculosis ward, where the SS would not find me. And that is where I stayed, with the dying and the dead, and I listened to them crying for water but there was none to be had, and at night the past ran its drowned fingers across my cheek, and on the afternoon of the eleventh of April, when we heard the heavy machine-gun fire a matter of metres away, we didn't know if the Americans had finally come or if the SS were finishing us off. Then, later in the afternoon, clicks and whines from the loudspeaker, and a single blown breath – and a prisoner's voice: *Attention! Attention! This is the Camp Senior speaking. Comrades . . . we are free.* The SS had fled, and American tanks had entered the grounds. From inside the infirmary I heard the cheering, and as word travelled around the ward a few men tried to clap, but they were so weak that the sound was nothing more than rain on leaves. The Muselmänner did not register the news at all, already staring into their own deaths. And still I wasn't sure I was safe, and I waited until Wirth came and told me himself: we were free. In his hands the rolls of film he'd shot in secret, and the hidden photographs. When I emerged I saw a hole cut in the barbed wire, and five or six prisoners who still had the strength were throwing an American soldier into the air and catching him again, throwing him and catching him again, until he had to shout, 'Stop!' A white flag hung from the gate-house tower, and the electrified fence was dead, the power shut off. And all the Jewish children had emerged from their barracks – hundreds of them, hidden for months on end.

But that was not the third miracle, Lotte. And I did not feel like cheering.

I was still at Buchenwald when General Patton ordered one thousand citizens of Weimar to view the camp at close range. Perhaps they thought we couldn't understand German; they spoke right in front of us, as if we weren't there. 'This can't be true,' some of them said. 'This can't have happened.' Others said, 'They must be actors. Aren't there such things as hunger artists?' And others, holding their handkerchiefs in front of their mouths and noses, said, 'It's not right, that decent Germans should have to see this.'

I was still there, too, when a group of former prisoners found a former guard in civilian clothes in one of the nearby villages. They brought him back to Buchenwald and handed him a rope, and then they told him how to tie a noose. After that they stood him on a table and made him tie the rope to the electrical fitting above, then test his weight on it. When it held, they told him to place the noose around his neck and pull it tight. They moved the table so he balanced on its very edge, and while they were still talking to him, he jumped. They caught him and returned him to the table, and then, following their instructions, he took a small, small step off the edge, and they pulled the table away.

I suppose I could have said something.

When I returned to Frankfurt, our building had disappeared. I'd thought that someone else might be living in our apartment, or that it might have been ransacked – but it simply was not there. All the smart red sandstone façades in our street, built in the first affluent years of the German Empire – all gone. I found a single unbroken tile on the ground, which looked like the tiles from our bathroom. Didn't it? Or perhaps it was a tile from the bathroom of another missing building; I couldn't quite remember.

Your little hands, splashing at the water. The kick kick kick of your plump little legs.

I chalked your names on the broken foundations, and my own new address, in case you came back. I checked and rechecked the lists of survivors, and made sure I appeared on them too, so you could find me, but all of you had died: you and Anna, Anna's parents and brother who went to Shanghai – and David Hirsch, too, the man she had married. Eventually I stopped checking, because whenever I thought of someone else – one of Anna's cousins; a former neighbour – the Red Cross told me the same thing.

I am writing this in my new flat in Nordend, which I share with three others. It's not so far from where we used to live, Lotte, and when they replace the bells in St. Bernhard's, I think I'll be able to hear them ringing. One day a woman came to the door looking for a man who used to live here, but I didn't know the name and couldn't help her. She asked why I was living there, and I said the housing office had assigned it to me, and she sniffed and said how *lucky*. And afterwards and still, I ask myself the same question: Why am I living here? And I suppose, when they replace the bells, they may not sound the same. But I have a comb. I have a tin opener and some tins to open. I have a pair of shoes that fits me and a pair that almost fits. I have a splinter of wood to remind myself of an oak. I have a bed, which probably is the bed of the man who used to live here. I have work, in a temporary location, while they rebuild the hospital – the Holy Spirit was badly damaged. I have a pen, and I have ink. I have my neighbour's old calendars to write on, all the way back to 1933, the Führer's every birthday ringed in red.

In unguarded moments I think about you and Anna. She grows no older, but you do. I imagine you becoming more and more like her: a high forehead and a narrow chin, dark hair curling all the way down to your waist. I think about Greta Hahn, too, and remind myself that I was never going to save her; that she was already lost by the time I came to Buchenwald. But was I more attentive to her than to any other patient? And what of the thousands I didn't treat in the camp? They come to me in darkness, those transparent men. They open their arms, press my ear to their breasts so I can hear the beating of their needle-thin hearts.

One day, when I was walking in the Taunus, I saw a falcon circling. It must have been looking for mice or small birds; it glided above me, scanning the ground, turning its sleek head this way and that. I stopped, stood dead still. Lower it came, lower and lower, until I could see the black shine of its eyes and hear the whistle of its wings. Until I could feel it pushing the air against my face.

At home, I took Greta Hahn's bible from the shelf. She had underlined certain verses, and I remembered reading them to her when she asked me – the only thing I could do, in the end, all the while listening for footsteps in the hall. *In the Lord I put my trust: how say ye to my soul, Flee as a bird to your mountain?* Some passages I did not recognise. These she had marked with thick, deep lines that pressed through several pages and in places tore the paper: *God is jealous, and the Lord revengeth; the Lord revengeth, and is furious; the Lord will take vengeance on his adversaries, and he reserveth wrath for his enemies.*

The following morning I slipped the bible into my satchel – something to pass the time on the train ride to work. And at lunchtime, too, when I saw one of my colleagues coming to sit with me, I took it out and began reading so I wouldn't have to answer her questions about Buchenwald. *But it was only a labour camp, wasn't it? There were no gas chambers, were there?* I found the Saint Peregrine card tucked inside, the holy man raising his eyes to something beyond the edges of the picture, his black robe framing his sick leg. Why show him unhealed? Why the moment before the miracle? This I had never understood. The card marked a page at the front of the bible: the family tree of the original owner. I traced down the generations, down through the Marias and the Beates, the Johanns and the Michaels, until I reached Peter and his wife Ottilie, who'd had no children. Except there at the very bottom, branching off the two of them, where there was hardly any room, someone had added new names. I squinted to make them out – my eyesight is not what it once was – and thought I must be mistaken. I hurried back to the laboratory, and as I passed Baumhauer in the stairwell he nodded a friendly greeting.

At my table, where I dissect tumour tissue to estimate how long my patients have left, I slipped the page under my microscope and brought the names into focus. There were Dietrich and Greta Hahn, and their son Karl-Heinz, their birthdates signalled by a star. No dates of death. I shifted the page across, and right next to the Hahns, in the place of a sibling, was my own name. Underneath it, a question-marked year, also starred to signal my birth: *1903?* A colleague entered the laboratory then, and I jumped and tried to hide what I was doing, but he glanced at the bible under the dissecting microscope and said good morning and began his work. Yes, I thought. I am here. *Here.* No need to hide. And I focused the lens once more. Beneath Anna's name was the correct date of birth, starred, and then, marked with a cross, the correct date of her death at Theresienstadt. The same date I'd learned from the Red Cross. And I shifted the page again and found you, Lotte, also with the correct dates: *6.4.1935 †2.3.1944.* What was I doing on the day Anna died? On the day you died? I often ask myself this, as if I can change the past by remembering the answer. And I can't remember, not for sure, but I think I was treating Greta Hahn.

Through the microscope, which made the names ten times bigger than real life, I could see the fibrousness of the paper: all the little splinters of wood pressed back together. All the little pieces of tree. I turned that word over and over: tree. Tree. The echo of something that wouldn't quite come. I could see the tremor in the handwriting, and the uneven edges of the ink; the way it had seeped ragged into the texture of the paper. And further over to the right, a capital A, just past the end of *Lotte Hirsch*. A beginning. I moved the page, and the word – the name – spelled itself out – A s t r i d. *Astrid Sara Hirsch, *16.2.1943.* Born nine months after I last saw Anna. And still living.

I remembered the final conversation I'd had with Greta. That small lucid moment when she gave me her bible – insisted I take it – and then turned her gaze to the windows.

'Look at the tree,' she'd insisted, her eyes on the glass, and I had knelt next to the bed and followed her gaze, except I could see nothing but rain and fog. All the same, she kept on repeating the phrase, and I held her hand and agreed that I could see it, her phantom tree.

Except this was the tree she had meant: the one under my microscope; the one she had finished. The one made of names.

For a week I did nothing. It was likely, I told myself, that Greta had imagined the child; hadn't she said, towards the delirious end, that she'd always wanted daughters? She was nothing more than a ghost, this little girl. An opium wish.

But she would not leave me alone.

The Red Cross had no record of an Astrid Hirsch in Theresienstadt, nor an Astrid Weber.

'It's possible the records were destroyed, though,' I said. 'Isn't it? Didn't they burn as many as they could?'

Yes, it was possible, said the Red Cross. In theory it was possible, but I shouldn't hold out hope.

And still, she would not leave me alone.

There were no Hirsches left in Frankfurt – I had already checked and double-checked – but there was a Leah Wohl, née Hirsch. The sister of David.

'I know who you are,' she said when I started to introduce myself at her door. 'I suppose you'd better come in.'

Her flat was a jumble of things salvaged and saved. A rag rug on the floor, and on the table a cut-down bedsheet in place of a cloth. Mismatched candlesticks and dining chairs, and a clock without a minute hand, and half of the windows without their glass. In three wicker baskets, piles of mending, and an open box showing spools of thread of every colour. While Frau Wohl made a pot of tea, I waited in the living room. It overlooked a park where families were eating picnics and walking their dogs; one little boy was trying to climb into the empty fountain, and his mother grabbed him by the back of his collar just before he toppled. A brother and a sister were flying a kite, the yellow paper panels shining like church windows in the October afternoon.

'No sugar, I'm afraid,' said Frau Wohl.

'Thank you,' I said, taking the tea. The cup rattled in its saucer; they were not a pair. 'You mentioned you knew me?'

'I know your face,' she said, but didn't elaborate.

I began to wonder whether I should have come at all. On the piano, a small cluster of photographs watched me from their frames.

'That was David,' she said, pointing to one of a dark-haired young man standing at the bottom of a staircase – and yes, I recognised him.

'I met him once,' I said. 'I came to the flat in Ostend.'

'I remember,' she said.

'You were there too?'

'We all were.'

'He let me sleep in his bed.'

She nodded. 'We did wonder . . .'

'Wonder?'

'If his marriage to Anna was real. But we thought, even if it wasn't, they might grow to love each other. We hoped.'

'I'm sorry,' I said, though there was no hostility in her voice. 'What happened to him?'

'After a few months in Theresienstadt they sent him on to Auschwitz. He died, along with all the others.'

'All except you.'

'Yes,' she said. 'I survived.'

'How?'

She looked at me sharply. 'Luck, of course.'

'I'm sorry,' I said again. 'I didn't mean to suggest—'

She sighed. 'I'm ashamed of it myself, most days,' she said, refilling our cups, the steam fogging the air between us. 'You haven't come to see me, though, Doktor Weber.'

'No,' I said. In the corner of the room, a dropped doll made from scraps of flour sack and ends of wool, with cut-glass buttons for eyes. 'I think Anna had a second child. A daughter. I think she named her Astrid.'

For a moment Frau Wohl did not speak. A boy in the park shouted: *Stop it! You're not allowed!* She placed her cup and saucer down, and then in a quiet voice she said, 'I wanted to believe she was David's, but I think I always knew.'

The words pulsed through me, shook my every cell. I would crack, I thought; I would shatter.

'What did you know?' I said, and the eyes of the doll glittered in the corner of the room, and Frau Wohl said, 'Come with me.'

It was difficult to make out anything in the bedroom at first; a blackout blind still covered the window in place of curtains. I stood in the doorway, strangely fearful of what the dark might hold, and Frau Wohl went to the bed and touched the sleeping figure on the shoulder. 'It's time to wake up now, darling,' she said, and raised the blind a little way.

The child opened her eyes and blinked, then sat up. She stared at me. I wondered if she might begin to cry, but she continued to stare, as if unsure I belonged to the waking world.

'This is Astrid,' said Frau Wohl, pulling the blind all the way up. 'Astrid, this is your papa.'

She climbed from her bed, clutching a rolling pin carved with snowflakes. The pattern had pressed into the side of her face as she slept, and I wanted to touch my fingers to the little flushed cheek and ask if it hurt – but I stayed where I was, watching from the threshold as Frau Hirsch dressed her and combed her hair. It was fine and straight and yellow-blond, just like mine, and her eyes were my own dark blue. There was nothing of Anna in her, and not a scrap of you either, Lotte: she was all me. She cradled the rolling pin against her chest, still eyeing me. Pinned above the bed like a holy picture, the postcard of the Transparent Man. Once I had thought he told me everything about being human, that bright being. Limbs alight, arms raised in supplication or surrender. The heart exposed.

'Shall we have some bread and schmaltz?' said Frau Wohl.

'Yes,' said Astrid.

'Yes what?'

'Yes please.'

I moved aside to let her pass, and she peered up at me and prodded my leg once, twice. Then she handed me the rolling pin – warm, solid, smelling faintly of nutmeg – and I followed her back down the passageway to the living room.

And I admit that a rage flared in me; I didn't understand why Anna had never let me know about her pregnancy. She'd sent word of her remarriage; surely, through some intermediary, some coded letter, she could have told me. Couldn't she? On the day that I saw the two of you across the street, Lotte, when you patted the little dog, she must already have had Astrid.

Then I remembered the night she told me she was pregnant

with you: she came into the parlour, where I was still thinking about how I might refine the Vitaliser, persuade Baumhauer to allow a second trial. She placed a silver rattle on my desk without speaking a word, right on top of my papers, and I picked it up, and I could hear the little beads sliding around inside, clicking one against the other – and when I looked at her face, I knew. And I remembered thinking that I would do anything for this little life that hadn't even begun, and that nothing was more important. And then I understood why she hadn't sent word to me of your sister: she believed that it was too dangerous; that if I found out I would not be able to keep the secret of our sham divorce, and we would both be punished for race defilement, and then what would happen to us? And what would happen to you? Something terrible.

But it happened anyway.

Hahn must have known too. And chosen not to tell me.

When Astrid had finished her bread and schmaltz, Frau Wohl said, 'I have a lot of mending to do, Doktor Weber. It was nice to meet you.'

'It was nice to meet you too,' I said. 'Both of you.'

I was still holding the rolling pin, so I gave it to Astrid, and she took it and said, 'Thank you,' then handed it back to me. 'You're welcome,' she said.

'Oh . . . no, this is yours,' I said, passing it back, and she said, 'Thank you,' again and returned it to me. 'You're welcome.'

'She can do that all day,' said Frau Wohl. 'Stop teasing, Astrid. I have mending to do. Now come to the kitchen, and I'll wipe your face.'

A voice calling from the park: *It's my turn now! Let me!*

'If you're busy, Frau Wohl,' I said, following her across the passageway, 'why don't I take Astrid to the park for a little while?'

'The park!' said Astrid, already heading to the front door to find her shoes.

'I don't know . . . ' said Frau Wohl. She wrung out a cloth, twisting it again and again, her knuckles white.

'It's just across the road,' I said. 'You'll be able to see us from the window.'

She went back to the living room and looked out as if to make sure.

'Half an hour,' she said.

'Half an hour,' I said.

'She likes kicking up the leaves, but don't let her get too muddy.' She wiped Astrid's face and buttoned her into her coat, then gave her a little push towards me. 'It's all right,' she said. 'I'll wave to you from the window.'

Off we go. Down the stairs and through the courtyard, stop at the side of the road, hold hands, wait for the bus to pass. Hold hands, look left and right, make sure it's safe. Quickly now. Hold hands. And yes, there is Tante Leah, waving to us from the window, and everything is all right. And yes, what a pretty leaf; shall we keep it?

A woman walking alone stops to touch Astrid's hair, and to murmur how lovely she is, how precious, and another woman who is also alone stops to stroke her cheek and to smell the smell of her.

I told you, Lotte, that there were three miracles in this story. Herr Erling was the first, but only for a time – his miracle didn't last. And Greta Hahn was the second – but again, only for a time. You understood that, didn't you? That she couldn't live, never could have lived? Let me tell you, then, about the third miracle; let me write it down so I believe it myself: this early autumn day, this damp grass darkening our shoes, this bright-throated wren singing to save the world, this pale sun in this white sky. This yellow kite, this empty fountain, your sister Astrid tracing the veins of this leaf. All of it so close.

AUTHOR'S NOTE

There are many accounts of Buchenwald, some written during or immediately after the war, and others decades later. Over the course of researching and writing this book I consulted a wide variety of sources in German and English, from prisoner interviews, letters and memoirs to official records and historical analyses, and I have tried to provide as realistic a representation as possible. When faced with conflicting accounts, I took into consideration political agendas and potential distortions of memory over time.

I based the public hanging of Polish men described on p. 342 on the 1942 executions in the forest near Poppenhausen, carried out by Buchenwald SS. The original Transparent Man from the 1930 exhibition in Dresden was destroyed when the German Hygiene Museum (Deutsches Hygiene-Museum) was bombed in 1945.

Johanna Haarer's child-rearing manual, mentioned by Greta on p. 158, is *The German Mother and Her First Child*. The Goethe poem Lenard quotes from on p. 217 is 'To Charlotte von Stein', and the one Dietrich quotes from on p. 329 is 'Gingo biloba'. Karl-Heinz's book, which Lenard recalls on p. 306, is *The Story of the Rabbit Children* by Sibylle von

Olfers. The first line of Herr Heller's poem on p. 424 is adapted from a line in 'Heimkehrende Krieger' by Nazi poet Heinrich Anacker, published in the *Thüringer Gauzeitung* on 23 August 1942. The quote on p. 432 from Karl-Heinz's schoolbook comes from a 1941 primer, *Fibel für die Volksschulen Württembergs*. All translations are my own.

I have used some real names – Ding, Katzen-Ellenbogen, Pister, Schiedlausky, Schmidt, Schwartz and Prinz zu Waldeck von Pyrmont, for example. My description of these figures is imaginary, though the deeds described are mostly factual. Herr Baumhauer, my director of Frankfurt's real-life Holy Spirit Hospital (Hospital zum Heiligen Geist), is entirely fictional, as are Lenard Weber and his machine, although the latter was inspired by others that were in existence around the same time. Lenard's colleague in the photo department, Foucher, is based on the French photographer Georges Angéli. The prisoner who carves the face from the salvaged Goethe oak is based on Bruno Apitz – a towering figure in the history of the camp as well as in the post-war East German interpretation of that history. His carving, *The Last Face*, is held in the collection of the German Historical Museum (Deutsches Historisches Museum) in Berlin. Dietrich Hahn is loosely based on Otto Barnewald, in that they share the same administrative position at Buchenwald.

Dietrich's quotes from his post-war trial are taken verbatim from the American Military Tribunal's 1947 war-crimes trials at Dachau, in which Otto Barnewald was sentenced to death. Later his sentence was heavily reduced, like those of most other Buchenwald defendants. He was released from Landsberg Prison in June 1954.

ACKNOWLEDGEMENTS

I wish to thank my publishers, Fergus Barrowman and Ashleigh Young (Victoria University of Wellington Press) and Christopher Potter (Europa Editions); my agent Caroline Dawnay and her assistant Kat Aitken; my copy-editor Sarah Ream; my colleagues at the University of Waikato; Creative New Zealand, who provided me with an Arts Grant; Jann Medlicott and the Acorn Foundation; and the Janet Frame Literary Trust.

Sincere thanks to Harry Stein (Gedenkstätte Buchenwald), who gave me the ammonite fossil, and graciously answered my many questions about the history of the camp. Any errors are my own. I am grateful to Roland Bärwinkel (Klassik Stiftung Weimar); Frank Boblenz, Stefanie Dellemann and staff (Landesarchiv Thüringen – Hauptstaatsarchiv Weimar); Benedikt Burkard (Historisches Museum Frankfurt); Monika Flacke (Deutsches Historisches Museum, Berlin); Petra Graupe and Katja Lorenz (Herzogin Anna Amalia Bibliothek, Weimar); Beate Meyer (Institut für die Geschichte der deutschen Juden, Hamburg); Jens Schley (Berlin); Maximilian Strnad (Stadtarchiv München); Carsten Timmermann (Centre for the History of Science, Technology and Medicine, University of Manchester); Manuel Vojtech (Deutsches Hygiene-Museum, Dresden); and

Wolfgang Wippermann (Freie Universität Berlin), who won't remember me, but who took my university class to Buchenwald in 1996 and told us about the Goethe oak.

Thank you to Annie and Detlev Brandt, Anne Ferrier-Watson, Matt Grace, Thorsten Harms, Maria McGuire, Helen and Fred Mayall, Stephen Murray, Kimberley Nelson, Michael Norris, Nathalie Philippe, Brigitte Ruesseler, Bernd Schmidt, Jonathan Scott, Alison Southby, Michael Steven, Cheryl Pearl Sucher and Claudia Williams.

For their unfailing support and encouragement, special thanks as ever to Alan Bekhuis, Alice Chidgey and Tracey Slaughter.